INVENT

The Completionist Chronicles Book Seven

DAKOTA KROUT

MOUNTAINDALE
PRESS

This book is dedicated to my tiny new deadline, Michael Krout.

ACKNOWLEDGMENTS

Many thanks to all of my supporters, especially those that have been here since the beginning.

To my Patreons, thank you for wanting to be the first to have eyes on the work, and for giving me tips to make it all better.

Finally, to William Merrick, Samuel Landrie, and Zeb Foltz... thank you for doing so much, and asking for so little in return.

PROLOGUE

"The Lord of Slaughter took the field, his first intervention in half a century culminating in the losses of the Ninth Celestial Army of Light, *five* Shaper High Councilors, as well as one Shaper Scion: The Lady of Light, Elfreeda." The Elf lifted his eyes from the document, but not to the person he was speaking with. He had been granted the authority to *speak* to the Ascetic, but certainly not enough to *look* at her. "This concludes the report."

Silence filled the air, and sweat poured down his regal Elven face as he waited patiently for the Ascetic to either ask him questions or dismiss him. Several hours passed as the ultimate ruler of the Elves pondered deep thoughts. Her melodious voice eventually moved through the intervening space—at the same moment, a breath of fresh spring air swept through the open windows—and reached his ears.

"There *is* more." Those three words from her lips were enough to cause direct damage to the waiting Elf, passing effortlessly through the barrier spell he had prepared specifically for this occasion. Blood erupted from his eyes, ears, nose, and mouth. In the same instant, he was healed by her divine presence; the Ascetic fully understanding the impact her words would have on his physical form. "The light is shining ever brighter... but darkness has swept through the Oligarchy to counteract it. How is it possible that those godless Dwarves...? Ah... I *see*."

This was the second reason the regal male Elf didn't dare raise his eyes. To the uninitiated, it would appear that the Ascetic was speaking to herself, but the true fact was that the pantheon of Elven Deities spoke to her directly. Often, they would even physically manifest in this bare room, and laying eyes on a vengeful deity was simply begging to be returned to the light in the same moment.

As the Ascetic's voice rose again, it was muted; the dulcet tones were sung by the stone below, so that he *felt* the words instead of being sliced apart by the flesh-shattering force of her breath. "The *humans*. Much has changed. The Dwarves even now have a burgeoning pantheon which has begun multiplying the troop readiness of their people. It appears that they have been far more... *enthusiastic* with their recruitment and integration efforts. Tell me why you think they have been more successful at this... why your failure has begun to turn the warscape to their advantage."

"This servant has failed you." The Elf leaned forward, kowtowing with his head against the stone, as though this task that mere recruiters had been burdened with had instead been a personal and intentional crime. "The humans are... *resistant* to the teachings of the Theocracy. They have strange desires, such as rising through the ranks or gaining access to restricted knowledge based on their completion of quests alone. It was determined that the tasks they perform, which any Elf would be filled with joy to accomplish, are insufficient for such advancement and enlightenment."

"It is not unknown that they come from outside of Eternium." The Ascetic's voice could never be called impatient, nor anything other than perfect and measured, but there was still *something* that set the waiting Elf on edge. "Here are my teachings, Ecclesiarch. Prepare to receive them."

Utter delight filled the second-highest ranked Elf in the entire nation. It had been more than a century since the Ascetic had issued an edict. His hours of waiting had *absolutely* been worth it. The King of the Elven nation, known to his people only as the Ecclesiarch, lifted his head fractionally from the hard stone floor of the small cave as a prophecy and successive orders filled his very being.

"Havoc has been unleashed; his soul-deep longing has been completed. The Lord of Slaughter taking to the field is a harbinger of great destruction in the months to come. Even worse… for the first time in centuries, he has taken a True Apprentice." Here the Ascetic trailed off momentarily, and the King's face twisted in disgust as her next words explained *why*. "Keeping to the old ways will usher in the destruction of our people, culminating in our nation being overrun with Dwarven influence. At this time, by my decree, *all* locks on knowledge will be assigned a value that can be paid, and the key to unlocking them will be the destruction of our enemies or the empowerment of our people."

"You… we are to follow in the footsteps of the *Dwarves*? Let the humans gain access to the highest levels of knowledge, just so that we can defeat this age-old foe?" The King gaped as he tried to wrap his mind around this command. "I just don't understand."

"Do you need to *understand*… to *obey*?" The King was flung back as divine mana suffused the air. "I tell you now, they *will* gain our knowledge. It is our choice whether that is through mighty deeds or terrible crimes committed against us. It has been *seen*."

The King, the Ecclesiarch, King and Head of the Elven Theocracy, simply returned to pressing his head to the stone floor, shivering in terror. "It will be as you have spoken."

"One last thing." The Ascetic allowed the King to breathe through his shakiness and find a semblance of calm before finishing her thought, "Find the *best* of the humans. Pull them close to the Theocracy. Give them everything they've ever wanted or needed, and ensure that they will remain true to the Elven cause. They *must* work to the benefit of the Elven people... no matter the cost."

The image of a man in a trenchcoat—a human who had earned rank through a style of combat hitherto unknown to the Theocracy—flashed through the King's mind, and he nodded fractionally. "I already know *exactly* who to contact."

"Then *go*, and prepare yourself to atone for your impudence."

CHAPTER ONE

"You mean to tell me that you think we can fit three *thousand* different buildings in this area?" Joe stared down at the map the city planner had handed him with eyes full of suspicion. "How in the *abyss* did you come up with that number? You're full of it."

"It's simple, human." Ciril, the city planner, answered flippantly as he sharpened a chisel. "When buildings are higher tier, they take up less space. More bang per building, as you humans say. Less clutter. This is the reason why it is so important to rank up your town into a city and start making improvements—in the *correct order*."

"We can discuss that, but how are we supposed to pull in those kinds of resources?" Joe impatiently demanded, tapping the map that detailed *very* high-Tier buildings clustered around the Pharaoh's Pyramid of Panaceas, the Artifact-ranked alchemy building whose recent creation had saved thousands of troops in the Dwarven Legion from drowning in magma. "You're planning this out as though we're going to be able to push this whole section into Unique or better... *how?*"

"*Candidate...* I just plan the city. I don't do logistics to make it come together," Ciril scoffed as Joe's bald head began reddening. The human took a few deep breaths, remembering that calm words returned better results. "After all... it's not *my* fault you used all the resources from capturing this place to fix your mistakes instead of making the place less of a shh—*hello* there, Major General Havoc!"

Joe turned to look at Havoc, who seemed to be dead tired and wobbling on his feet. More smoke was coming off his beard than usual, the gray hair slowly turning to ash. "Ciril. *Civilian* Ciril, who was hired to do this job, perhaps you should make an effort to actually *do* the job correctly. Just because you aren't in the Legion doesn't mean I can't pull you up on charges for negligence. You don't wanna work for humans? That's fine. I'm sure some *other* city planner would literally slit your throat for the chance to plan an entire city from scratch, but you can just *give* them the job instead."

"S-sir, that's not-" Ciril nervously tossed his chisel from hand to hand, glancing between Havoc and Joe, "-necessary. Not necessary, sir. I'm more than happy to do this. I just suppose I hadn't taken the... lack of resources into account."

"Look at it this way." Havoc pointed at the map, detailing parts and circling sections Joe hadn't even looked at yet. "That can be a Tier-five *City* plan. Get him one through four, and earn yourself five times the experience by starting from a town and expanding outward accordingly."

"Oh. *Oh.*" The oddly owlish Dwarf blinked at the map, his demeanor resolving into craggy smiles and excited squirming as plans started flowing through his mind. "Oh, I like *that.*"

"Before you go..." Havoc used his lit cigar to circle a section of the map, nearly a quarter of the entire area, then put a burning 'X' over it. "Section that off as workshops for Joe and myself. Don't wanna destroy the *entire* city if things go bad."

"What could you *possibly* need all that-" Ciril started to huff, then froze as he remembered who he was talking with at the moment. "I'll, uh, see that it happens."

"Good. *I'll* review the next *option* before you present it to

Candidate Joe over here," Havoc informed the man with a toothy threat-smile. Joe expected Ciril to pale, but the Dwarf simply nodded distractedly as he pulled out a fresh parchment and began drawing on the spot. "Don't worry, Apprentice. You'll learn to bargain with their greed, and not their logic. There's a reason our nation is ruled by Oligarchs and not charities. Now walk with me."

They began to stroll toward the Pyramid, waving at a few people as they went. The area as a whole was subdued and near-silent, but not in a bad way. There was just practically no one living in it yet. Those that remained in the region were simply a skeleton crew, a token force meant to hold the campground against medium-sized wandering monsters. Joe eyed the prolific rubble that remained, all that was left of the tightly-designed Elven fortress that had once stood here, muttering his thoughts aloud. "I gotta get started on fixing this place up."

"No, you need to do *much* more than that. You gotta reinforce it, set up traps, get some rituals going, and begin building a full-blown militia," Havoc rattled off, much to Joe's surprise. The curmudgeonly Dwarf whom he had needed to provide with terrifying results for just a fragment of information was now offering advice rapid-fire? It was very welcome, just… strange. "You're gonna have an interesting time. Building up a town is a whole different volleyball match than we're used to doing. Dwarves, Elves; neither have built a full town, much less a city, in half a millennium. Gets killed off too fast. Mostly just forts for the last few… centuries."

"You don't build towns? Is that a 'war' thing?" Joe wondered as they paused and leaned on a pile of rubble just the right size for lounging.

"Kinda. Far as I know, each of the different zones, planes, or whatever you wanna call 'em, comes with different challenges for constructing cities or towns." Havoc offered a cigar, which Joe turned down in favor of *not* getting sick or possibly turned into a golem. "Here, on Svaltarheim, when you start to tier up a settlement, the other side gets notified. They have a certain amount of time to destroy the place and gain rewards as though it were a tier higher. Busting down a camp that got too big for its britches and tried to become a hamlet? That gets paid out like they killed an entire village, savvy? That only gets worse the higher up you go in the tiers."

"I see." Joe considered the town his guild had purchased for a moment. "Couldn't tell you what it was like back on Midgard. I wasn't in charge of it, even though I was directly responsible for getting a Town to Tier one."

"Oh? How would you say that turned out for you?" Havoc questioned him mischievously.

"It was fine, I… ah. I see. Yeah, I kicked off a war that Shattered the Wolfman race, and accidentally committed a war crime that got me banished for a year." Joe chuckled ruefully along with Havoc. "I see your point. There must've been *some* benefit to the Wolfmen to make them drop everything else and come running."

"Good self-reflection. On that note, here's a question for you." Havoc took a long draw, then spoke along with a cloud of hot pink smoke. "Now, you've got good skills. You're powerful, draw people to you, and seem to make for a pretty good leader. Feces for a Charisma score, though. Tell me, why *weren't* you in charge of the area on Midgard when it got attacked? Why were you putting in that effort to build the place for someone else?"

Joe shifted uncomfortably on the stone 'bench'. "I prefer being able to focus solely on the things I *like* to do, I suppose. You know, I actually have a land claim token and noble title on Midgard, and I never got around to using them?"

"Huh." Havoc nodded in understanding. "Well, I can tell you that you'd better get used to not running around and making a nuisance of yourself. We're gonna work out a proper training program for you. We'll improve your strengths and shore up your weaknesses. Now, are you opposed to working toward golemancy? I'd say that your biggest flaw when it comes to crafting is detail work at a very fine level. All the support skills for the class give a pretty wicked boost to dexterity."

"While that sounds… *amazing*, to learn that from a Grand-master in the field…" Joe shook his head and decided to spill his thoughts out in a rush. "I just have so many *other* things I want to do. I'd absolutely *love* to learn more enchanting, or anything like that. I just think that perhaps golems aren't my style?"

Havoc shrugged and waved someone over. "No hair off my teeth. Listen, you know Captain Cleave-"

"Yes." Joe cut the Dwarf off before he could say the Captain's actual name. "We're well acquainted at this point, but I think she was supposed to leave for-"

"Nope, she's here. I reassigned her as your escort, 'cause you have a bad habit of doing strange human things, like ignoring orders from Major Generals and yelling at people that outrank you. Her job is gonna be to make sure you don't do something to tank your career and get chucked off a cliff without being properly warned that you're about to castigate the wrong person." The grizzled Dwarf cut off as Captain Cleave arrived and saluted. "Good to see you, Captain. Joe, too bad about the golemancy, but if sculpting and other physical skills get in the way of completing your class quests, I understand."

"Thank you for pointing him out, sir." Captain Cleave eyed Joe with distinct relief. "I've been wandering this place for hours looking for him. You'd think that shiny pate would stand out more, but-"

"Wait… *wait.*" Joe was on his feet in a flash, reaching out to Havoc. He pulled back just in time. A needle extended from Havoc's shirt, glistening with gold-flecked purple poison. Ignoring the deadly barb, Joe locked eyes with the incredibly powerful Dwarf whom he had never known to lie. "What do you mean, *'class'* quests?"

"No." Havoc narrowed his eyes in return, then pulled up Joe's status, reminding the human that he had never revoked access to it after it had been demanded the first time they had met. The Dwarf's eyes scanned both active and completed quests; what remained of his eyebrows rose ever higher over each line. Finally, he clamped his cigar in the corner of his mouth, reached forward, and cuffed Joe in the side of the head, getting a shadowy slap in retaliation, even though Joe hadn't even bothered to flinch when his Exquisite Shell flared. "You have *got* to be joking. Everything you can do, and you haven't even *started* your first class quest?"

"I didn't even know it was a thing, and no one has *ever* mentioned it to me," Joe protested as he attempted to peruse his quest tab. Nothing appeared, even though they were talking about it.

Havoc stood in considering silence, the smoke from his cigar slowly drifting toward the top of the enclosed volcanic space. "Alright. Let's go figure this out."

CHAPTER TWO

"Just make an easy ritual," Havoc demanded of his Apprentice. "I don't care what it is, or what it does, just that you make one in front of me while I'm watching your status."

The Reductionist stood over the simple ritual diagram, rolling his eyes at the ease with which he could now generate Novice-level rituals. A single circle? No need for anything but Damaged aspects, and an eighty-five percent discount, thanks to his class? Even with triple-checking his work just to be as safe as possible, the ritual took less than thirty seconds to complete. Joe arched a brow at his mentor. "What is this supposed to prove, Havoc? I've made literally hundreds of these at this point."

"Then you're clearly doing something *wrong*, brat." The Dwarf leaned back and kicked Joe in the chest, sending him flying as a shadowy copy of himself appeared and slapped Havoc in the face. "Heh, that spell of yours is so nice and refreshing. It's like taking a cold shower."

"What the *abyss*, Havoc?" Joe roared as he vaulted to his feet, his Ritual Orbs springing into the air to swirl around. He was fully prepared to attack... but Havoc wasn't even listening to him. The Dwarf was inspecting the ritual circle, muttering under his breath.

"Alright. I think I know what the issue is, but you aren't gonna like it." The Dwarf looked up at the human, and a smarmy grin crossed his face. "You know why no one ever brought the class quests up to you? It's because almost everyone gets them as soon as they select their class. It should have been one of the first things that appeared in your menu when you arrived in the world. In other words, everyone else is way ahead of you."

"That's not ideal, but I've been able to manage so far. What's the problem?" Joe groaned as Havoc leaned back and rubbed his beard, the mirth in his eyes informing the human that he was refusing to answer. "It's never easy with you, is it? Can't you just *tell* me?"

"Where's the fun in that?" The Dwarf pointed at the ritual circle and smiled. "Think about your class. What it does; what it *needs*. It'll be obvious in hindsight. Ah, don't look at me all upset like that. I'll give you one hint: your type of class was never meant to be a base class, which means it has *prerequisites* to gain its class quest. If you can't figure it out on your own, I got advance notice of a situation coming up that *will* fix it for you. Good thing, too, else you'd need to return to Midgard to even *start* your class quests."

"Ooh! That sounds fun! What's a class quest?" Joe turned toward the new arrival, smiling as he spotted Jaxon walking toward them with his odd, very straight-backed stride. "Can I have one, too?"

"You don't have it either? That's not right...?" Havoc puffed on his cigar as he looked between the two of them, deep in contemplation. "This is... strange. Maybe humans *don't* gain access right away... no, I'm pretty sure there's just something wrong with the two of you. Dino-hands guy, you want help, then give me access to your status."

"Sure thing!" Jaxon narrowed his eyes in concentration, and Havoc grunted in acknowledgement a moment later.

"Huh." The Dwarf tapped at the air, wincing as he perused the *mess* that was all the seemingly unrelated skills Jaxon had, as well as the utter and unbelievable lack of basic abilities. "Well, I can tell you that you have a similar problem to Joe's. Yours is easier to fix, though; come along, and I'll let you know how. You go with me; Joe, you go away."

"What? Why won't you tell me, too?"

Havoc turned and winked at him. "More fun this way!"

Joe threw his hands up in frustration as the two men vanished around a corner, accidentally sending his orbs rocketing away from his hands as his attention wavered too much. They thudded to the ground at varying distances, and he sighed as he started picking his way around the rubble to find all of them. "I really gotta bind spells to all of these so they automatically return."

He wiped a whole lot of sweat off his shiny head as he collected the last of the orbs, belatedly activating Neutrality Aura to passively return himself to prime condition. The sound of pounding feet drew his attention as a Dwarf ran at him like an unstoppable freight train, only for the barrel-chested newcomer to be swept off his feet as Captain Cleave slammed into him and sent him to his back. She swung her war axe down, pulling the blade to a stop just before lopping off his head guillotine-style. "Why are you assaulting the Candidate?"

"Whoa, it's Cleave Dudette in the flesh!" The Dwarf reached up and flicked the axe, making the metal ring. "Sweet moves! Listen, I got orders to bring Teamkiller Bro to the triangle building. Whole place is melting, yo."

"The *pyramid* is falling apart?" Joe didn't wait for any further information, knowing the Dwarf wouldn't have it. He vaulted into motion, practically employing parkour as he launched himself toward the Artifact-ranked building—the only thing that was keeping this place from sinking into the superheated liquid rock below them. Thanks to his Strength characteristic, each leap launched him forty-four feet, if he moved perfectly. He didn't always, but he still crossed the distance to join a group of harried officials in practically no time flat.

"There he is," one of the Dwarves called in obvious relief. "Candidate, we've received intel that the interior is reaching untenable levels of heat, although the exterior of this space is in no danger of failing. If we don't find a way to drain off the heat in the near future, this camp is going to return to molten slag in short order."

Joe caught his breath as he considered the issue. He already had a way to drain heat, since he had used zombified aspects to escape from this place in his original visit. The question was how to use that ritual *safely*, and then sustain it. "I have a solution that may work short-term to solve this issue, but its current iteration is dangerous. Do we have anywhere we can vent the heat?"

There was a collective sigh of relief, and Joe felt a swell of pride as a few muttered snippets reached his ears. Things like 'I told you he could do it' and 'see, nothing to worry about when he's around' reached a deep part of himself that had been craving positive feedback. Between Joe's compounding failures on Midgard and his responsibility for the accidental death of hundreds of Dwarves, he had been nearing a breaking point of self-doubt. His resolve to make this place *awesome* intensified.

That all started with not letting it melt.

"What we can do is set it to vent up into the open air, similar to an actual volcano," the Dwarf offered with an easy smile, "until you find something you want to use the excess heat for, at least."

Joe fist-bumped the Dwarf in greeting as the group collectively started discussing the best location for a coolant system. "Nice to meet you…?"

"My apologies!" The Dwarf pulled a set of documents out of a leather messenger bag. "I just transferred here; my name is Bauen. I'm an engineer, hoping to learn from the Lord of Slaughter during what are certain to be his *many* improvements for the first place that hasn't placed restrictions on his... residency."

A vivid set of memories flashed through Joe's head: Havoc screaming at the thundering sky, releasing the equivalent of magical nanites to slay hundreds of Elves, converting his own body to golem-form despite knowing it would mean his death, defeating an Elf and setting off the failsafe that would have wiped out thousands of Dwarves... Joe slowly nodded, "I see. Yeah, I can understand why most places might... 'restrict' him."

"Bauen, we've decided that the best place to vent the heat, for what should be obvious reasons, is as close to the top and center of the settlement as possible," one of the other Dwarves announced, giving Joe a doubtful once-over. "It'll allow for a natural convection current and possibly generate a fresh, cool breeze, if the heat reduction factor is great enough. We'll need to be watchful of isothermal expansion if Havoc's designs are-"

"*That'll do*! Thank you!" Bauen cut off the other engineer with great haste, going so far as to clap a hand over his mouth. "Mixed company here. Ah... Candidate, what can we do to assist with this?"

"I'm guessing you're under orders not to tell me what's going on?" After the Dwarf nodded with clear relief that the human wasn't pressing him for information, Joe paused to consider for a few moments, then motioned for the engineer to follow him. "There *are* a few things I could use help with. I'm used to doing this all myself, but perhaps having a greater insight on how my rituals will impact the matter around them is exactly what I need. Who knows that better than an engineer?"

"*I* have the chance to teach Havoc's direct apprentice?" Bauen's chest swelled with pride as he hurried to follow the human. "I have so many ideas! If we make something truly remarkable, perhaps you might... put in a good word for me?"

"That could only be counterproductive." Joe shook his head slightly and chuckled at the thought of Havoc whisking Jaxon away to teach him secrets. "Trust me, if you want him to give you direct tutelage, all you need to do is make it seem like the information would be exceptionally beneficial to me and pretend that you're going to spend time to help me understand it. *Then* he'll start teaching you."

"Um…" The Dwarf raked his hand through his combover, pulling attention to the fact that he actually did have hair atop his head, even though it was exceedingly thin and fair. "That seems… unusual."

Joe shrugged ruefully. "That's Havoc."

CHAPTER THREE

Even though he knew that there was currently only a single permanent structure standing in the town, Joe still searched for somewhere they could work in peace. Remembering his conversation with Havoc and the city planner, he led Bauen to the northeast quadrant of the settlement and started drawing out a ritual diagram.

"Pardon my intrusion… can you explain to me what you're doing right now?" Bauen nervously questioned as the human continued with his work. "I was under the impression that you wanted to have my advice, and that you were going to be casting your spell at the roof of the cavern?"

"Yes, I will be. Not exactly a spell, however." Joe glanced up after completing a particularly tricky symbol, then ran his eyes over the ritual diagram he was drawing. Due to using aspects as the ink, it appeared as though he was sketching a ring of equations in fire on a large chunk of fallen stonework. "This looks pretty neat, not gonna lie. It always seemed so bookwormish to do this with ink. Imagine how many more people would learn calculus if the numbers lit on fire when you got something correct?"

"Yes, multiple rings of light that aren't vanishing despite having no internal energy source… very concerning. I mean, exciting." Bauen chuckled nervously as he watched Joe work for a dozen minutes, who had apparently forgotten that he was there. Perhaps this human had more in common with Havoc than he realized?

"I'm trying to make a Common-ranked workshop. It should only take about an hour more, and then we'll get whatever benefits to productivity that doing this *not* out in the open will afford us," Joe explained to the Dwarf, who relaxed minutely when he realized that he hadn't been forgotten. "Ah… shoot. I can't make chairs. Abyss, yet *another* thing we'll need to shop out to someone else."

The engineer, now that there was a clear reason behind Joe's behavior, was far more interested in the diagram Joe was producing. They ended up having a good conversation on the differences between having a team of skilled contractors build the workshop by hand versus generating it with a ritual. By the end of the chat, Joe had quite a few concerns that he knew he would need to pour time into researching.

The largest benefit of having skilled people create structures was that they could account for changing circumstances as they built, while Joe got *exactly* the design for whatever he cast. It hadn't been an issue thus far, but who knew what the future held? As Joe got closer to finishing his ritual diagram, the discussion petered out and was replaced by the static yet satisfying **crackling** of stone being etched with energy. As the final symbol completed, Joe reached down to activate it… only to be met with a blaring red warning.

Unauthorized attempt at creating a structure on the territory of the Dwarven Oligarchy. Continuing with this action will result in bounty hunters being dispatched to your location to halt your infringement on this territory. Proceed at your own risk.

Joe reread the message, attempting to understand why he had never seen something like this before. It slowly dawned on him that he had never constructed a building in Dwarven territory. He had only ever done so in Elven-controlled areas. He tried to remember if the pyramid had gone up while this place had been considered Oligarchy-controlled… but no. It had been labeled as 'contested' until they had calmed the volcano and managed to secure the safety of the Legion. "So, I have a small problem…"

"Can't build because of the ownership restriction?" the engineer bluntly questioned him. Joe's eyes drilled into the Dwarf, asking why he hadn't mentioned this issue ahead of time. Bauen tapped the stone and gestured around them. "I thought you knew, or you already had control of the area. Commanders of major incursions tend to be gifted the area that they first conquer for development. This leads to productivity at no cost to the Oligarchy, as well as increased revenue and such for the commander. Why haven't you claimed it yet?"

"I'd have to go see General Court-Martial." Joe stared at his completed, and yet currently useless, ritual, his lip twitching in displeasure. "Well, that was a waste. I certainly don't have the kind of time I'd need to go and claim this place; there's way too much for me to do here. This place is melting, the rubble needs to be cleaned up, and-"

"You can't do much of anything here without the authorization to actually *make* changes, right?" Bauen gently reminded the human. "Let's get to work on the cooling system, and then —if I may offer my opinion—you should go and claim this area so we can get to *work*."

"*Fi~ine*," Joe grumbled as he rubbed at his head. "Why is it that I always seem to be surrounded by people that are smarter than me?"

"You know, I've always believed that if you surround yourself with people smarter than yourself, you have the most opportunity to grow." Bauen offered an outstretched hand. Joe took it and pulled himself off the stone. "That's not a terrible place to be, is it? Also, I'm paid a premium to be the most highly skilled and intelligent person around, so don't be trying to edge in on me."

They both chuckled at that, then started slowly walking around while discussing the best way to attach the cooling ritual to the roof of the cavern, and Bauen had some useful thoughts on the process after observing Joe make the ritual he hadn't been able to activate. One of the most helpful suggestions from the engineer was the fact that perhaps Joe should fuel the ritual with higher-ranked materials than needed, simply to improve the longevity and functionality of the final product.

"I had never even *thought* about using my resources like that. I gotta say, it seems wasteful when the final product already does what it's supposed to do," Joe admitted as they rejoined the remainder of the Dwarven engineers. "Do you think it's really worth augmenting like that?"

"I would say," Bauen carefully worded his thoughts, "that when you are developing critical systems, creating the minimally viable product is not a *good* idea. If you are using a short-term item, such as one of your 'rituals' that generates a specific outcome and then stops forever, minimum viable all the way."

"That makes… too much sense to ignore it even a little." Joe slumped with a half-smile as he tried to recall any active rituals that should be patched. Nothing in this Zone came to mind, so he shrugged and got to work with the other Dwarves. Soon enough, they were installing piping along the ceiling of the cavern, and moveable scaffolding was being erected so that Joe could gain access to the ideal area to write out the ritual. By the time he was allowed to go up, they'd designated multiple fracture points, areas for venting, and ideal locations for his ritual.

After looking over the options, Joe had a sense that *this* one would be the best spot. He created a Field Array that was only half an inch in height, but ten feet by ten feet wide. The Reductionist activated the array, converting a thin but wide area into trash aspects, and subsequently gained a perfectly flat area for creating the ritual.

The next few hours were used to set up the ritual in such a manner that it would absorb ambient heat at a constant rate, then funnel it up and away. There was far less emphasis on *speed*, and far more attention placed on safety and consistency. When he was finished, Joe stared at the ritual and decided to add in one final circle based on his conversation with Bauen.

This fifth circle included no additional symbols, being only a quarter-inch thick ring around the exterior; it was a common ritual addition that was only used as—essentially—structural support that he had noticed in several ritual designs before, but had ignored in favor of efficiency. If his idea and the sympathetic connections were compatible, the important sections could take the higher-tier aspects and use them to reinforce or replace the lower aspects if the ritual began to deteriorate.

At worst, it would make the ritual more expensive to create and activate. The best case would be the ritual *not* failing at an inopportune moment and drowning the residents of his new town in magma. Joe was willing to risk a few aspects, but he wasn't going to gamble with lives.

Now that the ritual was ready, all he needed were a few willing volunteers and a bit of a Tier-four Core to empower the ritual… but he only had a single Rare and ten Uncommon Cores in his possession. It took a bribe of a full *two hundred* reputation with the Dwarven Council to get a grumbling Major Cleave to part with the needed Core, but the group of excited Dwarves and the single human were finally ready to make the magic happen.

Joe placed his hand on the ritual and activated the newly redesigned diagram. "*Frigidus ex monte fratris!*"

The ritual, though potent, was still only at the Journeyman ranking. Between the group of highly specialized engineers and the Reductionist, the activation went off without a hitch. Joe had been worried that he wouldn't have enough Zombified aspects, but the ritual only accepted twenty of the twenty-three that he had available.

Energy swirled and spiraled as the air in the immediate vicinity began to rapidly decrease in temperature. The group left the ritual to do its work, and the engineers remained up on the scaffolding only long enough to tear it down as they went.

Bauen and Joe gazed up at the energetic patterns set in the ceiling, feeling a surge of pride in a job well done. "I hope that takes care of the issue."

"I'm sure it will," the Dwarf smoothly stated. "Any idea what you'll do next?"

"He's gonna get off his rear and go claim this place as his own!" Havoc roared from the distance. The shout drew a lot of attention to the fact that the Dwarf was staring at them through binoculars, but most people simply averted their gaze and returned to whatever they were doing as the cantankerous Major General's bellows echoed in the open cavern. "Right now, he's a useless lump of potential resources, and I'm sending a golem to turn him into nutrient paste if he's not going to do what he needs to do!"

Joe looked around the leveled area, noting all the rubble and destruction, then glanced back up at the perfectly ordered ritual that would ensure the area remained livable. "I dislike how accurate his words are... but I *am* looking forward to seeing what I can do when I have free rein to make amazing things happen."

"I can't wait to be a part of it." Bauen grinned in wicked delight.

Joe simply nodded and headed to the exit of The Shoe, Captain Cleave keeping pace with him. "I wonder if they'll let me rename this place."

"They won't! Now get outta here, and hurry back! You're too slow, I'm gonna make you suffer for ignoring me-!" Havoc's voice echoed around the chamber, as did the scream of twisting metal. Joe softly screamed and started running toward the exit without stopping to see what kind of monster the crazy old coot had sent after him as 'motivation'.

CHAPTER FOUR

Joe entered the city at a light jog, with Captain Cleave easily keeping pace. They had made excellent time, knowing that there was a decent chance that Havoc had sent his golem to chase them for the entire trip. Joe hadn't *seen* it anywhere, but that had merely served to ramp up his tension until he was using Omnivault as often as possible; never knowing when a creature might pop out of the ground, or a tree might turn into a whirling dervish of metal had kicked his paranoia into overdrive. Even though he was currently in the city proper, he was still hesitant to slow down… but he needed directions.

He approached the first resident he could find, and learned that General Court-Martial was holding his sessions near the Legionnaire's main fortress in the city center. Joe loped along the road in the 'walking' lane, since people were *moving* today, for some reason. Large numbers of Dwarves and humans alike were clogging the roads, more than he had ever seen at once, with the exception of troop mobilization.

"The Elves have made a public statement that they will be attacking our forests and delving into our territory!" a town crier was yelling from a flipped-over box. "All people are called by the Oligarchy to volunteer to defend our lands as these dastardly foes *invent* reasons to slaughter our civilians!"

"Don't get involved, Joe…" he muttered to himself as he rushed along. "Got *plenty* to do; too much going on in the first place. No more random wars for this guy, no sir."

Even at his 'slow' pace, he found himself standing in the administration hall in almost no time flat; he had to wonder what travel in higher-tier zones would be like. Did people just teleport wherever they wanted to go? He approached the Dwarf that was stamping papers as though she had a grudge, her mustache fluttering due to her furious muttering. "Beanpole Elves make an abundance of paperwork. Why can't they just roll over and get flattened like they *should*? We all know what the outcome is going to be after they lost their most prominent invasion forces."

"Pardon me…" Joe struggled to find the proper way to address her, so he settled on his meager knowledge of Legion culture, "…Dudette? I'm here to see General Court-Martial."

"Name, rank, reason for attending," the Dwarf muttered in the same tone as her complaints, not bothering to look up from the flashing paperwork.

"Joe, Candidate, here to get a proper rank… pretty sure." He smiled grandly as the Dwarf looked up and let her eyes rove over him. She winced, making Joe sigh internally as his smile fell away. His lack of facial hair did him no favors with the ladies. Not really an issue, as he had no romantic interest in Dwarves even slightly, but the *flinching* was starting to get to him.

"Take a seat if you need to, else you can stand there while he's informed." She dropped her gaze once more, though the muttering continued. "Not sure why you needed to attend a basic rank advancement. This is all calculated before you even get here, so it should at least be quick once they're ready for you."

"Thanks, that's good to know." Joe let out a sigh of relief at that revelation. "I really had no idea what to expect, and I've had… *issues* with authority in the past. They tend to get… I don't know, nervous? Who knows? Seriously, I'd love to just vanish for a while and make neat things."

"Yeah, no *joke*, he might get vanished." The muttering was slightly more stress-inducing this time. It appeared as though the Dwarf didn't realize that Joe could hear her. "Happens every once in a while, when you kill enough people on your own side."

Unsure of how to respond to that, Joe went and sat on one of the most uncomfortable chairs he had ever had the misfortune of experiencing. Based on what he had gleaned from Jaxon, this chair would be a welcome addition in any Wolfman's den. After the first bruise, he reactivated his Exquisite Shell—he had needed to turn it off when he'd entered the city, else he'd be arrested—and floated an eighth of an inch above the chair's metal surface. A moment later, he activated Neutrality Aura and Retaliation of Shadows as well. Being clean and presentable was never a bad thing, and the shadows would help if he were getting 'vanished'.

An hour passed, then two, and Joe began to get antsy. Just as the third hour rolled by and he was preparing to leave and come back another time, two Legionnaires stepped through the doorway, locked eyes on him, and motioned for him to follow.

The higher-ranked of the two addressed him. "Candidate, usually this process is a simple and easy transition. As a courtesy for what you have accomplished, I am allowed to explain to you that there are a few problems with your promotion. Not only are you the first human to get to this point, but you caused enough collateral damage that there are many opposing your advancement. This simple trial has been pushed up to a full tribunal."

"I'm guessing that's not a good thing." Joe sighed as they closed in on a set of double doors with dozens of shouting voices pouring through the slight opening.

"Dude." The Dwarf on Joe's left grabbed his shoulder roughly enough to get a shadowy slap to the face. "Heh, that never gets old. Don't know if you recognize me; I was in the

Shoe with you. You're the only reason we got outta there, so I wanted you to know I'm pullin' for ya. Good luck."

Joe was touched by the sentiment. The next moment, he was shoved through the doors by the first of the guards. He managed to catch himself and walk through the boundary under his own power, even if his steps were a little… springy. The Reductionist looked around, surprised by the normality of the place. When he heard 'tribunal', he had expected to be looking up at Dwarves behind a table, standing in judgment of him.

This place looked more like a simple room with a table designed for staff meetings, and there was even a seat for him. All the Dwarves stood and went silent as he walked into the room, none moving -though some were openly glaring—until he was also standing by his assigned chair. Only then did one of them clear their throat and announce, "With the Candidate present, we can begin. All remain standing for General Court-Martial, the final voice on any subject relating to the Oligarch's Code of Military Justice!"

A door opposite to the one through which Joe had entered was slammed open, and a Dwarf whom Joe could only describe as a Dwarven silver fox strode inside the stark room. His stern face was lined with age and experience, his every movement clearly practiced and graceful, and his voice was unexpectedly smooth.

"Thank you all for attending this utter farce."

Joe blinked at the opening statement. That was *not* what he had been expecting to hear. The silver-bearded General pulled out his own chair and sat down, followed by everyone else.

More than a few furious glares were being directed at General Court-Martial, but he ignored them and began laying out the issues they had gathered to discuss. "The fact that this has risen to a level where I must get directly involved is a mark against our people, the military process, and the OCMJ. I have *very* little patience for this foolishness. By all accounts that *matter*, the Candidate has done an excellent job, and I am confirming his advancement to a Major General right this moment. The remainder of this tribunal is now officially to determine additional rewards. If there are those among you that have something to say, for or against, it will all be taken into account."

A massive smile uncontrollably curved Joe's mouth. He had been expecting his success to be downplayed and to miss out on cool rewards. The fact that he was guaranteed his position caused a wash of relief to flow through him. It had been a... hard few months. He had desperately needed a win.

Other people were less than happy.

"Hold on! I have a *number* of grievances against this *Candidate!*" One jowly Dwarf slapped a large scroll of parchment on the table and began listing off all of the trouble Joe had caused, from killing a swath of the Legion, all the way down to demanding the attention of Grandmaster McPoundy—and getting it multiple times—in a public setting.

"I also have my concerns!" Another Dwarf, this one in unadorned armor began spouting off other *tiny* things the first had missed.

Nearly forty minutes passed before the two ran out of things to complain about, and General Court-Martial started to move for the first time since the rant had begun. To Joe's dismay, he was nodding along with them. "I see. I shall rebut these issues myself, without need for additional testimony. But first: a fine of one hundred reputation with the Dwarven Oligarchy for you, Major, as well as five days of extra duty."

"What! How *dare*-" The jowly Dwarf swallowed back his bellow as he rose from his seat and remembered who he was speaking with. "On what grounds, sir?"

"For ignoring rank and intentionally belittling a superior officer." General Court-Martial's words were calm, but the steel in them could have been forged into a set of matching swords. "I *just* confirmed his rank as Major General, and you referred to him as a 'Candidate', not to mention spitting in *my conference room* as you did so. Such disregard for rank is a terrible precedent, and the insult to myself cannot be ignored."

The Major sat down, his face twitching. General Court-Martial looked around the room, then knocked on the table once. "Send in Major Infraction, General Information, and High Priestess Dawnesha. Major General, these three have asked to speak during this tribunal."

Joe, in a daze, nodded at the odd confirmation. "Should I-"

"You have no speaking lines in this play group, sir." General Court-Martial informed him respectfully. As the three Dwarves entered the room, only General Information was staring at Joe maliciously. "The three of you have requested to speak. Please feel free to explain your interactions with the newly advanced Major General."

The announcement of Joe's rank made General Information's stare wither slightly, and his eye twitched as he rapidly calculated how to reword his forthcoming comments into respectful and succinct concerns. He didn't get much time to plan, as he was called on first, due to his rank in the Legion. General Court-Martial stared him down, "You first, General. Your thoughts on the matter at hand?"

"All I can *say*, due to apparently changing circumstances," the General growled through gritted teeth, "is that when the person on trial was at the *Candidate* rank, he held zero respect for military authority. He intentionally harmed his people, and allowed anywhere from dozens to hundreds of soldiers to die, even at his own hand, to secure small victories."

"I see." General Court-Martial nodded at this assertion, making notes on a pad of paper. "In order for this to be held against him, I must confirm a few facts. After these deaths, the Major-General then abused his authority as a Candidate, and forced the Commissioned Officers in the area to pay the resurrection costs. Further, his actions did not aid in the overall victory, but were simply small successes for personal honor and gain?"

General Information's teeth ground against each other hard enough that Joe was almost certain he would need to find a specialized healer sometime in the near future. "He *did* contribute to the overall victory. He did use his personal resources to resurrect the Dwarves that died due to his actions."

"Understood. His actions then were only *somewhat* helpful, and he resurrected only the Dwarves that were directly slain by his actions." This time, the Major-General didn't write, instead waiting patiently for more from Information.

"That's... he..." General Information went silent, his hands clenching and unclenching along with the rhythm of his heartbeat. "I have no more to say on this matter."

"How very interesting that you would leave off pertinent data, doing your best to sully another's reputation by intentionally refusing to clarify the information; your namesake. I'll need to ensure that your reports for the last few years are audited for authenticity after this. It seems you are willing to punch down and hurt those under your own rank, but not to build up people that are incredibly useful but 'slighted' you, perhaps? I'll make a note to look into the individuals in your chain of command that have been requesting promotions, and those that have received them. You are ordered to remain on the premises until this investigation has been thoroughly carried out. Major Infraction, your thoughts, if you so please."

The room was so silent that Joe could hear his pulse racing in wild exultation. Just as the atmosphere shifted from shocked to oppressive, Major Infraction coughed and began enumerating how Joe had pulled off an overly complex spell, going on to explain how—even though this action had caused death—it had likely saved the entire deployed Legion from falling to illusions and trickery. She then gave a *thorough* accounting on the way that Joe had saved the Legion and brought back *all* the Dwarves that had fallen through the entire area, as well as pulling all the fallen Elves to their side as newly-recruited Dwarves... all out of his personal war spoils.

Princess Dawnesha stepped up next, not waiting to hear orders or commands. The high-ranked people in the room all stood and bowed as she did so, making Joe feel the need to reassess her importance to the Dwarven people.

After she explained Joe's actions in bringing the deities to step in on their side, and how thousands of previously unfit-for-duty Dwarves now had productive roles in the military and society, thanks to their new classes, she made a statement that shook the group at large. "Finally, not only am I recommending the highest rewards for Joe, but I have put forward my personal sponsorship for him as a Noble Candidate based on his contribution to the Oligarchy. I have already filed the necessary paperwork with the Oligarchs."

The collective gasping around the room, and the reddening faces of his detractors, clued Joe in that this was something… *wildly* out of the norm. General Court-Martial took it in stride. "Princess, though he has done well militarily, what you are proposing is outside of my power to grant. As of this moment, he already outranks me. I-"

"He is already gaining the Shoe to be turned into a fortress, yes?" the Princess interrupted without hesitation. "On my authority, assign him the most stringent of Noble assessors to gauge his prowess, and allow him to convert the enclosed cavern into a settlement instead of a fortress."

The demand was greeted by a long moment of strained silence until General Court-Martial shrugged, once more standing and bowing with the rest of the room as she retook her place in the line. "As you wish. This *will* impact the additional rewards he is allowed, as there are rules restricting how much the military can offer any individual Noble."

"I trust that he would rather have long term success over a short-term influx." She turned her eyes to Joe and widened them fractionally. "*Right*, Major-General?"

"Honestly? I'm kinda hoping for a big ol' payday." Joe offered the group a weak smile. The room went totally still as General Information's face gained an excited, hungry expression, and the Princess glared at him. Joe let out a tired sigh. "No, no. I'm joking. Cultural differences; my apologies. That sounds amazing."

A low rumble rose from the assembled Dwarves, and

General Court-Martial began speaking before anyone else could take the floor. "Good. Very good. With all this new information, Joe... I shall hereby officially confirm your rank and title. Welcome once more to the Legion, Major-General Pyrrhic, Noble Candidate for Baron."

Each of the assembled people, no matter if they had been against him to that point, stood and clapped loudly. Joe heard a notification but ignored it in favor of listening to the people speaking.

"As an additional reward for your service and merits, you will be granted five thousand reputation with the Dwarven Oligarchy, as well as ten Rare, fifteen Uncommon, and twenty Common Cores. The Legion hopes that you will continue to use your talents for the betterment of Svaltarheim and the Dwarven Oligarchy." The General motioned Joe forward as a few of the people around the room stopped clapping and began choking on their attempted words. Joe simply saluted and stood forward. He was handed a box, and the General leaned forward and whispered, "*Run* back to your town and stay away from the gossip mills for a few weeks. Public opinion's gonna be rough on you."

Joe stood tall, saluted, and practically skipped out of the room, missing the moment where Captain Cleave—his guard and chaperone—was pulled aside by General Court-Martial.

CHAPTER FIVE

Joe ran, jumped, and skipped—anything necessary to get ahead of any pursuers. He was over halfway to the Shoe before he remembered to stop and look at his notifications, so he hopped to the top of a tree and pulled them up.

Quest complete: Ranker. You have achieved the highest possible marks of any human!

Title gained: Major-General Pyrrhic, Noble Candidate for Baron (Upgradeable). This is both an active and a passive title. Passively, this title allows you to hold official and Noble rank in the Dwarven Oligarchy, as well as the ability to own land for creating a settlement.

This title activates automatically! In active use, this title increases damage dealt by yourself and any troops under your command in a one-hundred-foot radius by 100%, solely when you have lost at least half of your forces, or you are in a situation where there is a greater than 50% chance that you will die.

At any time this title is active, if you do not have at least half of the original number of units within range, you will take double damage from all sources.

Upon your death, if the title was active, all troops under your command deal 150% bonus damage for one hour.

"Celestial feces... now anytime I win, it'll literally be a pyrrhic victory? No one is ever going to want to be under my command." Joe grunted as he read over the activation conditions. The branches of his tree creaked loudly, swaying slightly as a breeze rolled past. He ignored it as he kept reading.

Quest gained: Ranker II Peerage. You are tasked with creating, maintaining, and defending a settlement within the land you have been granted through your actions in the first portion of this quest. Your progress will be judged by (Pending). In order to join the peerage as a Baron, you must complete one of the following two options:

1. *Take an Elven city for the Dwarves.*
2. *Flawlessly fend off five major Elven incursions into your granted land.*

Joe nodded along as he absorbed the details of what he was only now realizing was a chain quest, and adjusted his position as the branches moved slightly more aggressively. "This makes sense. At least I'll have all the Cores I need to build up a solid little town right away..."

Grant of land approved! You now own the internal cavern system of 'Gramma's Shoe', and have full authority to develop the land in any fashion you so desire.

"Perfect. Let's get moving, Cleave! All we need to do is..." Joe peered at the ground and frowned. He looked up the trail, scanning the area, but couldn't find Captain Cleave. He began shifting his position in order to look behind himself as well. "Drat, I must have lost her when I was leaving the city. I suppose I should-"

Blam!

The sound of a gunshot going off next to Joe's ear was enough to deafen him, and the sneak attack's critical impact to his skull dealt massive damage to his Exquisite Shell. The shock sent him tumbling out of the tree and to the ground, bouncing off branches and scattering leaves. He hit the ground heavily, stunned and confused from the sudden and brutal attack.

Four people suddenly leaned over him with malicious grins on their faces; in the next moment, they were beating on Joe with a variety of weapons and skills. His only defense was his Retaliation of Shadows slapping them away, but the reactionary spell wasn't able to dissuade the men from bringing his health down to a fraction of full in only a few moments.

Joe's watery eyes focused just enough to spot a man sitting on the branch he had fallen from, holding a smoking pistol and smiling widely down at Joe as the men stepped back for a moment. "Who are you? Why did you—*Mend!*"

The Reductionist's health shot upward, and the smile weakened fractionally on the strange man's face. He spoke with a strong put-upon German accent as he hopped out of the tree and fired three rounds into the arm and hand that Joe had used to heal himself. "Oh, now, *that* will just not do. *Tsk, tsk, tsk*. Hello, Joe of the Dwarves. I… am Herr Trigger, and I have been tasked with taking down high-value targets for the Elven nation."

"A bounty hunter? More like an assassin. How did you even find me?" Joe flipped off the ground and healed himself once more, sending two of his Orbs flying at the relaxed man at the same time as the thugs backed off.

"What can I say? I am highly trained, exceedingly well-paid for my time, and have a love of hunting monsters such as yourself. I know of your crimes on Midgard; things like mass murder of half the plane of existence tends to follow you no matter where you try to hide." Herr Trigger spoke with an infuriating calmness as he dodged Joe's attacks contemptuously, dashing across the ground at full speed while avoiding the flying metal balls with ease. He dove forward and tackled Joe to the ground, one barrel pressed to his heart and another to his head. Joe froze, ingrained instincts from his life on earth overpowering him.

Herr Trigger lifted the pistol off Joe's chest and waved the barrel under his own nose, taking a deep sniff. "Oh-h-h, *ye-e-es*. I just *love* the smell of gunpowder in the evening. Now, little *mage*, I'll answer honestly, for that is who I am. I found you purely by *chance* today, and you were too distracted to even attempt to keep yourself safe. I was hunting another reviled human target by the name of 'Jaxon', who has a standing bounty with my mentor, BackAttack Beastbane. My team has already neutralized the Dwarf that was following several miles behind you, and this was simply a lovely chance encounter. Now, it is time for you to go to respawn, and for me to collect your bounty."

The man paused as he studied Joe's face through his perfectly round sunglasses, "What is it that used to be popular with you Americans? Ah yes... *Trigger Warning.*"

The blond assassin unloaded his weapons into Joe, each blast shaving off a solid fifth of the Reductionist's health with each impact.

You have died! As this was player vs player combat, you lose 5,250 experience! You will respawn in 12 hours!

Skill increase: Mental Manipulation Resistance (Beginner II).

Joe blinked and found himself in his respawn room, and—after a moment of shocked realization—started flailing around on his beanbag chair in a rage. He calmed down quickly, taking deep breaths and reminding himself that everything else had been utterly awesome today.

Over the next few hours, he messaged his mother and her new husband, answered questions from his Coven, and even found a few pending queries from his guild: The Wanderers. Aten had reached out directly, evidently hoping they could meet up soon. Joe messaged back and resolved to check his mail more often. He normally only did so when he died, and it had been quite a while since the last time that had happened. As he typed one final message to Jake the Alchemist, informing him that the Artifact-ranked Alchemy building was ready for him, Joe muttered, "Hopefully, the next time I die will be even further away."

As soon as his resurrection timer ended, he *sprinted* out of the portal and beelined to the command tent, basically the nicest non-permanent structure in the Shoe. He grabbed the Ledger of Souls, finding Cleave right at the top, and paid the cost to bring her back. A glance confirmed that a few additional Dwarves had shown up in the Ledger, far too many for day-to-day accidents. "Gotta give my people a warning about Trigger... ugh, now *I'm* doing it. I *hate* that he found such a good catch phrase!"

The cost for Cleave was higher than expected, and as she appeared in front of him, he discovered why. Her full title had been updated to *Major* Cleavage. She had been promoted, and higher rankers were more expensive to bring back. He cleared his throat and mumbled, "Congratulations on the promotion."

"Sir." Her eyes were obsidian daggers as she glared at him. "My *duty* is to make sure you're safe. You can enable me to fulfill my duty by allowing me to be with you at all times, especially when traveling outside of the Shoe, or I can toss you in a pit and make sure you have just enough food and water to prevent you from accidentally dying off or defecting to the Elves in secret. Your choice, Major-General."

"No threats, please. I don't do well with those." Joe rubbed at his head and groaned as he pondered where exactly he had dealt damage to this relationship. "Major, I'm not wonderful with people. This is reflected in Charisma being one of my lowest stats. If that hasn't come across by now, please realize that although I love what I do, and how it helps people in general, I've always run face-first into my inability to be political. There's a *reason* I don't pursue relationships, or lord my abilities over people. I just want to do what I do, and stay out of the way."

She remained silent, her mustache wafting slightly in the artificial breeze. Joe shrugged and began studying his hands, flexing the powerful digits as he continued to verbalize his thoughts. "All I have going for me is that I'm highly *skilled*. I am *not* highly attuned to people's wants and needs, so... take that as you will. I'll do better if you remember to treat me as a proper member of your party instead of expecting me to act like a convict who is constantly trying to escape."

"Yes, Major-General," came the bland reply. Joe realized that he had likely burned this bridge too badly by letting her die alone in the woods while looking for him. Unable to find any more excuses, and unwilling to debase himself further, he simply grunted and walked out into the open area of the volcano, getting slapped with a new tab in his character sheet as he emerged from the tent flap.

Gramma's Shoe, Hidden Camp (Tier 0)

Town Level: 0

Residents: 0

Morale: -125 (Dissatisfied.)

Resources: none.

Living areas: 0 (-25 morale).

Air Quality: Livable (poor, increasing. -25 morale).

Heat: Dangerous (Hot. -25 morale).

Water Sources: 1 (Mineral Water. Tainted. -25 morale)

Light: Poor (-25 morale).

Now that he had the ability to use his personal resources, Joe was determined to get to work right away. He was wavering back and forth between what building should be the first he raised: he'd finally narrowed it down to either a barracks or an apartment building. It finally came down on the side of 'make someone else choose', which motivated him to go talk to the city planner.

He set to it right away, asking around until he finally found the man drawing something out on the ground in the distance. As he hurried over to the Dwarf, the Reductionist passed by the chunk of rubble that he had originally set up with his construction ritual. He glanced at it, then the city planner, and decided that there were still plenty of great reasons to go ahead and generate this building first.

With a few extra minutes spent on using his inscriber to bring the quality of aspects—as well as the building cost— higher, Joe pulled out the highest-value of the ten Rare Cores and activated the ritual 'Architect's Fury'. The four circles blazed out, and since he had charged it previously, he was able to simply power the entire process himself.

He now had an immense mana pool—a great benefit of getting Tatum free—which meant he was constantly struggling to find ways to use it all effectively. With so much power just sitting around unused, he kept finding himself feeling lazy by casting whatever came to mind; a stark contrast compared to the days when he'd needed to carefully control each individual spell that went out so that he would have enough for the next one that was needed.

That aside, the project moved quickly and efficiently. Aspects flowed out of his Natural Aspect Jars while he checked his bound core.

Core energy: 4,198/5,498 (Rare-ranked core)

Everything was within expected parameters, so Joe ignored the pain and pushed through as the drain started sucking away the last of his reserves. His brand-new workshop was being built right in front of his eyes, and a huge part of himself was cheering at the fact that he would *finally* have a place where he owned the land *and* the building and could therefore work at without interruption. As the ritual came to completion, he inspected the structure and smiled at the messages that appeared.

Magical workshop (Ritual-focused): Common-ranked, reinforced.

Architect of Artifacts activated! All building characteristics increased by 10%,

Durability: 1,650/1,650.

Features: enhances ritual power, decreases time required to create a ritual, and decreases cost of all rituals by 1.1% for all rituals made inside the building.

Joe admired the workshop, inordinately pleased with the results. It was no Pathfinders Hall, but it was all *his*. Nothing short of a war or criminal act could take it from him… the grim thought filled his mind as another message popped into his vision.

Class quest prerequisites fulfilled!

- *Own a plot of land.*
- *Build or buy a building to use as a workshop on that land.*
- *Have 'Ritualist' class.*

You have gained a quest: Ritualist Novice.

Ritualist Novice: You have taken the first steps on the path of the Ritualist! In time, no magic will be able to hide its secrets from you. To advance down this path, create 100 Novice rituals! Reward: New Novice ritual module!

Novice rituals created: 0/100.

"Yes! I got my class quest!" Joe whooped as he skimmed the details, his excitement waning slightly as he reread how many rituals he had to make. "Feces! Nothing I've made up to this point counts? Not even the Pathfinder's Hall…? Ahh… abyss, I didn't own the land. What an *aggravating* requirement."

He frowned at his new building, at the city planner who was gaping at the fresh structure in horror, then at the morale ratings for his eventual town. "No… I can use this. Let's make lights; that's an easily solved issue. Making them as Novice rituals? Please. I can make a hundred of those in… thirty seconds each, that's fifty minutes. I've got this."

He rushed into his workshop, eager to get started and allow the unhappy memories of the day to rapidly fade into background noise.

CHAPTER SIX

Just over an hour later, Joe was inscribing the final circle of Damaged Aspects onto a flat square tile. His plan of working for a solid hour to complete the first quest had been only *slightly* thrown off by his desire to explore the workshop.

The majority of the building was an open space designed for any number of magical craftsmen; the only reason it was specifically created for rituals was due to his intent upon creating the building itself. The main working room had three offshoots: first, a smaller workspace that was heavily fortified on the interior, designed for containing volatile projects. Section B was a small office for research that could hold two or three people at a time. Finally, the ending area resembled a large walk-in closet with a bank vault-style door; essentially, a heavily defended storage room.

To get into his workshop proper, Joe had gone through the first door and found himself in a small room with another door leading to the main workshop. When he touched the second, sturdier door, he had been required to register his mana signature and claim ownership of the building. Since that had been exactly what he wanted, he had hurried through and locked the door behind him.

After exploring, he had pulled out a stack of flat stone tiles and got to work. He glanced at his quest counter as he finished the tile he was working on.

Novice rituals created: 99/100.

Joe took one last stone out of his storage ring, ran his inscriber in a circle around it, then made a perfect equilateral triangle that broke through the circle in three places. "If these were words... the circle would be 'hold energy' and the three points the triangle pierce would be 'intensity', 'color', and 'type of energy converted into'. This last one will be essentially daylight, but..."

He had been monkeying with the other triangles, slightly altering everything except the final point of 'type of energy', as he didn't want to accidentally produce flames or lightning. He was already planning on using that concept to create this world's version of a magical Bunsen burner, both for black-smithing and alchemy, but he had no interest in scorching himself when he was merely trying to brighten up the area.

Novice rituals created: 100/100.

Quest complete: Ritualist Novice! Congratulations, you have completed the Ritualist Novice class quest in a record time. You are competing not only against yourself, but all previous Ritualists throughout history, so this is a truly exceptional record to break!

Rewards increased. You have gained: one module of Student circle effects (Increased from Novice to Student). Record breaker reward: Somatic Ritual Casting!

Skill gained: Somatic Ritual Casting (Novice V). This skill allows you to create a ritual in midair! No longer will you need flat land or perfectly smooth paper; you can draw out a ritual in midair! Increases ritual instability by 30%-10n% per ritual tier, where n=skill level.

Caution: this skill is usually granted as a reward in the Student Ritualist class quests. Earning it early will be a great boon in training it up, but it may be very difficult to use as a Novice Ritualist!

He wasn't overly worried about the difficulty of the new skill, since he wasn't *actually* a Novice. He couldn't wait to raise this skill to a high level and teach it to his Coven when he saw them again; something like this would even allow them to create rituals in combat someday. The practical applications for this skill were *whirling* through his head, and he almost missed the moment when a half-orb with a button atop it appeared in his hand. "Hello, there... what are you?"

Burble? Mate, his coffee elemental, poked its head out of the stain on his sleeve, peering at the object in disappointment for a moment before absorbing back into the stain and vanishing.

Module of Student circle-effects. Press the button to upgrade Ritual Lore skill. (Must have Ritual Lore skill.)

He stared at the unassuming half-orb, which looked like an old-school 'easy button' from earth. "Should I save this? Give it to a student, since I'm already getting close to-"

The information updated, and he sighed as he realized he shouldn't have been muttering plans aloud.

Module of Student circle effects. Press button to upgrade Ritual Lore skill. (Must have Ritual Lore skill.) Usable by Joe 'Tatum's Chosen Legend' only.

"Well played, system." Joe slapped the button, and the entire item shattered into glittering motes of light, which then filtered into his body.

Ritual Lore (Apprentice II -> Student IX). Your study of rituals via trial and error, study, or other arcane means has borne incredible fruit. You are now able to 'read' ritual circles up to the peak of the Student ranks and are able to alter them to achieve a desired effect with high certainty.

He glanced at the light-tiles he had just made, and simply sweeping his gaze across them revealed what color and intensity each would emit. He had been *pretty* sure of their individual details before, but now they held no secrets at all. He felt fairly confident that Beginner rituals would appear the same, Apprentice would be slightly harder to read, and Student would be similar to the level of effort he had just employed to inspect his fresh Novice rituals. "I'm totally fine with being *pretty* sure. Celestial guacamole, I feel like I've been flying *blind* compared to how they look to me now. Hope this helps me blow myself up less frequently from now on."

Quest gained: Ritualist Novice II. You've shown that you can create rituals! Now, how much trust do you have in your work? Activate 50 self-made rituals, Reward: 500 experience. Rituals activated: 0/50.

"Hah! I bet this task sent a ton of Ritualists back to the drawing board back when this class was more common." Joe chuckled as he deposited the inactivated rituals in his storage codpiece. He let himself out of the workroom, locking the inner door behind him with a mere thought. Looking back at the building fondly as he exited, he muttered, "I think I might love this place already."

Then he had a thought. He turned back to the doorway, crouched, and jumped straight up onto the roof. "If this is gonna be my place, it needs some personal flair."

He pulled out his inscriber and pondered the knowledge that he had gained with Somatic Ritual Casting. Lining himself up to stand directly over his doors below, Joe drew a circle of fiery light-gray aspects in the air. His brow furrowed in concentration; this *was* a lot harder than inscribing it on a surface. "Gotta keep each side of the circle aligned... wow, that *really* wants to droop. Mmkay, don't let that part go too far forward. Stop *shaking*, fingers! Since when do my hands shake?"

Sweat was dripping down his face, cleared away after a moment by his Neutrality Aura, and he hadn't even inserted the triangle yet. Happily, three straight lines were understandably easier to create than a perfect circle. He set the intensity of the light to 'high', which would have been approximately a hundred watts back on earth, then connected it to a point that would tint the light a royal purple, and finally the point that directed the ritual to convert mana to light.

He stepped back, admiring the circle that shimmered lightly over his workshop, then reached forward and activated it, gaining an insight into the ritual that he had never before gleaned.

Ritual of Glimmering (Royal Purple).

Rank: Novice.

Activation cost: 210 mana.

Time until ritual requires replacement: 179:23:59.

"This is *awesome*." His eyes shone with reflected light as he truly felt magical once again. "I want more."

Rituals Activated: 1/50.

Joe scanned the rooftop, trying to select the best locations to affix the remainder of his light rituals, and his eyes landed on the scaffolding set up in various places where Dwarves were attaching tubing and pipes to the ceiling to circulate air up to his siphoning ritual. His gaze brushed the clunky inscription he had designed, and he winced as he instantly spotted a dozen ways guaranteed to improve it, and at least as many more about which he felt *pretty* sure would make it at least a little better.

Ritual of Heat Collection, Zombified to become Ritual of Heat Draining.

Rank: Rare, Fortified.

Activation cost: 5,003 mana. (Inefficient diagram, mana invested: 5,519)

Time until ritual requires replacement: 50:13:45.

"Less than two months before that fails? Ugh… nothing to do for it right now." He casually vaulted along the broken ground, reaching the scaffolding Bauen was shouting orders from. He waited for a break in the bellowing, then waved the Dwarf down. "Two things for you: first, the cooling ritual has fifty days before it fails. Let's make sure to have a backup ready. Second, I have a hundred lights to install on the ceiling, if you can think of good places for them."

"Fifty days? That's…" The engineer nodded from side to side as he juggled a few thoughts. "An acceptable time frame. I'll put out a bounty for a core that would work. You'll have to pay the reputation cost for it, though. As for the lights, do you need to do it yourself, or can you just hand them over and we can place them as we go?"

"I… huh." Joe grinned as he realized that there *were* perks to being the leader of an area. "I hadn't even *considered* not installing them myself. Yeah, give me a bit; your people can take them as I go."

The human separated the tiles into two stacks, then used each hand to activate a Ritual of Glimmer at the same time. He had more than enough mana to accomplish this, so he flew through their activations. In no time flat, the Dwarves carried off the final rituals.

Quest complete: Novice Ritualist II. You had a lot of faith that you wouldn't get some backlash, huh? Great! Confidence is needed if you choose to walk this path to completion. Record breaker reward: experience gain doubled. +1,000 experience.

Then Joe got the next notification, one he had been expecting.

Quest gained: Beginner Ritualist. You have shown remarkable dedication to the tedium of highly particular magics. Now do it again. In order to prepare for higher rituals, you need to understand rituals exceedingly well, in addition to possessing the massive number of resources needed to complete them. Raise the skill of Ritual Lore to Novice IX, and collect enough resources to complete the work on 100 Beginner rituals.

Ritual Lore (Novice IX): 1/1. Resources gained: 0/1,000 Common Aspects, 0/5,000 Damaged Aspects.

"It's not counting what I've already collected? Good to know." Joe was sure this was intended as a method to keep people from simply accumulating a massive stockpile and *then* achieving this class. It was a cute attempt, and he knew that it was going to fail to slow him down; he was a *Reductionist*! A second notification appeared, one he very much had *not* been expecting.

Prerequisites for Class Quest met:

- *Have Novice base class quest completed.*
- *Have the Rituarchitect class.*

- *Have some form of Ritual Lore at Beginner rank, minimum.*
- *Have some form of Architectural Lore at Beginner rank, minimum.*

Class quest gained: Novice Rituarchitect. Using a ritual, scan ten Common buildings and create blueprints for them. Reward: Blueprint for Ziggurat, a ritual-based area buff landmark.

"Hold on… *every* class has class quests?"

CHAPTER SEVEN

"Bauen, sorry to say, I have another request to make." Joe skidded to a stop atop a pile of rubble, his leap over to the Dwarf culminating in landing on some shattered roofing. "I need to find someone that can help me design a building. You have any architects in your entourage?"

"No…" Bauen paused, visibly hesitating to speak further, but he finally couldn't hold back his concern. "Joe; that is… Major-General, I need to explain something that is a bit of a difficult conversation. We're here, and we're completing various projects based on an amount of reputation offered by the Legion before this place became yours. That amount is beginning to run dry, and if we aren't given proper payment for future projects… the vast majority of my team will need to leave. *I* plan to stay and attempt to get Havoc to teach me some tricks, but there's only so useful a single Dwarf can be to you."

"I see. It's just a money thing?" Joe was disappointed, but that wasn't fair to the Dwarf. It was likely that he had a well-paying career as an engineer that he was considering giving up for a *chance* to learn from a Grandmaster. "I guess I'll need to figure out how to earn some serious reputation."

"Will... how much do you spend every day?" Bauen tapped at the railing he was holding onto, eyeing Joe as if the human were making a joke in poor taste. "Will taxes not be enough?"

"Taxes? Oh, *snap*! I'll get the taxes from this place?" Joe almost smacked himself for acting the fool. "Of *course* I will. I own the town. I'm guessing there's a tax that the Oligarchy takes as a whole, but I'm a landowner with a large amount of land, and I don't even need to hire other people to build or invest in the buildings?"

He walked away from the Dwarf slightly as he muttered to himself, but his eyes snapped back to Bauen in the next instant. "If you had an unlimited budget... what improvements would you make to this place?"

The Dwarf shrugged as he ran his eyes around the cavern. "I mean... this could be an amazing fortress, completely impenetrable. You could *invent* a sanctum for all of Dwarvenkind out of practically nothing, if the buildings were a high enough tier. Problem with impenetrable fortresses: no way in means no way out. If you wanna go that route, you'd need to make this place entirely self-sufficient. Food, greenspaces, workshops... mines, cropland, air and water purification."

Joe interrupted as politely as possible. "I can't make it a fortress; I need to build it up from starting out as a town. It needs defenses, of course, but..."

"Yikes... that's gonna be tough, so close to Elven territory." Bauen waved Joe off. "I need to work; you need to find ways to build things and hire people."

"Understood. Let's have a conversation later, though? Have a good one." Joe called distractedly. "I need to gather resources and scan Common buildings. I have a ton of interesting blueprints, but I had specifically gone after Rare or better in the last Zone, and I can't think of any structures there that would be helpful here."

"Can I make a suggestion?" Major Cleave offered, her unexpected interruption causing Joe to shout and vault fourteen feet away before whirling to gape at her with surprise etched onto his face. "You *forgot* that I was here… sir?"

"Did you improve your… stealth skill recently?" Joe grabbed at his wildly beating heart and frowned. He flexed his mana, collapsing his active skills, then pulled Exquisite Shell and Neutrality Aura back into full power. Feeling more comfortable in his own skin and secure in his passive defenses, he nodded at Cleave. "Pardon my rudeness. Please, go ahead?"

"The city planner almost certainly has connections with architects." Cleave's voice bore just a *hint* of a begrudging tone. "I'm certain that you could get introduced faster by going through him. Beyond that, someone like you should hire an administrator that can manage day-to-day choices for this place as soon as possible. Someone that can promote it and hand you a schedule of tasks that need your personal attention."

Joe studied her in amazement. She had never spoken this much to him, and he realized that he had a very weak grasp on her abilities. "I suppose they wouldn't have promoted you to Major if all you could do was hit things. Thank you. Please let me know how I can be doing better, and… I hope we can have a cordial relationship going forward."

A corner of her mustache was twitching, either in rage or mirth, but Major Cleave merely nodded at him. Joe thanked her again, then excused himself to locate the city planner. He found Ciril glaring at his workshop with bloodshot eyes. "Hello, Ciril! I was hoping-"

"This is in the wrong spot, *Joe*," Ciril the city planner spat, his unblinking eyes zeroing in on the Reductionist. "It's six centimeters too far to the left, and the angle of the foundation is thirty-eight degrees off. Do you know what this *means*?"

"That… the plan you had drawn up needs to be altered?" Joe shrugged, but he couldn't feel too bad. "I'm sorry, I thought it was correct. I must have missed my-"

A bark of anger cut him off. "*No*. It means that the roads planned through this area will not be wide enough to move

large projects. That means fewer buildings will fit in the designated zones, and-"

"It *means*," Joe growled at the Dwarf in turn, "that the *plan*
will need to be altered. I'm sorry; these things happen. I *apologize*. Putting this here without double-checking was an accident,
and I will endeavor to ensure that future projects align
properly."

Ciril stared at Joe, eventually looking away with a sneer.
"What do you want?"

Awkwardly clearing his throat, Joe mumbled a few words,
then looked up at Ciril. "I was hoping for a favor-"

"*Ha!*" The Dwarf scowled back at the building and started
walking away.

"Oh, that's fine." Joe spoke nonchalantly, turning and
walking away. "I was hoping to use your recommendations for
building design, material selection, and so on. I guess I'll just
figure it out on my own and slap the building down as soon as
I'm ready."

"Let's not be all hasty." Ciril was at Joe's elbow in the same
instant. "Accidents happen, and tempers flare at odd times. We
can always work for the betterment of the Dwarven nation.
Together, like. See?"

"I sure do. Let's be friends," Joe aggressively asserted as they
got down to discussing details. A few minutes later, Ciril had
written out a letter of recommendation and described how to
find the 'best construction company in Svaltarheim'. They
wrapped up and went their separate ways, but Joe mentioned
one small thing just before he hustled to the tunnels leading to
the surface. "As soon as I get back, I'll try to raise some apartments and a barracks. Make sure you know where you want me
to put them. Also, get a few work crews to start gathering all the
rubble into one localized pile! I'll clean that all up!"

"Yeah, yeah," came the grumbling reply. "I got one more
week here, then *someone* is gonna be payin' through the nose."

Joe and Major Cleave were once more on their way to the
city, but as they weren't being chased by an unknown murder-

golem, they were able to step into the command tent and tele-port directly to the Capital by paying a hefty sum of reputation.

By the time they got through the teleportation customs check -something he noted that *Havoc* had never been bothered with—twilight was approaching. Joe paused for a moment, real-izing that he hadn't slept in days. He had died once in that timeframe, but that hadn't exactly been restful. "Major, do we need less sleep as we gain a higher Constitution?"

"Yup. I sleep only about once a month for about four hours at a time," she replied instantly. "That's how we can work long hours and not complain about no free time."

"I see." He inspected himself, realizing that he didn't even *feel* tired. "Status."

Name: Joe 'Tatum's Chosen Legend' Class: Reductionist
Profession I: Arcanologist (Max)
Profession II: Ritualistic Alchemist (1/20)
Profession III: None
Character Level: 21 Exp: 236,309 Exp to next level: 16,691
Rituarchitect Level: 10 Exp: 45,000 Exp to next level: 10,000
Reductionist Level: 2 Exp: 4,636 Exp to next level: 1,364
Hit Points: 1,864/1,864
Mana: 4,955/6,788
Mana regen: 52.7/sec
Stamina: 1,524/1,524
Stamina regen: 6.46/sec

Characteristic: Raw score

Strength: 146
Dexterity: 146
Constitution: 142
Intelligence: 152
Wisdom: 133
Dark Charisma: 100
Perception: 137

Luck: 79
Karmic Luck: 15

Nothing appeared wildly different from previous checks, but his eyes lingered on his massive mana pool. Even though he held a solid fifteen hundred mana in reserve at all times for his three almost-always-on spells, he had more mana than he knew what to do with. "I gotta get some huge cores and make a few utterly massive Mana Batteries."

They soon found their way into the city and located the recommended construction group, which was open despite the hour, further proving Major Cleave's point about higher Constitution. It took a solid hour of negotiation and a hefty cost of a thousand reputation with the Dwarven Oligarchy, but they finally approved a limited license for Joe to scan any of the buildings on a list they provided, so long as such structures were only ever built in his own area.

Joe, finding that he appreciated the group, hired them to design a Rare or Uncommon building, whichever would work best. After describing the garbage-to-aspect building design he had fabricated during his last stint in the dump below the city, and shelling out another five hundred reputation as a down payment for their work, he wandered out into the street.

"Back to the Shoe?" Cleave inquired with a *tiny* groan.

"No, not quite yet." Joe turned toward the city center, which was still well-lit and full of life. "Haven't hired someone I can shuffle all my work onto yet. Let's go find ourselves an administrator so I can get back to being neck-deep in magic. Mate, two coffees, please. It's gonna be a long night."

Burble...! came a strangely sly reply from the stain on his sleeve. Joe was pleased to see Cleave jump back in shock, then less pleased when he needed to dive out of the way of a great axe zealously intent upon cutting off his arm.

"Something's on you!" The swings were coming rapid-fire, and only Joe's Exquisite Shell kept her from dis-arming him.

"*Whaa!* Wait! It's just my coffee elemental!"

CHAPTER EIGHT

Joe and Cleave stood next to each other, staring up at the rickety sign with 'Temp Agency' scrawled across it. The human looked at the Dwarf askance. "Are you *sure* about this place? As far as I can see, people don't come here because they're… skilled."

"Take my advice as you'd like, sir." Cleave pointed at the window, where a few indistinct forms were moving around. "This is where people go when they aren't able to build their own business, acquire an apprenticeship, or just don't want to join the Legion. They don't have a reputation, but they *might* be skilled."

Taking a deep breath, Joe stepped forward and grasped the door handle. He pulled the door open and stepped inside with a smile on his face. "Good evening…good *morning*, that is, seeing as it's well after midnight."

His cheery tone was a massive mismatch for the room, and he received more than his fair share of glares for bursting in as he had. A thickly bearded Dwarf waved them over to a desk with very little enthusiasm. His voice exhausted and monotonous, further sinking Joe's hopes for this place. "Good morning, I'm Stan. Welcome to the *Stan*-dard Workhorse. Our people may not be the best, but they never stop plodding along until they die. How can I help you today?"

"I'm..." Joe's thoughts refused to come out after that congruous introduction, and he turned to gaze longingly at the door.

Major Cleave kicked him in the shin and took over with precise military professionalism. "We're looking for an administrator with a skillset of logistics and city-building. We are offering a long-term contract, with low pay but high opportunity for advancement, both in terms of payment and class leveling."

"What is the reputation rate that you'll be providing?" Stan quizzed Joe directly as he reached for a quill.

Before Joe could open his mouth, Cleave interjected firmly. "Room and board of at least Uncommon quality, with reputation based on effort and success. We are building a town with permission from the Oligarchy. This is not only a chance to gain long term success, but to increase the skills of whoever gets this position to the Master rank or beyond. They will start at the ground floor and eventually become the number two in charge of the administration of a Tier-five city. This is a fully unique offer."

Stan sighed and set down his quill. He glanced up to find a bevy of interested Dwarves that were starting to crowd forward, and he glared around the room. "Everyone get out. We're closed for the morning."

When no one moved, his chest began to rumble and energy started to collect in the air. In the next moment, every waiting Dwarf was lifted and tossed from the building at the same time. Stan's eyes came back to them and he started shaking his head. "A minor question; pardon the inconvenience. Are you attempting to get me killed by coming to a place like this and offering a path to pseudo-nobility?"

"We aren't. I'm not. She might be, but if she is, then I don't know her motivations. Look, do you have someone that fits our needs?" Joe wondered aloud at the depression-inducing Dwarf.

"…I do." The Dwarf studied his paperwork, and his quill flashed out and flew across the page in contrast to his slow-paced diction. "Your offer isn't enough. There *needs* to be reputation involved. How do you feel about a five percent monthly dividend based on tax revenue generated?"

"One percent quarterly. You trying to rob us blind, *bro?*" Cleave half-stood, her hand on the haft of her war axe. "We'll leave right now."

"No, no, one percent is fair when factoring in the other perks." Stan skimmed the sheet, then tapped the housing allotment. "In that case, set housing at *least* at the average rank of the buildings in town as it upgrades?"

"When *possible*. The administrator will understand the finances and such that are involved, yes?" Cleave slowly sat down when Stan didn't even glance up at her outburst.

"Agreed." The paper glowed, and he turned the job offer around to allow the two to read over it. "If I can provide the person, you'll give them a six-month minimum trial."

"This looks good." Joe read over all the details in a flash, his Ritualist as well as Occultist abilities giving him no cause for alarm. He signed the document after Cleave finished reading and nodded her agreement as well.

Stan reached over and shook their hands. "I only have a single person who has the skillset you need, as well as being someone that I know would want the job. So… I look forward to working with you. Please give me one full day to sell this building and join you."

Joe snorted, then burst into laughter. After a few moments, he took the offered hand and shook it. "Well played, Stan. You'll be working for me directly, so I'm glad to know that we can get along without a problem."

Stan cracked a smile for the first time that morning as a glint of light and hope appeared in his eyes. "Looking forward to it, boss man."

As Cleave and Joe walked out onto the street, Joe outlined his next day for the Dwarf. "Tomorrow, I'll be scanning buildings with a representative of the construction company, so tonight... wanna go to a hotel? I feel like we could both use a good night's sleep."

"If you're buying, as well as getting us separate rooms, why not." Cleave shrugged and motioned for him to lead the way. A short while later, they were settled in, and both managed to get a few solid hours of rest.

Thanks to an oddly snickering Mate, they both started the day right and headed out to meet the rep with a pep in their step. The sun slowly crawled above the walls of the city, and the appointed time approached. Joe heard the clicking of heels on stone, striking at a measured pace that he considered a normal human speed, and turned to discover a head of frazzled brown hair surrounding a familiar face. Joe squinted, unsure if his mind was playing tricks on him, until her eyes bounced up from the clipboard she was carrying and met his. "Daniella?"

She screeched to a stop and stared at him in shock that slowly turned to recognition. "Joe? *Joe*! You *aren't* in prison! So good to see you again! Are you... oh, this is going to be exactly like what happened in Ardania, isn't it?"

"Um... yes." Joe chuckled and rubbed at his bald head. "I'm planning to build a city, and I need to get a few scans of more Common buildings."

"Yeah, that certainly sounds nothing like what you did back... oh, I'm so rude. Major, I'm Daniella, your representative for the day."

"Major Cleavage," the Dwarf rumbled with a nod. Daniella peered down at the outfit she had chosen for the day in concern, but the Dwarf powered on unabashed, "Still strange to say, since I was only a Captain for forty years. Got promoted *way* ahead of schedule."

"Oh, it's your *name*... ahem." Daniella lifted the clipboard like a shield and started walking. "Shall we get started? It looks to be a long day ahead of us."

The three of them started working their way through the city, with Joe intermittently activating Architect's Fury and pulling in a blueprint. As the quest drew closer to completion, he became more animated in his conversation with Daniella. Soon they were discussing what he was actually planning to do with all of the scans, and it came out that Joe was already actively working on constructing an entirely new settlement, not just 'planning' to make one.

Daniella went quiet while Joe scanned the final building he needed, and the quest updated.

Class quest complete: Novice Rituarchitect. You have scanned ten Common rank buildings and are prepared to use them!

Buildings scanned:

Barracks (150 units), Apartment building (50 units), Administrative Office (25 stations), Warehouse (10,000 feet of storage), Smithy (3 forge stations), Shop (General Goods), Tannery (3 positions), Warehouse (Perishable goods, 6,000 feet of storage), Bathhouse (10 wash stations), Butchery (5 stations).

Reward: Blueprint for Ziggurat, a ritual-based area buff landmark. Record breaker reward: Ziggurat blueprint upgraded to Rare rank!

The bathhouse had been the most fun to scan, as it had been in use, and the attendant had determined that there was no need to warn the patrons. Water had been sloshed everywhere, and shouting and laughter had soon followed.

Class quest gained: Novice Rituarchitect II. Using a ritual, create each of the buildings you have scanned at least once. Reward: 500 class experience per building.

Even though the reward was only experience, it made Joe wildly excited. He couldn't remember precisely the last time he had rapidly gained class experience for his specialization—since he had only crafted two buildings the entire time he had been on the zone—and he was *yearning* for new abilities and increased power.

The truth was, Joe was underleveled and underpowered for this entire plane. He could defeat monsters one by one with trickery, but the Elven foes were able to smack him around like a pinata. Even when Francine had been saved and the fortress destroyed, his contribution to the war effort had been blocking an illusion—and he was able to see his weakness written in the Dwarven blood price that he had needed to pay. Now that a path forward was presenting itself, he didn't want to *walk* it… he needed to *sprint*.

"I had a question for you." Daniella squared her shoulders and looked Joe in the eye. "I saw the company start a new project this morning… was that you?"

"Yes, I requested a custom building," Joe admitted slowly, unsure where the conversation was heading. "What's on your mind?"

She nodded a few times, then offered him a sheet of parchment with a set of skills written out on it. "I came here when the Bifrost opened, but the only work I was able to find was Assistant to an Apprentice. Climbing the company ladder is a matter of *decades* here without great feats of valor or other major accomplishments. Can I come work for your city?"

Joe looked over the list, fully ignoring the wide eyes that seemed to draw him in even at a distance. The more he read, the more interested he became. "How in the world do you have all of these skills at Journeyman?"

"I had plenty of schooling, as well as practical experience before my entrance to Eternium." Her voice was pitched to be as professional as possible, and he could tell that she was treating this as a job interview. "I honed my skills on Midgard as well, before being transferred here with a few specific advancement quests."

Swallowing dryly, Joe hesitated and waffled over how he should respond. Completely unsure whether he wanted to say yes so that he could see her more often, or if it was because of her *excellent* resume, he decided on the safe course of action. "Major, I know where I stand; what do you think?"

Major Cleave took the list, scanned it, then nodded at Joe. "Her skills close at hand would make our life much easier."

"When can you start?" Joe held out his hand to shake Daniella's.

Seemingly ever practical, she glanced down at her papers and thought for a moment before reaching out. "What if I deliver the blueprints for your new building, then just… stay there?"

"Done." The last thing Joe wanted was to have to make another trip to the city in the next few days. The fact that he was finding it hard to breathe had nothing to do with the reason he turned on his heel and started marching in the general direction of the Shoe with a smirking Major keeping pace beside him. "See you soon!"

CHAPTER NINE

The day was sinking into late afternoon by the time Joe and Major Cleave were approaching the main entrance to the Shoe. In a bid to take their time slowly so as to get to know each other better, they had taken the long route home. Joe had found that even though she seemed cold and distant, that was simply the veneer that had been put in place over her years of service in the Legion.

She had a certain gallows humor that made him chuckle, and the formal military bearing she kept up at all times had eased as the travel day stretched on. Joe was about to make a joke that he was sure she would appreciate, when he caught a whiff of schnitzel and gunpowder. His stomach began rumbling at the same moment that he dove at Major Cleave with a full-powered Omnivault and sent both of them rolling.

The ground where they had stood erupted from the impact of a veritable wall of metal shards slamming into it, followed shortly by the sonic booms of shots fired. As the echo came, so too did a deep German accent. "What a terrible shame to make me waste all of my precious babies! Shame. On. *You!*"

Joe had his Ritual Orbs out and flying as soon as he had a line of sight on the unfortunately impressive assassin. Herr Trigger was prepared for his attacks and simply began dodging as he crossed the ground between them, his larger weapons set aside in favor of more close-range pistols. Joe forced the man to shy away as he activated Cone of Cold through his Orb and caught the man's legs from an unexpected angle. "Why are you still coming after me? Don't you have better things to do?"

"You have an *impressive* bounty on your head. Once I got a taste, I felt the need to dine again and again at my new favorite restaurant." Herr Trigger had a wide smile gracing his lips. "Now I *must* know, how did you escape our first volley?"

"Our…?" Now that he was looking for them, Joe spotted a half-dozen people dropping what appeared to be flintlock rifles and closing in on his two-person group. "Well, *that's* not good."

"*Finally*," Major Cleave snarled as she whirled her axe around, charging as soon as it settled in her palm. "Assassinate me once? Shame on me. Show yourself before I'm dead…? Prove yourself a fool!"

In the next few moments, Joe realized that he might need to spend a *whole* lot of time increasing his physical ability. All the Dwarf did was *run* at the assembled humans, nothing fancy or wildly skill-oriented. Her attack was also very simple and straightforward, but the power behind it was at a level that Joe hadn't ever been able to experience up close. At least, not with this kind of characteristic point discrepancy.

When he had attacked the Shoe, the Elves had been ready for the Dwarves and had centuries of practice in fighting them. Direct blows were turned away by spells and summons, which meant that combat had looked similar to what Joe had seen against the Wolfmen. Here? There were assassins and fighters, humans that had gotten good at killing… but they were nowhere near ready to be exposed to Major Cleavage.

As her namesake suggested, a single attack traveled through multiple enemies, but Joe hadn't *really* known what that meant.

'Cleave' sounded pretty basic. The reality was… disturbing. If an axe hit multiple enemies, that meant it had gone *through* all of them.

Three humans dropped to the ground as six chunks, sent to respawn by the time Joe managed to flinch away from the ranged blood splatter in shock and disgust. The Major's axe swept back and forth with less effort than a human whipping a twig around, dealing maximum damage to the attackers' gear before finally taking them down. Joe had no doubt that the repairs for all that gear would be extensive and *expensive*.

His mind returned to the battle at hand, and he performed a backward handspring with Omnivault, barely managing to escape a flare that erupted from Herr Trigger's pocket and blazed where his head had been a moment earlier; he guessed it was likely a combination of a flashbang and intense flame damage.

Joe's hands swept around, directing his mana into a Dark Lightning Strike that lashed out soundlessly, catching the assassin even as he dodged. With the minor paralyzation that took the man, the Reductionist sprayed out a wash of acid that he tried to direct at the weapons in the man's hands. His aim was good, but his actions utterly *infuriated* the bounty hunter.

"Do you have *any* idea how long it takes to create custom firearms and individually enchant every bullet?" Herr Trigger bellowed as he tossed his guns into the air above him. Joe landed on the ground, thinking he had a moment before the assassin would be able to attack. His assumption was that the man was throwing away the damaged weapons: he was wrong.

Herr Trigger pulled out a second set of handguns that looked like oversized six shooters and tossed those in the air as well, finally drawing one last pair and shouting with a strange authority, "Thirty-six Six Shooter!"

The last pair of handguns were fired at Joe, then tossed up as the first pair came and landed in his hands. Those fired, and were tossed. Just going by the speed of the shots, there was clearly a skill involving a spatial inventory at work, but Joe didn't have time to examine the technique. He simply broke it down to the most basic level. Six handguns, six shots a pop, which all fully reloaded when they were tossed up.

Bullets flooded against his Exquisite Shell so rapidly that he barely had time to think. He dodged around, back and forth, jumping and rolling; but no matter the action he chose, bullets were constantly clipping him—if not directly smashing into his defenses. Joe hit the ground, blood pouring out of his minced body.

Damage taken: 10,406 (121 penetrating damage x86 hits.)

Exquisite Shell: 0/9,842

Health: 1,300/1,864 (bleeding. -34 health per second!) You've got holes in you!

There was only one saving grace, one thing that kept him from getting hit perfectly with each shot and cut off the storm of bullets: with every bullet, Retaliation of Shadows went to work, slapping the absolute *abyss* out of the bounty hunter. Eighty-six total rounds had pinged off Joe until his shield failed, but the same number of little slaps of enhanced darkness eventually sent Herr Trigger flying, his weapons following him as he tumbled.

Damage dealt: 3,731 dark damage.

"That *hurt*, you *bounty*." Even with the sheer amount of damage he had taken, the man was on his feet a moment later, rolling with the force and checking to see how his team was doing. Coughing blood, his eyes wobbled back over to Joe. "Oh, we are doing *poorly*. Here's today's Trigger Warning: next time, I will be prepared for you… and for *him*."

"That's a *female* Dwarf," Joe snorted as he directed his Orbs to slam into the sides of the assassin's head from either side, pumping a Cone of Cold into the man's ear on one side and simple, pure, concussive force into the other. "One win for each of us; next kill decides the winner."

Damage dealt: 541 (158 x2 blunt, 225 cold).

"It'll be my victory." Herr Trigger managed one last predatory grin before being sent to respawn with the rest of his team.

Joe dropped to the ground, heaving for air as he pumped healing spells into himself. A slew of messages tried to take over, but he only had eyes for the *wildly* expanded usefulness of Exquisite Shell. "Double mana means more placed in the spell, and I haven't found its upper limit for mana usage yet. How had I not even *thought* about how much damage that blocks now? Have I been so busy that I haven't even *considered* my combat spells? What's wrong with me?"

"Physically? Nothing, except your lack of any identifying hair," Major Cleave informed him after considering him for a moment. "I do wonder how you survived that series of shots. That skill the strange human used was *clearly* an Alpha Strike, and it must have had a massive cost to use. Without permanent defenses of a certain level, I'm having trouble remembering another time I've seen someone survive one. Skills such as that tend to end lives when they are as single-target and point-blank as that one was."

"Alpha Strike?" Joe blinked owlishly as he mulled over the title. "I'm learning that I may be further behind than I thought I was, Major. What's an Alpha Strike?"

"The... torrent of destruction you just survived?" The Major peered into his eyes with concern. "Did you take a brain damage debuff? You *must* have some form of ability... oh! I have also heard them called an 'Ultimate' by your race?"

"An ulty? People have ultimate abilities?" Joe glanced at his skill list, not finding anything that could count toward that. "How do you know what an ulty is? I mean, how do you know if you have one?"

"How do you *know?*" Major Cleave huffed in surprise and shook her head. "If you don't know how to rank skills and spells, I suppose you would know them by their massive cooldowns? A day, or twice-a-day usage, is at the lowest level of an Alpha Strike. Once you see week-long, month, year, or even longer... that is when you know you have gained a truly powerful strike. I heard a rumor that you saw two of Major-General Havoc's known Alpha Strikes. His golem form is one?"

Joe's eyes went dull as he recalled the horror that his mentor had turned into with the full knowledge that he wouldn't survive. Somehow the knowledge that that particular skill couldn't be called on at will gave him a sense of intense relief. "I see... I suppose I have something that might count. I have an ability called Resurrection which can only be used once a day before cooldowns."

Major Cleave held his gaze for a long moment, before slowly nodding. "Yes, the ability to return someone to life with only a cost to your mana is... fairly ultimate, as you say."

"Yeah. But... how do you get them?" Joe tapped on the ground in thought, then remembered that his Exquisite Shell was broken. He dumped his entire pool of six thousand, seven hundred and eighty-eight mana into the spell. For a long moment, the spell crackled and sparked like lightning, before settling into a patina that looked like a glitter bomb gone wrong. He was so used to it that he didn't notice anymore, but the Major rolled her eyes.

"How indeed." She shook off her attitude and tried to give a proper answer. "While there are people that may be able to teach them, Alpha Strikes are usually gained through a combination of class levels and class quests. At some point, you will either learn or be granted one."

"Oh." Joe frowned at his level, which had remained near twenty-one for several weeks at the minimum, and his other classes, which had barely progressed in months. "So there *are* still reasons to level up. I had kinda stopped worrying about that in favor of grinding skills."

"Yes, sir," Major Cleave informed him drolly. "You're correct. Levels aren't just numbers that stop carrying meaning as you get stronger. That would kind of defeat the entire purpose of having a quantifiable system of advancement in the first place."

"Huh. I figured that at some point, it just wouldn't matter anymore." Joe smiled and hopped to his feet. "Nothing for it! Let's get awesome!"

"He's just been using *basic* abilities this entire time? What kind of imagination does he have that lets them push the limits of skills this successfully?" Major Cleave watched as Joe skipped down the road toward the Shoe, shivering lightly. "This man is a monster."

CHAPTER TEN

Dark Lightning Strike has reached Apprentice IX.
   Lay on Hands has reached Student III.
   Retaliation of Shadows has reached Journeyman IV.
   Assisted Ritual Orb Usage has reached Beginner III.
Joe's eyes flew across the information as he entered the tunnels and raised his arms to let the Dwarven guards on duty wave an Elf Alignment Rod—an EAR—over his body. It was an incredibly basic test that listened to his mana frequency to ensure spies weren't slipping in, but until this city became wealthy enough to have more potent security measures in place, they worked with what they had.

As expected, the check came back clean, and they progressed to the interior of Gramma's Shoe. Joe blinked at the dazzling lights that had been arranged across the ceiling in a pleasing gradient in five distinct sectors: daylight, orange, green, blue, and violet. Surveying the ground under the lights, Joe could see that the lights roughly correlated to the areas the city planner had zoned out.

The 'daylight' area was one of the largest, and was designated to be set up for livestock, farming, and a small park. The violet would be the area which Havoc had claimed for Joe's magical experimentation, but Joe hadn't paid much attention to what the other areas would eventually be. For now, his eyes came to rest upon the only real landmark besides his personal workshop and the Artifact alchemy-building: a huge pile of fragments and building material.

It appeared that the Dwarves had been busy. The ground was clear from rubble, and several teams were working to excavate the last few remaining sections of stonework that had been buried even slightly underground. All that remained at this point was cleanish, bare stone—a solid foundation that they would use to build a new and powerful community. Before kicking that off, Joe was fully planning to use the destroyed materials to jumpstart his settlement—his class quest would shoot ahead in the near future.

Hurrying over to the pile, he started setting up a Field Array. No one was guarding the waste material, for fully understandable reasons, but it still felt like an oversight that he should correct. For him, someone else's trash was literally his own treasure. Banana peels could become walls, dirty diapers were destined to be shingles, and... "Now that I'm thinking about it... maybe I *shouldn't* tell people what I'm going to be making their houses from?"

The Field Array came out to be about ten square meters, which meant he would need to shift it around and redo the work a few times, but it should be worth it in the end. He tapped the lines that remained glowing in the air, sending a pulse of mana along them to get an idea of what he was getting into.

Item: Approximately 10 cubic meters of Rare and lesser material. (Rubble; most aspects reduced in aspect value.)

Reduction value: 291 Rare aspects, 2,648 Uncommon aspects, 24,097 Common aspects, 72,291 Damaged aspects, 144,582 Trash aspects.

Total mass: 23,490 pounds of material.

Reduction cost: 112.5 mana per second. Estimated reduction time required: 81 seconds.

"Yikes. That's heavy. Nine thousand, one hundred and twelve mana if I do it all in one go?" Joe assessed the material and nodded as he realized that a goodly amount of it was stone and other dense material. "That's about a third more than what I have, so I'll just have to deal with standing here and slowly converting it. Huh. Must be a lot of air in there, too. If it were tightly packed, I bet this would be *way* more expensive and dense than that."

The idea of 'dense material' brought his mind back to the cube of material that had dropped out of his codpiece when he had reached this zone. He was waiting to reduce that until he had a proper reduction room; essentially, a large warehouse with a permanent oversized Field Array. Until then... Joe closed his eyes and felt at the Ritual of Reduction that was literally written out in his body.

He only had two aspect jars with him, a Natural Common Aspect Jar and a Natural Unique Aspect Jar. Joe placed them strategically along the Field Array and directed all the other aspects to enter into his Codpiece of Holding. Plenty of Aspects would be lost, but he *needed* to get to work on this project. Also, while there were no Unique aspects in this batch, he was hoping that the ritual would eventually uncover some. With everything in place, he started gently pushing his mana into the lines.

Over the next few minutes, the pile of rubble slowly shifted and settled as it was converted into aspects. The original eighty-one second timeline came and went, and a frown started to build on Joe's face. Aspects were streaming into his storage device, the Common aspect jar *long* since full. His mana regenerated at just over fifty per second, meaning he had regenerated over four thousand at the point the process should have ended.

"Feces... it's shifting down from above!" Joe hadn't even thought about how that would impact the reduction. Now he was *glad* he hadn't simply pushed for completing it in one burst —the stone may have all toppled onto him, or at the very least, not been stacked in such a nice pile anymore. "How did I not think about that?"

Releasing the array, a flare of the mana lashed out and vaporized a good amount of the stone, reducing it to trash without granting him any aspects. "Ugh... what a waste. Still, I can do this at *least* another three times without any issues. I should save it for when I get access to my Reductionist class quests."

Quest complete: Beginner Ritualist. Ritual Lore (Novice IX): 1/1. Resources gained: 1,000/1,000 Common Aspects, 5,000/5,000 Damaged Aspects. Reward: access to Beginner Ritualist II. Record breaker reward: Reward for Beginner Ritualist II increased.

Quest gained: Beginner Ritualist II. Now that you've prepared your reagents, quills, and likely went on a shopping spree of epic proportions, it's time to do some actual work and prepare for combat! Higher-tier materials aren't going to rip themselves out of monsters for you; you've got to do it yourself without dying! Create 25 offensive and 25 defensive rituals for use in combat! Minimum: Beginner rank. Reward: self-protection is its own reward, but you specifically will also gain access to Beginner Ritualist III! Offensive rituals: 0/25. Defensive rituals: 0/25.

"What the abyss...? Wasn't the reward from the first quest a boost to the next reward? But this one's reward is just access to the third one?" Joe pored over the rest of the information, then looked at the charged Aspect Jars. He gathered them up, letting the Field Array fade into nothingness.

Natural Common Aspect Jar: 1,820/1,820 Common aspects.
Natural Unique Aspect (Unique) Jar: 1,201/9,558 Unique aspects.
Aspects gathered
Trash: 141,581
Damaged: 74,373
Common: 25,926
Uncommon: 3,390
Rare: 418
Special: 3 (Zombified). 100 (Anima). 111 (Molten)

Unique: 1,719
Artifact: 357
Legendary: 0
Mythical: 0

Looking at the list, Joe could only bite his lips to keep from being frustrated. Weeks of effort, the sacrifice of a half-dozen impressive weapons, as well as the material from another Artifact building had all been devoted to creating a single building that no one could even access yet. "Only reason this place is still standing is that upside-down pyramid… that was a *great* return on investment. Keep that in mind."

He scowled at the pyramid and felt his eyelid twitch. "I suppose I can only wonder what an Artifact-ranked Reduction Warehouse would look like. For now. It's *fi~ine.*"

"Major-General, if I may-" Joe screamed and vaulted away from Major Cleave, who stood stock-still as he clutched at his heart. "Sir. You *need* to stop doing that."

"If I gave you a bell, would you wear it?" Joe muttered too softly for even her enhanced senses to pick it up. He cleared his voice and spoke in a normal voice, "Sorry about that. I was lost in thought. Would have screamed at anyone who came up on me right then. What were you… ah, what's your suggestion?"

The impressive mustache twitched as Major Cleave struggled to swallow her harsh words. "I was saying that perhaps you might want to consider getting a few buildings in place for housing the people in the area. While we *do* have the ability to go for a long time without sleep, simply having the option may sway the minds of the people considering staying here long-term in your favor."

"An excellent idea." Joe nodded vehemently, *totally* not agreeing because he was afraid that annoying her too much would bring her axe to bear and turn him from regular Joe into 'Espresso Joe' by slicing him up into fine bits and applying heat and pressure in the form of hiding the evidence in the lava pits. "Let's find Ciril and get a team of mana-rich Dwarves together. Also, please feel free to remind me whenever I'm going off on tangents. I *know* I have things to do, and I'm always glad to toe the line in the Shoe!"

"Sir…" Major Cleave's voice was pained. "Before you came here, what sort of things did people throw at you, and how many times a day did it happen? Just for research purposes."

CHAPTER ELEVEN

Quest updated: Novice Rituarchitect II. Buildings created: 3/10.

Eyeing the message as he listened to the odd sound of brand-new screws biting into wood all by themselves, Joe licked his lips and whispered, "Soon, my sweet class experience. *Soon.*"

To be fair, each of the buildings he had raised with the ritual had added fifty experience each to his Reductionist and Rituarchitect classes, but those drops in a bucket only added up over time. He needed nine thousand, eight hundred and fifty to reach level eleven as a Rituarchitect, but under five thousand for his Reductionist class. At five hundred per completed structure, each of which he could soon charge rent on, he'd be over halfway to his next class level.

Title 'Architect of Artifacts' increases base stats of Common Apartment Building (50 units) by 10%, increasing Common Apartment Building to 55 units. Durability: 3,300/3,300.

"Look at *that.*" Ciril stared at the perfect, burnished orange glow that seemed to hang around the building due to the lights directly above. "I swear, every time you've made one of those, they look better the longer I look at them."

Joe chuckled internally, knowing that he'd never reveal that he had a title that improved the buildings after initial construction. It was too much fun to watch the Dwarf trying to figure out if he was going crazy. He looked around the area, noting the other two buildings he had managed to bring up over the last few hours: a barracks and the bathhouse.

As it turned out, the lighting had been coordinated with the planner after he saw the tiles being placed all willy-nilly, and Joe had managed to take a look at the new plan. He had been correct about what was planned under the daylight and purple lights, then been informed that areas under the blue light were for crafters, green was for administration and cleaning, and finally orange for housing the civilian, militia, and military members that were moving in.

"I think we should call this place 'Eternal Sunset Acres'," Ciril informed the people around them. "A name like that lends the area a sense of mysticism, and it should draw people looking to relocate."

"Huh. I was thinking of 'Empty Shoe Estates', personally." Joe shrugged as his suggestion gained him a few disdainful glances. "What? You guys think that'd draw in the wrong crowd? People that want you to get off their lawn or something? 'Shoe' does sound like 'shoo', I guess. You win this one, Ciril."

He continued rambling until the staring became withering glares, then promptly looked down at his list and decided that they had done enough for the day. "Now that we have a place to sleep and clean up, let's take off and meet up tomorrow. I have a few things to attend to."

Various Dwarves who had volunteered to help muttered their farewells and drifted off. Joe watched where they went, observing that the population of the area was rapidly declining. Practically all the civilians in the area were tourists that had been living in seclusion in the nearby caves, and had come out only to find that the Shoe had changed drastically. The remainder were leftover Legion units who were planning to leave over the next few weeks. There would be a token force remaining, but Joe needed to build up the defenses of the fledgling town as part of his Ranker quest, so he wasn't expecting too much help from the existing military.

"I've done my duty for the night; now on to *other* things I want to do." Joe shot off, leaping along the ground yet doing his best to stay as low as possible. He hadn't earned any progress with Omnivault recently, so he knew he needed to spend plenty of time practicing with it in new and interesting ways. He turned and headed toward his space, the area that was just for him.

His purple light hanging in the open air was a welcome sight that drew him to his workshop, but the person hitting the door with what looked like a reinforced handbag was not. "You open this door right *now*, Jimathy!"

The lady continued hollering as she battered the door. Joe wanted to chuckle at first, but then he realized that the blow had caused a full point of durability damage. She was swinging that bag with the force of a maul and hitting *his* workshop!

He was next to her with one more jump, just as she was beginning a fresh attack. Joe grabbed the bag but was thrown into the building as it swung forward. He hit the door with a *crunch*, woozily appreciating the fact that at least the building didn't take further damage. "Yay, I'm softer than a brand-name handbag. Lady, why are you attacking my workshop?"

"Help! A thief is trying to steal my purse!" The words that blasted out of the painted lips could have been a sonic weapon back on earth, and the bag that swung down at him could have been mistaken for a warhammer. The first blow slapped Joe into the door, but he managed to get his wits about him as she tried again.

"*Stop that!*" he commanded in a voice resounding with pure authority. "You're attacking a Major-General. Any further violence against me will get you… chucked in the lava or something. Knock it off."

He resolved at that moment to make holding cells. The nice kind, where the detainee had books and such for entertainment. While the Legion *could* take care of any issues, being sent to the

Ledger of Souls for a year was apparently a common punishment. That did make him wonder how they would handle the humans' constant respawning…

"Oh! Then you can help me." The lady shrugged back her bright pink boa, which she was wearing in a volcano… *what?* "Jimathy ran off while we were playing, he said he decided that it was time for him to learn magic. He came to this house to start practicing, only to find that he was locked out! He got so upset that he refused to let me into the entryway to help him break down the next door! You've gotta let me in so I can help him smash the doors all the way in."

There was a whole lot to unpack in that statement, but Joe started with the easy stuff. "Why would he… no, why would you think it was fine to break into my workshop and start messing with my stuff?"

"Don't you get snippy with *me*, turtle-head!" A perfectly manicured, hot pink fingernail jabbed at Joe, only stopping at his Exquisite Shell. "*What?* how did you stop me? Are you using *magic* against me? Elf! There's an Elf here! Legion! Come kill this Elf!"

Taking a deep breath, Joe peered through the small window on the door to find a hulking brute of a man slamming his fists into the reinforced inner doors, ignoring the fact that blood was pouring from his knuckles and staining the white stone floor. "Whoa. I haven't seen someone act this entitled since I gave up eating fast food a decade ago, when I saw that lady slap the seventeen year old cashier because the ice cream machine was broken. Ya know, I really thought people would have changed when they had the ability to constantly improve themselves."

"What did you just say?" The painted siren followed his eyes and shifted her tone into a sickly-sweet one. "I get it; you noticed his gains? Jimathy has been in the gym lifting almost *endlessly* since we came to this realm. He has one of the highest strength stats out of all the humans in this, like, totally weird world."

Joe tapped the door, and it swung open. He wanted to enjoy

the benefits that came with owning the building, but the lady blasted past him and started yelling at the man for ignoring her 'again', then started swinging her bag at the closed door. Joe took a deep, calming breath… then bellowed, "Both of you, get *out*!"

"Whoa. You *don't* get to talk to me like that." The lady whirled on him, pointing her sharp fingernail at Joe's face. "Babe, are you gonna let him talk to me like that? Aren't you gonna be a good boyfriend?"

The constant **thud** of meat against metal paused, and Joe was thankful that he had taken the time to reinforce his building. He was unhappy to see the man turn around and look at him through eyes that could have been marbles: perfectly round, tiny, and solid black. Like a miniature shark. "Yo. You want some of this, *bro*?"

As the man flexed, Joe reflected that the guy had somehow gotten to this zone and joined the side of the war that was a perfect fit for him. Just as he was about to mouth off, a tiny asterisk appeared over him. Now that he noticed it, he saw it over the woman as well. Unsure what the image meant, he focused on the anomaly and it expanded into a message:

Private (PV1) Kettlebell. Crime: Threatening a superior officer. Punishment options…

The *massive* list that appeared next shocked Joe to his core. Some of the options were marked 'Major-General', meaning that he could only select them due to his rank. His mind reacted on autopilot, filtering the options to things he actually *wanted* to do. In an instant, he had found and selected 'Ban from premises' for both of the humans. They found themselves lurching out of the building under their own power, shocked expressions on their faces.

"*Du~ude.* Is that what magic can do? I wanna piece of that." Kettlebell ran back at the door like a linebacker charging a quarterback, only to be forced to stop. He fell on his face and rolled back until he was considered 'off the premises'. "Ha *ha*!

That's what I'm talking about. Yo, Baldy. Teach me the magics."

"Babe, you don't wanna learn from *him*." The lady, 'Pink Flying Flamingos Are My Jam'—according to her Legion punishment option—hissed at her boyfriend. "Look, he's all gross and weird. I bet he can't even do magic. You can't even do magic, can you, gross bald man? Hey, I'm *talking* to-"

Joe firmly closed the door and took a few deep breaths. "I'm gonna need to talk to the people who're letting newcomers into the Shoe. I have no interest in allowing an infestation of fungus like that."

Doing his best to put the strange people out of his mind, Joe turned his attention to the parchment waiting for him. "Twenty-five attack and defense rituals. Beginner rank. This should take no time at all."

Using his newly improved understanding of lower-ranked rituals, he slowly decided on the effects that he wanted to see come to fruition. Once he had a goal and actionable steps, he would begin the process. He had learned that if he simply jumped into it without thought, he would only be annoyed at the result. "A goal without a plan is just a wish, so let's begin."

The first step was going to be determining what the quest considered 'defensive'. He supposed that he could simply try to make twenty-five versions of his Exquisite Shell, but he wanted to gain experience as well as complete the quest. After looking over his spells… he realized that he might not have another choice. That was his only defensive spell, and it wasn't as though he could turn his *skills* into ritual diagrams. That thought made Joe pause in excitement, but he eventually shook his head. "I'd have no clue where to start on that. With spells, it's just rejiggering a known diagram to make it work. Skills? No idea."

Feeling slightly self-conscious, Joe got to work making twenty-five variations of his Exquisite Shell.

CHAPTER TWELVE

Joe had finished with his defensive rituals and was eagerly looking forward to testing them out. As they were his first try, and he had designed them to be Beginner rank, they were kind of… weak. For use in Svaltarheim, they were practically useless by themselves. Having realized this well in advance of making them, Joe had found a way to do something hilarious, which would cause the rituals to come up to a sufficient level of usefulness at the same time.

Ritual of the Exquisite Shell (Beginner) (Linked* x5): This ritual mimics the effects of potent arcane magic mixed with the divine. When activated, a ritual circle appears beneath the user, which will block all damage that crosses the boundary of the circle in either direction. Total damage that can be blocked: 3,000.

Linked Ritual: This ritual is linked directly to another ritual. Upon expiration or destruction of the original ritual, the next linked ritual will automatically activate.

Quest update: Beginner Ritualist II. Defensive rituals: 25/25. Offensive rituals: 0/25.

"I cannot *believe* I didn't blow my head off after I managed to put five of them on each parchment scroll," Joe muttered to himself as he looked over the vibrating scrolls, very carefully lifting them up and storing them away in his spatial ring, where they shouldn't accidentally activate or get damaged. "This'll give me a solid safety net against that trigger-happy assassin that's been stalking me, at least. I can see why this is a required class quest for everyone. Even at the Beginner rank, I managed to learn something new."

He hadn't had the opportunity to scribe the offensive rituals yet, and he didn't think he was going to be able to make it happen right away. Keeping the parchment and rituals stable while he had been expanding them into linked versions had been surprisingly taxing, even though it was absolutely worth learning that he could do so. Rubbing his tired eyes, he stepped out of his workshop with five new scrolls ready to be used whenever he had an emergency. "Or I could give them out to someone else that could activate them, I guess?"

The rituals were primed, but they still required at least a basic understanding of how to use a magic item. The Ritualist looked up from his feet and stumbled to a halt as he found himself face-to-face with Private Kettlebell, Pink Flamingo, and a seriously upset Major Cleave. She was smiling, baring all of her teeth under her extra-bushy mustache. "I don't suppose you forgot something important when you rushed into your office and slammed the door behind you? Perhaps someone that had to wait out here with these... absolutely delightful specimens of humanity?"

Thinking quickly, Joe shook his head somberly. "I am sorry, Major; I do not have more comfortable accommodations for you. However, I left you out here on purpose. I was attempting new ritual diagrams, and there was a good chance I was going to create a contained explosion in the building. I could not, in good conscience, allow you to wait in there with me."

Sweat trickled down his face as Joe waited to see if the Dwarf would buy that load of malarkey. There was no way that he could tell her that he had once again forgotten that she existed. Not trusting that he could be quiet enough, he simply kept his thoughts to himself. *'Seriously, wallpaper in a building I've worked at for a decade keeps my attention more than she does.'*

"I see…"

The Major went silent, her eyes narrowed in suspicion as Kettlebell stepped forward. "Yo. I'm in this volcano because someone told me I could learn the magic, and if I'm gonna do it, I'm gonna be in a totally rad volcano that could kill us all at any second. Really adds a sense of urgency, you know? You going to teach me, or what?"

"While I would love to help you… 'learn the magics'…" Joe shook his head at that thought, then sobered up as the deadly shark eyes of the huge man locked on to his own. "Let me ask you something. Are you trying to learn magic because you *want* to learn it, or because you think that is the only option? I have to tell you, there are *way* better options if you've already started going down a purely physical build."

There was a long pause as Kettlebell considered the question, surprising Joe by seeming to *really* think about it. Perhaps he had misjudged this mountain of muscles? "Nah, I'm only wanting to do it because my gal here said I should."

"You *should*," Pink Flamingo barked at him, turning to glare at Joe. "Why are you going out of your way to kill his dream like this? I'm going to make you *pay* for that. No one treats my man like this. He gets what he *wants!*"

"I mean… if this is what *he* wants, I'm sure you can find someone to teach him. I don't use standard magic all that much, so I wouldn't even be a good teacher." Joe threw his hands in the air helplessly. "Frankly, you both need to leave before I start blasting you into puppy kibble. Why do you think you can barge into my town, try to break your way into my building, order me around, then get mad at *me*? First of all, I'm a *Major-General*, and you're each a rank one Private. I could put you in prison for literally eight years every time you talk to me like this. It's an option that appears every time-"

"How about you-" Pink Flamingo was cut off with a yelp as Major Cleave grabbed her by the hot pink boa and started dragging her out of the area. Since she couldn't breathe, she couldn't yell at Kettlebell for help, and he hadn't even noticed her plight—his unblinking eyes had never left Joe.

"Only way to get promoted is to do something these Dwarves can't. That means purely physical is out," Kettlebell informed Joe with a strangely thoughtful tone. "Right now, I have only basic classes. I'm not going to leave you alone unless you either promote me so I can get out of the Legion, or give me something I can do here."

"Just... *fine*. Why don't you go find Jaxon?" Joe took a moment to describe the man, then tried to shoo the enormous bodybuilder of a human away so that he could test out his new rituals. After he described some of the things that Jaxon could do, Kettlebell seemed at least interested enough to blink once every eight seconds.

"Thanks, man. I won't make you regret helping me like this." Kettlebell paused, looked around, and shook his head. "*I won't. But unless you go groveling to Pink Flamingo, you better watch your back. She really likes to claw people's eyes out, then turn them around so her victim can watch themselves get sent to respawn.*"

"Utterly terrifying," Joe deadpanned as his stomach turned, easing away from the huge man and going off in search of an empty area where he could try out his new defensive parchments. Even though they were perfect, and they would have been expensive if he hadn't just 'eaten' several buildings' worth of material, the idea of going into combat without testing his weapons gave him cold sweats.

After verifying that he was alone, his personal Exquisite Shell was in place, and there was nothing in the area that he might accidentally damage, Joe unrolled the first set of linked rituals and activated it...

Then there was darkness and pain.

Only when he checked his combat log, after peeling open blurry eyes and finding himself lying on a bed wrapped in bandages, was he able to learn what had happened after their activation.

You have empowered a damaged, unstable magic item. Ritual is activating: Warped Ritual of Exquisite Shell (Linked x5).

Warped ritual is approaching critical instability!

Warped ritual has gone critical!

Linked ritual is activating: Warped Ritual of Exquisite Shell (Linked x5).

The messages went on like that for a while, so Joe ignored them and used Lay on Hands to rapidly bring his body to normal condition; happily, his efforts brought the spell up to Student four. Around a dry throat, he croaked, "Silver linings."

Once he was clear of pain, Neutrality Aura was hydrating him, and he was able to think clearly, he tried to figure out where he had gone wrong. Yet, no matter what avenue he tried to walk his mind along, he could not find an answer. "When there is just no way for me to figure it out on my own, I have two options. I could ask Havoc, since I am supposed to be his Apprentice and all… I think?"

After pondering that conundrum for a long moment, Joe shook his no-longer-aching head and instead decided to go to where he *knew* he would get answers. Wiggling his bandaged fingers, he activated Query and sent a message to Occultatum, who was no longer being hit by the banhammer for giving him freebies. "Tatum… what went wrong there?"

Query received! Minor answer allowed: Rituals aren't spell scrolls. Don't roll them up, you nitwit.

Skill increase: Query Novice III -> Novice VI.

Joe stared at the answer long enough that by the time he looked away, he had already stopped feeling like he should be bashing his head against the wall. "Right. That makes… sense. Well, I guess now I have these nifty, um… traps?"

That brought up an entirely new realm of possibility, but the facts of the matter remained: first, the defensive rituals that he had made would not be able to keep him safe. He would need to make new ones so that he had a few proper protections.

Second, his class quest had registered the linked rituals as complete, meaning that this method was viable… so he just needed to ensure that he had inscribed them on a rigid structure or target before he tried to use them again.

Joe muttered aloud as he planned out what to do as soon as he was out of the bed and bandages that were keeping him tied down. "Straight back to the workshop, and we'll take another try at making proper defensive rituals. When those work like they're *supposed* to, I'll go straight into making offensive ones. All I need to do is get out of here… seriously, I've been here for *how* long, and no one has come to check up on me? How do I get out of these bandages?"

Ahem. Major Cleave cleared her throat from the chair next to Joe's bed—where she was reading a book—eliciting a muffled scream from him as he thrashed around in his bandages. She met his wild eyes with her resigned ones. "You know, sir, I just don't think we're ever going to be able to be good friends."

CHAPTER THIRTEEN

"It's not like Dwarves are known for their stealth and subtlety. When she's practically invisible, how am I supposed to know if she's there or not?" Joe grumbled to himself as he calculated his defensive rituals once more. He was using the remainder of his rigid tiles, stone that didn't need any special qualities beyond 'flatness'. He amended that thought, remembering that they also required the special property 'no bendiness'. Though he understood that there were proper terms for these things, like malleability or some such, he was currently too grumpy to search his memory properly.

Major Cleave had released him from his bandages after letting him know that Jaxon had been the one to find him—thanks in part to recognizing that the blast wave associated with Joe's failed invention was not an attack on the town. When he hadn't seen the Reductionist around anywhere, Jaxon had been quoted as saying, 'I'm betting that Joe blew himself up again. I need to go'.

"Note to self: Set up Mend as a ritual, and do something really nice for Jaxon. He's a good friend." Apparently, the man had rushed to what remained of Joe's side and had used acupuncture to stop his bleeding debuffs, giving himself enough time to rush the mangled Ritualist to a combat medic. Sure, Joe wasn't exactly happy that the first assumption when there was an explosion was that it was his fault, but this time… well, it usually was, if he were being honest.

"A Ritual of Mending. Hmm. Not sure if healing would be categorized as a defensive ritual or a utility one, but I'm gonna figure it out. It's a good idea." This time around, Joe hadn't bothered with pausing to test things. He had simply made a single set of five linked Exquisite Shell rituals, then dived into making three linked sets of Dark Lightning Strike and two Acid Spray linked rituals. He finished the last set, noting the vibrating stone with worry. "Making a smithy next. I bet if I make a few spell stabilizers and embed them in the stone here and here… yeah, that would work. Maybe I *should* take up sculpting with Havoc?"

There were always new things to do and test, but for the first time in a long time, the growing list didn't feel overwhelming. He was back to doing what he loved, and there was a difference between scrambling and tinkering. There *should* have been far less of a chance to blow himself up as well, but he had figured out a solid way to test out his new rituals without getting injured. He could only do it once a day, for now, but whenever he put together a new design, he was going to Query Tatum and get his advice on whether the thing was going to blow up in his face.

Otherwise, he'd need to hook it up to a Ritual of Remote Activation to determine if it worked properly. That would be a waste, but only if he didn't have a target to test it out on.

Quest complete: Beginner Ritualist II. Offensive rituals: 25/25. Defensive rituals: 25/25. Congratulations! You made yourself into a better-protected individual! Reward: Access to Beginner Ritualist III! Record breaker reward: Reward for Beginner Ritualist III increased.

He was still making good progress toward being the speediest Ritualist Class Quester in history. Maybe he should recommend to other people that they should front load all the hard work of their entire class, with very little direction... for an unknown reward. "Eh. Never mind. They probably wouldn't go for it."

Class Quest gained: Beginner Ritualist III. This is a timed, optional reward quest! There are benefits to finding success quickly, and those benefits are more success, faster! You've made your rituals; now use them in combat! Strike a blow with your offensive rituals against at least fifty different hostile creatures. Dying before this quest is complete will automatically fail the quest. 0/50 creatures impacted by your offensive rituals. Time limit: 10 days. Reward: For each creature impacted, if killed within one minute, you will gain a core at their same tier.

Note: They do not need to be killed <u>by the ritual</u> for you to gain the reward. You are allowed to work with a team!

Class Quest gained: Student Ritualist. Congratulations! You are a Student of the path of rituals! Students must learn: For you, this means plenty of fun things to do! Personally draw out and activate twenty Student rituals which you have never used before. 0/20 rituals activated.

"A reward quest...? A core for *all* of them? Two quests at once?" Joe gasped as he realized he was wasting time with the opportunity. "*Havoc!*"

He started running, knowing that the ten-day time limit was deceptive. He *could* go out and beat down a ton of monsters without too much difficulty, but he would earn a core of their same tier. That meant that going against weak creatures would be near worthless. But if he went against creatures that might be too strong, and died, he got nothing. That meant he needed to join an expedition and find that fine line between challenging and deadly.

It only took Joe a short while to locate Havoc, but the high-powered Dwarf initially had very little interest in speaking with him. As he came running up, Havoc literally flipped over the table that he was working on so that Joe could not see what he was doing. The crowd of Dwarves and humans around the table were tossed across the room in some cases, but not a single one of them uttered a word of complaint. Joe glanced around, highly concerned by the guilty looks on multiple faces. "What's going on?"

"Nothing you need to concern your bald little face with," Havoc informed him coolly as his cigar burrowed its way out of the mess, climbed up his pant leg, and jumped into his hand. "Something I can help you with, Apprentice?"

The Grandmaster Dwarf directly calling him 'Apprentice' garnered a few gasps and reactions that literally chucking a table had not; making Joe wonder if there was something more to the term which was more important than he currently knew. Joe shook off his concerns and opened his mouth to tell Havoc about his quest, then paused as he registered all the other people in the space. "Can I have a private moment?"

"Yes, *absolutely*; how about you and I step away from here right now and have a chat?" Havoc's rapid reaction and movement only increased Joe's curiosity about what they were working on, but that conspiracy would just have to wait until he was caught up with his own concerns. They hurried away from the large group, soon finding a much more secluded area. It wasn't hard, as the interior of the volcano was practically a ghost town at this point. "What's got your knickers in a bowtie, kid?"

Joe took a moment to mentally translate the query to 'what has your undies in a knot' before he could answer the Dwarf. "I need your advice and help. I just got access to a new quest, a 'reward' class quest."

"You're *joking*." Havoc's slightly-less-ragged-than-usual beard caught the breeze as he turned his head to stare at Joe in utter shock. "Why, the last time I heard about a reward quest was... I can't even tell you how many centuries ago at this point. I thought those pansy deities had written that out of classes already; that's how long it's been. What do you need, and what is the reward?"

Before Joe could respond, Havoc shook his head and muttered, "Never mind, I have direct access. I'll just look for myself... oh. Oh, *my*."

"Exactly why I came running." Joe smirked at his 'master', who simply nodded slowly in return. "What should I do?"

"Here is *exactly* what you should do." Havoc's eyes were practically dancing in delight as he twirled his ever-present cigar over his knuckles. "You go back to your little workshop, make the biggest, most powerful, most numerous area-of-effect rituals you possibly can… and in three days, get ready to ride the Lord of Slaughter wagon. I'm going to take your work to the most dangerous areas in all of Svaltarheim, point your rituals at creatures I want to attack, and then immediately destroy them. I'll be taking a quarter of your reward for my part in this, and you are going to be fine with that."

"Um. Yes, I sure am." Joe gulped as he took in the flames that were swirling in Havoc's eyes. They did not look like the reflection of lava. They looked like the promise of death and dismemberment. "I guess I'll… go get to work?"

A long stream of smoke curled out of Havoc's mouth, even though he hadn't even had his cigar in his mouth since they first started speaking. "Yeah. You do that."

The Ritualist rushed off toward his workshop, stopping only a single time—to grab a ring-full of stones that would serve well as ritual slates. He would need to take a few minutes to set up a Field Array and make some precise slices, but he needed to restock anyway. Once he had accomplished that, the next several days were a blur of creating rituals both to hit other things, as well as to keep himself alive.

When Havoc pounded on the door to his building, Joe took a swift glance at his stock of rituals, nodded in acceptance, and hurried to join the Lord of Slaughter on his quest.

Ritual of Dark Lightning Strike (Beginner) x30.
Ritual of Dark Lightning Strike (Beginner) (Linked) x6.
Ritual of Mending (Student) x5.
Ritual of Exquisite Shell (Beginner) (Linked) x10.
Ritual of Spraying Acid (Beginner) x10.

"You're ready?" Havoc questioned him with a wild gleam in

his eyes. "You'd better be; teleportation ain't cheap. Next one won't be ready for another week."

"I'm good to go. All my attacking rituals are set as an area-of-effect, so I'm pretty sure we'll be fine," Joe confirmed with equal excitement. "I also made sure to put together plenty of things that'll keep me alive as we-"

"Hold on tight to your horse's hat. Let me explain how this is gonna work." Havoc chuckled darkly. "You're going to *activate* the Rituals, hand them to me, and then I'm going to teleport away to the most dangerous monster-infested territory on this plane. Your quest will complete, and you won't be dead. I'll be back in a week to pick up my share of the Cores. Savvy?"

"What? No!" Joe nearly stamped his foot in indignation. "I need to be there to... to... feces, it never said I needed to be there. Just that I needed to activate the rituals and damage hostile creatures."

"*Now* you're getting it." Havoc laughed as he hurried Joe along to the Caves of Solitude and their apparently overpriced teleport array.

CHAPTER FOURTEEN

Joe looked on wistfully as Havoc was struck by lightning and acid sprayed away from him in a nova. The Dwarf vanished, and the people maintaining the area swore heartily as they moaned about the damage the Dwarf had done to their spell diagrams and teleportation hall on the way out.

"I swear, if he was anyone *except* the Lord of Slaughter, I wouldn't go through the trouble of fixing this and bringing him back," The Dwarven mage that had activated the teleport enchantment grumbled heartily. "Why would someone even go *to* the Deathyards? What was with all those active effects? His entire ticket price is going to have to go back into making this functional again!"

Not wanting to get caught up in Havoc's monetary issues— or get charged on his behalf—Joe hurriedly made himself scarce and went back to his hole in the ground that would one day grow up into a full-fledged town. Before he got halfway home, he was already getting spammed with quest updates informing him that his rituals had hit 'hostile creatures'.

By the time he was back to his workshop, the quest had been completed.

Class Quest completed: Beginner Ritualist III. Congratulations! I'd call you a dirty cheater if it wasn't likely the most intelligent choice you could have possibly made. Here's your reward; don't expect to get off so easily ever again! Reward: Unique Core x49. Artifact Core x1.

Joe stared at the vast amount of wealth that had literally just appeared in his Codpiece of Holding in total shock. This quantity of Cores would let him either create weapons at the Expert rank in the form of war rituals, or simply generate massive long-term investments by raising a swarm of Unique buildings. "Not even gonna think about that Artifact one… there's no way that one is gonna stay with me. Sure, I *could* use it for a Master-ranked ritual, but I'd never survive the experience. Havoc must have gone to a dungeon and cleared it or something. That's a Boss Core, if I've ever seen one."

He desperately wanted to know what had happened in the 'Deathyard'. Yet, currently, time wasn't his friend. Joe knew precisely what he wanted as soon as he saw the tally of all of the Unique Cores. There was one long-term investment that he could make immediately. "Aspect Jars… specifically Natural Aspect Jars. From the looks of these, even though they're all 'Unique', they're all identical and *right* at the cusp of stepping into becoming Artifacts themselves, with each of them being worth a whopping ten *thousand* experience to absorb."

He shook his head at that thought. It was one thing to know that Havoc was practically a force of nature, and another to see the results of it in action. "Set up a Field Array, ensure I have the required aspects… a thousand each to make their Natural Aspect Jars? A worthy investment, but *ouch.* Start small; I'm not gonna bother with a Trash or Damaged Jar… so an upgrade for Common, it is."

Joe's Field Array was altered to match the exact of the Core, and then he started flooding the blazing ball of light with aspects. The radiant daylight emitted constantly by the Core slowly and subtly shifted to a pure white emanation, swallowing down a thousand aspects in an instant.

Item created: Natural Common Aspect Jar. 0/10,000 Common

aspects. This jar can be used to store and retrieve Common aspects. As it is a naturally formed aspect jar, it will collect Common aspects from its surroundings over time. Current rate of collection: 7 Common aspects per hour.

"Six days until I get a return on my initial investment." Joe shook his head in dumbfounded glee. "If *only* I had enough Artifact, Mythical, or Legendary… no, I need to just see where I am now and be happy. Okay, I don't have enough Rare, but I do have the rest."

Using the same Field Array, he slotted a new Core and set up an Aspect Jar for both Uncommon as well as Unique aspects. "Just like that, now I'll be ready when I go to set up my secret building in the dumpster of the capital. No one will expect a secret landfill building. But getting there… and going up against the monsters that live in there… abyss. Havoc took all my attack rituals."

He seethed for a moment, frustrated that he hadn't been able to see his last several days' worth of work in use. Joe acknowledged that frustration and moved on, knowing *logically* that he had made the correct call. Still, he wanted to watch magic streak through the air and reduce his enemies to slag. "Slag… ahh, I should perhaps practice summoning or… no, I need to do more with my Ritual Orbs. Having only one that can use a spell against Elves or humans is getting tiresome."

Joe pulled out the Orb assigned with Cone of Cold, and a quick glance at it made him wince.

Ritual Orb 1: Spell trapped within: Cone of Cold. Bound Core Power remaining: 375/1,545. Cost per spell use: 195.

"Glad I checked." Joe called up his memory of how to remove the Core and place in a new one, happy to remember that he could just slot a new Core as needed. "That's inefficient, though… Mana Batteries work just as well and are much more highly stabilized. Oh, and they're rechargeable. I guess I know what I need to do next."

Joe stepped out of his workshop and paused, ensured Neutrality Aura was active so that he wouldn't offend anyone's senses, then started looking around to see if Major Cleave was nearby. He found her a foot and a half to his left and smiled at her instead of squealing like a stuck pig. Improvement! "Hello, Major. I'm on my way to bring a Smithy up; would you care to join me?"

"Huh. Polite today, aintcha. Do you want something from me…? Anyway, the Legion says I go where you go, so you're stuck with me until that changes." There was a long pause, so Joe started walking, almost missing the quiet follow up of, "Still, nice to be invited for once. You should know, Stan's here, and he brought a wagonload of goods that you need to go pay for."

"Stan… Stan… oh! The newly-hired administrator who roleplays a certain purple depressed donkey from a children's show." Joe nodded sagely, rubbing at a non-existent beard. "I hope he brought along a few cores and other such essentials; I have no idea how I'm gonna get these other buildings up otherwise."

He certainly wasn't going to be spending *Unique* cores on raising Common buildings. On that note, he hurried over to the clearly visible wagon in the distance and waved at Stan, who was vigorously—for him—shooing off overexcited engineers. "No. Stop. Go away. This is for the town. I am an official of this place."

Joe wobbled as though he had been hit with a sleep spell when he heard the Dwarf speaking, managing to put on his professional face just as the new hire saw him. "Hello, Stan! I'm so glad you made such good time! Can I help with anything right away?"

"Need a place to store all this stuff." Stan scowled around at the crowd of Dwarves, who were trying to catch a glimpse of what he was hauling. "Perhaps you could send off the vultures?"

"I need a core; Uncommon should be fine. Used my last one making an apartment building." Joe chuckled softly as Stan blinked slowly at him. "I can use just one to bring up six individual structures, including a warehouse and apartment building. So, got one on you?"

"Oh, I get it. Hard to get rid of the vultures when you are one. Fifty reputation each. Discount applied, as you're using it for the direct improvement of the town," Stan told him a moment later. He reached into the wagon, dug around, then handed over a Core. "Did I hear you made an 'apartment building'? What level of rent have you specified?"

As soon as that question left the merchant's lips, the clustering engineers all let out loud groans, except one that directly shouted at Stan, "Why would you *do* that?"

Stan looked around at all the freeloaders, and his eyes narrowed slightly. "How are we going to increase the reputation of the town if we don't have the funding to improve it? Are you fine with this being an unranked *Camp* with a poor reputation? I'm not. Joe?"

"I'm not either," Joe agreed after he had waited *just* long enough to get the engineers' hopes up. They walked away, muttering that they should 'get moving before they started getting *charged* for loitering or something'. "I'll leave all that to you, Stan. Make the prices fair, please? We really need to start getting people to move here so we have defenders, crafters, and-"

"I'll take care of that," Stan informed him firmly. "Feel free to trust my judgment. I have business contacts, connections with high nobility, and understand the value of land and work better than nearly anyone in the Oligarchy. Don't worry; I only need to sleep once per month."

Joe pondered the soul-crushing business which Stan had been running for who-knew-how long, and simply decided that since he had chosen to hire the man, he would trust him all the way. "I'm all in, Stan. You tell me what you need, and I'll make sure it happens."

"What sort of structures do you have access to right now?" Stan inquired directly as Joe started leading him to the area marked out in chalk by Ciril; Joe knew better than to just plop a warehouse down in an arbitrary area. Instead of answering, the human handed over a list of buildings that he had prepared

exactly for this occasion. Stan inspected all of the special buildings Joe had marked down, shaking his head. "Only thing on
there I want to see you bring up are the Common buildings you
found when you got to this zone."

"What? Why? I think that a trophy hall would go a long way
to building morale!" Joe argued instantly, then paused and
rethought his rebuttal. "Of course, *you* know what is best for city
functionality, and I'll lean on that knowledge, but I'd love to
know the reasoning behind your choices."

"All of those special buildings are useful in a *City*. A Tier-five
population center." Stan emphasized his words so they would
stick in Joe's mind. "If you put those up in a Camp—a Tier-
zero population center—which you're trying to turn into a
hamlet, Tier one, you're just *asking* to be forced to knock down
every building and start over. You only have a set amount of…
let's call them 'upgrade points' per city tier. If you don't meet
the requirements for going up a rank, even if you have 'neat'
buildings, then you'll need to smash them and put in less 'neat'
ones and replace them with more 'functional' versions."

"Ah…" Joe eyed the Pyramid of Panacea nervously. "Is that
going to work against us?"

"Big time." Stan nodded at Joe, then crooked his version of
a slight smile: the edges of his beard wrinkled minorly. "But
settlements spring up around large, important structures all the
time. At least, they did before the war. Now? Forts spring eternal. Is this the place?"

"Looks like it. Hold on." Joe sent his mind through his
storage ring and searched until he found what he needed,
pulling out his little-used Rituarchitect Survey Grid. Touching
the wand-like item to the blueprint he planned to use, a translucent blue gridline appeared in the air. He worked to line it up
with the outline that Ciril had put on the ground, fairly
surprised when the lines matched up almost perfectly.

"You must have gotten assigned a great city planner," Stan
deadpanned. Or, Joe realized, that might have been his 'excited'
voice.

"I honestly think the two of you would hit it off." Joe didn't mention how badly that made him want to groan internally. One endlessly grumpy human-disdainer, and one verbally anhe- donic. The staff he was building for this city was *so~o* fun. "Please 'Stan' back; I'm gonna get this building up."

There was no reaction from the Dwarf. Joe *tsked* under his breath. "Another person without a sense of humor."

CHAPTER FIFTEEN

Joe was originally going to attempt to raise the warehouse by himself, but when he looked at the overall schematics of the ritual combined with the blueprints, he grew concerned that the mana cost would be as large as the structure itself. "Stan, I don't suppose you have a big ol' mana pool, do you?"

"I'm here to administrate, not to subject myself to the rigors of magecraft. If I wanted to do intensely laborious work, I would have remained in the Legion," Stan informed Joe with his unfortunate voice. Before the owner of the area could voice his displeasure at his new employee's view on pitching in, another voice cut into the conversation.

"I have roughly twenty-five hundred mana! Does donating it to you get me a free room?" Daniella's chipper tone reached Joe's ears, and he perked up instantly.

Turning to face her directly, Joe pretended to think about his answer as he tapped on his chin. "I suppose I could set you up for tonight in the barracks for a single mana donation like this. Now, if you would like to get on the regular schedule, I'm sure my fine City Administrator here would be *more* than happy to-"

"No reputation offered, no room granted," Stan stated firmly as he crossed his arms and glared at Daniella. "I'm not going to be known for taking care of a city that has a poor reputation pool."

Both of the humans stared at the Dwarf with frozen expressions, knowing that they had both simply been joking around. Joe took in a deep breath, exhaling slowly as he forced a proper smile back on his face. "Stan, I am more than certain that since I own the land and am putting up the buildings, I get to decide what to charge for rent, correct? All of that money is going to go to *me*, and I will give a portion of it as taxes to the town at large?"

Stan's face shifted to slowly dawning horror. "You mean to tell me that you are not just *donating* all of these buildings to the town?"

"Stan. *Stan*, why in *Eternium* would I do something like that?" Joe chuckled softly, though his eyes were as hard as flint.

"But you can just put a building up in a few minutes! Why would I assume that you are not giving ownership of them to the town?" Stan jabbed a finger at Joe's chest. "I even gave you a discount on that Core!"

"Not sure why that would matter, but let's review the facts. Stan," Joe looked his administrator in the eye and held his scandalized gaze, "not only does it take a mess of mana investment, as well as a core, but I also need blueprints, a ritual diagram, and all of the materials to construct a building, just like any other construction crew would. Now tell me: if I have all of the expertise, resources, ability to use them, as well as own the land... why would I give up control of what I make to a third party?"

"...Exposure?" came Stan's weak reply. "Then people can see what you can do?"

"People die of exposure, Stan. At least now I know why your building didn't have any art in it. They can see what I can do while also paying me rent." Joe was chuckling softly at this point. "Wanna try again?"

"Altruism? Patriotism?"

"No, Stan. *Capitalism*," Joe rebutted, his word pulling a **hiss** out of Stan, who clutched at his chest like a vampire that had just been staked.

"People always want to be *paid*," Stan muttered as he shook his head sadly. "Why do they need my reputation more than I do?"

"Well, look at that, Daniella! I just found a job for you. Besides your normal work as an architect, can I pay you to make sure that Stan is paying people promptly and fairly for the work that they do?" Joe's chuckling died as he noted the horror on Daniella's face. "You okay over there?"

"Joe, set me up with a room here, and I will do that *for free* for the next three months," she assured him firmly. "That should be long enough for people to get used to arguing for proper salaries."

"See, not everyone wants to be paid for the work they do!" Stan tried desperately to convince Joe. "We shouldn't pay them if they don't *require* payment!"

"I *really* want to like you, Stan. Help me make that happen." Joe motioned for Daniella to join him in his expanding ritual circle. "Anyway, meet your new assistant! Daniella, this should not do anything funky, since it is only a Common-ranked building. This should result in minimal flying through the air for us, no bodily implosions, and very few surprises overall."

"Have those... been *issues*... in the past?" She regarded the shimmering ritual with sudden concern.

"The issues mostly took care of themselves. If not, I could always use the practice in Resurrecting people." Joe waved his hand back and forth. That was all they could say before the ritual started and the mana began to flow out of them. Daniella cried out, and Joe realized that she may have never channeled so much mana for such a sustained amount of time before. "Direct the flow of mana! Don't just let it tear its own way out!"

Of course, *he* was not having that issue, since his mana was diffused through his entire body and not locked into any single core area. He hadn't found any downsides to this, beyond the fact that his Coalescence skill had seemingly stagnated. He wasn't sure if it was his advice or something else that got his new partner to succeed, but her jaw firmed up and no blood was trickling from her lips. Joe quietly congratulated himself. "I must be getting better at teaching this sort of thing!"

The walls of the massive storage warehouse came together in the strangely organic look that all of his buildings had, his aspects converting into stone, wood, metal, or glass as needed. As the final touches came together, Joe pushed to take the full mana burden on himself, knowing that there was no way that someone other than a Champion of a Deity could have a mana pool like his at this level.

Quest updated: Novice Rituarchitect II. Buildings created: 4/10.

Rituarchitect Class experience gained: 50.

Architect of Artifacts has increased the structure by 10!

Warehouse (11,000 feet of storage). Durability: 5,500/5,500.

Daniella was panting as she looked over the building that had a *slightly* strange aesthetic. "This is *amazing*. How did you learn how to do it? This is a class, right? Can you teach the class to others? What sort of base class do I need?"

"I suppose I shouldn't be surprised that an architect wants a class that can create buildings," Joe chuckled as they walked forward to inspect the building properly. "I'm sorry to have to tell you that this is actually a combination of *three* classes that work together. If you had the first specialization alone, which allows you to raise structures, you'd have a serious disadvantage. The actual cost for all of this is *astro-abyssal-nomical*. My main class gets an eighty-five percent cost reduction on rituals, and my *third* class makes it so that I don't need to have the exact materials needed to build it. Instead, I can convert other things into what I need."

"I'm guessing that's why these walls are grainless, even when they're clearly wood?" Daniella ran her fingers over different sections of the building, noting how smooth the surface was. "It's almost like the hives those carpenter wasps made back on earth… or a cartoon drawing of a building. It looks almost unreal."

"Huh. Maybe a lack of shading, or texture?" Joe scanned the walls of the warehouse, then the other buildings in the distance. Now that he was thinking through things from her perspective, the buildings he had made *did* almost look two-dimensional. There was a kind of 'material' look that just wasn't present, and the walls were all perfectly smooth. "I can see that. Happily, they work as they should. Stan, feel free to start storing materials here. Daniella, make sure the city pays me a fair, if reduced rate, for rent of the warehouse space."

"Yes, sir!" She threw him a mocking salute, winked, and followed a grumbling Stan into the building.

Joe watched her go, a corner of his mouth quirking up into a smile. Something about her resonated with him very well. He shook off the feeling, trying to analyze it. "Maybe she just has a lot of points devoted to Charisma, Joe. Don't do anything stupid. She's shown nothing but professionalism to you, so don't take that as anything else."

He made his way out of the green district, and into the blue-light district. "Okay, self. Let's get the smithy up so I can make a core enchanter, then convert a few cores to batteries. That will allow me to upgrade my weapons, all so that I can protect against monsters as I convert garbage into making more buildings. Ugh. Haven't had a task list like this since I used to play video games."

CHAPTER SIXTEEN

Raising the smithy was far easier than raising the warehouse, since he was able to bribe a few Dwarves with no rent on the smithy for the next two weeks if they helped him out. After the forges were created and set to the proper heat, Joe easily crafted a Beginner gyroscope out of aspects using an Aspect Ingot Hammer.

There was something about not needing other materials that made him laugh out loud as the Dwarves grumbled about not having access to metal. The downside to all of this was the jeering they sent his way as he started on the third layer of the gyroscope and it fell apart immediately, nearly lighting the new building on fire before he managed to put out the aspect-driven flames. Joe scratched at a few small burns he had taken, unsure what had happened.

He made another attempt and got further, but then the ring fell apart again clattering onto a large boundary of stone rubble the Dwarves had set around him as if to ring a campfire in the woods. "What is happening? I know *how* to do this…?"

A third try, and another failure. This time, he got a notification of a skill increase.

Ritualistic Forging (Beginner V) -> Ritualistic Forging (Beginner VI).

"Ah…" Joe skimmed through his skills, noting the fact that even though his Smithing Lore was at the Apprentice rank, his actual skill was still lagging behind. "Nothing to do but grind, I suppose. Anyone wanna point out my issues with forging as I go? Also, I need someone to run to the warehouse and order metal from Stan. I'm paying, if someone can help me with a project I have going on here."

A Dwarf offered his expertise, at an *interesting* rate per hour of teaching: a mere twenty-five reputation with the Oligarchy. Joe made sure to inform them that he would remember that these Dwarves thought that was a reasonable hourly rate when they were charged for using the forge. The price mysteriously dropped to *ten* reputation for the entire day.

Now that he was doing everything possible to move through all the forms properly, and utilizing a paid instructor, the aspects began happily converting to metal at a rapid rate. Joe spent the next few hours making stabilization baubles, tiny pyramids that he planned to embed in his ritual tiles. He could only craft Beginner versions with a decent success rate, but he still managed to make two sets of Apprentice stabilizers by the time his skill increased.

Congratulations! Ritualistic Forging has reached Apprentice 0! Reward: Aspect Ingot Hammer technique. Hammering using this pattern will increase the chances of a successful item creation by 20% when used at the same tier of your Ritualistic Forging. No additional benefit will be given when attempting to create something of a higher tier!

Joe looked at his skill list, confused that the new technique was not appearing. He decided to ask his instructor about it. "Pardon me… it seems that I increased my forging, and I got a hammering technique. It isn't showing up when I look for it in my skill list, though?"

"Oh? Congrats, kid." The Dwarf nodded at the anvil Joe had been using. "As to why that is, just try making something. You'll see."

Joe pulled out his gyroscope and started working on the next ring, silver aspects converting to metal with each strike. His eyebrow rose when he noticed that he was unconsciously hammering in a new pattern. His loss of focus cost him the ring, and it converted back into aspects with a flash of light and heat. "Ahh!"

"Yeah, just wait till you see what it looks like when you try to make something at the Unique rank and mess it up." The Dwarf shook his head and started waving his hands. "Grandmasters don't have subspaces in their smithy *just* for privacy. Something goes wrong on a Legendary crafting attempt? *Boom*."

"Why does everything have to blow up? Can't it just fail?" Joe grumbled as he set up the space to try again.

"It can. If you *aren't* making something magical." The Dwarf tapped the side of his nose knowingly. "When you're pumping magic into something, putting it in sideways makes the whole thing unstable. In fact, it can be preferable to have it go wrong at the start. Often, an instant failure saves a ton of material, time, and keeps people alive. Imagine you make something that looks right, but you get all the way to the end and find out that there was an incorrect magical matrix in the first part you made? Then the entire thing is a natural disaster waiting to happen. You just don't know when."

"That happens?" Joe paused as he pulled back his hammer.

"Oh, *ye~eah*." The Dwarf sounded far too close to a certain juice commercial for Joe *not* to chuckle at him. "That's why most anything made by a Master goes straight to an appraiser. Failure can mean an explosion, a curse, or something... wonky coming out of it."

The Reductionist's mind immediately recalled a powerful sword that only wanted to cut feet, but he managed to keep his mouth shut and nod, getting back to work on the gyroscope. His next attempt at the third ring met with success, but that meant that his skill increases also stopped rolling in. The fact of the matter was that the Dwarf was just too low-skilled at his profession to artificially boost someone through teaching. Joe had fully expected this, as it was *very* unlikely that a Master Smith was going to leave the city and come to an unknown campground without good reason or even better compensation.

That left Joe with an issue: he needed two more rings on his gyroscope if he wanted to produce a firm foundation for his ritual of enchantment, and there was no way that he could make it happen. He left the smithy with both his completed and partially-completed works, having decided to find Havoc. He was fretting about the choice, and thus worked to psych himself up. "He called me his Apprentice. That's gotta mean something, and... he won't be able to ignore me forever on this stuff. He wants something out of me, and of this land. Why else does he have secret projects going?"

He went searching for Havoc, but instead came upon Bauen handing a group of engineers something; something that he made them hide as soon as Joe was within earshot. "The human's almost here. *Move*, ya blighters! Havoc'll slice open our gizzards and pelt us with the stones inside 'em!"

Joe simply paused, took a deep breath, and decided to put the strangeness out of mind. After the rapid shuffling had subsided, he approached with his eyes firmly locked on the sweating engineer. "Bauen, I'm looking for Havoc... a~and I just remembered he's gone for the rest of the week. Drat. How did I forget that? You know metalwork, right? Could I have your assistance on a project?"

Bauen stood in a 'totally casual' position and took a long moment to look Joe over. "Hmm. Why not? How about we go to your workshop?"

"I need some metal work done; I got the smithy-"

"To the workshop!" Bauen cheered as he marched away at twice the speed a normal human could run. Joe had no choice but to hurry along after him, even though he knew the Dwarf was just trying to keep him away from what he was doing.

"Major Cleave, anything you need while we're out and

about?" Joe questioned the empty air around him, knowing that there was a strong probability of his minder being next to him.

"I'm fine," she informed him stoically from her position just to the right of his elbow. "I appreciate the concern."

They hurried to follow Bauen, who was studying the door to Joe's shop without attempting to open it. The Dwarf shook his head in wonder as he turned to Joe. "This... it's a masterwork of trickery, Joe. I have no *idea* how you managed to trap this place in such a way that I can't even figure out what will pop out at me if I go in there without being invited. Care to share?"

"That's easy, Bauen." Joe slapped the door open with a tiny effort of will, walking inside along with the other two. "It isn't trapped. I haven't made anything in here that I haven't taken with me."

Bauen squinted his eyes at Joe to see if he was being toyed with, then his face started to go red. "You're going to *fix* that, yes? No crafter worth their salt is going to just... let people *in* without protections in place. Just... right, what do you need now?"

Pulling out his gyroscope, Joe pointed out the design and explained about needing two more rings. He and Bauen went over a few ideas, including just having the Dwarf make them, until the engineer grinned and snapped his fingers. "Why do you even need the metal? I saw that fancy light you put up on your shop; didn't see anything under it. You've got a new trick, right? Use that."

Joe considered the possibility, but slowly shook his head. "No... it would require a *lot* of time to get that properly made. I need an Expert ritual circle, and that skill *really* hikes up the instability when trying to make something free-floating. At the Expert tier right now, the instability would jump... thirty per tier... I think that's the math on it, so something like one hundred and eighty percent. Guaranteed explosion."

"Huh. That *is* an issue. I suppose you could grind and get that skill up, or find ways to stabilize the ritual as you were using it." Bauen noticed Joe's flinch, and a wide grin appeared on his face. "Oh? You're holding out on me so you can be lazy, aren't you?"

Joe reluctantly pulled out his ritual stabilizers from his time in the smithy. "I can make these. I have a skill for ritualistic forging, but-"

"But you wanna cut corners to beat your class quests." Bauen smiled gently, reaching over and patting Joe's shoulder. "That's a great way to get yourself trapped and unable to complete the *next* quest, lad. Rushing ahead is gonna ruin your foundation if you let it."

"I just want the nifty bonuses." Joe let the Dwarf see his defeated smile, though he slowly nodded in acknowledgment of his assessment. "Havoc told you I was challenging the record?"

"He warned all of us to stay out of your way, more like." Bauen shuddered, a dark expression covering his face. "That man is a genius. Insane, perhaps, but a genius."

"So... help me to stay on track?" Joe offered brightly, deflating as Bauen shook his head.

"I was recently hired for a, um, job. I recommend sending an order to the Capital if you *really* don't want to do it yourself." Bauen raised a bushy eyebrow, and a knowing look showed on his face. "That is, if you're gonna offload all your problems?"

"I mean... if possible." Joe's attempt at keeping a straight face failed in response to Bauen's confused expression. "No, fine, you're right. Time to rise and grind. Time to show the world that I don't have a mindset. I have a *grind*set."

"Please don't." Major Cleave saw where Joe was going and attempted to head him off. She failed. Joe slapped the table and stood erect, already planning his next move.

As the human rushed out to get to work, Bauen met Major Cleave's annoyed stare as she grumped at him, "Why are you encouraging him to fail? There's a reason the Legion rarely allows people to rank up so rapidly. Trying to do all of these things at once is a mistake, and he's going to get himself killed."

"He can respawn for just a small cost of experience." Bauen ignored her glare as he sauntered leisurely out of the door.

"Hey, they say you learn from mistakes, so maybe he'll be a genius soon."

Major Cleave growled and ground her teeth as she stomped off to follow her charge. "I'm gonna die in this volcano again. I just *know* it."

CHAPTER SEVENTEEN

Fire poured out of Joe's fingers as he traced lines in the air, using both hands to rapidly draw out the ritual diagram with light gray aspects. When that was completed, blazing white aspects replaced the gray, and he flipped to using a Common-ranked Inscriber in each hand.

Sweat rolled down his face, wiped away in the same instant by his Neutrality Aura, as the second circle rapidly approached completion. Then his left hand twitched, sending the aspect he was using nearly a half inch out of the correct pattern. Joe *vaulted* backward as both circles erupted into blazing flames that melted the stone below and ignited the air. The circles burned in reverse order of their creation, like a fuse on a powerful firework.

As the stone settled into a solid mass once more, Joe stepped forward and began again. Major Cleave sighed and continued watching the surroundings for any threat, completely ignored once more by the Reductionist. This time around, Joe set out both his Beginner and Apprentice ritual stabilizers in a pleasing pattern around his feet. "This is only a double circle. Stabilizers at a rank above the intended diagram should fully offset the instability… right?"

He only had eyes for the ritual as he started over. His test ritual had failed exactly as expected, and now he wanted to see what it felt like to be in a 'stable' environment. His hands moved again, but this time, the air itself almost felt like a solid as he pressed his Inscribers forward. He knew that he *could* push through it, but also that it would be a bad idea. To his satisfaction, the double circle completed without issue.

"That was a good test. Perhaps something a little harder, just to see how unstable this really becomes?" Joe inspected the ritual that was hanging in the air above the rubble pile one last time, unable to spot any issues. He turned on his heel and started walking away, only to falter as Major Cleave called out.

"What is this? Are you just going to leave random magical effects laying around for people to stumble into?" The Dwarf's question had merit, so he slowly walked over and activated the ritual, pushing on it slightly to make it hang in the air about eight feet off the ground at the lowest point.

"No stumbling into this for people." Joe's distracted utterance made Cleave bristle. "Good call on that."

"What does that *do*, sir?" She watched warily as the ritual ever-so-slowly rotated in the air.

"Cleaning service," Joe muttered as he pulled out a book and thumbed through it. "It'll grab any garbage and collect it here. If there's no trash, it'll just keep things organized for people."

"You just made a garbage collection service for the town? That easily?" Major Cleave gaped at the ritual in wonder, suddenly happy that it existed instead of the emotion she *had* been feeling toward it: pure annoyance. "What kind of range does it have? This place has been turning into a vermin paradise. No one's been bothering to take their filth to the lava pits like they were supposed to."

"Uh… range." Joe glanced up at the ritual, his eyes becoming unfocused for a moment. "I altered that, pushed it up, and added aspects… looks like about a mile or so? Didn't need a zombie brain; I just used Uncommon aspects for that section. Yeah, should be pretty effective. But, ah… this isn't what I'm excited about."

His eyes wandered to his notifications, where a bit of his confusion was focused. "I'm gaining skill ranks too fast. Not sure why."

Somatic Ritual Casting (Novice IX).

"Too fast?" Major Cleave questioned him. "That isn't right… typically, your skill levels only increase rapidly when you are doing something that you can demonstrate a higher skill level than you should have, or if you've earned bonuses."

"In that case," Joe considered his Expert rank in Ritual Circles and his clothing set of the Silkpants Mage, which granted twenty-five percent magical skill increase speed, and narrowed his eyes, "perhaps it is actually a little too *slow*."

"Are you often called a maniac, sir? Just wondering for my, uh, report on people that are insulting toward you." Major Cleave coughed as she frantically backpedaled. Joe glanced at her and smirked. "Just… most places don't have magical garbage collection. Certainly not due to a random test of your skills."

"It tends to just happen around me." Joe shrugged and started walking. He needed some distance from his new, about-to-be tiny landfill before he started on the next ritual diagram. The one he had been practicing… he stopped, turned, then ran back and collected his ritual stabilizers while Cleave watched him critically.

"I'm just having fun while I still can." Joe hurried over to his next set-up point and started strategically placing the stabilizers. "Soon enough, I'm going to need to devote time and effort to either fortifying this place, or I'll have to push to help with the war effort. Until then, I'm going to run with making super cool magic."

"'Super cool'… magic," Major Cleave deadpanned as she dodged a half-eaten mango that was floating toward the new dump. "I suppose you do make 'interesting' practical effects, such as your garbage collection, but I've seen magic that would grow hair on even your head, turn it white, and make it fall off again. Also, we're only on Svaltarheim… I can't even imagine what people in higher planes have accomplished."

"Not all magic needs to be terrifying and part of a grand design." Joe chuckled darkly as he started planning his next ritual in a specifically non-grand-design sort of way. He made no promises on the 'terrifying' portion. "For instance, this is going to be a ritual that collects moisture from the air and turns it into usable water. Normally, I'd only need to make this a Novice ritual, but we're inside a volcano. So, Uncommon at the least. The inner circle condenses water, the second one collects it, and the third will increase the range to the entirety of this enclosed space; allowing none of the water to escape."

"Essentially, you're making this place into a giant terrarium?" Cleave chuckled at that and pointed into the distance. "People were wondering when you were gonna bring in water for the bathhouse. Is this what that's for?"

Joe paused long enough that the ritual almost went out of control. He hurried to make the next few marks, muttering grimly. "How did I forget to add water to the bathhouse? Forget that; why did no one mention it till now? Disgusting."

Over the next few minutes, the Reductionist finished the third circle. It completed with a flash of light and hung in the air, waiting to be activated. "Now all I need is a… no, a well would be a bad idea. Hard to dig that out when there's only magma below the surface. Either a cistern or a water tower, then?"

"Until you make one of those, why not set it up at the bathhouse? Let the fresh water flow into the tubs, and then leave a stream of water for anyone that needs it?" Cleave offered when she noticed Joe struggling to find a use for the ritual.

"Thanks!" Joe pushed on the floating ritual diagram with his mind, moving it along until it hung where he wanted it. He angled the ritual so that the collected water would fall into the currently-unused pipes, leaving plenty of room for the water to be diverted if needed. Devoting some mana to the ritual, he activated it and watched as a slight fog rose around the center of the diagram. "Huh… may need to bring in a few water mages or get people to start dumping a lake or three in here. Something to kick this off."

"You think that would work?" Cleave wondered aloud, unsure if she wanted the answer or not.

"Fog… that reminds me, I could go drink a lake or three with… um, ignore that. To your question, we can wait until people sweat or use the latrine enough that the collected water is usable, but I think more people would be comfortable if we…" Joe looked over and realized that Cleave's eyes were boring into him. "You know, I think I'll keep the details of how we'll accrue liquid in here to myself."

"Yes."

"In that case, I'm going to create a backup system and not tell you what it does." The Reductionist chuckled as Cleave came to a stutter-stop, closed her eyes, and took a calming breath. The human ignored her for the most part, only glancing over at her intermittently as he spent an hour in the open, slowly creating a Ritual of the Ghostly Army while she watched his back. He would need to find a source of water that was unclaimed so that he wouldn't cause any problems with the locals, but he could hold onto the ready-to-use ritual diagram nigh-indefinitely.

Was it wasteful to use this ritual in such a manner? Maybe. Should he hold off on using what the system had once classified as 'dark rituals'? …Perhaps. Would it be fun to use it in here and scare the population witless for a few minutes? Most definitely.

With a water source secured, or at least knowing it would be *eventually*, Joe browsed his quests and decided that he had put off creating the remaining buildings long enough. The two of them walked around the space, collecting anyone they ran into. Soon Jaxon, Bauen, and all of the others whose names he hadn't yet learned were gathered. Only Stan absolutely refused to participate.

"Hello, all! This should be the last time for quite a while that we need to gather like this." Joe started, earning a few jeers and cheers in response. "I need some helpers, and I'll pay twenty reputation per person for each hour you give me tonight."

"What's the job?" someone called from the back.

"We're making this Camp into a proper hamlet!" Joe firmly announced. "Over the next short while, we're going to create six new buildings. If we have time after that, we'll put up a wall around the new village, followed by a few more residences or workshops. We'll vote if it comes to that. After that, if anyone has a particular request, we'll try to get to it then. Helping me out now means we get to a building you actually *want*, sooner rather than later!"

The promise of useful buildings was what got a few to work, though there were some that only wanted to pad their reputations. Joe made sure to carefully memorize the few people that offered to do this project for the sake of doing it: he was going to ensure they earned the best rewards of all.

CHAPTER EIGHTEEN

Quest complete: Novice Rituarchitect II. You have created all ten of the buildings that you scanned in the first part of your quest! You sure can follow instructions well! Reward: 5,000 class experience. Record breaker reward: You have completed this quest faster than any other Rituarchitect in history! All ten buildings have been upgraded to Uncommon rank and Tier.

Joe and the Dwarves were cheering as the final building was completed, but they went still and silent as *all* of the new buildings were upgraded. The changes were minor to the naked eye; simply a tightening, a shifting, and finally ornamentation added to each building. To determine what the full difference was, the Reductionist scanned the perishable goods warehouse they had just created.

Warehouse (Perishable goods, 13,200 feet of storage). Uncommon. Durability: 11,100.

"The storage and durability *doubled*?" Joe frowned at the building, unsure how that was possible. "The building looks the same, so there's magic involved?"

"Buildings are buildings." Ciril was sweeping wide eyes around the area. "The space they take up is always the same, but the space they *capture* can differ greatly. Even so, I'm shocked you would let this happen at this juncture."

"What do you mean?" Joe's question had barely passed his lips when a notification with the sound of a massive gong arrived, causing everyone in the area to wince.

A new hamlet dares *attempt to exist!*

Area quest: A new Dwarven camp is getting delusions of grandeur and is attempting to break into becoming a Tier 1 hamlet!

- *For those aligned with the Elves, destroying the campground before it tiers up will give rewards as though it is a Tier 2 town!*
- *For those aligned with the Dwarves, defend your newly hatching settlement for one week to gain a hamlet!*

"Ah. That's what you mean." Joe read over the information one more time, then closed it with a shrug. He had known this was coming; he just hadn't expected it so soon. "Anything we can do about this?"

"Literally: no," Ciril told him sadly. "Just defend for a week, and then you can start creating more buildings to improve this place further."

"I can't make more buildings for a *week*?" Joe gasped in horror, staring at the next item on his agenda: the Ritual Ziggurat. He had been practically foaming at the mouth to get that particular structure up and functioning.

"Nope." Stan walked over with his hands in his pockets. "Good job on these buildings. I can charge half again as much rent for an Uncommon building as I can a Common one."

"I don't care about that so much," Joe muttered as he tried to mentally rearrange his plans for the next few days. "Now what?"

"Now we hunker down and get this place ready for a siege," Ciril replied, eyeing him sternly. "The destruction of a Tier-two town is worth *thousands* of resources. Even split by a raiding party, it'll be a juicy target."

"We don't even have a wall," Stan's monotone rang out. "Next week, make a wall. Then make a town hall or something. Anytime you rank up a town after Tier one, the town hall is automatically upgraded. Don't waste that; it's free. Free is great."

"I have plans for a Guildhall. Would that work?" Joe looked to the other two for confirmation, but both of their faces were as neutral as possible, with just a hint of disgust.

"You *can* have a Guildhall as your town hall... if you want to make this a *guild* town. Somewhere that even people aligned with *Elves* can just walk into, if they're part of your guild." Ciril spat the explanation with a sneer. "You have any guild members aligned with Elves?"

"I... I don't know?" Joe pulled up his status, noting that he had a few quest notifications to look over. "I am the 'First Elder', or will be when my guild gets strong enough to upgrade to a Sect. Does that change things?"

Stan and Ciril looked at each other, and Stan sighed heavily. "I suppose all things come around again, given enough time. Sects are coming back into style? Ugh. That was a nightmare last time."

"If you have the power to refuse entry to people in your guild, then *yes*... a Guildhall can work." The admission was clearly difficult for Ciril to spit out. "You're going to have some pushback from the Oligarchy."

"I understand that." Joe smiled brightly, then decided that he should hurry along. He paid each of the Dwarves that had helped with the rituals, then rushed back to his workshop. "No defenses, possibility of a lot of people attacking. No real militia. My weapon usage at the... Beginner rank. Whoo, *boy*. Now what?"

He tapped on the golden eye tattooed on his forehead as he contemplated his options. "I can set up defensive rituals. I can't get good enough with my weapons in a week with no trainer, but what I *could* do is make them stronger. Maybe I could get out word that I have Uncommon housing for anyone that wants to be here? I never saw more than Common ranked for anyone in the Legion, so that should be a big draw?"

Joe examined his Ritual Orbs, feeling minorly frustrated with them. The only way to empower them in short order was to bind them to a characteristic, and that made him... nervous. "I could start with one that I don't really need to worry about so much? Like Charisma?"

There was nothing to do but get to work, even if it was reluctantly. Since he was attempting to increase his skills and spells at the same time, Joe worked to create the ritual diagram entirely free-floating. The first two circles went without issue, and he switched over to only using a single Aspect Inscriber for the third circle. When he reached the Student-ranked ritual circle, he spent long seconds agonizing over each mark that he made with his dwindling Rare aspects.

He was in an enclosed building at the moment, and even a single mistake would turn his workshop into an oven. "I *really* should have done this in the reinforced lab area..."

"Or opened the door so I could leave if I needed to do so," Cleave interjected dryly. To Joe's credit, her words didn't cause him to flinch and burn down his workshop, which had remained at the Common rank, as it was not constructed during his questline.

"Almost done... then I'll have a Student-ranked ritual diagram and be ready to use the Rare ranking to help keep the subsequent enchanting work stable," Joe whispered to himself as he completed the final line. It held in the air as he backed off, then a light blue energy drained from the outermost ring and connected to the remainder of the ritual, lightly dyeing the entire thing. "Success!"

"You can use the ritual to help with enchanting?" Cleave wondered aloud as she stared at the inert floating diagram.

"Not this one, but it was a good way to psych myself up," Joe informed her with a goofy grin. "No, I need to enchant my Orb directly, and this won't help in the slightest."

Cleave shook her head, moving to the other side of the

room and slumping to the ground. "You should get some chairs in here."

"Magic is done on your feet! It's a real stand-up profession," Joe quipped as he pulled out a few chunks of scrap metal. "I need to practice this enchantment before I actually attempt it. You wanna go to sleep for a while? I'm going to be at this for *hours*."

"Just do your magic." She waved at him while cradling her head in her hands. "I'm getting paid even if you aren't doing anything interesting."

With a shrug, Joe turned to his *wildly* exciting work. "I'll speak out loud so you can get an idea of what I'm doing."

"*No~o.*" Cleave moaned into her palms.

"As I was saying!" Joe loudly spoke over the complaints. "This enchantment is… an interesting thing. I need to create a sympathetic link between myself as well as my understanding of the characteristic that I'm attempting to bind. Now, some of this is formulaic and can be widely applied. For instance, I'm human, so that means the enchantment uses a shape like… *this…*"

He spent the next twenty minutes creating an enchantment diagram for 'basic human'. "There we go; not entirely terrible! Now I need to add in things that hold meaning regarding the characteristic I'm trying to bind from myself and onto the Orb. Let's see, how about… Charisma?"

That was when Joe ran into the hurdle that would be impeding his work every step of the way from that moment on.

"Feces, how do I create an enchantment that means *Strength*, much less 'Charisma'?" Joe gently slammed his head on the table as he tried to think of anything that could possibly work. "I suppose I can think of something for Strength… that's just moving stuff with physical might. Even intelligence has some-thing to do with the mind, and I can kludge something together."

After testing a few more diagrams, he found that he could even generate a form for Constitution, by making the sketched body 'resist outside influences'. When he tried to do the same by showing two people interacting, there was a magical backlash because the image was no longer drawing from *him*.

"I can do basic Strength, Constitution, Intelligence… everything else is not gonna work for me." Joe thought about trying to assign Karmic Luck to something and just ended up shaking his aching head. His knowledge would need to advance far beyond its current level in order to make those characteristics viable for ritualistic assignment to an Orb. "On that note… Knowledge, Architectural Lore!"

He had chosen to increase this particular section of his lore skills because it was the only one he *could* increase at the moment. That changed in the next instant, as two thousand mana drained into his skull and opened his mind to new information.

Architectural Lore has reached Beginner IX.

Knowledge has reached Apprentice 0! Cooldown decreased to 18 hours. This skill is not impacted by cooldown reduction from spells, skills, or items under Artifact rank!

Congratulations on reaching a new rank with a Legendary skill! Reward: Compendium of Skill and Spell Rankings up to Rare rarity.

For a long moment, Joe stared at the five different lore skills that he would be able to start increasing again, starting only three quarters of a day away. Then he looked at the book that had appeared in his hand. Barely able to hold back from opening it and investigating his skills, he placed it in his ring for some light reading at another time.

"Too much to do right now; I can't just start perusing random articles." Joe turned his attention back to his Orbs and decided that it was time to make his choice. "I'm going to assign…"

CHAPTER NINETEEN

"Major Cleave, I've decided to assign my Intelligence to this Orb and hope for the best!" Joe declared as he began lightly coating the entire exterior of the Orb with the purest of white aspects. "Don't try to stop me; this is something I need to do!"

"No, no…" Cleave called out as Joe *scritched* away at his Ritual Orb, drawing out a fair likeness of himself and high-lighting the interior of his head. "I think likening your Intelligence to a chunk of dead metal is fairly accurate."

"*Thank* you. See, in the past people have—hey!" Joe chuckled at what he hoped was a joke coming from the Dwarf. "That's a good one, but you aren't gonna make me mess this up that easily. Here's the interesting part: did you know that the thickness of the lines on the X, Y, *and* Z axis are important? Enchantments are three dimensional at all times, even when they're 'flat'. You see, the sympathetic…"

Joe waxed eloquent as he worked, doing everything he could to tamp down his own nerves over the process. He remembered all the warnings that were assigned to the Ritual Orbs, and how dangerous it was to do what he was attempting. If something happened to this orb, he would need to repeat the process on another orb, with his intelligence effectively halved. "Gotta find a way to automate this... just in case."

"Can you *stop*?" came an unexpected cry from Major Cleave. "I just gained Enchanting Lore at the Novice rank, and I have *no* interest in this subject!"

"You did?" Joe blinked at her owlishly, and then a wide smile shot across his face. "That means you were *really* listening... you *do* care!"

"I'm requesting reassignment right now," she grumped at him half-heartedly.

"You'd lose your promotion! I'm guessing you would, at least," The Ritualist called back as he finished his final few markings. "This was a Beginner enchantment... I'm kinda surprised by that. Perhaps it was because this is such an easily understandable concept? Or is it because there's such a clear downside to using this enchantment?"

"Perhaps each one you make will require higher tier aspects." Major Cleave finally gave up and decided to just get invested in the conversation. "You know, I will always cherish the initial misconception I had about you. You seemed so professional, intelligent, and ready to do anything necessary to stop the Elves."

"Glad you got that out of your system, then." Joe tossed back his head and laughed over-exaggeratedly. "Magic time! We see if my brain gonna do work hard."

"Fill out form PH ten thirty-one EZ for transfer to a front-line combat unit," Major Cleave muttered as she wrote on a notebook she had pulled from a storage space. "That'll let me stay a Major."

"Don't be like that!" Joe walked over to his hanging ritual and willed his Ritual Orb into the center. Using his sole Rare-rank core, he powered up the ritual and began pouring mana into it. Eschewing his previous antics, he watched each and every reaction with hawkish attention.

As the ritual came fully online, for lack of a better term, the enchantment on the Orb lifted away. The mathematical equations, sympathetic lines, and various formulae were drawn off of the Orb and into the ritual, which slightly shifted its configuration to hold all of the new information it was being fed. After a few long, question-filled seconds, the ritual shifted its focus and roughly grabbed Joe.

He was held as still as if he were in a Ritual of Stasis as his mind was scanned, poked, prodded, and tested by the ritual. Thanks to the Ritual Orbs coming with the first diagrams that he had needed for this particular experiment, Joe knew that he hadn't created them incorrectly. Yet, it was a terrifying feeling to have something of his own design hold him in a way where there was no possibility of stopping; even though that was *supposed* to happen.

Mana flickered from the ritual and sunk into his head. A moment later, a ghostly image of a brain was etched on the side of his Orb. Power streamed out of his head bit by bit, increasing until a flood of blue lights was connecting him and his Orb together. As the ritual finished, both Joe and the Ritual Orb dropped to the ground with a *thump*. With a final spark of power, the ritual ignited itself and burned away in an instant: a not-so-subtle reminder that this process had completed... and it was permanent.

Skill increase: Enchanted Ritual Circles has reached Beginner 0! Congratulations!

Words of Power (Written) has reached Apprentice II.

Somatic Ritual Casting increased significantly to Beginner V as you have proved your personal ability!

Magical Synesthesia has reached Beginner 0! You are now able to better understand how magic is noticed by your senses!

Essence Cycle has reached Beginner IV due to being forcibly cycled through your brain without causing permanent damage!

Quest updated: Student Ritualist. 1/20 rituals activated.

Joe blanched as he looked at all the skill gains that seemed... slightly ominous. Something told him that an error in his work would have resulted in even worse consequences than he had been expecting. As he glanced at his orb, he had the strangest feeling that it, too, was contemplating him in return. He touched it gingerly and read the description that appeared.

Ritual Orb of Intelligence (Masterwork). This Ritual Orb has gone through an Alchemic treatment as well as an extra round of enchanting via rituals.

Base Damage: 100 blunt -> shifting in progress.

Characteristic assigned: Intelligence. Any spell assigned to this Orb will have the primary damage effect increased by 10% on spell cast. Base damage will shift over time to be the damage type provided by the spell.

- *Automatically grants Orb the 'recall' ability; it will return to you after five minutes if left behind, forgotten, or stolen.*

Core assigned: 375/1,545

Spell assigned: Cone of Cold (Beginner V, awaiting unbinding for skill upgrade).

Ritual Diagram captured: None.

"That's a lot more information than you used to give me," Joe breathed in wonder as he induced the Orb to fly over and hop into its holster on his bandolier. "If I'm reading that correctly, this is working on changing the damage type for hitting someone with this from blunt, to *cold* damage?"

The etched brain on the side of the Orb caught his eye as it gleamed, and he wondered if that meant that it would eventually have thoughts of its own. Joe didn't know how he felt about that, but... too late now. His next thought was to upgrade another Orb, but the invasiveness of the process made him shudder. He wanted to see how effective this first one was in combat before he put himself further at risk.

Name: Joe 'Tatum's Chosen Legend' Class: Reductionist
Profession I: Arcanologist (Max)
Profession II: Ritualistic Alchemist (1/20)
Profession III: None

Character Level: 21 Exp: 236,309 Exp to next level: 16,691
Rituarchitect Level: 10 Exp: 50,500 Exp debt: 2,300
Reductionist Level: 2 Exp: 5,186 Exp to next level: 814
Hit Points: 1,864/1,864
Mana: 4,955/6,788. (1,832 reserved)
Mana regen: 52.7/sec
Stamina: 1,524/1,524
Stamina regen: 6.46/sec

Characteristic: Raw score

Strength: 146
Dexterity: 146
Constitution: 142
Intelligence (bound): 152
Wisdom: 133
Dark Charisma: 100
Perception: 137
Luck: 79
Karmic Luck: 15

"You know, maybe one of the reasons I was having so much trouble with Charisma is that I have *Dark* Charisma." Joe pondered that for a moment, reflecting on the change and what the resulting notification had told him. "I'm more easily able to influence people toward actions that cause fighting… I'll keep that in mind. Maybe I should go and incite a riot? No, that's a bad idea. Might be good training, though…? No! Must keep attention on making traps, alarms, and… oh, shiny notification! I got a new quest?"

Beginner Rituarchitect. Gather enough materials to create 10 Uncommon buildings. Damaged aspects: 0/20,000. Common aspects: 0/10,000. Uncommon aspects: 0/1,000. Reward: +3 to your choice of relevant Lore skill. Current options: Architectural Lore.

"I can use that to save a ton of time." Joe stared at the reward, telling himself that he could hold off on completing the new quest until the town upgrade quest was completed. If he did so, and used Knowledge as much as possible, he could jump the Lore skill to the Student rank. With his plan set in stone, he turned to his currently empty workshop table.

"I'm almost out of Rare aspects, so I need to focus my rituals on three circles or below." Pulling out a notebook, he wrote out the things that he thought would be the most beneficial, cost-effective defenses. "Major, would you mind taking a look at this?"

She took the paper, reading it with increasing concern for each list item. "What is this, Joe? Alarms, barriers, healing rituals, holding rituals, attack rituals, explosion… *collapse*? Are you planning to kill us all?"

"No, I was just writing down what I could start working on for defenses. I put it in order from least to most dangerous." Joe tapped the paper and showed his teeth as he smiled at Major Cleave. "We're *going* to be attacked, which means I'm gonna fall back on what some people might see as bad habits. Where do you think I should start?"

"Alarms, if you'd be so kind," Cleave answered in an instant. "Least number of chances to accidentally murder us in broad daylight."

"Ooh, *so* close." Joe tapped the bottom of the page. "I'm gonna rig every tunnel to collapse based on the proximity alarms going off, so that actually has the *most* chances to take all of us down. Great advice, Major Cleave!"

"What if there are others? Noncombatants? Hostages?" Cleave didn't bother to hide her displeasure. "You aren't a Candidate anymore. War crimes against your own people will not be so easily forgiven going forward. Don't you think this is too… ruthless?"

"Yeah." Joe's sclera flashed black for an instant as he gazed out at the myriad tunnels that had been dug through the volcano by the Elves. "Being ruthless is what The Wanderers are good at. We even get a bonus for it. That's why I said I'm falling back on old habits."

"You said they were *bad* habits, sir."

"Did I?" Joe muttered softly as he imagined lava rushing along the enclosed passages, incinerating human and Elven aggressors alike. "I think I said *other* people saw them as bad habits. I just call it keeping my town safe."

CHAPTER TWENTY

One of the things that Joe had learned during his time in the military was that engineers were only ever a gentle push away from shifting into full-blown sappers. Anything that promised even the *potential* to step away from creation into beautiful, cascading destruction was a career path that all but the most satisfied were ready to step onto. Happily, there just so happened to be a large team of engineers in the volcano who were waiting on Havoc's return to begin the next phase of their secret current job.

All he had needed to do was walk out of his workshop, locate the nearest cluster of engineers, and explain that he essentially wanted to install some devices that would collapse all but five of the tunnels leading into the Shoe and thereby eliminate any invading Elves. He had made no offer of payment, long-term contracts, or anything resembling a tangible incentive. Even so, without missing a beat, one of the Dwarves had whipped out a map that she had put together in her spare time. She rapidly outlined six different areas that they could target to accomplish his goals.

The only reason Joe did not take her up on the offer immediately was that every single other engineer in the group began offering alternatives at high volume. They all had good ideas, so Joe had been forced to come up with a plan on his own. Using his authority over the area, he created a quest worth a hundred reputation for any engineer who could design the most detailed plan for collapsing as many tunnels as possible with the fewest 'charges' without collapsing the volcano on the town.

The only stipulation given by the other Dwarves was that Bauen was not allowed to participate, or even know what they were doing with their free time. A very confused Joe had agreed to this, and the engineers had scattered into the volcanic shafts like children on a scavenger hunt.

While they were out perfecting their maps, Joe took a few hours to go over his personal plan for collapsing the tunnels. What he eventually settled on was a variation on his gravedigging ritual. The main difference was that it did not have any particular living target; it would simply begin intensely vibrating the earth and stone within its range. In essence, it was a very low-powered earthquake ritual. He liked that idea so much that he scrawled it atop the paper he was using to design the ritual diagram. "You know what, I'm going to name it that. There's no one around to stop me. Ritual of... Minor Earthquake. Done."

+1 Wisdom.

"Well, that's an ominous gain." Joe's brows furrowed as he tried to puzzle out what earning the random stat meant, but he could only assume he had gotten it for planning against an attack. "Hope I'm correct in thinking that this was just due to planning a wise defense. Guess I'll find out?"

Words were not enough anymore, so he took himself to the rubble pit, or landfill-to-be, and started smashing rocks with his Ritual Orbs while wondering if he was doing the right thing. When he eventually calmed down, he realized that he couldn't remember the last time he had gained a characteristic point, and that worried him greatly.

He had already been behind where he should have been

when he joined this plane, and if he was falling behind again, the next plane that he had access to would figuratively crush his spirit, and do the same much more literally to his entire body and mind.

"Add Characteristic training back to the ever-growing list, I suppose. What I really need to do is find a hobby that makes it fun," Joe mumbled as he tried to put his game face back on. The first of the gleeful Dwarves were beginning to emerge from the tunnels, and they were clearly looking for him, even if they were trying to do so subtly. "Also add 'Find out why they wouldn't want their boss to know about my quests'."

All too soon, he held a stack of maps pointing out the best areas to blast. In order to find the *actual* best one, he made everyone secretly vote on a map that they had not made. Whoever won would get a small bonus for their vote. After tallying, there was a clear winner. Joe paid the celebrating mustachioed Dwarf and had her guide him through the tunnels to each location that would be outfitted with a Ritual of Minor Earthquake.

It took surprisingly little time before he was all alone once again and preparing to… "Wait a moment. Major Cleave?"

"Need something?" she quizzed him in her curt, gruff voice. "Or just checking to see if I still exist… yet again?"

"No, I was, um, going to ask you something." Joe's mind whirled as he tried to come up with a believable query, and his thoughts dredged up a concept he had been pondering only a short while previously. "I need to take some time before completing my next class quest, and I was thinking about how I needed to increase some of my characteristics. The issue is, I have so many things that I want to do, so how am I supposed to increase my base characteristics as well as getting things done?"

There was a short pause as Major Cleave chewed on his dilemma. "Well, if you are looking at a hobby… can I interest you instead in a profession?"

"Please, do tell." Joe actually was interested, despite the fact that the conversation had started as a way to avoid confirming her suspicion. As she explained, he began drawing out his ritual diagram at the. "I need to find a way to hide the inactive ritual, since these aspects glow no matter if it is active or not…"

"I suppose my answer should be more than a simple 'do this'." Cleave stroked her mustache as she considered how to give him proper instruction. "You understand, of course, that high-level crafters are some of the most revered people in the Oligarchy, yes? You should also know that it is very difficult to hold on to something if you do not have the ability to protect it properly."

"Makes sense." Joe answered her, only half-listening as he started sketching the second ritual circle.

"Let me ask you this, do you have any skills or spells in the Master ranks?" The question she postulated gave Joe pause, though luckily not enough to interrupt his concentration on the ritual.

"Not… anymore," he grimly informed her. "I used to, but I found some other skills with high synergy and combined them into a better version. At least, I *think* that the combined skill went up a rarity rank, but it also brought the individual skills down into the Expert ranks."

"Had you ever increased any skill while it was in the Master ranks?" Cleave pressed him, thankfully pausing and allowing him to collect his thoughts as he worked.

The fact was, while Joe was happy with his new skill, the loss of a Master-rank skill was likely impacting his guild's ability to work with the nobility or recruit new members back on Midgard. The guilt about that was eating at him slightly; it was one of the reasons he had earned his rank in the guild in the first place. Since he was silent so long, Cleave took his answer as a 'no'. "If you had a Master skill, you should have noticed that every so often when using that skill, you suddenly gained large increases in your characteristics even without increasing the skill level. Specifically, the main characteristics in use as you activated the skill."

"I'm guessing that is why so many Dwarves are happy to

apprentice themselves to Masters and Grandmasters for what is essentially a pittance?" Understanding was beginning to dawn on Joe. "If that is the case, bringing your skills in alignment with a profession would mean more rapid advancement and extra rewards as you progress, as well as interesting new options for the profession?"

"Precisely." Cleave looked at him with newfound respect. "No matter what everyone else is saying about you, every once in a while, it *is* nice to be around someone that can extrapolate from incomplete information."

"Thanks. *Wait…*" Before he could follow that conversational landmine any further, the Major hurriedly pushed forward with her explanation.

"It should be obvious that combat gives the most consistent characteristic increases. However, constant combat also significantly increases the opportunity to become injured or slain. With crafting and gathering professions and skills, there is typically less immediate danger, which would allow for more rapid growth." She held both of her hands in the air as if she were mimicking a set of scales. "For every benefit, there is a cost. Just like with all things in life, there are three major considerations: Time, talent, and cost."

Joe took over at that point, having just put the finishing touches on the second circle. "If you have unlimited time to work on something, you'll get there eventually, no matter what else happens. If you have greater talent for the task you are attempting, it will require less time and money to accomplish. If you have more money, you can… I'm thinking of delegating or hiring someone else to do the work?"

"Yes, but for our example, my meaning is this: if you have the reputation to make it happen, hiring a Grandmaster as your instructor will allow you to fly through the early ranks of any skill or spell," Major Cleave explained eagerly. Clearly, this was a topic she was invested in for some reason. "An average person has time, talent, and cost in balance. As an example: a warrior has to be good at fighting, take the time to learn their skills properly, and earn enough money to afford the gear they need. In that regard, there is a medium requirement for all three considerations."

"Which means that as a crafter," Joe stepped in once more after catching where she was going, "typically what you need is a large monetary investment as well as... I'm guessing talent is the most important secondary?"

"Learning a full profession is almost entirely a matter of how many resources you can bring to bear. Let's take... *table making*, for example." Cleave's selection made Joe want to roll his eyes, but he simply stopped his break and started on the third and final circle of his ritual. "If you wanted to make a table out of stone but had no talent for it, you would waste much more stone than someone who had that talent."

She paused for a moment, evidently wanting to clarify a point before going further. "Of course, hiring an instructor would help mitigate some of the resource cost, but it would inversely alter the cost of learning. However, if you decided to make the table out of wood and had a great talent for it, that would be a better way to reduce the cost of materials, and learning how would be necessary to bring your vision to fruition."

"Are you wanting to be a public speaker or a teacher when you get out of the Legion?" Joe asked aloud without thinking. When Cleave remained silent, he risked a glance back at her. "Actually, I have no idea if you have any plans to ever leave the Legion."

"No." Her reply was as short as she had been with him over the last few days, informing Joe that he had messed up once again. "I plan to stay in just long enough to gain a high enough rank that I will be able to inform policy decisions for training new recruits. You have gone through basic training... you should recall that all the Legion does for the first half a year or longer is throw fresh recruits against monsters. It is the cheapest, most basic way to increase their skill levels. Yet, I feel we could do better as a society at large if we took the time to properly train each Legionnaire."

"Interesting." Joe put the finishing touches on his ritual, then stared at it in consternation. "I know that I certainly would have enjoyed having a trainer instead of... that hot mess. Let me know if I can help with that someday. Now... how in the world am I supposed to... I guess I could set up a Ritual of Remote Activation, but on *what?*"

"Do you actually mean that?" The earnestness in her voice pulled his full attention back to her. "You would actually help me push through my designs for the Legion?"

"I mean... yeah. You have good ideas. To be fair, I tend to be biased in favor of people that are keeping me alive, even if they are simply ordered to do so." Joe shrugged as he turned back to his current conundrum and tapped it with his inscriber. "Realistically, all of these could be bound to a single activation ritual, since I don't want to have to set them off in sequence or at different times. One single ritual... bound... carry with me."

"I need to think about this," Cleave muttered as she considered Joe in a new light. Light that unfortunately reflected off his bald head and made her wince.

"Take all the time you need. I just had a breakthrough." Joe floated one of his Ritual Orbs up in front of his face, smiling at it in a good approximation of the look Jaxon had on his face at all times. "Hello *bound* weapon that I always have on my person, and will return to me no matter what. My bright and shiny orbs of power that can each carry reusable, reactivatable ritual circles within themselves. Imma turn you into a detonator."

CHAPTER TWENTY-ONE

It seemed to take almost no time at all for Joe to complete the next four Rituals of Minor Earthquake, as well as the associated receiving ritual portion of the Ritual of Remote Activation. Major Cleave, apparently now holding him in a higher regard, also helped by taking a few moments to smash large piles of rubble out of the tunnel walls.

They stacked the rubble around the free-floating rituals, very effectively hiding their glow. As they were inactive, No magical fluctuations or feelings were being given off by them, not even when Joe stood right next to them and focused his entire attention on his Magical Synesthesia.

"When they aren't active, they may as well be ordinary paint! Beyond the glow that can only be seen with the naked eye, no matter what ability I'm looking at them with, I can't tell that they're magic," he gleefully informed his companion, guardian, or minder—depending on how he thought about the situation. "Even an Elf coming through here should have no reason to start shifting random detritus around, right?"

"Who knows or cares what those pointy-eared…" Major Cleave took a deep breath, forcing a smile onto her face. "That is, using proper *Dwarven* logic, no; there would be no point in doing so."

"*Excellent.*" Joe rubbed his hands together as he considered his next move. "I think I'm going to go to that section and add alarm rituals near the end of each tunnel, as well as... ooh! You know what I should try? I bet if I set up an alarm ritual, which goes off based on a proximity sub-ritual, I could set that sub-ritual to activate a Ritual of Remote Activation at the same time! I haven't done redstone wiring in a while; this should be a lot of fun!"

"What is redstone? Some kind of tripwire?" Major Cleave took in their surroundings, noting that all of the rocks in the area had a red tint to them, either from an excess of iron in their makeup, or just the glow from the few pools of lava that were still open to the air. Joe's Ritual of Heat Draining—though inefficient—had been even more effective than he or the Dwarves had been hoping for. Now, even the large pools of molten rock that had been threatening to turn the town area into a kind of lava peninsula had hardened. This was going to allow for more area upon which to build the town; the only remaining question was whether it would be zoned as a building area, some kind of park, or a demilitarized zone in order to allow them to see enemies trying to sneak in.

"Redstone is from an old game. Yeah, it'll act like a trip-wire," Joe mumbled distractedly, daydreaming about *his* personal preference—turning the unexpected extra space into a peaceful green space, or maybe a nice walking track around the town. He was saving that proposal for a time when he was able to find both the city planner and the city administrator only partially conscious. "Perhaps a serum of suggestibility whenever Jake the Alchemist gets to work?"

"You say something?"

"Yes."

"Anything that mattered?" Cleave's tone held a jesting quality to it, something that had certainly been missing from her presence over the last few days.

"Ah… no," Joe admitted with a wry chuckle. "Just making mental jokes about being far more devious than anything I would actually follow through on."

After a few more hours of setting up extremely minor rituals throughout the tunnels and especially near the tunnel entrances, he was truly exhausted. Worse than that, he had no idea what to do next. He couldn't complete his Ritualist class quest without quite a few more resources—specifically Rare aspects—but if he went out to collect them, he would be leaving the town mostly unprotected against an assault. Not only that, but he would be wasting some of the viability of the reward for the Beginner Rituarchitect quest, as gathering Rare aspects was guaranteed to provide him with all of the lower-ranked aspects required for the quest to complete.

"Knowledge, Architectural Lore." Joe practically heaved as he flopped down onto a chair made entirely of stone. He knew that the seat would have hurt him when he had first arrived upon this world, but his Constitution was high enough that the blocky seat actually felt comfortable. Mana flooded into his mind, and suddenly, he understood buildings at a deeper level.

Congratulations! Architectural Lore has reached Apprentice 0! You now have enough theoretical knowledge regarding the creation of structures that you may be able to start detecting anomalies or benefits inherent in a blueprint or created building, as well as being trusted to understand what is needed to create Common-ranked buildings of nearly any origin. To help you get a job somewhere, have +2 luck!

"That seems like such a backhanded compliment," Joe softly muttered while silently cheering over the boost to his Luck. He had been eyeing that characteristic nervously recently, as he was two thresholds above the characteristic with his Intelligence, and he remembered what had happened to him the last time he was too far out of balance. "Still, it is really nice to be progressing rapidly again. Especially with my lore skills, I really feel that I have something special going on here."

He skimmed the short list that he had arranged to only show lore skills. Joe was rather pleased with their overall growth since he had gained Knowledge, which he only included in the grouping because it was the skill that directly allowed him to increase the others.

Alchemical Lore (Beginner IX)
Architectural Lore (Apprentice 0)
Enchanting Lore (Apprentice 0)
Knowledge (Apprentice 0)
Ritual Lore (Apprentice II)
Smithing Lore (Apprentice 0)

"Ahh… alphabetized and easy to understand." Joe stretched out over the stone seat and twisted side to side. "I have no idea why that matters so much to me, but it does. Now, I *can* see the use and appeal for gaining lore skills. Yet what I really need to know is… are these so useful and so hard to acquire that people will throw things at me if I tell them I had it? Or perhaps throw me in a room and only let me out to write textbooks and technical manuals for them? I suppose I… should *probably* just go ahead and keep it to myself."

Low on resources, remaining on constant alert for a possible attack, and without many people in the area to interact with, Joe was uncertain what to do. He had been focusing on ritual circles so extensively in recent days that he was starting to get sick to his stomach whenever he saw curved lines. "What to do, what to do… Mate, an espresso for me, please."

As the elemental filled a small mug for him, Major Cleave looked at the brown liquid and shook her head. "Never got a taste for that stuff. It's not good for me."

"You're in the legion. You probably never *had* any of the good stuff. Would you like to try this, which is from the elemental plane of coffee… or something?" Joe got another mug ready and offered it to her. She eyed it, shrugged, and tossed it back like a shot of grog. Joe waited to hear her response, but the Dwarf merely stood near the huge stone like a statue once more. "Let me know when it hits you."

Ignoring the usual reply-grunt, his eyes fluttered around the mostly open area, coming to rest on a chunk of stone that must have been imported by the Elves when they had originally burrowed into the volcano. The block was a long rectangle of what appeared to be marble, at least a dozen feet long and eight feet wide, standing waist-high on him despite laying on its side. There were large visible flaws which had likely caused crafters to deem the stone unusable, cracks and damage to the surface that would make it undesirable for most things.

However, he couldn't see any damage that went all the way through, and he was *itching* for something new to do. His conversation with Ciril and Stan was troubling him; how would his guild members be able to get along if they were also loyal to opposite sides of this ancient conflict? He, and all other guild officers, would be running around stamping out arguments at all times of the night and day; that is, if they *too* were not arguing amongst themselves.

"Major Cleave, I can only blame you for making me think of tables. Time, Talent, and cost." Joe grinned at his own joke as he started imagining the stone block as a huge, ornate table in the Guildhall that he would be creating after the town upgraded. "I've got lots of time, no talent at present, and the stone is free. Two outta three isn't bad. If I cut it there, there, and round that section off… maybe I can get Havoc to clean up the design a little bit after he gets back?"

A simple use of his Field Array made the top of the stone block perfectly level and cut-glass smooth. He checked it, double checked, and triple checked before he was completely certain that the polished surface would be able to hold the entirety of the enchantment that he had gained as his level twelve bonus for following Occultatum way back when. "Nice. You're gonna be a gorgeous centerpiece… and I *really* need a hobby."

"If you need something that takes up your time, you should start dating that lady architect," Major Cleave commented as Joe ran his fingertips gently over the entirety of the roughly-shaped table. A glance revealed that her cheeks were rosy, and she was dancing back and forth as though she were about to explode from overabundant energy. "She seems to like you even with your glaring, reflective, obvious issues, and you do seem to have many things in common."

Joe's fingers slid to a stop, and he continued moving only after a moment of perfect stillness. The Dwarf was unable or unwilling to ascertain that this meant Joe had no interest in continuing the conversation. For a few minutes, she waxed eloquent upon the fact that Daniella had thus far been instrumental in forcing Stan to do the work that he was supposed to do, in the order that he was supposed to do it. She brought the conversation back around after going over all of the positives of the new hire, reiterating that Joe should see if she was available to go monster hunting with him.

Eventually, the human had enough and braced his hands on the tabletop to heave himself upright. "Cleave, you should go ahead and sit down. I think you're having a bad reaction to the caffeine."

"No I am not." She informed him firmly. The creeping flush spread to her bald pate, and she started bouncing up and down. "I just think that people should have more in their lives, and you clearly need a person."

"Major. While I appreciate what I *think* are good intentions, I have no plans to do something so foolish as to split my focus away from magic and town construction. If I were to start dating, you may as well light my research notes on fire and expect me to give up on my goals of city building for the next few decades. I would appreciate no further-"

"Not big into commitment, are you? Or is it that you're *very* into commitment?" Cleave chuckled at her own joke, touching on the fact that Joe had just said he wanted to spend literally decades on a single facet of his abilities. The Dwarven logic in her approved, though she decided to needle him a bit further. "You know, in my society, we just fight with our partners until we have gained enough bonds of friendship and camaraderie to commit to them for a few hundred years."

"Cleave." Joe's tone was harsh and completely different

from how the Major had ever heard him speak to anyone before. "I have *magic*. I get to do things that I have always dreamed about, with unique resources, power, and amazing discoveries almost every single day. I am also essentially immortal, so I see no reason to rush into a commitment with a single person. Not now, and not again."

"Ah. *There* it is," she stated knowingly, her voice and posture returning to normal as the rush of energy faded thanks to Joe's Neutrality Aura removing the abnormal status.

"I would be an absolutely *terrible* partner. No one else will be as willing to invest their time and efforts into the same things that I want," Joe stated calmly, his hands beginning to trail around the previously damaged surface of the stone. "When you are in the pursuit of something, something you want so badly that you are willing to give up anything to get it… you might start to understand what I have here. I am a *Ritualist*, and I do not want to have to compromise upon expanding my magic. That is what a relationship with another person is: *compromise*. I don't have that in me anymore."

"Listen, Baldy. If you don't want to date her, don't. I don't need your entire life story," Cleave grunted at Joe in displeasure as she sat down in his vacated stone seat, rubbing at her suddenly-throbbing head. "For someone that literally has to work with other people all of the time, you sure do seem against working with a *special* someone. It's just confusing to me, that's all."

"I have my reasons, Cleave. Let's look at the facts." Joe found a small crack and set the Field Array to shave off a slightly deeper section to extricate it. "I meet people all the time, but so far I have only found a single person on Svaltarheim whom I used to be in a longish-term party with: Jaxon. I've already gone through two different parties, five people in each. Let me ask you something… where do you think those other eight people are? I know for a fact that they're all powerful enough to be here, at least if they *wanted* to be."

"Probably gearing up or getting ready for the warzone before they make the jump-"

"*Wrong.*" Joe turned to face Major Cleave for the first time since the conversation had started. "They all fell off their path of progression for different reasons. It's true that some of them stopped looking for resources, and a couple simply didn't have the mentality they needed to progress further. But three of them —more than half of my entire previous party—stopped because of the people in their life."

Cleave merely raised an eyebrow, rolling her eyes as Joe went on.

"One of them had *excellent* reasons to stay and absolutely did the correct thing. Poppy, a sublime Duelist, is working back on Midgard to prepare for his child. Setting up a life for someone he loves and is responsible for." Joe shook his head at the memory of the next words he had to say, "But Bard and Alexis? They stopped progressing entirely because they wanted to explore their relationship more than they wanted to explore a literal new *universe*. A universe where they could be anything they wanted to be, have anything they wanted to have!"

"Sounds like they *wanted* to be together." Cleave met his eyes calmly. "Seems more like you resent them for not joining *you* than you do for them being together."

"Don't get me wrong." Joe slowly let out a long breath, wondering if there could have been a better way to explain his feelings. "I am happy for them. *Especially* for Poppy. To him, being a parent was the most amazing thing in the entire universe. I get that, and I respect it all the way down to my soul. I *also* know that humans that joined this world cannot have children while they are in it. I read the terms and conditions for coming to this existence. We're immortal while we're here, in that we will never die or pass away permanently from time passing. That means *any* relationship formed here will eventually end."

Major Cleave allowed him to work in silence for a short

while before breaking his concentration one last time. "Could it be that you're just running from your own feelings?"

"Must we continue this? Abyss, you made your point! I'll never give you coffee again. Besides... you're missing the entire point of this little tirade, Cleave." Joe shook off his grumpies and gave her a half-cocked grin. "I have *magic*. I'm not running *from* anything. I'm running *to* everything I've ever wanted."

"You are going to end up being one of those lonely wizards who locks themselves in a magic tower somewhere." She sighed as she held up her hand to let him know that she was done with the conversation.

"A magic... tower?" Joe's eyes started dancing as he imagined it. "A massive building devoted to generating resources that I could use to make this entire universe better? Well-protected, far off the ground so that experiments gone wrong don't hurt anyone, a great landmark so people wouldn't get lost, and reality-changing magic pouring out of it for time immemorial...? That sounds *spectacular*!"

"I should have just kept my mouth shut." Cleave growled as Joe's eyes went vacant, and a hint of drool appeared at the corner of his mouth. "I told you coffee wasn't good for me."

CHAPTER TWENTY-TWO

Joe fiddled with his table, joined a group of Dwarves that were gambling in an effort to boost his luck stat, and prepared a few more rituals for town defense. Each ritual that he made came *ever* so slightly closer to the town proper, which meant they were starting to become very difficult to hide.

The glowing manifestations of power simply hung in the air, waiting for anyone foolish enough to enter their proximity. To mix it up, he made sure to attach some rituals directly to the surface of the volcanic floor, then covered them with ash and dirt when they were complete. He wouldn't want someone to win a fight simply because they could see where he was defending.

The week went by slowly, and when the timer showed only a little more than a day remaining, Joe finally perfected the method for placing a ritual in his Ritual Orb. The only reason it had been so very difficult for him was because—as a Reductionist—he was forced to use aspects for every personal creation, from dinner to ritual circles. Too bad for him, the Ritual Orb was a physical object, and he could not simply replace the entirety of the wires that made up its internal structure.

To his great embarrassment, he finally stumbled upon the answer by mere chance, rather than any kind of research or understanding. He had created the Novice ritual, leaving it free-floating in the air so that he could at least *activate* the preset Rituals of Minor Earthquake if he needed to do so. Several days of attempting to draw out the wiring and arrange it had only netted him frustration, especially after he found that he needed to replace the wiring manually when he opened it with his hands.

To be fair, the shape of the Orb had shifted significantly, turning into something that looked much closer to a frozen-metal icicle than an orb. It had taken *hours* to figure out how to close the outer shell of the not-exactly-an-orb-but-he-was-still-gonna-call-it-that-out-of-convenience when he was sick of trying.

Even then, the only reason everything had worked out was because the casing of the icicle-orb had popped back open after he'd thought he had it. In abject frustration, he had thrown the Orb at the wall with a low growl-scream of frustration. The orb's trajectory had passed it through the ritual diagram, and the tangled mess paused in mid-air and arranged all of its wires neatly, using only a portion of them to mimic the diagram as it drew the ring of fiery light into itself.

Ritual Orb of Intelligence (Masterwork). This Ritual Orb has gone through an Alchemic treatment as well as an extra round of enchanting via rituals.

Base Damage: 100 piercing cold.

Characteristic assigned: Intelligence. Any spell assigned to this Orb will have the primary damage effect increased by 10% on spell cast. Base damage will shift over time to be the damage type provided by the spell.

- *Automatically grants Orb the 'recall' ability; it will return to you after five minutes if left behind, forgotten, or stolen.*

Core assigned: 375/1,545

Spell assigned: Cone of Cold (Beginner V, awaiting unbinding for skill upgrade).

Ritual Diagram captured: Ritual of Remote Activation (Sender)

"Do I really need to just make a ritual, then throw an Orb into it like I am trying to catch a flying fish with a net?" Joe pulled the Orb back to himself and examined its surface, exceedingly leery about opening it up and inspecting the wiring once again now that it had closed. "I don't understand why it is so easy to pop it open to remove the core if needed, but pulling out one little wire turns the whole thing into an unraveled ball of steel wool."

"Hello, Joe!" Jaxon's muffled voice reached Joe's ears through the door as the man pounded on it. "I'm here to ask for a building where I can offer my chiropractic services! Havoc told me that I need something like that to get access to my class quests, and I could only ask when you had brought the town up to a new level. I figure we're close enough."

"Just you out there?" Joe quizzed as he started opening the door.

"Oh, my, yes," Jaxon cheerfully intoned as Joe pushed open the door, revealing both the slender chiropractor and Kettlebell. "Just me and this *wonderfully* attentive student. Do you know he's almost to Student rank as a chiropractor already? His attention to detail, love of twisting people, and the musculature to back up the skills? He's a *prodigy!*"

"He's also banned from my workshop." Joe rubbed his head as he snuck a glance at Cleave. He had the feeling that she wouldn't be amused that he had let someone in without even checking to see if they were alone. His glance revealed that she appeared upset, so he let out the breath he had been holding. Thank goodness; nothing had changed. She always looked like that. "Run that by me again... you need a building?"

"Yes!" Jaxon stepped in happily, slamming the door in Kettlebell's face. "I'd like it to be out near an environment where animals will be living. Cattle and the like. Or a beast training area. Then I can give classes and test things on people and creatures alike!"

"Efficient," Joe stated dryly. "But starting a whole practice here seems-"

"Exactly! *Wonderfully* efficient!" Jaxon clapped his hands together. "Now that I have a student, I don't even need to worry about what would happen to the practice if I went out on a hunt for a few weeks! Once he is trained up a little more, I could leave my patients to him without a single concern in the world! Just between you and myself, Lefty and Terror need some tender love and care; I've only been able to let them out to eat *twice* in the last week!"

That caused Joe to pause, and he glanced dubiously at Jaxon's hands. "Do they *need* to come out and eat?"

"I don't think so? Why does it matter?"

"The way you said that made it seem like… never mind." Joe always had trouble understanding Jaxon's motivations, but he had long since chalked it up to the multi-generational difference between their mentalities. "We can make it happen, but you need to gather all of the resources you need for it. Blueprints for the type of building you want, especially, since I'm sure this is going to be a custom structure. You've always gone out of your way to help me, so I'll make sure that most of the cost is taken care of. Problem is, I've got no idea what will suit your needs best, and so ya need to do that research yourself. Sound like a plan?"

"Excellent." Jaxon twisted to the side, covered his eyes with one hand and extended the other. "When we agree on something, we are supposed to do this 'dab' motion, right? That's what I was told by-"

"No, Jaxon." Joe shuddered at the cringefest in front of him. "That was… no. No one has *ever* done that to seal a business deal."

Before they could discuss the intricacies of popular culture, and how far away from popular culture both of them were— and should stay—the sound of a gong echoed through the entire enclosed volcanic space. That was soon followed by a siren reminiscent of a klaxon call mixed with screaming pigs.

"What on Svaltarheim is *that?*" Jaxon wondered idly as he tried out a few new 'dab' positions.

"I think that's one of my alarms? Are we under attack?" Joe cracked the door and searched for the origin of the noise, unable to spot anything amiss other than a pillar of black smoke in the distance. Then something appeared in the volcano that never should have been able to form under natural circumstances: a massive sheet of ice.

The frozen coating was followed by an explosion, which cracked the surrounding earth deeply enough that fresh magma bubbled up to the surface. Jaxon nodded sagely as he looked on. "It certainly appears as if we are under attack. Should we do anything about that? Or just head to the speakeasy you don't know about, grab a cup of tea, and wait for it to blow over?"

"*Jaxon!*"

"What?" The chiropractor put his hands out to the side in a 'what did I do' gesture. "The last time you got involved with defending a town, you got banished for a whole year! How am I supposed to know if you want to be a part of town defense again?"

"To arms, Bros and Dudettes! There's *hundreds* of 'em coming through!" A pained scream echoed through the cavern. "It's a full-scale invasion!"

"Is he serious? What are we supposed to even do about that?" Major Cleave stepped forward and put her hand in front of Joe, stopping him from proceeding. "My last headcount showed us at thirty-eight *total* people living in this Hamlet. We might have a few more by now, mostly due to whatever traders have started trickling in, but a full invasion of hundreds of people? This is over. It's time to evacuate, sir. Let's get you somewhere secure."

"So they can chuck me in a room and make me write technical manuals until I finally escape in a blaze of glory?" Joe hollered to no one in particular, ignoring the confusion that she exuded. The Reductionist was determined to choose his own fate. "How about we try things my way first?"

He swung his arm out in front of him, his Ritual Orb floating up to hover in front of his outstretched palm. "Activating bound ritual."

The Orb twisted in place. Over the next half second, it unlocked with a *click* and released a huge amount of spooled wire that popped up into an oversized version of the Ritual of Remote Activation. The wire rapidly sucked back in until it had shrunk down to the proper size, with Joe's hand resting directly in the center activation portion. Taking a deep breath, he began pouring mana into the ritual.

It could have been his imagination, but he could have *sworn* that the air in front of him vibrated as his ritual came into effect. Upon activation, the Ritual Orb's open form only lasted an eyeblink before collapsing back down to its standard combat form. Joe smiled grimly, knowing that the ritual had been successful. After all…

The effects were hard to miss.

CHAPTER TWENTY-THREE

As his Ritual Orb returned to its standard icicle shape, notifications began trickling into Joe's combat log. At first, it was indeed a trickle, but it rapidly became a *flood* of notices telling him the same thing: reputation had been gained with the Dwarven Oligarchy.

He was too far away to hear anything directly happening with combat, but a rumble—followed by the vast majority of tunnels beginning to spew lava into the chamber itself—told him everything he needed to know.

"I'm going to have to give that engineer a bonus if we survive this," Joe muttered to himself, watching the other tunnels that were supposed to remain unaffected. There was a chance that, even with the assurances of the engineers, those tunnels would directly collapse due to the adjacent tunnels falling around them, or melt down thanks to the influx of fresh lava. He held his breath as he watched; so long as they had at least five tunnels remaining, they had options.

With the ambush out of the way, and no ability to determine how many Dwarves, Elves, and humans were currently in combat, Joe shoved the Major's arm out of his way. Against her protests, the man started sprinting toward the still-sounding alarm. Knowing he was moving too slow, especially since everyone else—including a disapproving Dwarf—had already caught up to and passed him, Joe began using Omnivault as rapidly as he could without draining his mana and stamina.

Even with as nervous as he was—his budding town was at risk—he was still excited to test out his upgraded weapon, as well as the defenses that he had put into play. "I hope Herr Trigger is somewhere out there. He and I have a rubber match to settle. He's won, I've won, and now it's time for me to establish dominance."

"*Down!*" Major Cleave grabbed Joe out of the air by his ankle and slammed him to the ground. He bounced once but managed to avoid the crescent of force that had been generated by someone's sword swing a few dozen meters away. Joe managed to turn in time to see the crescent lose momentum and crash to the ground—where it impacted like a truck hitting the side of a building. A miniature volcanic eruption occurred at the point of impact, with molten rock erupting into the air and splattering across the group.

Shield damage taken: 15 Environmental.

"Celestial avocados, what level of skill with a sword do you need in order to do something like that?" Joe whispered so softly that he did not expect an answer, thanks to the din of battle.

"If it isn't a spell? Expert, at the absolute minimum." Jaxon squatted beside Joe, his ever-present smile slipping slightly. "I'm sorry to have to tell you this, but that wasn't a sword. That was a knife."

"*Jaxo~o~on!*" a man bellowed as he stepped out of the rising cloud of dust. "You ruined everything! Come here so I can kill you!"

"No, but thank you for your interest in my existence. I like life!" Jaxon called out as he stepped forward and began working through the motions that Joe recognized as the 'serious combat warmup' his friend always did before a major battle. "You know, I think there is a fundamental difference between us that sets us at odds. How about you and I start over? Hello, my name is Jaxon. I like to help people's spines stay in the position that they should be-"

"You know better than anyone that I am planning to rip your spine *out!*" The man shifted to the side, somehow breaking Joe's line of sight and vanishing in the same instant. Jaxon swept down and to the side, his hands raising with open palms and slapping away the man's wrist and elbow in a clean block.

"Backattack, you predictable brat, why you always gotta attack the back?" Jaxon taunted the man. Joe felt his jaw drop; he had never seen his friend acting this way toward any enemy before. Jaxon had always been polite and offered chiropractic services the entire time he fought, often ending combat by passing a self-made business card into his enemy's hand if they remained alive. "If this is the way it's got to be, that's just fine. Also, if you still have anyone in your guild... I'm going to charge them ten percent more than anyone else for the same care!"

Their altercation devolved into fluid motions, rapid swings, and taunting back and forth. Joe had no faith that he would be able to intervene without damaging his friend. In fact, he was almost certain that he had spied Jaxon literally wrapped around his opponent at least twice so far. If their combat had not been so brutal and bloody, especially when the T-Rex head hands popped out and sank their teeth into Backattack's shoulders, their closeness and motions would have looked intimate enough to make him blush.

"I'll take care of him; you guys get going!" Jaxon cheerfully announced as Lefty tore off a chunk of flesh and swallowed it with a happy **Nyah!**.

That left Joe, Cleave, and strangely enough, Kettlebell, to their own devices. The three of them hurried to the front lines, where a meager handful of Dwarves were fending off a much larger group of humans. Joe recognized most of the defenders, but his eyes were drawn to Bauen as a large caliber bullet slammed into his stocky arm—taking it off at the elbow in a spray of blood and gristle. Something about the injury screamed 'piercing enchantment' to Joe's magical senses, but he didn't stop to think as he vaulted forward, caught the falling arm, and reattached it to the Dwarf with a rapid Mend. "Couldn't let you stay in battle disarmed!"

"Do you have any idea how many *times* I have heard that joke over the years?" Bauen shouted back in mock anger. "Thanks for the assist, but I don't think we're going to be able to hold out."

Since he was now able to see where exactly the combat lines had been drawn, Joe rolled forward and dug his fingers into the dirt and ash. A moment later, a ten-foot-long barrier tall enough to reach Joe's chest popped into existence, giving the Dwarves a much-needed fortification. The pitiful number of remaining dwellers stacked up behind it, able to see through it from their side, whereas a bright light was blinding the people attacking their hamlet.

Bauen looked at Joe questioningly, but the human kept his eyes on the situation. "Dark Lightning Strike!"

A large group of people shuddered involuntarily as their muscles spasmed, and a half dozen bullets slammed into the barrier mere millimeters from Joe's face. He stared at the enchanted bits of metal as they attempted to drill through the protection; clearly the projectiles had been designed with breaking enchantments in mind. If his barrier *had* been an enchantment, it would have worked. Happily, the ritual barrier was slightly different. Not only would it break down in a *fraction* of the amount of time in which a proper enchanted barrier would crumble, but it was also constantly refreshing itself— similar to a computer monitor with a prodigious frame rate per second.

All together, these factors meant that the barrier was *absolutely* going to fall, but only to the unrelenting march of time. The bullets would reduce the amount of time during which the hard-light fortification would continue to exist, but it was still more than enough: they only needed it to remain in place until the enemy was defeated or fled. Joe pulled out a Ritual of Mending, which he had intended to use during an exciting outing with Havoc, and activated it as quickly as possible. A moment later, the damaged Dwarves within range started rapidly healing to full health. "Don't let any Elves near; that thing heals anyone in range."

"As if they'd be foolish enough to enter melee range." Bauen chuckled along with anyone else that heard him. Finding a moment to breathe, Joe pulled out his Aspect inscriber and rapidly drew a circle in the air.

Novice ritual circles took him anywhere from ten to twenty seconds in total to draw if he wasn't triple checking his work, which was a huge amount of time in combat. Even so, he took every single second that was necessary to form the diagram correctly. He turned his eyes to the cavern ceiling and noted that he was under the Daylight section of The Shoe, then factored that location into the fractal that he used as the focus of the circle. "They only made it twenty meters out of the entrance. That means I need to activate sections one *and* two over here…"

The first circle was completed, so Joe rapidly devoted enough mana to activate it. A moment later, three rituals activated at the same time and began sending lines of compressed, sharpened air at the attackers. He had used this method before to defend a breached gate back on Midgard to great effect, and subsequently found himself rather disappointed at their effectiveness against higher-leveled and skilled people. The blades were enough to slow their attackers down, but the humans and Elves were still able to push through while taking little to no damage.

"I suppose most people won't be taken down by Beginner-level rituals going forward; note to self has been *made*," he grumbled even as he worked with all the speed and efficiency he could muster. Even though the auto-wind-claymore ritual wasn't heavily damaging the enemy forces, it was still pushing them back through sheer force of impact. It was also kicking up huge clouds of dust and ash into the attacker's eyes, giving the defenders some much-needed relief from the hail of spells, arrows, and much more rarely: bullets that were zipping through the air.

As Bauen had pointed out, *very* few of the attackers were making the mistake of engaging the Dwarves in close combat. At this point, the only people Joe could see, who were still fighting man-to-man, were clearly exceptionally skilled with their weapons. Joe finished his second Ritual of Remote Activation, complete with the slightly altered fractal that worked almost exactly like a radio antenna would have back on Earth. As he activated this particular diagram, he felt a large sense of satisfaction.

Eight barriers popped up, slicing the combat zone into three distinct areas. Even so, Joe was studying the new additions. He was staring straight up. The attackers were forced to funnel into one of the three areas if they wanted to continue the battle, and just as they regrouped, the effects of other rituals became noticeable. The stone above the battlefield momentarily became almost liquid every five seconds, which delayed the end result of his stealthy placement. Just as the attackers were getting back into their battle rhythm, thousands of pounds of oddly-shaped rock collapsed from above and devastated their formations.

Then rose a sound that Joe had been waiting for, a demand that came just in time, as he was already out of tricks.

"Retreat!"

CHAPTER TWENTY-FOUR

The Dwarves began cheering, and Joe dropped to the ground panting as the attackers fled into the single remaining volcanic shaft that led back to Elven territory. Only moments later, dozens of tiny reputation gain notices appeared in his vision, and he allowed a slightly cocky grin to appear on his face. "Oooh, looks like they chose to try to escape down the super-deadly, over-trapped path. That was a bold move; let's see how it plays out for them."

"Joe!" Jaxon called as he ran over and swept his human friend up in a hug. "I beat Backattack! Sure, he's a shadow of his former self—apparently he's started believing all of the hype his people are putting out as propaganda—but it is still a big win for me! I was thinking we should-"

Crack.

Joe was abruptly dropped to the ground as Jaxon spun in place, blood flowing freely from his head.

Crack. Crack. Twice more, rounds impacted the man before he fell low enough to be protected by the shimmering barrier.

"*Jaxon!*" Joe cried out as he caught the man and slapped a

heal onto him. It didn't take, and Joe knew exactly what that meant.

"Ah, I missed." Herr Trigger's voice echoed out of the tunnel that Joe hadn't bothered to secure. "Still, that one has quite the bounty on his... *head. Ohh*-hoo-hoo-hoo!"

"He's laughing at his own jokes after killing my...!" Joe was seeing red, but he still set Jaxon gently on the floor before turning to the mouth of the tunnel.

He took a single step before his arm was roughly gripped by Major Cleave. "Sir, chasing after an unknown number of enemies, especially as they are taunting you directly, would be the height of foolishness."

"Major. Stand down." Joe's response was deadly calm as he turned back to face his fallen friend. He took a deep breath and began making the necessary motions, slowly, ever-so-terribly slowly finishing the somatic components of his spell by breathing out, "*Resurrection.*"

Skill increase: Resurrection (Novice VIII).

"Celestial Feces, I keep forgetting you're a *cleric* under all that mess you call a magical class." Cleave shrank backward as a portal opened above Jaxon's body, and the man stepped out a moment later. His corpse disintegrated, and he cracked his neck twice as he got used to his new body.

"Thanks for the too-late heal, Joe!" Jaxon's words popped Joe's tension like a balloon. "Hey, is that kinda what necromancers do? Just heal *really* late?"

The Ritualist shouted at the air for a moment, then started chuckling. After a quick breather, he turned to Major Cleave with a wide smile. "I order you to not follow me into that tunnel."

"Major-*General!*" Cleave bellowed in shock as Joe vaulted away from the small group, reaching the tunnel entrance only seconds later. He slapped his hand against the mouth of the passage, and moments later, a barrier covered the egress in its entirety. "*Sir!* You can't do this! You're *going to die!*"

"Most likely!" Joe grinned as a notification popped up, then turned and jauntily waved at them. "Back soon, one way or another!"

"What can you possibly hope to achieve?" Cleave shouted as she slammed her axe into the barrier. "You get back here this instant!"

"There are some rituals in here that need a *personal* touch to use properly, Cleave! Trigger will be waiting for me, and everyone else is gonna run. This is my best chance at a fair fight against the man." Joe shook off her concerns like a duck ignoring rain. "Besides... you know as well as I do that it's already started."

Cleave paused, and Joe knew that she was reading the same notification that he had received just a moment ago.

Major-General Pyrrhic's fuse has been lit! The countdown to victory or death has begun! For the next ten minutes, all allied troops in a 100-foot radius of Major-General Pyrrhic gain 100% increased damage!

"Ehh. Glad I'm testing this out without putting my own people at risk." Joe winced as he noticed bloody footprints that he could follow even if he were half blind. "Not a huge fan of losing half my people just so I can hit a little harder."

He hurried after the fleeing forces, knowing that there was only one direction they could be moving. The Reductionist contemplated his choices, grimacing as he realized that he should leave this route intact in order to make it *extra* deadly in anticipation of the next time they tried to pull something like this. He knew that there *would* be another attempt, and even with the awareness that the tunnel was trapped, more people would want to attack through an easy access point instead of opting to dig out their own entryway through a volcano. "That takes a total meltdown off the menu..."

You have gone more than 100 feet from at least half of the people that had been boosted by your title! Damage received will increase by 100%!

"Forgot about that little disaster waiting to happen." Joe grimaced as he vaulted along. It wasn't long before he found the ragtag rear scouts, a bloodied group that had clearly been left behind to 'guard'; they *definitely* hadn't been abandoned so that the others could move faster. Once again, Joe was *very* happy that he had Darkvision. He commanded his Orb to float out of his bandolier, a bloodthirsty grin on his face as he finally found the perfect opportunity to test out his newly upgraded weapon. He willed the 'Orb' to attack, narrowing his eyes in surprise when it didn't instantly fly away.

Instead, the icicle-shaped Ritual Orb spun in place for one full second like a drill bit on a power tool, then *blasted* away easily three times as fast as Joe had ever managed to make his weapons fly. It impacted his target, an archer that was staring into the pitch-black tunnel with sharp eyes. The Orb went *through* the man's chest armor, delivering the damage directly to the man's heart and effectively nailing him to the stone wall.

Critical Damage dealt: 356 Piercing Cold damage! (Base 100 + 37 physical damage, modifier + 30% critical damage increase) Damaged doubled due to Pyrrhic bonus!

The fact that the man was still alive was a testament to the massively boosted stats of anyone that had made it to this world. Before the man could do more than gasp in shock, Joe activated the final use of Cone of Cold that the weapon had charged, dealing an additional… he gasped as he looked at the damage output. "Give me the full breakdown!"

Overkill!

Critical Spell Damage dealt: 2,683 Cold damage! (Base 225 + 38 magic damage modifier, + 460% critical spell damage increase) Damaged doubled due to Pyrrhic bonus!

"Wow." Joe frowned at the frozen corpse of the man, which he knew would vanish within an hour if no one was able to revive him. "Looks like I really am a… cold-hearted killer."

"We're under attack!" someone bellowed as they felt the wash of cold air in the dark tunnel. "Someone cast some lights out there!"

Joe tried to order his Orb back to him, but it appeared to be frozen to the corpse, and he couldn't manage to get it to budge. He snarled in frustration as he pulled out another basic Orb and sent it flying at a Mage that had raised glowing hands. The weapon bounced off a gem-shaped shell of mana around the man, alerting Joe to the fact that he should have used his main weapon on this guy first.

A warrior with blood slowly streaming down his face ran at Joe, bellowing a war cry. The tunnel was fairly empty, and Joe knew that taking on a close-combat focused warrior head-to-head was asking for a rapid death. When no other options presented themselves, he panic-jumped away, flipping in midair to land against the ceiling. As his knees bent to absorb the momentum, he realized that he might have just discovered how to use one of his highest-level skills in combat.

"Dark Lightning Strike!" Joe snapped out, dropping power onto the Mage and blocking his view for a precious moment. His hands pointed down at the warrior, and he devoted mana to Acid Spray as he started to fall. Just before he reached open air, he vaulted off the ceiling and arced over the mage; trailing acid the entire way.

A thick mana bolt just *barely* missed him, impacting the wall of the tunnel and sending shards of stone pinging off his Exquisite Shell. With one of his mainstay combat spells locked in his currently unusable Ritual Orb, Joe was down to lightning, acid, or battering his opponents to death with his Orbs. As he tossed out another Dark Lightning Strike, he hissed, "I need to get more personal combat rituals up and going!"

Ultimately, he decided that the best course of action was to ignore these two and continue on the hunt for Herr Trigger. He turned and ran down the tunnel as his two shocked opponents bellowed at him to stand and fight. As Joe entered into a section of the shaft that curved, he paused and touched the wall where a pale gray light was shining through the ash that he had spread over the hidden ritual.

Activate Ritual of Proximity (Wind Blades)? Yes / No.

"Yes."

Defensive charges used: 0/500.

"That should hold those two in here until I can come back and clean them up." Joe wanted to let out an evil laugh, but he also didn't want to warn his opponents about the trap. Instead, he simply ran down the tunnel as fast as he could, only letting out a *tiny* chuckle when he heard a scream of wind followed by a bellow of rage echoing along after him.

"Now all I need to do is follow the smell of gunpowder, but I'm not willing to drop my Neutrality Aura to make that happen… I hope they haven't made it out yet." Joe mentally traced the tunnel which he had left open when he'd set the earthquakes up. This one *should* be an *unholy* long tunnel with a ton of switchbacks seeded with countless traps, but there was always the possibility that the earlier collapse had impacted this tunnel more than planned, either by opening a new escape, closing this one off entirely, or simply rendering his rituals useless by dropping too much rubble in the way if the tunnels only *partially* collapsed.

"Next time, *all* of these get set with a remote activation tied to them." He grumbled as he found himself needing to gasp for air. Even with all his boosted stats, running was still often a mental game, and pushing through that mental blockage was imperative if he wanted to force his body to keep moving. "Mind over matter was right, I guess."

As Joe vaulted around the next corner like a rubber cannonball bouncing through the enclosed space, he learned where the attackers had retreated. They were *all* waiting for him.

"He actually did it! He came by himself! *Trigger warning*, Joe." Still in midair, Joe's eyes flicked over to Herr Trigger, who was dropping his left hand in a harsh chopping motion as he shouted an order. "All troops… *fire!*"

CHAPTER TWENTY-FIVE

Curling into a ball in a vain attempt to impact his attacker's aim, Joe slammed into the wall and fell to the ground as a dizzying array of projectiles were launched at him.

Fire, ice, pressurized air, arrows, bolts, bullets, throwing knives... whatever someone had, they used it against him. If Joe were a fan of psychology, he would have cursed them all with the knowledge that they were taking out their inadequacies and failure on him in various fits of rage. Yet, he couldn't find it in himself to speak as his defenses were blown away and the terrain around him was turned into a cratered mess.

"You think we *didn't* know that you were arrogant?" Herr Trigger bellowed over the howling of dozens of spells being discharged. "That you would come after me to prove your superiority in the little game that you play in your mind? This is *our* tunnel now! With you out of the way, we will use this as a staging ground to turn your little town into-"

A klaxon call answered him, an alarm in such close proximity that at least a half dozen spells were interrupted and backfired as people slapped their hands over their ears. Herr Trigger bellowed over the outpouring of noise and friendly fire as he tried to push through the crowd toward Joe. "What did you *do?* Another of your little barriers and alarms?"

Joe had been pinned to the wall by an oversized bolt through his gut, and blood poured from his mouth as he chuckled at the assassin. "You... *ptooey*... you're right. I thought I'd only find you. You got me. But if I'm going down... *hack*... I'm taking *all* of you with me."

His hand dropped down from the wall, trailing a smear of blood pointing to a glowing ritual diagram. The alarm was emanating from the sketch, blaring so loudly that it was vibrating the air. One of Joe's attackers had a realization and turned to run, screeching, "That's the same alarm that went off just before those tunnels were flooded with lava and collapsed! He's trying to kill us all!"

"Run for it!"

The second person to move started a panic by shoving an archer into the wall as he barreled past. "Get out of my way! I *just* hit level twenty-three! I'm not going to lose two levels over this!"

That was all it took to create a full-blown evacuation attempt. Herr Trigger, caught in the middle of the churning mass, was being swept away in the tide. "No! *No!* Someone at least finish him off! Do you have *any* idea how long it takes me to enchant each individual bullet? I've spent days on the ammo you just wasted! Make it worth it! Kill him! *Kill-!*"

Any further command was lost as the packed tunnel was vacated, the howling assassin desperately trying to push against the much stronger warriors that were shoving him along in their escape attempt. As the last of them vanished in their mad scramble, Joe managed to fight through the weakness that his massive blood loss had induced, calling up his mana and sending Lay on Hands into his thoracic cavity directly to restore three hundred and seventy-eight health: a mere drop in the bucket.

Exquisite Shell: 0/9,299
Health: 599/1,864. Organs pierced! -23 health per second.

"Eleven thousand damage in two seconds... and most of them *missed*." Joe coughed up and spat out a thick wad of phlegm and blood. "Ugh... a stiff breeze would have killed me. Thank the celestials that people wanted to survive more than they wanted to take me down."

He looked over at the Novice Ritual of Alarm that had required his manual activation. The alarm that somehow no one had gotten close enough to set off, and wasn't connected to anything whatsoever. It was just noise. "I need to get the abyss out of here."

Luck +2! Great bluffs can lead to huge paydays!

Joe frowned down at the bolt that was still holding him in place, trying to figure out the best way to remove it from himself. "I really need to start carrying around a knife of some kind so I can cut my way out of situations like this."

He swept his awareness over his weapons, pleased to discover that his icicle Ritual Orb had appeared in his weapon bandolier at some point without him noticing. Even so, he was going to need to do things the hard way. He gripped the bolt and tried to break it off, only to find that the entire shaft was some kind of metal. "Well... that just makes too much sense for this world."

A check of the fletching convinced him that this was going to hurt. He couldn't get the bolt itself out of the wall, which meant he had no choice but to pass over the solid metal fletching and tear his way out.

Damage taken: 68 secondary!

Joe groaned and poked his organs back into place as best he could, then started alternating casts of Mend and Lay on Hands. As his health approached maximum, he prepared to replace his Exquisite Shell... but a strange sound reached his ears even through the klaxon call of his ritual that was blasting out his senses. "That means it's not my standard senses? Something... *magical!*"

He vaulted forward in a roll, a huge—clearly enchanted— sword slamming into the ground where he had stood a mere moment ago. The massive blade cut clean through his right leg, taking his foot off just above the ankle. Joe's scream couldn't be heard over the siren, but he made a valiant attempt. As he landed, he looked back and found a huge warrior staring at him with bloodshot eyes. "Fecal matter; they must have got through the barrier. This is why you *never* leave enemies behind you, Joe!"

Damage taken: 100 slashing. Right leg crippled! Fully heal or reattach limb to regain use of [Right foot].

The warrior's mouth was moving, and he clearly expected that Joe was able to hear him. He had launched into a grand, impressive monologue; but all it did was give the Reductionist enough time to tie off his open wound, stop the bleeding, and respond with a Dark Lightning Strike. The man lazily swept his sword up and *through* the spell, the weapon flashing brightly as the strike was dispersed. Then the man rocketed toward Joe, moving so quickly that he left an afterimage; a subtle reminder to Joe that he needed to increase his perception.

Joe vaulted straight up, his form wobbly as he was only able to put weight on one leg. As the ceiling neared, the blade sliced into his stump, taking another few inches of that leg. Even though the pain made him want to scream, the sound that came out was mostly fury.

He had lost the use of his limbs before. It had changed how he experienced life in so many ways, and had driven him to do objectively terrible things—like leaving his body behind for another chance. It hadn't occurred to him how deeply that decision had impacted the things he did even now, how it would make him react in situations like this where someone was actively taking cross-sectioned circle steaks off of him.

Joe's icicle Ritual Orb left his belt and pointed down at the man below, starting to spin in place as the Reductionist pushed off the stone ceiling and started falling at an angle. He specifically *hadn't* jumped—and the warrior was waiting for him, pulling his sword to the side like he was about to hit a home run and Joe was the slow-moving baseball.

Since his eyes were on Joe, the man's throat was exposed. Just before the Reductionist fell into perfect range, his Ritual Orb raced past him and *blended* into the unarmored space just below his assailant's Adam's Apple. The piercing weapon kept traveling until it hit armor that it couldn't bore through. The fighter dropped to the ground and grasped at his neck, panicking upon feeling his lungs rapidly filling with blood.

Damage dealt: 178 piercing cold. Critical! Massive internal bleeding damage. -89 health per second.

Joe grabbed his fallen foot, taking a moment in an attempt to put it in the right spot. His healing didn't work, and he realized there was another fleshy frisbee lying off to the side. Holding both of those in place, Lay on Hands managed to bring him back to pristine condition. Standing and savoring the feel of both functional legs, he looked at the warrior, a man that clearly had no way to heal the huge hole that had literally been drilled through his neck. The guy also had so much health that he likely would be suffering for a long time before going down.

That wasn't okay with Joe. Not even slightly.

Even so, he took the necessary time to get Exquisite Shell back in place before approaching the man. Joe moved with slow motions so that the warrior didn't lash out, then, with a single sharp order, pulled his Ritual Orb out of the man via his willpower. A flash of blood leapt in the air, and Joe grabbed the man's neck with both hands, pumping him full of healing water using Lay on Hands.

At that moment, the klaxon ended, even though it almost seemed to continue ringing in their ears. A new voice arose at that moment, and Joe's head whipped to the side. "What in the blazes did you *do* to him? You don't have that kind of grip strength; how are you choking him so hard that the skin bursts?"

Joe looked over his shoulder to see Havoc carrying a slumped mage, then back down at his own situation. His pure white Silkpants Mage's set was soaked in blood, and he was clutching a barely-breathing warrior's neck as if he were trying to knock him out. As the Reductionist let go and stepped back, the warrior crashed to the ground and gasped for air, shuddering in horror and coughing out wave after wave of blood. Knowing this wasn't the right time for it, Joe still went with a joke. "What can I say? He talked too much."

"In that case, remind me to keep quiet around you when you're in a mood," Havoc muttered as he tossed the mage down next to the warrior. "Whaddaya want to do with them, then?"

"There's no point in killing or keeping them. They might be worth some reputation, but why?" All Joe could do was shrug, then lean down to talk to the warrior. "Hey. Listen. There are better things to do. Better ways to spend your time. Just leave us alone, man."

"I will *never* come back here," the warrior rasped at him with terror in his eyes as he nodded and pawed at his unmarked throat. "I owe you one."

Joe shrugged noncommittally, healed the mage just to make sure he would wake up after whatever Havoc had likely done to him, then turned to the Dwarf. "Are you late, or right on time?"

"Quiet down and give me the cores you owe me," Havoc snorted in reply as they turned and walked back toward their settlement. "Also, I found that atrocity you've been performing terrible deeds on. The… I'll generously call it a 'table'? After seeing that, I realized that it's likely past time that the two of us did some hands-on training together."

CHAPTER TWENTY-SIX

Even though Havoc protested, the first thing Joe did when they got back to the settlement was take a nap. Something about combat—perhaps getting his foot chopped off—had really put him in a bad place mentally, and he needed to sleep it off. "I shouldn't have gone after Trigger… why did I ever think that was a good idea?"

When he woke up, he felt wildly refreshed and ready to take on the entire Elven Theocracy. Before he could head off, he had *dozens* of notifications to go over. He collapsed them so that he could choose to read them based on their categories. After that, he had only three broad choices: reputation changes, quest updates, and skill increases.

Reputation gained: 8,000 Legion, 2,000 Dwarven Oligarchy.

Quest updated: Ranker II Peerage. Major Elven incursions fended off: 1/5.

Skill increases:

- *Acid spray (Apprentice V -> Apprentice VI).*
- *Dark Lightning Strike has reached (Student 0)! This spell can*

now be recast a second time in the cooldown period for an additional 10% mana cost. This will not impact cooldown time.

- *Exquisite Shell (Student V -> Student VI).*
- *Lay on Hands (Student IV -> Student V).*
- *Neutrality Aura has reached (Journeyman 0)! Congratulations! You really made this poor skill do some* **work** *with all that blood! Journeyman bonus: The range of this aura has doubled, but the extended range is only half as effective as the main area of effect.*
- *Retaliation of Shadows (Journeyman IV -> Journeyman VI). I hope you enjoyed the slap-show!*
- *Ritual Magic (Expert IV -> Expert V).*
- *Somatic Ritual Casting (Beginner V -> Beginner IX).*

"Ugh… all this shows me is that I need to go out and participate in heavy fights more often." Joe chuckled at that thought as he settled on his plan of staying inside and crafting for the foreseeable future. "Let's add the last chunk… Knowledge, Architectural Lore."

Architectural Lore (Apprentice VII -> VIII).

Knowledge (Apprentice 0 -> I).

With all his goals met, Joe heaved a sigh of relief. Now he could get back to completing his class quests and maximizing the bonuses that they gave him. He rose to his feet and crossed the room to the door, throwing it open and gasping in shock at what waited on the other side. "What the abyss…?"

"Well, good morning, sleeping whatever!" Havoc called from his position around the table which he was sitting at. Joe eased out of the doorway and gaped at his room, which for whatever reason now opened to an outdoor meeting area. A moment later, the 'room' began to shift, collapsing into a flat cube that picked itself up and walked away. "Havoc… did you turn my apartment into a golem?"

"No, that would be ridiculous," Havoc 'reassured' him with a casual wave at a chair, "Sit down. If you must know, I had that golem *mimic* your room so that you would be here as soon as you were up and at 'em. Now we can get started right away."

"How big can you make… no, why would you waste…" Joe gave up on trying to suss out the intentions of the mad Dwarf and simply drew near to inspect the table he had been working on for the last few days.

"To answer your question, I can make my golems as large as I need to make them." Havoc grinned around his cigar, tracing some of the lines Joe had lightly drawn on the tabletop. "I just need a good enough reason to justify the expenditure. Now, I see that you're planning on enchanting this… rock. I'd call it a table, but that would be like calling a landslide 'landscaping'. Disasters don't get pretty names."

What followed was a mix of Joe showing Havoc his plans for the table and enchantment, back-and-forth bellowing on turning the town into a *guild* town, as well as a discussion on the basics of sculpting, followed by debating the finer points of what Joe was trying to accomplish with the inscribed enchantment.

Due to having no desire to spend too much time making a table when there were so many other things to do, Havoc eventually handed Joe a cube that reminded him of the training device he had given up in order to achieve his Reductionist class, though this one was a much larger, thirty-six-sided version where each face was a hexagon.

"This is a training tool that works well for enchanters," the Dwarf explained as Joe fiddled with the device. "It'll *slowly* boost your intelligence, but its main purpose is training Mana Manipulation. That's the most difficult part of most high-level enchantments: getting your mana to go where you need it to go."

"How does it do—*bleahgh*." Joe managed to activate the cube, and it drained his mana to nothing in an instant. He sagged and almost fainted from the intense headache it imparted but managed to hang on through the shock.

"Aww. Most people pass out the first time they use one of

these." Havoc actually seemed upset that Joe was still upright as he tossed a coin to a Dwarf that 'just happened' to be passing by. "You need to stop costing me money."

"How about you just stop betting against me?" Joe growled around the mana deprivation headache. "Why isn't my mana regenerating?"

"Oh, it is." The Dwarf pointed at the device, where one of the hexagonal faces had lit up. "But you only get one point of mana to work with at a time on the first face. There are internal pathways that you need to *massage* your mana through, and the most difficult part for *you* is always going to be manipulation. You have so much mana that you can just flood any magical device until it's so saturated that it activates. That ability makes an enchantment... how to put it... higher level enchantments almost always correlate directly to your ability to manipulate your mana. Too much in the wrong pattern, *boom*. Too little mana, and the extremely expensive matrix fails and nothing happens other than losing those resources."

"How do I do this, then?" Joe set the device on the table, instantly feeling his mana begin to regenerate at the normal rate.

"Mana speed, flow, convergence, divergence, input, and finally *output* are the six variables that make up enchanting, and therefore Mana Manipulation," Havoc informed him succinctly, his eyes twinkling as Joe put his hands back on the device and went green as he had his mana drained away again. "Each face has different requirements for the six variables. Some of those sound similar to each other, but they aren't. They're paired opposites. Mana speed is how fast a unit of mana moves when you control it, but *flow* is how ambient mana moves and finds the pathways you made to keep the enchantment alive near-permanently. The next two are easy, so explain them to me."

Joe thought for only a moment, since Havoc started twitching almost as soon as he ordered an answer. "Convergence... that would be how the mana moves through the model at various angles, eventually coming together."

"Coming together *without*…?" Havoc puffed on his cigar and motioned leadingly.

"Blowing it up?" Joe guessed, getting a nod of affirmation for his trouble. "Or without colliding the mana and making it spill from the model, I'm guessing. That would mean divergence is taking it from a single flow and splitting it off to fill other areas? Also without causing a catastrophic failure."

He added the last part because Havoc had started glowering at him, but the Dwarf nodded when he finished. "Good enough for where you're at, Apprentice. Input and output, now. These are special cases. One you are testing; one you are *guessing*."

Joe didn't interrupt, knowing Havoc was baiting him. The Dwarf paused, then continued with a dissatisfied grunt. "When you activate an enchantment, you add a lump sum of mana, then send it along the pathways you've carved. If you haven't poured in enough, it fades away and you can start again. That's input. Even the same enchantment, made by the same person, has tiny variations that need to be accounted for when they are being activated. You need to learn a new pattern every single time, meaning input is gonna be *hard* for you, Mr. Mana *Ocean* instead of mana *pool*."

Deciding not to mention the perfectly cloned enchantments that his rituals could make and activate without his Mana Manipulation factoring in, the Reductionist simply nodded and continued to listen. "Output is the final effect of the enchantment, as well as how long it will last. It *could* be permanent. Every enchantment *could* be. That would be a problem; tell me how."

"Because…" Joe thought back to the first time he had ever needed to get his enchanted gear fixed up. "Enchantments are at least a little bit alive, and slowly gain a mind of their own?"

"Yup." Havoc didn't take his eyes off of Joe's. "That means that each and every mistake you make will cause that enchantment to lose its mind just that much sooner. Until you are a Master enchanter, you won't be able to take out the built-in self-destruct sequence that every low-level enchantment comes with.

Otherwise, you'd be making cursed enchantments that will one day destroy themselves and everyone that interacts with them."

With that happy thought, and Havoc insisting that Joe needed to be at least a Journeyman Mana Manipulator to complete the enchantment he was working on, the Dwarf pulled them away from the table and started walking. Joe looked into the distance, seeing nothing but flat stone. "Where are we going?"

"You have at most an hour until the settlement finishes upgrading," Havoc told him with a hearty slap to the shoulder that sent him tumbling through the ash. "Whoops. Moving on. It's important for you to maximize your efficiency, and that means getting the next buildings up as soon as possible. We're going to the spot where you're going to build your town hall-"

"I can't." Joe hopped to his feet as Neutrality Aura cleaned the last of the ash from his clothes. He could see the question in Havoc's eyes, so he hurried to explain properly. "I can't afford it. I'm too low on aspects."

"What in the bloody abyss have you been *doing* this last week?" Havoc rumbled in a low, threatening tone. "No additional buildings, the cheapest rituals I've ever seen you produce, barely holding together a defense even after you managed to wipe out nearly the entire attacking force?"

"I was holding out for a quest reward." Joe winced as Havoc's cigar went from barely lit to a stick of charcoal as he heaved in a huge lungful of air.

The only fragments Joe could remember about the resulting dressing-down were that he probably shouldn't ever let himself get so low on resources in the future, and there were going to be some changes regarding how and *who* managed his time. There was also a short—but vehement—recommendation that Joe should never reproduce. At some point, the Dwarf tossed 'compliance powder' in his face and reached for his neck.

Joe came back to consciousness a short while later, only to find that Havoc was stuffing him sideways into a garbage chute in the capital city. The Dwarf bellowed in his face, "Don't come back 'til you're ready to be worked to the edge of death at least three times!"

As Joe slipped down the slimy tube, he could only mumble, "My ears *really* hurt."

CHAPTER TWENTY-SEVEN

"Wait, this shouldn't be happening…?" Coming fully to his senses, Joe managed to flip around in midair as he shook off the final lingering effects of whatever it was that Havoc had dosed him with. "I don't even have *defensive* rituals ready! Havoc, you son of a-!"

Then he landed in the middle of a house-sized pile of rotten vegetables and slammed his mouth closed just to ensure that none of it slipped in. His initial reaction, destroying everything around him with acid, was only curbed by the idea that he may melt something of actual value that was in the mess. 'Swimming' out of the partially liquefied plant matter, he once more thanked his lucky stars that he had Exquisite Shell and Neutrality Aura keeping him clean as well as parasite-free in this goo.

After breaking through the surface and screaming like an alien tearing its way out of a human chest, Joe tried to tamp down his rage and take stock of the situation, preparing himself as well as possible. He had a few major concerns. Firstly, he had no edible food prepared, although hydration would not be an issue, thanks to his aura. Second, he had only his spells as offensive and defensive measures, and had hardly anything usable to his name beyond them. He was almost certain that Havoc knew this would be an issue, as the Dwarf had been keeping tabs on him.

Speaking of people keeping tabs on him, he looked around carefully but was unable to find Major Cleave.

"Not only am I low on attack and defense power, but I don't even have an escort who can help that situation even slightly." The Reductionist rubbed his bald head in consternation, unknowingly leaving a trail of moldy beet juice across his skull before it was whisked away by his aura. A quick peek into his storage devices confirmed that he didn't even have nice, clean tiles available to build out his rituals on. "So, my mentor must want me to be forced to be as efficient as possible? Or maybe he just wants me somewhere that I can train without blowing up things that actually matter…"

Joe ignored the fact that the *most* likely reason Havoc had sent him down here was simply as petty revenge for delaying the plans he had set up in his head—plans he had failed to share with his Apprentice. "Guess all I can do is hope that everyone is going to be okay out there."

The Shoe (Unnamed campground) has officially been upgraded from a Hidden Camp (Tier 0) to a Hidden Hamlet (Tier 1)!

A Hamlet is allowed to have up to:

1 Town Hall or Guildhall (not filled)

1 Unique or higher rarity building (filled)

2 Rare or 1 higher rarity building (not filled)

10 Uncommon buildings (filled)

20 Common buildings (not filled)

5 monuments (not filled)

To improve from a Hamlet (Tier 1) to a Village (Tier 2), the following conditions must be met:

All building slots filled.

Residents: Minimum 50

- *Current: 17*

Morale: Minimum 1,000 (Satisfied)

- *Current total: 127 (Neutral) (375 positive morale x 17/50 residents)*

Resources: 1 major export/trade good

- *Current: none (-100 morale)*

Living areas: Space for 100 permanent residents of at least Common quality

- *Current: Space for 110 civilians + 660 troops = 770 (Excess! +200 morale)*

Air Quality: Decent

- *Current: Barely Decent (+-0 morale)*

Heat: Uncomfortable

- *Current: Comfortable (+200 morale)*

Water Sources: 2 potable water sources

- *Current: 1 Mineral Water, tainted (-25 morale)*

Light: 60 lumens at least 8 hours per day

- *Current: Constant (+100 morale)*

Looking over the requirements, Joe could only be glad that he had set someone else in charge of starting to make things happen. Otherwise, he would be very concerned that by the time he got back, people would be calling for a change in leadership. Almost everything made sense on the list, except for the fact that having constant light only gave half the bonus that the other living conditions did when being provided in excess.

"Maybe I need to work out a day and night schedule? Also, only seventeen residents? I distinctly remember having at least thirty-eight," Joe muttered aloud, then shook his head and reminded himself that he was in a potentially deadly, but undoubtedly dangerous, situation. "The first thing I need to do is set up a protected area; Predator's Territory should work perfectly for this."

Knowing that it was only a Beginner-rank ritual, he pulled out two inscribers and began working on the circles. He used his left hand for the less-intense Novice interior circle, and his more dexterous right hand for the second circle. Using Somatic Ritual Casting, he drew the ritual diagram out in the air. Using both hands increased the time of each circle by a quarter, but reduced the overall work time by more than half; a joyful smile came to his face, as per usual when a nifty magical shortcut opened up to him.

With a flex of his will, the double circle turned horizontal and dropped beneath him. Joe stepped on the activation portion and channeled the required mana through his foot, activating the ritual with ease. A feeling of intense bloodlust abruptly rippled through the area, centered on the ritual. Joe got chills for a moment, both from the feeling, as well as from being impressed with just how much more potent the ritual was even without going out of his way to improve it.

He was ever so slowly closing in on the Master ranks with Ritual Magic, and it was to be expected that an Expert's ritual just had more *oomph* than one a Novice could manage—and that had been his skill rank when he had made this particular diagram for the first time. "The perimeter is now set; let's get some defenses in place, then set to reducing everything to useful components again."

As Joe slowly set up rituals that would attack, barriers that would block, and a few last resort diagrams to flood the area with acid, he realized that he had never put significant effort into considering the results of what each rank of ritual could accomplish. The Reductionist had been correct in his thinking, and he needed to follow that line of thought: he was going to be a *Master* of this discipline soon… and he currently couldn't even clearly differentiate the ranks. For such low-level rituals, he didn't need to invest all of his attention. "Let me think. What exactly can Novice-rank rituals accomplish?"

The short answer that his brain teased him with was 'nearly anything', but that wasn't quite accurate. Thinking over all of the times that he had created one of the single-circle rituals, a pattern slowly started to form in his mind. "Little Sister's Cleaning Service moves things around and organizes them. What *can't* it do? It can lift them, move them, put them in alphabetical order, or organize them in any fashion I tell it to arrange them… can it sort by rarity? How much weight can it lift when it comes to an individual object?"

He paused his hypothetical thinking as he finished working on the Ritual of Acid. Messing up on this one would cause a backlash that he did *not* want to deal with, so he gave his full attention to the project. When that one was finally complete, he sat down in the muck and looked around. An oversized double circle rested on the ground, generating a barrier at each of the primary compass positions, followed by four wind blade Rituals of Proximity at equidistant intervals between the barriers, and a Student-ranked Ritual of Acid hanging in the air above him.

"I remember, once upon a time, walking into a house in the grassland where giant bugs were flying around," Joe softly reminisced as the multi-hued rituals slowly spun around him. "There were so many connected rituals, floating in the air just like this, and I had no idea how it had been possible for them to be created like that. Now that I can do it, maybe not easily or at that skill level, but still…"

The Reductionist shook off the odd feeling, letting a faint grin flash across his face. "That just means that there's still plenty for me to learn! Now it's time to go for a swim."

As he shimmied deeper and deeper into the garbage, he

continued his line of thinking on rituals as a whole. Making sure not to open his mouth too widely, he muttered softly to himself as he descended, "What can other Novice versions do? Emit a simple light, activate a different ritual, or project my voice to another ritual that is set up to receive it. The only thing these all have in common? They have one specific effect on the world around them."

You have begun delving into the mysteries of your class in a serious and thoughtful way, answering a question you've had deep within but have been unable to articulate, until now. Intelligence +5! Wisdom and Charisma +3! There will be no more bonuses from this sort of introspection, but you're on the right path toward achieving Mastery!

Pausing in his shimmying, Joe stared at the notification in wonder. Only after he had read over it three or four times did he manage to keep moving. "Celestial feces… when was the last time I gained such a large number of stat points in one go? I knew that it was important to focus on your own class, but I thought that meant doing class-related things. Having to get all philosophical? That's ridiculous."

His original plan had been to sink all the way to the bottom of the garbage piles, but only a short distance in, after maybe twenty minutes, he found that he was suddenly standing knee deep in liquid. "Ugh, that is *disgusting*. Oh no. Don't tell me... the city uses this as their *sewer* as well, don't they? *No~o!*"

The Reductionist screamed and rapidly climbed a few feet higher, shudderingly deciding that he had delved deep enough for one day. Then he paused as a realization struck him: he was mere feet above an unclaimed… not *exactly* a lake, but there was certainly at least a lake's worth of water below. As he reached into his storage ring and pulled out the inactive Ritual of the Ghostly Army, he swore to himself that he would never tell the people of his town where their new water source had come from.

Joe activated the ritual, targeting the fluid that lay directly below him for absorption. The glorious thing about having a ritual that was already complete, charged, and ready to use: he could ignore it while he did other things.

Taking a deep breath of aura-sterilized air, he began pushing mana out of his hands and formed the largest Field Array he could generate, managing to keep the array stable at eleven meters, a full meter further than he had ever been capable of before.

Skill increase: Mana Manipulation (Student V -> Student VI).

"That settles that; the size of the Field Array is almost *certainly* directly related to my Mana Manipulation skill." Joe dismissed the message and got to work. A quick check confirmed that there was nothing better than Common-ranked garbage in the area of reduction, so he didn't bother setting up his Aspect Jars. Feeding mana into the array, the garbage began dissolving into energy and collecting directly into his Codpiece of holding.

Joe thought about the blueprint that he had in his ring, hoping that he would be able to create the filter house and a permanent array in the near future. Then he made himself a promise. "I am only staying here until I get this building up and running… or until I have enough resources that Havoc won't chuck me right back in here."

CHAPTER TWENTY-EIGHT

The fortunate thing about having an excess of mana—or perhaps an unfortunate side effect, depending on how Joe thought of it—was that he could continuously work for extreme lengths of time when he was providing a simple trickle of mana such as converting garbage to aspects. With his bonuses, everything under Common aspects took only a single point of mana per second to convert. Frankly, he didn't even notice the mana loss unless the items being reduced touched on the Uncommon ranks at twenty-two mana per second.

Even so, it took time to convert all of the garbage as it shifted and swirled down into his Field Array. "I am fairly certain that I'm starting to learn all the rules here. Novice rituals have a single effect that they can create and output into the world. It is almost always a single, *physical* effect."

Joe looked up, even though all he could see was slowly slumping rotten things trying to plop onto his face. He knew that Predator's Territory was up there, a two-circle ritual at the Beginner rank. "The next tier up has an effect on the world, though it can have additional functions that are *not* physical in effect. This ritual gives off an... emotion? Is that the best way to describe that feeling of bloodlust?"

After thinking it over, he slowly shook his head. "No, evoking an emotion would make it mental manipulation of some kind, and that's just too powerful. What else could I use to compare the differences between a Beginner and a Novice? My... attack and defense rituals that I had to make for class quests? Yes. Leave off proximity, as that is an add-on, and you have a ritual that can select a target and then create a physical effect or an illusion of an effect."

Ritual Lore (Apprentice II -> Apprentice III).

"Got it in one, then. Thanks for the confirmation, system." Joe set that as a mental note to physically write down when he got out, as he would eventually need to teach these principles to someone. "Uncommon. That's where things turn... murky. Planar Shift uses an Uncommon ritual as a focus, but I don't know enough about summoning to make a good comparison. I know I've made a few of these, and the easy answer would be that it can target a person, create an illusory or physical effect, as well as a third thing. What the third thing is... that's the real question."

Leaning back into the heap of filth, Joe let all of his weight settle in and continued pouring mana out of himself thoughtlessly. "Or... am I looking at this incorrectly? It isn't about the rarity; it's about the circles themselves? First circle allows the effect to manifest in the world, while the second circle takes that effect and enhances it with the ability to target things more directly or at a larger distance? Then how would that third circle... oh! It allows for the caster to target something other than a living being directly, or it makes the ritual powerful enough to get past whatever initial defenses?"

He remembered fighting a Smith in the cursed instant dungeon on Midgard, specifically using a Ritual of Poisoned Vitality to target the powerful boss monster. That ritual had both created a physical effect, sinking the Smith, as well as a secondary effect that went after the creature's stamina. "Now is that target penetration, or is it the ability to impact non-physical things, concepts, or stats?"

At that moment, light filtered through and landed on Joe's face. He blinked in surprise and squinted up, spotting his rituals hanging in the air far above. "Hmm. Maybe I should have chosen an area closer to the center of this place? Going by all the rotting fruit and vegetables when I landed, Havoc probably stuffed me in at the outskirts. Nowhere near shops or crafters that would have been dropping high-aspect-value items."

Shadows flickered above him, and Joe flinched as he saw *something* get smacked from the air by a whistling wind blade. "What in the...?"

Moments later, the form—moving at a speed which a bullet train would feel intimidated by—tried attacking again, this time managing to avoid the wind blade and setting off the proximity barrier. For just a moment, Joe saw a Dwarven body highlighted against the electric blue of the barrier, until another wind blade scraped it off and sent it tumbling away. "Yup, *that's* a high-level zombie. Time for me to go."

After collecting the now-water-laden Ritual of the Ghostly Army, but before he made his escape, Joe had a sudden bright idea. He took a minute and created an alarm ritual that was keyed to his Orb's activation ritual, then left it in place and let his Field Array fade away. As stealthily as possible, he crawled up the steep, slippery slope he had created by draining all the garbage.

Nearing the top, he froze in abject terror as the zombie impacted and sank into the filth not even five feet away from him. Joe held perfectly still, not looking at it directly as it moaned and got to its feet, leaping at the rituals above once more and somehow punching its way *through* the first barrier.

The shield flickered, just long enough for the zombie to get inside. Then the failsafe went off. The barriers all activated, and the entirety of the Ritual of Acid released its contents at once. The barriers made a seamless sphere around the zombie as the space filled entirely with acid in an instant, making it appear as though the undead Dwarf were trapped in a fishbowl. The creature struggled mightily, but without proper leverage or the force from jumping, it was only able to make the barriers flicker and release some acid to splash with a *hiss* in the area below.

Joe never once stopped moving away. He remembered *vividly* what had happened the last time he had met a high-level zombie in here, and how rapidly it had taken down his protections. Then it had called for all its friends, and he had needed to skedaddle at high speed just to survive.

"I'm only here until I have what I need. That means not letting the zombies know I'm around, if possible, and setting up a fort that could keep them out... or... making them ignore it!" Joe's eyes brightened, and he breathily whispered, "That could work."

You have slain a Dwarven Zombie (Level 28). +700 experience. Drowning in acid? Nice. Classic. Resource-intensive, but what do you care?

"No idea why a zombie that level could come after the ritual I had there. That is... oh no. I guess it would make sense that they're immune to fear." Joe growled at the thought. That was yet another ritual he couldn't use down here now, and his list of options was growing thin. "I'm not saying I'm upset that I don't have access to the magic that Elves do, but it would be *nice*."

His trek across the miles-wide landfill was too eventful for him, and by the time he had put down the eighth two-headed rabid raccoon, tenth low-level zombie, and third swarm of rats, he was ready to start hunkering down again. Luckily, on his third hour of hiking, his Exquisite Shell informed him that it had failed. Joe hadn't needed the notice, as he could clearly see the blood dripping from around the shining nail that he had stepped on.

The one that was sticking out the top of his foot.

He managed to restrict his screaming to only internal just long enough to turn, toss his Ritual Orb into the air, and activate the alarm that he had set up in his first location. The klaxon call was intense, even from this distance—likely a mile away—and loud enough to cover his shriek of agony as he yanked the two inches of metal out. He inspected it with a glare as he healed his punctured flesh.

Radiant nail (Rare). Building material for energy-attuned projects. This nail is designed to move through potent materials with ease. Caution: sharp.

"Yeah, no joke," Joe growled at the 'helpful' message. "I'm gonna *enjoy* reducing this thing."

Now that he was looking for them, Joe could clearly see various broken tools and material that had been tossed down here by accident or to hide their existence. "Here's as good of a place as any, then. Not too close to that damaged city defender, not too far from the good stuff."

Once again, it was time to put his protections in place. But this time, he knew better than to put out anything that would act as a beacon for creatures, even when it was *supposed* to drive them off. He started with his barriers, breathing a sigh of relief as he finished fully encircling the area that he wanted to work in. He knew that wouldn't keep anything truly powerful out, but it gave him the security that he needed to activate the next layers. The next set of rituals was once again barriers, but this time, Joe adjusted the design slightly.

"If I can make it so that one side is blindingly bright but doesn't impact the other side, it stands to reason that I can make them so dark that it looks like nothing is here… right?" It took some tinkering with the design, but Joe was able to learn for certain that no, it was not possible. "Can't make it put out a lack of light, got it. What if I set light as another thing to absorb as an 'attack'? Eh, I don't know how to do that. Make it reflective? Bounce the light back? That shouldn't make it too expensive to maintain."

He went with that, managing to create a tiny version on his third try. He expanded it out and soon was able to make a second ring of protections. From the outside, since the light was already dim, walking toward his setup looked just like another large pile of trash on the ground. He had angled the rituals slightly so that they wouldn't show a reflection of whatever might approach, instead showing the ground right under them.

With that done, and feeling far better about his safety, Joe pulled out his Aspect Jars, set up a Field Array, and started to 'dig'. "Can't shimmy down through this… I just know I'd get a nail stuck somewhere unpleasant."

CHAPTER TWENTY-NINE

Joe let his head fall back, spotting his barrier rituals glowing far above him. He had only burrowed down about fifty feet this time, not wanting to destabilize his work above, nor get too far away from the scant protections that he had put in place.

Once he was able to get his new building up, a lot of this would be automated, and he was so very *much* looking forward to that. However, even though his building was going to be a glorified open-top dumpster, the blueprints labeled it as a Unique structure. A large portion of the resources would be allocated in order for the 'building' to maintain a permanent array, but the other reason it required such a substantial amount was that it was built like a bank vault.

Joe had requested very specific dimensions for the building, with extra attention paid to the walls. The finished structure would have a large opening up top, but once he was done with his work, nothing living or undead should be able to enter the building through that aperture without extreme effort. Each wall was extremely durable, and they joined to form a perfectly symmetrical nonagon. With this design, even if it sank to the bottom of the dump, it should be able to withstand any damage, work in any position, and ignore high pressure.

All he needed to do was gather the materials and put in the work, and then he might never have to do something like this again. Joe was unequivocally *over* being thrown into the dump, or coming down here on purpose just to search for the materials that he needed. "Oh, I could have just bought what I needed? That would have been so nice and easy, wouldn't it, Havoc? *What's* that? You got upset that I didn't have enough materials on hand to build a whole city in one go and threw me in here after knocking me out? How *strange!*"

Grumbling aside, he *was* pleased to finally have the requisite time to start generating aspects regularly and consistently. It was also very satisfying to watch the numbers tick upward over time.

Class quest complete: Beginner Rituarchitect. Reward: +3 to Architectural Lore skill!

Class Quest gained: Apprentice Rituarchitect. You have the material; you have the know-how! All you need to do now is find ways to practice your craft! Research each of the materials required to build five Uncommon structures, as well as the different methods involved in building them! Research percentage: 0%.

Architectural Lore (Student I). Congratulations! Any building you personally design will require 5% fewer resources for you to build!

As a reward for reaching the Student rank with a Lore skill, you get the satisfaction of knowing that you are an overachiever!

"Well, unfortunately both of those rewards are kind of useless to me right now, and it looks like I missed out on the bonus quests for speedrunning, abyss it. I *knew* I shouldn't have waited." Joe browsed his aspects and decided that he had enough to do the initial construction work. He started climbing out of the pit he had created, watching for sharp objects that could somehow penetrate his Exquisite Shell. "I don't even have an architect skill, and it's kind of hard to design a building without knowing how to do it. I've just been building them… but now I guess I should probably look into figuring out how to design them as well?"

Class quest gained!

Class quest: Novice Reductionist. You are a powerful, third-specialization individual. You must have power, influence, and resources to get to this point. Now you need to have a way to turn those resources into more resources. Create a Trash rank permanent array. Reward: 1,000 Damaged aspects. Array created: 0/1.

"Yes! I think I got it; I need to pass the Beginner quest to get the next one? Wait, why didn't it give me the prerequisites this time?" He tried to figure out what the difference was, but eventually gave up in favor of simply being happy that he had gained access to the next set of quests.

Once he had reached what passed for ground-level once more, Joe used his Rituarchitect Survey Grid to set out a ghostly version of the building. Then he created four more barriers, each of which would act as a support or foundation as he worked. In preparing the ritual, he devoted as little mana as possible in order to have enough remaining to start and continue the process. He was alone down here, and he knew for a fact that this would be an extremely draining process.

"Now comes the dangerous part..." He checked his status before temporarily dropping his Exquisite Shell, Neutrality Aura, and Retaliation of Shadows in order to maximize his mana. The Reductionist was immediately assaulted by dozens of tiny debuffs, but nothing that would be life-threatening in the small amount of time he needed to keep them inactive.

Name: Joe 'Tatum's Chosen Legend' Class: Reductionist
Profession I: Arcanologist (Max)
Profession II: Ritualistic Alchemist (1/20)
Profession III: None
Character Level: 21 Exp: 237,109 Exp to next level: 15,891
Rituarchitect Level: 10 Exp: 50,500
Reductionist Level: 2 Exp: 5,186 Exp to next level: 814
Hit Points: 1,898/1,898
Mana: 3,194/6,945
Mana regen: 54.3/sec

Stamina: 1,546/1,546
Stamina regen: 6.48/sec

Characteristic: Raw score

Strength: 148
Dexterity: 148
Constitution: 144
Intelligence (bound): 157
Wisdom: 137
Dark Charisma: 103
Perception: 140
Luck: 83
Karmic Luck: 8

It took thirty-five seconds for his mana to fully recover, and in that time, he wondered why his stats had improved even when he had not seen a notice for them. Specifically, his body stats. Each of them had improved very slightly… "Right! The bonus I got when I entered this plane of existence: Mind over Matter. Ten percent of my mental stats are added to my body. Nice; that means that those are just about to break through the next limit."

As soon as he was topped off, he began the ritual.

The ritual circles appeared as normal, and the massive drain on his body began. Just as always, he only had eyes for the work that was being done: it was unique and amazing to observe each time. Aspects roared into the frame of mana that had been created—standard ones as well as all of the Special Anima aspects that he had collected—creating a single glorious dais that hung in the air for a few seconds. The dais was studded with dozens of small, modular sections that could easily hold an inserted Aspect Jar. He was looking forward to inspecting those up close very soon.

The floor was created next, starting at the base of the dais and rippling out like the surface of water hit by a raindrop.

Each 'ripple' increased the thickness of the floor another millimeter, until the solid metal nonagon side was fully in place. From there, the sides were raised all in one go, moment by moment, as if a massive three-D printer were working at insane speed. Once finished, the 'ceiling' was created, leaving a hole large enough that Joe could have driven a truck through it.

If he were being honest with himself, it looked like it belonged here. The 'building' was a huge, hollow metal capsule without a single noticeable purpose. It was simply a massive, intricate dumpster.

Building created: Anima Supported Prodigal Entrepot Containment Tower. (Unique Building).

Architect of Artifacts has come into effect! All building stats increased by 10%!

Joe felt a deep sense of pride as he admired the building that he had not only created, but had a major role in designing. This was going to be the linchpin to all his future success, if he did it correctly. "Oh, *feces*, I just remembered that I might not have been able to build here."

The human grimaced as he recalled the building restriction that he might have run into, a restriction that would potentially force him to continue doing everything by hand. This *was* Dwarven-owned territory, and there had been no guarantees that he would be able to establish his structure. "Maybe the dump is designed so that anyone can put stuff down here? I guess I should just be glad that worked out?"

There was no door to the building, but that was perfectly acceptable to him. Crouching down, Joe gathered his strength and jumped straight to the top of the A.S.P.E.C.T. A quick glance at his skill reminded him that he could jump fifteen feet straight up, as his Omnivault skill was based on his raw strength. Peering down into the hollow tube of the tower, Joe selected his landing spot and hopped in. "Okay, now I just need to figure out how to add in a permanent aspect array…"

A moment later, a paperclip with googly eyes appeared in his line of sight and began speaking to him. "Hi there! It looks like you are trying to add an active effect to this building! Would you like some help?"

"I can't... feel my hands." Blinking rapidly, Joe realized he head collapsed and was currently on the ground, foaming at the mouth. He put all of his dwindling attention behind the reactivation of his Neutrality Aura. His vision stopped tunneling as he started to heal, and the quietly accruing debuffs began vanishing. The mirage went away as well. "Ugh... that would have been great, but I know for a fact that's outdated, retired technology. Good to know that hallucinations go straight for our deepest desires."

Health: 219/1,898

Chuckling nervously at his close call, Joe healed himself a few times and soon found the strength to stand back up. There was only a single point of interest in this building: the dais with modular compartments for his jars. An easy decision was made; Joe walked over and put his hand on it. He expected a notification, but even so, he was surprised by the details that sprang up after claiming the building as his own.

A.S.P.E.C.T. is awaiting a permanent reduction array. To begin the process of creating a permanent array, please select which array layer you would like to begin with. Please note that all values shown are the total number of aspects that will be required to complete that array level. It is highly recommended that you complete them in order, thereby gaining the optimal degree of experience with the creation process.

Trash: 100,000.

Damaged: 10,000.

Common: 5,000.

Uncommon: 1,000.

Rare: 500.

Special: 250 (Rare).

Unique: 250.

Artifact: 100.

Legendary: 25.

Mythical: 5.

A quick mental scan of his codpiece informed Joe that he

had already collected nearly eight hundred thousand Trash aspects. As he had not only an abundance of aspects, but he also should learn how to do this correctly, he chose to begin the creation process for the Trash layer. As soon as he activated it, mana slowly began trickling out of him, creating an energetic outline similar to his survey grid which began to swoop and swirl around the circumference of the open-air tower.

He began tracing the closest line with his finger, trying to understand how he was supposed to build up the layer. Joe began musing aloud, "It did tell me that I needed to use aspects with this... should I try my inscriber? Can only hurt a lot to get it wrong."

His Trash-aspect inscriber—resembling nothing so much as a basic number two pencil—appeared in his hand. With a simple *swish* of the implement, Joe traced along the lines of mana that ran through the air and along the ground. As he had hoped, the strange energy stayed in place. The process was similar to creating a ritual diagram, but it felt rather strange—he wasn't used to moving across such a large area to do this kind of work. Just as he grew more comfortable with the process, he made a grave mistake: he stepped on one of the lines he had already filled with aspects.

All in the same instant, he began to fall over as his foot was vaporized, the filled line snapped like a spiderweb that had been walked through, and the rest of the aspects in the array destabilized. Joe cursed like a sailor as he frantically dumped mana into his forgotten Exquisite Shell, hoping desperately that he could reactivate it before the flaming energy landed on him.

CHAPTER THIRTY

The last of the flames guttered out, leaving behind a scarred and pitted metal floor. Joe gazed around hollowly as he inspected the damage, regrew his foot, three fingers, and his left arm; finally getting a notice as the structure itself stopped taking damage.

A.S.P.E.C.T. durability: 113,333/150,000.

"How in the *abyss* did that deal over sixteen *thousand* damage to the structure? I had barely even started!" Joe slammed his hand on the only undamaged portion of the floor: where he was sitting. His Exquisite Shell had been wrecked. Aspect damage—being True Damage—went right through shields. Even so, the protective layer had saved him from the super-heated air and molten metal that would otherwise have sizzled his skin. Right now, he was waiting for his mana to regenerate enough for him to reactivate the lifesaving skill once more.

"Even worse, that was using *Trash* aspects? No wonder the system told me that it 'recommended' doing them in order. I can't even imagine the level of damage that could have happened if I would have started with something like *Rare* aspects."

The framework that he had put in place, the ghostly mana scaffolding, had vanished when he had pulled his attention away in order to save his skin. Reluctantly, he reactivated the dais and watched as lines were traced over nearly the entire available space inside of the nonagon. "Right. There is no *way* that I could possibly do all of this tracing by hand... especially once it goes up the walls? There's nowhere to stand. I can't exactly move the building around so that I'm able to do the work that needs to be done. Think, *think*."

An answer to his concerns, more of an idea perhaps, filtered across his conscious mind. "If controlling a Field Array is directly correlated to my Mana Manipulation, what's to say that I can't directly use that skill to fill in this grid?"

He had been getting quite a bit of practice in using his mind much more directly when it came to handling objects—thanks to his Ritual Orbs—and even if it was absolute fractions of milligrams; energy *did* have mass. Settling into a firm stance that he knew he would be able to maintain for a good chunk of time, Joe pushed the tip of his inscriber into a mana line on the wall and tried to get a feel for the way aspects flowed out of his storage device and then through the tool.

Slowly, ever so slowly, he guided the inscriber along the line and began to get a feel for the way his power and the essence of what was once an item interacted.

Skill increase: Magical Synesthesia (Beginner I).

Skill increase: Essence Cycle (Beginner VI).

Even though he could see no progress in controlling it, Joe knew that he was moving in the correct direction once more. Over the next few hours, while maintaining his concentration only on the walls within arm's reach, he began to get a solid feel for how to control the flow of energy directly. The moment of truth finally came: as far as he could tell, he was not going to get any better without actually practicing it. Taking a deep breath and double, triple, quadruple checking his Exquisite Shell— then preparing to jump out of the nonagon if needed—he began forcing the Trash aspects along the lines using only his mind and his inscriber as a catalyst.

The only thing that saved him from detonating the entire place with his first attempt was the fact that the untraced lines were perfectly straight. Dark gray aspects *blasted* along the intervening space, collecting and slightly pooling at the end of the lines as he pulled back how much mental force he was using. He stared at the flickering, nearly destabilized energy and reached up with his off hand to wipe away the cooling sweat that even his Neutrality Aura hadn't immediately gotten rid of. "Oookay, got it. This requires a *very* light touch."

Narrowly averted destruction was a great motivator for rapid improvement, and there was even a hidden benefit to the pooled aspects: instead of drawing additional energy directly from his storage device, he was able to direct the excess from the pooled forces to flow along the lines closest in proximity. This allowed him to keep the lines consistent, both in thickness, depth, and placement along the walls. Getting a better feel for how to make his new strategy work, Joe slowly began feeding additional aspects into the array.

The design he followed with his eyes slowly filled with energy, all with Joe staying in one space. So single-minded was his focus, he did not even realize when he had completed the project. If it were not for an intense flare of gray light that broke his concentration, he would have been attempting to add too much power to the system once more, and he did not want to experience the devastation that would be wrought by the array breaking down at such a juncture.

Joe blinked his eyes to clear away the afterimages that had burned into his retinas, then examined the design that he had been working on for... he wasn't exactly sure how long. "It turned into metal?"

He ran his fingers along the intricate, impressive filigree that spanned the entirety of the walls and floor. The Reductionist found that he had been incorrect in his initial assumption; this was not metal. At least, not a type of metal that he had ever seen before. It shifted beneath his touch as if he were playing with a vein on the back of his hand; the line remained in place, attached to the wall and floor, but seemed closer to mesh tubing than malleable metal.

Array layer complete: Trash.

Class quest complete: Novice Reductionist. Reward: 1,000 Damaged aspects you can claim at any time, in any storage device that will accept them.

Class quest gained: Novice Reductionist II. Create a Damaged rank permanent array. Reward: 2,500 Common aspects. Array created: 0/1.

Congratulations! Your A.S.P.E.C.T. will now be able to convert materials into trash aspects if they are placed within the open area and the array is supplied with energy. Before you begin to worry, there are several methods available for powering the array.

- *Active Conversion.*

You are able to directly supply mana from your mana pool to convert items into aspects.

- *Directed Conversion.*

Using a mana battery or mana collection methodology is an effective way to empower the permanent array. Access points for indirect mana supplies are built into the exterior of the building.

- *Aspect Convection Direct Conversion.*

After initial powering of the array with mana, the array can be directed to use gathered aspects to fuel the reduction of items without requiring further energetic input. Each rank uses aspects at a differing rate. Aspects gathered when an empty storage device is not available will automatically be used as an AC/DC power supply if this option is selected.

"Well, that's easy enough; burn anything below Rare to fuel

the conversion process," Joe muttered to himself as he debated whether or not he wanted to set up the next layers of the array immediately.

His Constitution told him that he could keep going. His Strength informed him that he would have no issue if he chose to remain standing in this position for days if needed. Unfortunately, his Wisdom suggested that he should probably take a break.

"Forget *that!*" Joe chuckled as he dove into the 'Damaged' aspect layer. "The vote is two for continuing to work, one for pausing. Working has it!"

A new layer of 'scaffolding' appeared, but this time, the lines were not running along the wall and floor, or... a better way to put it would be that the lines were not directly touching the walls and floor anymore. It appeared that this layer would only connect to the first in a few areas, giving Joe the slightly uncomfortable feeling that he was weaving a massive spider web. "I don't suppose the original Reductionists were spiders, were they?"

With his ever-so-slightly more impressive inscriber, Joe began filling out the new layer with potent aspects. A frown touched his face as soon as he began, as he realized that even with such a minimal difference between the two rankings logically, the fact of the matter was that Damaged aspects were much more mentally 'heavy'. While Joe wasn't sure if it was due to the fact that he was already tired, or if they were truly that much more dense in comparison, the strain on his mind caused him no small amount of struggle in the beginning.

After the initial input, as he adjusted to the 'weight', the momentum of the energy's movement made it far easier to progress. It did make him slightly concerned over future attempts to work with higher-rank aspects, but that was a problem for future Joe. Right now, he was working on grinding these skills and making them more effective in order to meet the goals awaiting him when he was assigned the next challenges.

As he reached an extra tricky portion, he grunted, "Classic skill grinding, gotta love it."

He was pleased that there was no day or night cycle down here, otherwise he would have likely given into mental fatigue before completing the second layer. Over the next few hours of feverish creation, Joe managed to complete the dark gray portion of the array in one fell swoop.

Array layer complete: Damaged.

Class quest complete: Novice Reductionist II. Reward: 2,500 Common aspects you can claim at any time, in any storage device that will accept them.

Class quest gained: Novice Reductionist III. Create a Common rank permanent array. Reward: 500 Uncommon aspects. Array created: 0/1.

"It still considers the next layer as a Novice quest? This set of class quests might be… **yawn**… a lot more intense than my other ones. At least the reward is about half of what I need to make the next layer every time I succeed." As soon as he was done reading and mulling over the notification, he leaned against the viney, oddly organic layer he had just created and closed his eyes.

"Just a tiny nap… then I'll get the Common section done and do a test run."

CHAPTER THIRTY-ONE

Array layer complete: Common.

Class quest complete: Novice Reductionist III. Reward: 500 Uncommon aspects you can claim at any time, in any storage device that will accept them.

Class quest gained: Novice Reductionist IV. Create an Uncommon rank permanent array. Reward: 250 Rare aspects. Array created: 0/1.

"Oh, come on! Another *Novice*-rank quest? It's gotta be higher than that!" Joe glared at the white, sticky strings that composed the Common tier of the aspect array. He didn't want to touch them, he didn't want to think about them, and he now fully expected spiders to randomly spawn inside the structure at some point. "You know what? It's time to see what this bad boy can do."

Joe started inserting the Aspect Jars into their alcoves, which were denoted by the coloration of the array connecting to them. As far as he could tell, every aspect could have up to five jars along its path, except for 'Special', which had space for fifteen different jars. "In a landfill like this, Common and below are going to be by far the most likely to be found... probably why they are labeled 'Common'. Ugh. I can only blame poor-quality sleep for making me say that out loud."

On the plus side, since he had not yet constructed the array layers for the higher tiers, even if higher-ranked gear was found and collected, it wouldn't be broken down and he would be able to inspect it before deciding if it would be better served as aspects or used for its original purpose. The likelihood of finding a working treasure down here? Probably not worth mentioning, but still, having the option was nice.

"Next up, a ritual to start gathering everything…" Joe easily set up the Little Sister's Cleaning Service, hoping that the ritual wouldn't rebel when the artificial mind realized it was being commanded to sort the literal garbage of a civilization. He powered the ritual up, and it got to work right away, lifting, arranging, and neatly hauling things up and into the container.

Some clear restrictions that he had never encountered outside of this situation appeared almost instantly. The first was the fact that anything that weighed over fifty pounds was apparently regarded as 'landscape'. Either the ritual couldn't move them, being too weak to do so, or it couldn't recognize that they were valid targets. "Still… more than I ever expected out of such a low-rank ritual. Gonna need to find a way to upgrade this to a higher version."

Following that first restriction came the second: the sheer number of items it began moving at once was an *enormous* strain on the ritual. When Joe inspected the ritual's longevity, he found that it lost four seconds off the countdown per second. "Well, improving this just moved up the ol' priority list. Normally lasts a year; this will be lucky to last ninety days."

As the first load of junk started dropping in through the top of the A.S.P.E.C.T., Joe worked out how to pump mana into it. To power the permanent array directly, he needed to be standing at the dais with both hands in place. As used Dwarven adult diapers brushed gently across the barrier protecting his forehead, he resolved to make Mana Batteries as soon as he got out so that he could activate the array externally. "Four-point-five mana per second to do Common reduction; let's begin."

He had slotted the Common Aspect Jar made from a Unique core, granting himself room for ten thousand aspects. The array began powering up, dark gray light followed by light gray, then blindingly white light; as if the sun were hitting fresh-fallen snow. As incoming items swirled around the room, they bounced gently against the webs, ropes, and finally the walls. If an item was of the correct aspect rarity, it stuck in position as if it had been welded in place, then slowly converted to light and energy.

No Trash or Damaged aspect containers located. Would you like to use these aspects as fuel for reduction of higher aspects?

You may burn the same rarity aspect at a rate of 1 aspect to pull 10 aspects from an item. However, the cost of reduction is 100 to 1 per higher aspect. Burning 100 Damaged aspects will allow you to collect 1 aspect from Common-ranked items. Burning 1,000 Trash aspects will achieve the same. Yes / No.

Joe selected 'yes', then the only option that was available: reduce Common aspects. The lack of options made sense, as that was the highest rarity he had been able to set up. He had no need at all for these lower-ranked aspects, as he could gather more just from reducing rocks if needed. The reduction of the goods in the container sped up now that the power flow had found a balance, so Joe stepped away from the dais and watched for a while as the ritual dragged more debris in.

A.S.P.E.C.T. durability: 113,334/150,000.

"It's fixing itself? How?" Joe pulled up the building information and noticed that the 'Anima' portion of the name was click-able. "Unused aspects can be gathered and used to replace damaged portions of the building instead of burning away in the atmosphere.' Huh. Well, alright then."

One Omnivault later, he was perched atop the nonagon and observing the trash that was floating around his building. It was noticeable, but he didn't overly care. "Everything up to Common aspects is now taken care of by either fixing up the place or getting absorbed. Now I just need to wait until that Aspect jar is full, and then I can check out whatever is remaining in the storage area and break it down by hand if needed. I can only hope some Rare or better gear gets dragged in there."

Suddenly, he noticed something moving that was not a part of his designs. Motion off to the side drew his eye, which turned out to be an oversized two-headed rat sniffing around the barriers that he had erected. Another thing Joe noticed at the same time was that the klaxon call alarm that he had set off when he was escaping zombies had finally ended.

Either something had smashed the ritual, or it had just run out of juice. No matter the cause, the result was that any sounds caused by his attempts at combat or creation were going to be far more audible in the otherwise eerie silence of the landfill.

Tossing his icicle-shaped Ritual Orb into the air, he stealthily directed it to hover directly above the too-curious rat. He set it to attack, and it began its normal power-up moment, roughly half a second of spinning in place like a top to generate increased penetrative damage. A moment later, it crashed into the body of the oversized rodent, the sneak attack dealing bonus damage—and the force behind the weapon driving the furry vermin into the garbage where its death cry of surprise was muffled by a mouthful of slime.

Joe blinked at the space where the rat had vanished, slightly shocked by how effective and efficient that had been. He muttered under his breath, ensuring he stayed quiet in a space where almost everything had enhanced senses, "I'm guessing that where I'm standing right now is effectively a hunter's blind... no wonder they set them up; it *works*."

Moments later, a notification that he had gained thirty-five experience passed through his vision. He settled in to wait for his next victim and spent a few hours quietly chuckling as he practiced dexterous maneuvers and effective maneuvers with his Ritual Orbs. He didn't use the intelligence-bound Orb every single time, instead electing to practice with two or even three Orbs at a time.

Once, he even used one of his normal Orbs as a lure, inducing a rabid double-headed raccoon to chase after it like a cat following a laser pointer. Right as it jumped after the lure, he directed two other orbs to slam together and crush the small vermin. It exploded in a shower of gore. "Yeah! Critter? More like *crit*-ter. Ooh. I think I just invented a new game. Bad puns for the win!"

In his over-exuberance, Joe was slightly too loud and drew in a beast that he had been hoping to avoid for at least slightly longer: a Dwarven zombie. The undead hulk wandered into the area just after Joe's Orbs *cracked* together, and it began running toward the sound. As its undead senses latched onto the next still-breathing animal Joe was playing around with, the human simply let his Orbs fall to the ground like the inanimate objects they were.

The zombie completely ignored them, as Joe had expected, and tore into the warm, wriggling flesh that was left behind. The Reductionist saw the opportunity to destroy this creature, and he knew that he should probably take it. Yes, it was likely going to be harder than he expected; but he knew that if the zombie got a whiff of him before he took it down, it would be able to call a much larger hoard to assault his barely fortified position. Right now, he had the high ground, the potential for a sneak attack, and the benefit of the zombie's laser-focus on its current meal. With no small amount of trepidation, he ordered his icicle Orb into position and lined it up with the brainstem of the hunched mindless husk.

"These things have a massive amount of health... I gotta maximize the debuff when it hits." The Reductionist prepared Dark Lightning Strike and hoped for the best. More of his Orbs floated over to hang above the frenzied creature, "As ready as I can be."

With an internal scream of pure anxiety, he slammed his first Orb down with as much force as his mind could put behind it. For the first time in a long time, the secondary ability of Retaliation of Shadows activated, creating an icicle-shaped Orb that drilled in alongside the original. Joe ignored the notification of a sneak attack and critical hit in favor of wincing away from the wet, meaty sound. He grimaced as he thought, "If I didn't have my Neutrality Aura to get that clean, I would need to throw that whole Orb away."

Letting out a battle cry that he tried to keep as quiet as possible, Joe mentally began slamming the Orbs on the zombie's head. The combination of paralysis from having its spine severed, as well as enduring various Orbs bouncing against its rotten skull, came together in a glorious expulsion of fluids as the undead creature's head was fully removed.

He stared at the fallen being, not sure what to do next. An experience gain notification was pushed aside as he waited to see if other zombies would be drawn to the sound of combat, even as muted as he had managed to keep it. After a few long moments with no visible response, Joe fully relaxed from his combat-ready position and looked around.

"Ahh!" He screamed as he came face-to-face with… the zombie's severed head? Joe continued shaking as the Little Sister's Cleaning service dumped the rotten flesh into the Aspect Array, and it was permanently reduced. "Did… did a ritual just *prank* me?"

A howl from a nearby zombie was his only answer. Joe's eyes bulged as he realized that even though he had managed to avoid attention when slaying the first zombie, he might have brought the wrath of the landfill down on himself with his girly scream.

CHAPTER THIRTY-TWO

He knew that the horde would be surging toward him like a tide, and yet Joe could not find it in himself to move from his current position or attempt to fortify his location further. He peeked behind him, only to see that garbage was still flowing into the array. The only major difference that he could spot was that two columns of gray smoke were billowing out of the top of the building, as if it were some kind of refinery. Rolling his eyes at himself, Joe rubbed his shiny head and mumbled, "What am I thinking? This is *literally* a refinery. The smoke exiting the top must mean the building used all the aspects it needed for repairs."

The fact of the matter was that he knew *exactly* what he was doing: procrastinating. He wasn't sure how he was going to handle the incoming waves of monsters; there was a good chance that all of the work that he had been doing was about to get smashed. Joe chuckled to himself, "Well, if nothing else, if the building gets trashed, no one will know that I messed up this badly."

The first of the zombies crested a nearby hill of slimy waste matter and began searching the area. Upon finding the original zombie that had caused this mess, the advancing beast dove into its fallen brother and began tearing away strips of flesh. Apparently, whatever kept the zombies from going after each other during their undead state was no longer in effect after they were dead for good. More zombies were arriving by the moment, and the shambling creatures soon began fighting amongst themselves for the scraps.

As he looked on in complete shock, Joe's mind slowly began to remind him that he needed to get into that mix and figure out a way to take advantage of the situation. The creatures were already fighting among themselves, even if they were not fighting to the death. *Yet.* At present, it was more of a dispute for territory and a meal than it was truly brutal attacks. For the first time, he began wondering if these creatures did have some kind of pack mentality, and if not…

Bonk.

The metallic sound captured the attention of all of the feasting zombies. One of Joe's Ritual Orbs had shot out of the garbage pile, caved in a forehead, then rapidly drifted over to land in another of the undead Dwarves' hands. Each of them had immediately stopped to stare at an apparent imposter in their midst. When all of the eyes had locked onto the metal orb, Joe once more took control of it and sent it into another face.

The resulting chaos was exactly what he had been hoping for, as all of the undead started assaulting the 'perpetrator'. Moments later, more of his Orbs started to *bonk* zombies. After getting in a few attacks, Joe released control of his Orbs and leaned back against his building. The nearest beasts were tearing into each other, ever-so-slowly whittling down each other's hit points. Settling in, he decided to wait for an opportune moment to finish off the survivors.

He had forgotten that each of them had a massive Constitution. The battle went on long enough that he was nervous the sounds of combat would result in drawing in a much larger group of enemies. Luckily, he didn't have to worry. Every once in a while, another zombie would appear on a hilltop and take a gander at the commotion. For some reason, when they saw what was going on, they just... left. It did make Joe wonder how common of an occurrence this was; after all, garbage rained from the ceiling on a fairly regular basis.

Even so, he determined that there must be something he could learn, something he could use to keep his area safer. A few minutes later, the first of the zombies were beginning to stumble away. A glance at them was enough to determine that their health was low, and they were likely suffering from multiple debuffs: everything from torn flesh to loss of limbs. The winners were barely better off, and Joe knew that it was time to make his move.

"Dark Lightning Strike!" he hissed to entice the nearly soundless energy to storm down among his foes. A moment later, he regained control of his Ritual Orbs and sent them swirling around the head of the most damaged Dwarven corpse. Soon he received the first of what he hoped would be *many* experience notifications in the corner of his vision.

The remaining zombies had practically destroyed each other and were being held together by dark magic and sinew. The small group that had remained was easily defeated, nearly soundlessly, and Joe decided that he needed to get rid of their bodies. If the very first one had been any indication, a zombie seeing a corpse of any kind would be drawn to the location for a fancy feast. He tapped at his chin, trying to think of a discreet way to bring them in. "The ritual isn't strong enough to lift them... I can either go out there and haul them in myself, or I need to find a way to chop them into fifty-pound sacks of meat from a distance."

As much as he did *not* want to have to put his hands on them, the fastest answer was 'go do the work'. Joe moved as quickly as he could, hauling the corpses as close to his barriers as possible, then chucking them up and over the rim into the open-topped tower. A concerning point of note was that as soon as they touched the gray 'smoke' that was billowing out of the A.S.P.E.C.T., their exteriors began to dissolve.

"Good to know that clouds of aspect waste are still bad for your health." Checking the area, Joe ensured that—as far as he could tell—no one could see him or knew what he was doing. He re-entered the hidden area, climbed onto the side of the nonagon, and decided to take a small nap.

He was able to get perhaps two hours before his enhanced Constitution told him that he had received enough sleep and his conscious mind was no longer going to put up with being ignored. As soon as his eyes popped open, his stomach rumbled and his head started to hurt. A glance at his to-be-completed quests kicked his fear of missing out into high gear. "Okay, I *really* want to get back to the Shoe, but I know I can't go back empty-handed. I gotta put in some elbow grease and leg it back there, fully armed with everything I need to succeed, or Havoc will rip me a new… c'mon, Joe. Happy thoughts.."

With thoughts of Havoc going out of his way to find creative punishments driving Joe to take risks, he climbed the small tower and touched the Ritual of Little Sister's Cleaning Service to interrupt the flow of energy within it. All this did was pause the ritual—not destroy it. Over the next few minutes, the clouds of gray aspect byproducts began to vanish, and soon the air was clear. It was finally time to find out if anything had been found that couldn't be broken down by the array he had managed to build up.

It was strange to discover a smattering of gear that had clearly been thrown in the dump but was otherwise in a perfectly clean state. There was a mix of everything, from malfunctioning Alchemy equipment to bolts of cloth that had some kind of red wine stain across them. No single item was in large supply, as he had fully expected. Even so, a surprising amount of Rare material had been thrown away for no clear reason, other than some kind of discoloration or tiny imperfection that had likely kept it from achieving a Unique or better rating.

That reminded him of the way Grandmaster McPoundy had casually thrown out Unique swords and even Artifact-quality equipment, simply because it was either not what he wanted to see or was potentially embarrassing for such a vaunted individual to produce. "There's an idea: I should get a map of the city and mark where each Master craftsman has a shop. Then I can focus my attention on those areas for reduction and aspect collection!"

In the current moment, that brief memory of a Grandmaster's wastefulness served as validation that what he was doing had the potential for massive returns. He hurried to get to work and see what he had managed to gather.

Setting up a Field Array within the permanent array made him snort at the strange turns his life had taken, but it didn't stop him from sucking all the value out of the items. Soon his building was once again empty, and he was laying the groundwork for generating the Uncommon layer of the array.

He grunted in consternation as he began working with the higher-value aspect, finding that the energy had increased in mental weight significantly once again. Joe *was* able to force it along the mana path network that he had set out, but he was uncertain how many more layers he would be able to work with at this rate. On the plus side, each layer was significantly closer to the center of the room and covered a much smaller area in total. If nothing else, he should eventually be able to use his inscriber to trace each of the lines manually.

But that would feel like he was giving up on improving himself.

Array layer complete: Uncommon.

Class quest complete: Novice Reductionist VI. Reward: 250 Rare aspects you can claim at any time, in any storage device that will accept them.

Class quest gained: Novice Reductionist V. Create a Rare rank permanent array. Reward: 250 Rare aspects. Array created: 0/1.

"It'll give me Rare aspects again…? Ah! Everything I need for the 'Special' layer. Nice." Now that his mental exertions had been completed, Joe received five *excellent* reasons to continue working his mind rather than giving in to the 'easy' route.

Skill increase: Mana Manipulation (Student V -> Student VI).
Skill increase: Magical Matrices (Apprentice V -> Student VIII).
Skill increase: Magical Synesthesia (Beginner I -> Beginner IV).
Skill increase: Essence Cycle (Beginner VI -> Beginner IX).
Skill increase: Coalescence (Student IX -> Journeyman 0). Congratulations on reaching the Journeyman ranks with Coalescence! As a reward for your dedication to being dense, both mentally and magically, you gain +5 Wisdom!

The air around Joe brightened considerably, and he could hear harmonic singing just at the edge of his auditory range. The two bonuses that he had gained from the human monarchs confused him slightly, but apparently he had been receiving consistent and impressive gains from close proximity to not only the magically potent building that he was creating, but all of the various enchanted items that had been drawn in to be reduced. "It makes me wonder if the sight and sound of magical gear being turned into aspects is directly boosting these skills? Maybe I will catch the next seat that I see and stare down into the A.S.P.E.C.T. as it converts garbage…?"

Still feeling fresh, having plenty of mana, and now having the Rare aspects that he needed in order to make the next layer, Joe began organizing his thoughts in preparation of designing a Rare array. "It's strange to think about grinding skills the same way I do about watching a holiday parade, but… if something needs to happen to become more powerful, I'm gonna do it!"

Once again, the aspects felt 'heavier' than the previous layer, but it was surprisingly nowhere *near* what he was expecting. Joe quietly accepted the fact that his skills and characteristics being boosted were helping him significantly, and did his very best to actively train each of them as he struggled and strained to connect the bright blue lines of deadly energy to each other. Whenever he was able to find a straight line to send the aspects down, he was able to slowly build some momentum and reduce the mental strain on himself.

The downside was, the closer he got to the center of the building—where he knew Mythical and Legendary aspects would be collected—the more the scaffolding became intricate with fewer and fewer long, straight lines. Each time he had to follow a curve perfectly, the energy pressed against him as if he were ten pounds over his maximum curl weight at the gym. He could do it, and he *did*, but he knew that when he was done... he was going to be hurting.

He finished the layer, and frankly, he did not know how he had managed to do it. His mind was screaming from the strain, and his body was a shivering mess. "Why does everyone always cheer for people that hurt themselves to succeed, but nobody ever mentions how long it takes to recover?"

A distraction came at the perfect time, just as his mind started to collapse from exhaustion and strain. The blue lights flashed and coalesced into a more physical manifestation, just as the other layers had, and he knew that he was *done*. Not just with the most recent layer, but unable to continue on with the framework at all. As it stood currently, if he tried to press forward with the next portion, the Special layer, Joe recognized that he would most likely end up destroying the entire building and all the work that he had managed to complete so far.

Array layer complete: Rare.

Class quest complete: Novice Reductionist V. Reward: 250 Rare aspects you can claim at any time, in any storage device that will accept them.

Class quest gained: Beginner Reductionist. Create a Special rank permanent array. Reward: 125 Unique aspects. Array created: 0/1.

The Reductionist slotted his next few Aspect Jars, reactivated the overhead ritual, and started the aspect conversion that would keep this place running even when he was not here. As soon as everything was working as it should, he jumped to the top of his mini tower and activated Essence Cycle. He peered into the distance, where he knew he would be able to find an exit.

Thanks to his active skill, he was able to locate a few areas that were leaking a massive amount of foul energy into the air. Sheer force of habit made him glance at the control cuff on his wrist, where he had once worn a watch all the time. "I need to get out of here… but maybe I can raid just a *few* treasure pits on my way out? No one's stopping me."

He held his hands in front of his face and placed one index finger over the other, blocking his sight of the nearest plume of darkness. "X marks the spot. Arr, matey."

Burble?

"Not *you*, Mate. It's a pirate thing."

CHAPTER THIRTY-THREE

A door appeared in the wall of a dark alley. Before this moment, there had been no indication that such a point of egress had existed, and—unlike what common sense dictated—the door did not open into the building behind it. A rain of goop and filth splattered onto the floor as a white boot stepped out and touched the ground, at which time the filthy liquid vanished as if it had never existed in the first place.

Joe breathed out a sigh of relief. "*Finally* out of that place. Celestial feces, I need to find an assistant that can survive in there long enough to collect my aspect jars for me. But first, *food*."

The weary human made his way through the city, which was hustling and bustling even more than usual. In fact, the last time he had seen people this excited, this mobilized, the Dwarven Oligarchy had been staging an all-out assault on Gramma's Shoe. Joe hoped that was not the case this time; he was far too busy to join in on another attack.

Eventually, he found a food stall and asked the Dwarven attendant what was going on. The young-looking Dwarf ran a critical eye over Joe's bald head and face, shuddering lightly to himself as he tried to hide his revulsion from his current customer. "Not sure if you have been living under a rock or if you are just trying to verify whether people have been telling you the truth. As far as I know, the Elves just mounted a massive campaign against the Oligarchy."

"No!" Joe managed to mumble around what he hoped was a smoked turkey leg. "Where are they marching? Are they going after the Shoe again?"

The Dwarf shook his head in the negative. "You misunderstand. They aren't *going* anywhere; they *already* invaded. They snatched a buttload of land, nearly a five percent increase to the entire Zone than they had before. At least, if the news is correct."

"Didn't they just lose an entire division?" Joe shook his head at the foolishness of whoever was in charge of the Elves. "How can they *possibly* hope to hold that land?"

"Look, human, I just sell teriyaki Pteranodon legs. You want some kind of grand strategy, go ask the Legion proper." The vendor had apparently had enough of being polite, which was a thing that Joe understood. Frankly, it was rather refreshing to have people admit that they had their own area of specialization and preferred to focus on that, instead of offering their personal opinions. Nothing muddied the water like everyone commenting on the news of the day and offering their own take on what should be done about it.

Joe wandered toward the temples, a slight sense of urgency taking over as he observed more and more people losing their ever-lovin' minds. For Dwarves, being terrified about an invasion appeared in the form of a whole throng of short, muscular people standing in polite, straight lines while they waited on their chance to purchase goods and services that they might need over the coming days and possibly weeks.

Humans had different reactions to the same stimuli, and those present were starting to become a problem. Joe just happened to walk past a group as someone proudly and loudly proclaimed the fact that they had chosen the 'wrong side' and would be defecting to the Elves as soon as possible. Nothing quite got the Dwarves riled up like traitors in their midst, and soon the earth-toned cobblestones and walls received a fresh coat of bright red paint. Wanting to distance himself from the bloody conflict, Joe decided that it was time to stop being polite and waiting in the crowds, instead activating Omnivault and skedaddling toward the temples in search of more information.

When he arrived, the Reductionist learned that it was interesting to walk past the Juggernauts, knowing that they were not there to listen to his commands. Interesting, yes; not exactly fun. Many intimidation rolls were made at that moment. Hurrying past the constructs and over to the altars, he tapped on the large open book that represented Tatum's influence in the world. "Hope you are doing well up there, big guy!"

Please at least pretend *to be somewhat reverent while you are in the Temple. Good to see you as well, Joe. Ah… your accomplishments in my name haven't been increasing, so we're already out of time. Get to a crafting station and make a proper home for your Coffee Elemental. It's looking a little… decaf. I think-*

A new sweet but firm voice interrupted their conversation, and Tatum was cut off mid-sentence. *If you would like to make a direct connection to a Deity, please increase your relationship and provide DE for more monthly credit! Otherwise, as a Chosen, you can always spend a twenty-four hour period of prayer for one full minute of discussion.*

"Who or what was that? Hey! *Mate!*" Joe glared suspiciously at his sleeve, where his otherwise pristine white Shirt of the Silkpants Mage was stained a noticeable brown. "Is *that* why I have been having this nasty headache for the last week? You've been lowering the dosage of caffeine I've been getting?"

There wasn't even a conciliatory burbling; in fact, the coffee elemental refused to appear. Joe tried one more time, pulling out his list and showing it to the typically perky stain directly. "Look! It's right here on the list! I put in an order for a template so that I can give you a proper home as soon as I either learn how to craft one in the Forge or generate a cool flask for you! See? I even wrote down right here, 'ask Mate for a preference'!"

A tiny coffee bean appeared over the stain, appearing to browse the list. Joe rolled his eyes. "Come on, Mate. I know for a fact that you don't know how to read. But I'm telling you the truth."

A tiny stream of coffee appeared above Joe's wrist, lancing down to directly infuse caffeine into his bloodstream. The human took a deep breath as his blood felt like it was being set on fire, but moments later, he felt better than he had in an entire week. "Missed you too. I *will* make sure that we do something fun together sometime soon, okay?"

Burble!

"Any new information or spells that you think I should get access to?" This time, the Reductionist was speaking to the altar. A notification popped up in front of him as soon as he finished speaking, read off by the same sweet-firm female voice.

Your level is not currently high enough to grant you access to the next benefits designated for a Champion of Occultatum. Come back at level 25!

"Fair enough… bye, Tater-tum, Lord of potatoes." Joe jumped to the side and laughed as lightning struck where he had been standing an instant ago. "Ahh, blasphemy is even more entertaining in this world. We have fun, you and I."

The Ritualist proudly craned his neck to look around the large Temple. In a place like this—where the higher-ups in society came to mingle and gain benefits from literal Deities—there was always an opportunity to learn more about what was going on in the world. Soon enough, he spotted a few officers of the Legion murmuring to each other in low tones. He walked over and joined the small group as if he belonged there, until he remembered… he actually *did* belong there. He was a Major General now, and he didn't need to *hope* for information: he could order them to give it to him.

Within a minute, he had a fairly cohesive outline of the situation.

The Elves had attacked the Western flank of Svaltarheim, swallowing a massive section of forest as well as the barrier mountains that had sprung up when the two Zones had collided and joined together. To the Dwarves, those areas only had value as defensive locations. To the Elves, a huge forest where they could practice their druidic magic, as well as mountainous regions where they could summon more powerful types of Earth Elementals, was of grave concern.

"Let me get this straight..." Joe looked the sweating, bearded Captain in the eyes as he spoke in slow, calm tones. "With all of the land that they just grabbed, the Elves are now the majority land and resource holders. Instead of an almost-perfect split, they're now up two percent... and a pittance like that is going to require a full-blown military response?"

"Yes, sir, Major General Pyrrhic!" The Captain saluted crisply. "I hope you take to the field, sir! I understand if you need to sacrifice me to gain victory; in fact, it would be my honor to die for the cause, as many times as you need!"

The Reductionist recoiled from the bearded individual with a shocked expression. He looked around uncomfortably, only to realize that the small group which had originally been standing with them was nowhere to be seen. "Why in Eternium do you think that I would just outright sacrifice... *abyss*, I really hate the fact that *this* is the reputation that precedes me. At ease, Captain. You may leave, with my thanks for the information you provided."

Fully unsatisfied with how the conversation had gone, Joe decided that it was time to get back to an environment where he had at least a semblance of control over what was going on. He did not want to get sucked into combat, he didn't want to have to deal with strange logistics, he just wanted to build his little buildings and get cool rewards and accolades as he got stronger and progressed through the different zones.

The fact of the matter was, even though he had the odd trait that made it difficult to be around Elves, he really didn't even particularly dislike them. They were simply on different sides of this realm's conflict. At the end of the day, he would be living on another Zone and learning new and interesting ways to become powerful. Frankly, if he had the power and ability, he would *force* these two sides to reconcile.

"You know what?" Joe froze and gaped at the sky as if Tatum's lightning *had* hit him. He stumbled outside of the temple, pausing long enough that someone ran into him and caused him to fall. The human barely even noticed, so lost in his thoughts that the Retaliation of Shadows slapping a random Dwarf didn't even register as he got back to his feet. "The only way that the Bifrost is going to open is if the main Zone quest is completed. If we do it the standard way, either the Elves are going to need to be wiped out, or the Dwarves are."

Three eyes started shining in anticipation; the two that were peering out of his white half-mask, and the golden one etched on his forehead. "Since when have I ever done what I am told to do if I don't believe in it? Frankly, when has *humanity* done that? If I am able to find another way... I wonder if we can change the fate of this entire Zone."

CHAPTER THIRTY-FOUR

Finally returning to the Shoe after… Joe wasn't actually sure how long he had been down in the landfill. It felt like a long time? He had done a lot of things, but the lack of day-night cycles had really messed with him. He ogled his own lights, vowing to alter them when he had the opportunity.

"Joe! There you are!" Stan the despondent administrator ran up to him with the most aggrieved expression that Joe had ever seen. "Do you know what he *did?* Where have you been? That person doesn't just get to come in here and make decisions on your behalf; that's *my* job!"

"I know, Havoc is extremely hard to handle. He is also dangerous. Rude. Kind of smells bad-" Joe's attempt at calming his city manager down flopped spectacularly as the Dwarf clamped a hand over the human's mouth.

"Not *him*. Havoc has been nothing but a delight! In fact, he's been working on the sly to create structural supports throughout the entire Shoe, in addition to crafting a ventilation system that will keep the air purified down here even in the worst-case scenario!" Stan stomped on the ground, creating a miniature localized earthquake. Once more, Joe wondered if he should attempt to figure out his right-hand person's actual level and abilities. "The problem is *Checkoff*!"

"Chekhov? Like the gun? Is Herr Trigger back again?" Joe was ready to fight, and the Orbs that began floating around his head in the same moment proved it. "Let's go *get* that son of a-"

"Who, are *you*, supposed... to be?" A new Dwarf appeared, someone Joe had never seen or spoken to before. His voice was broken up in a way that reminded Joe of a too-dramatic space captain from an old television show. "City manager, Stan, I thought I told you, that your responsibility, was to ensure, that this settlement, had a beast enclosure. An enclosure, that could breed Beefs, up to level fifteen, for meat."

"I already told you, there's no need for that right now!" Stan managed to grind out through clenched teeth, "What we *actually* need is this man right here, the *City Lord*, to-"

"You? You are, the City Lord? Finally! Perhaps we can, finally get some, actual work done." There was an oversized clipboard in the strange Dwarf's hand, and he flipped a page over, tapped the top of the list, and ran his finger down until he found what he was looking for. "The first step, in the standard operating procedure, when meeting a new City Lord, is to give him a handshake—then congratulate him, on attaining, the city lordship position."

"With that in mind, congratulations, on attaining, the city lordship position." The Dwarf shot his hand out and waited for Joe to shake it. Joe waited, and waited, but the hand didn't move, nor did the Dwarf speak again until he took the proffered limb. As soon as he did, Checkoff pumped down once, dropped Joe's hand like it was a snake, and pointed at the list once again. "Step number two, is to introduce myself, and what my job is. Hello, City Lord Joe, I am Lord Checkoff, and I'm here—to assess your city readiness."

"Nice to meet-"

"As I'm sure you know, there is a clear-cut set of rules, and regulations, that you will need to follow, if you desire to advance, your current Hamlet of a settlement to a Village, then to a Town, then to a proper City. If I find, that you are unwilling, or unable, to perform the duties, at a comprehensive level, I will reject your application for lordship, though you may remain, in the Legion, indefinitely. Often, those who pursue military matters, are not well prepared for the maintenance, and duties, required of someone, who is leading people, who are not marching to war."

Joe had his hackles up, but the man spoke in such a clinical, overdramatized tone that there was simply no way to take his words as anything other than base truth. Trying to buy himself some time to get a handle on the situation, the Reductionist studied the Dwarf more carefully. Checkoff was clearly an oddity, based simply upon the manner in which he interacted with the people around him. There was more to it, though: physically, he was unlike most other Dwarves that Joe had met.

First of all, the man was clearly of high Nobility, simply based on the fact that he had a full head of hair in addition to a well-kempt beard. Unlike what Joe considered natural colors, his hair was a surprising shade of green. It could have been due to some kind of dye, but that was unlikely, as it was not only his facial and head hair, but also his eyebrows and eyelashes. Finally, something that truly grabbed his attention was that the Dwarf was wearing square-framed glasses.

Ever since he had entered this world, Joe had only ever seen one group of people that wore glasses. "Lord Checkoff, is there any chance that you have a... Scholar profession?"

Checkoff looked Joe directly in the eyes and nodded firmly. "Indeed I do, and yes, I have received notice, that we are supposed, to work against you, at every juncture. That I am supposed to go, out of my way, to ensure you fail, no matter what your task is."

"So...?" Joe gestured to the town around them while Stan's jaw dropped.

"Oh. No, you do not need to worry, right now." Checkoff shook his head in frustration. "You see, Mister *Occultist*, petty revenge against you, on behalf of the Society of Scholars, is so far down the list, that it would take until the end of two, or three, of your human natural life spans, for me to get around to it. I have my doubts, that you will be anywhere, under my power at that time. Yet, unless the Society, fills out the proper forms, to replace their edict against you, when I do get to that point, on the list… my assault against you, will be vicious, and sudden."

Joe stared at the clipboard that the Dwarf was wielding as though it were a sword and shield in one. For all he knew, it very well could have been an artifact that was even more deadly than the bureaucracy that the Dwarf was trying to drown him in. Before the human could think of a rebuttal, Checkoff continued, "Before any further, construction happens, you *must* build a town hall: a City Center. Without that, you will not, be able to properly regulate trade, showcase your trade goods, or resurrect fallen civilians."

"That was my plan-" Joe was cut off as Checkoff continued barreling down his list of talking points.

"One of the things, that I am quite impressed by, is the sheer number of people, which you have managed to draw, to the area. I do not think, I have ever seen, so many crafters practically *sprint*, to a new location, such as this." The Dwarf peered over the top of his glasses. "Perhaps it has something to do, with every single building being, at least, Uncommon? Do you know, what you have *done*, to the Legion? They are always very careful, to keep the barracks they have, as Common at the maximum. The troops in this area, have already ignored a request, for them to return to their standard positions."

"Ah." Joe was not going to apologize for improving someone's quality of life, so he decided to go for the nostalgia play. "I remember all too well how different it was when civilian contractors were in charge of creating lodging. There was actual comfort involved. Well then, please make sure to inform Stan of anything you need to tell us about, otherwise I will be off in the distance building a… town hall."

Joe hurried away from the incredibly efficient and simultaneously hostile Dwarf that was going to be... grading his performance? He knew if he stayed any longer, he would be pulled down into the sea of red tape and likely forced to go see this world's version of a PowerPoint. On his way to the location which the map helpfully indicated that he would be constructing his Guildhall, Joe glanced to the side and saw his table... except it was a beautiful sculpture of a table, instead of the blocky monstrosity he had left behind.

"Hey! Who set my table?" Joe pinched his nose as he rethought his wording. "Who finished crafting my table?"

"What do you expect to happen when you are gone for days at a time and just leave sad little projects like this behind?" Havoc's gruff voice reached Joe's ears as a cloud of purple cigar smoke engulfed his face. "I walked by that pitiful disaster at least a half-dozen times every couple hours. Every single pass, it was a reminder that someone had just started a project out in the open and expected no one to mess with it. Well, *I* messed with it! Finish what you start!"

"I was going to, but then *you* threw me in the garbage!" Joe growled at the Grandmaster Sculptor. "Aren't you supposed to be *teaching* me, not messing with my projects, my town, and *me*?"

"Just taught you." Havoc's right eye twitched as he searched for any severe wounds on his Apprentice. "Finish what you start, make sure you have enough resources before you start a project, and stay on task. That's *three* life lessons. It's not my fault if you don't understand what I'm trying to teach. If I just *tell* you the information in a clear, accessible way, any random passerby would be getting the same information, as well as the bonuses from having a Grandmaster as their teacher. *They* didn't pay for it! *You* paid for the full service by saving my daughter and myself!"

"How do I get a refund?" Joe muttered softly enough it may as well have been internal dialogue. He didn't *actually* want that. Speaking in a normal tone of voice, he addressed his mentor slightly more respectfully, albeit grudgingly. "I thought up some plans for the city, and I was hoping to run them by someone I trusted. Would you mind-"

"I'm too busy to-"

"-finding Jaxon for me?" As Joe finished his question, Havoc slowly crossed his arms and gave his human the evil eye. The Reductionist chuckled nervously and waved his hands. "Joking, I'm just joking! Do you *want* to take a look at this? I thought you might be interested to watch the town hall go up."

"Why not? I'll just be checking your status sheet to make sure that you have been making the gains that you need. If you haven't, I've devised some excellent... training... both for your characteristics, and your skills." The Dwarf's next statement confirmed that Joe had not gotten off the hook for his little 'joke'. "In fact, I'm thinking you have psionic potential, which means that if we can raise your Mana Manipulation and Coalescence to a high enough level, you might be able to lift a three-ton boulder with your mind. Of course, we need to run a baseline control test. What we're gonna do is see how much you can slow it down as I drop it on-"

Joe hurried to interrupt before the vindictive Dwarf could finish his thought and cement his Apprentice's destruction in his own mind. "Those two skills! Yes! I have questions for you about both of them. I was creating an array with the aspects that I've collected, and I noticed that as Mental Manipulation increased in skill level, I was able to fill in the requisite areas much easier, which was especially noticeable going around curves and tricky movements. For Coalescence, I only earned one increase to the skill while I was working, but it seemed to become easier to move the aspects. Do you have any idea why that would be?"

"You don't even have a basic education when it comes to mana, do you?" Havoc started chewing on his cigar, something that Joe had learned to associate with a bad time incoming. "Do you know why *any* mage with any kind of mentor, teacher, or book to learn from must learn those two skills?"

"I'm *assuming* it's because higher-level skills cost more

mana?" Joe offered up with a weak grin, getting a head shake as a reply. "But there must be more to it?"

"Mana cost factors in." Havoc started walking, and Joe hurried to keep up, even though his legs were nearly twice the length of the Dwarfs. "Let me put it like this. You can be an Expert spellcaster with the deepest of mana pools. You could generate amazing spells, send the masses running from you in terror at your capabilities... but you wouldn't even be able to deal a *single point* of damage to a Master."

That sounded fairly suspect, and Joe called him out on it. "Are the differences between the ranks *really* that different?"

"Yes. They are. The difference between the two is easy to quantify: a Master can do ten times as much with half of the mana. They can alter spell diagrams on the fly and are able to *precisely* customize the way they want to destroy or elevate the entirety of the Zone they are living on, if they so desire. Abyssal *cheese* has done it in the past, but it was..." Havoc paused, and a strange look crossed his face before he shook it off and hid behind a fresh cigar. "Ignore that last part. Look, kid. You can control mana all you want with Mana Manipulation, but without enough density behind your power, you won't be able to make energy flow in sufficient quantities to cast a Master spell or alter an Expert's attack."

"If there's a single thing you need to take away from this conversation," Havoc reached over and tried to burn Joe with his cigar to make sure that he was listening. Joe dodged the scorching stub, glaring as the Dwarf shrugged and finished his thought, "Those skills aren't just about earning a higher number on your mana bar. In the higher ranks, they are *literally* the two factors that determine whether you have the mental strength and focus to be *able* to cast high-tier spells. They need to be a major focus for you."

"In that case... can you help me with these skills?"

Havoc perused Joe's status sheet. "You've got one at Student, and one just reached Journeyman. Impressive, and good work. Journeyman is the benchmark for truly starting your training, even though *usually* it would just be under a Master, not a *Grandmaster* like myself. You got the mindset; all you need is the tools—and I've got the tools you need. In fact, many people even call *me* the sharpest tool on the Christmas tree!"

Joe swallowed his rebuttal and simply gave the Dwarf a thumbs-up.

CHAPTER THIRTY-FIVE

"I have a proposal to make this way more dramatic than it needs to be," Joe told the group of volunteers who showed up to help him install the Guildhall. "I just want to make sure that everyone is on board with having some fun with this project."

There were several smirks all around as everyone nodded. Only one person was shaking his head, but Havoc wasn't about to stop the human from having his fun. Seeing that the group was on board, Joe guided them all into position for fabricating the Guildhall, then showed off his prepared Ritual of the Ghostly Army. "Look here, everyone. What I'm going to do is make a giant fog bank inside this volcano. It's going to substantially boost the humidity for a few moments, but my water-collection rituals will turn it all back into water pretty quickly. No need to worry about it being an issue for any length of time."

"I can confirm that piping and water collection sites have been set up while you were gone! Any excess water will flow to them without issue. Stan had you pay for it and everything," Bauen called from his position in the second ring of volunteers.

Joe's finger shot out and he pointed at the Dwarf, switching it to a thumbs-up after a moment.

"Totally forgot that was an important thing to factor in! Without you, I might have just flooded our pretty new town!" Joe's response made the gathered people chuckle, as though he *wasn't* completely serious. "Everyone ready? Make sure not to move, otherwise you might miss out on being part of the ritual."

Without another word, Joe tossed his ritual diagram in the air, where it expanded into a massive cloud of fog that filled the entirety of the empty Shoe in moments. Sound began to act strangely, shapes appeared in the fog that Joe knew were not actually there, and the heat began to intensify as the fog started boiling away nearly immediately. Sweat tried to form on his body, but his Neutrality Aura wiped it away without issue.

He activated the next ritual in the sequence, the one that would pull up the Guildhall from practically nothing. Soon, mana and aspects were pouring into the ritual diagram, and the outline of the building slowly became filled in with matter. The construction process went off without a hitch. Joe had collected plenty of materials for the Uncommon building, the people in the area had a good understanding of what they needed to do to help him, and the ground had already been cleared for the work.

The dense fog stopped pouring out of the ritual, clearing away to reveal the shiny new building that would allow them to have diplomatic relations not only with their own people, but allies and potentially even enemies. Joe dismissed the message informing him that reputation had been paid out of his account to the people that were working with him. He didn't mind, not one little bit. "*Feces*, it's nice to work around professionals again. Is it weird that I started to miss people when I was down in the dump?"

"Why were you down in the dumps, buddy?" Jaxon called as he strode in to take a look at the new structure. "Your good friend Jaxon is here to help you become more well-adjusted to this new world! What can I do for you today: back, neck, shift your entire *abyssal spine*? Hold the gramophone… is it just me, or does this building look familiar?"

Most of the people in the area had flinched when Jaxon's voice took on a snarl, but Joe knew that it was simply his terrible dump stat of charisma coming into play. "It *should* look familiar; this is as close as possible to a clone of the Guildhall we built on Midgard."

"That was amazing! How cool is this place? I knew coming here was the right idea. That flier was really on point!" As Joe and Jaxon were speaking, a few people Joe had never seen before—a Dwarf and a human—wandered past, discussing what was going on in the world. The human was far too loud and wildly over-exuberant. "Looks like the show is over, but still… too cool."

There was nothing like a little bit of random admiration to really make a day happier, and even as his chest puffed up in pride, Joe tried not to look like he was listening to the practically shouted conversation. But it seemed like his moment in the sun had passed. They were already on a different topic.

"Did you hear about what happened near the border? The Oligarchy just took over two different small fortress towns in retaliation for the Elves grabbing a bunch of land!"

"*Fe~eces*, how are they going to fortify that, Bro?" The Dwarf held up his hand to stop the answer, deciding to make his own production instead. "Dude, I bet they just burn those two towns to the ground and walk away."

"How'd you *know*?" The human laughed, and their conversation faded as they walked away.

"Next time, if people just stand around and watch these go up, I'm going to charge them for the show if they aren't participating. Maybe we can get some bakers and street vendors to sell food and trinkets at the same time?" Joe shook his head at the peanut gallery's enthusiasm for destruction, knowing exactly how time-consuming and resource-intensive it was to bring buildings up to a livable standard. "Yeesh… it's hard to think that people are going to come here and try to destroy this town at some point."

"That's why we need to get you working on defensive systems!" Havoc grabbed Joe's arm and began dragging him into the newly built Guildhall. "Now that you have a town hall, you can *officially* set permissions, instead of 'delegating'. Go in there, designate Stan as your stand-in, and let's go practice your skills by devising new and interesting ways to destroy your enemies! I've got a great idea on how we can condense your mana further-"

"You already told me about the three-ton boulder; the answer is still no," Joe told the Dwarf curtly. "Please just give me a normal training method."

"How do you expect to grow if you don't take risks?" Havoc shook his head in disappointment. "Do you want me to send you to the warfront? Combat *is* by far the best way to increase your skills. Plus, we are on the precipice of an all-out war right now. If the Oligarchy gets their way, we're going to invade based on having an entire extra army compared to the Elves. All they have going for them is territory, and we can grind that out under our boots. Is that the sort of training you're hoping for?"

"No, what I'm hoping for is the ability..." Joe started tweaking the Guildhall's settings, "...to do amazing things and change the bad ending that is coming for an entire people."

Are you sure that you want to set 'Unnamed Hamlet' as a spawn point for members of the guild 'The Wanderers'? Linking a spawn point for your guild will allow potentially racially-unaligned members to spawn and tele-port into your town. Yes / No.

Joe accepted the bind point for his guild, setting a rule that would allow him to see who came in, who left, and if anyone granted access to another person. Of course, that would only work if they came through via teleportation, or resurrecting here after dying.

Then Joe did something that he had never tried before, as he had never needed to speak to his entire Guild at once.

Accessing the chat feature, he paid reputation to send a message to his current Zone, and a fee of gold to extend it back to Midgard. "Guild members of The Wanderers. I am Joe, the first Elder of what will one day be The Wanderers sect. For your information, I have created a guild-specific neutral town in the Dwarven territories. You will be able to spawn here upon riding the Bifrost; you will also be able to teleport here. Please note that if you do not follow the rules of the town, the large number of Dwarves present will quickly enforce the law."

He mused over what else to say, finally deciding on, "My goal with creating this town is to find a way to eliminate the hostilities between the Elves and the Dwarves entirely without bloodshed. The end of the Wolfman War soured me toward creating a Shattered race, and I would much prefer not to be a part of such wholesale slaughter ever again. If anyone in the guild knows of a way that we can attain peace, please contact me immediately."

Joe felt pretty good about that message, so he sent it and turned his attention to learning what other things he could do. One feature caught his eye immediately: as he had created a Guildhall on behalf of his guild, and if each Zone was only allowed one Guildhall, he could set a tax rate that would pull in money from all guild members on the zone, regardless of whether they were a part of the Dwarven faction or the Elven faction. He set the rate to eight percent, which was lower than the ten percent rate that had been set back on Midgard.

"Now I can set up a trade city that can deal in both Elven and Dwarven goods, while also acting as a currency exchange," he mumbled to himself before setting a few other small options such as rights, privileges, delegations, and laws for the town. As soon as he was done, he glanced to the side and noticed that Havoc was tapping his foot on the ground impatiently.

"Yes, yes, I *understand*. I will not take him away again. Not without notifying you, at least." The Dwarf was growling under his breath, clearly unhappy that he needed to make a compromise with anyone.

"Who are you talking to?" As soon as the question left Joe's mouth, a feeling of dread came over him and he looked back and to the left. "O-oh, you were speaking to Major Cleave. That's a normal thing to do, so of course you were. I just thought you were talking to me. I *certainly* realized that she has been standing next to me since I returned to the Shoe."

"Enough flirting, you two." Havoc tapped at the air in front of him. "Apprentice, why haven't you completed this class quest? The ritu-whatever. The builder one."

"The one that requires me to do a bunch of research? I haven't gotten a chance to get to a library since I got *onto* this Zone, so how am I supposed to-"

"Hold the calculator... what do you mean, you need to 'do research'? Don't you only use aspects and rituals to build your stuff?" Havoc's protest made Joe blink in surprise, and he slowly opened his quest log. As he stared at the progress bar, it rapidly ticked up until it displayed one hundred percent.

Class quest complete: Apprentice Rituarchitect. Research percentage: 100%. Reward: +2 to all stats! Record-breaker reward: You have completed this quest faster than any other Rituarchitect in history! You have gained access to Apprentice Rituarchitect II!

"Well? Explain yourself!" Havoc barked at Joe, who couldn't physically answer at the moment.

You have crossed the threshold for Strength! Try not to move as your muscles increase in density!

You have crossed the threshold for Dexterity! Your body will automatically begin testing your fast and slow-twitch muscles to ensure the incoming upgrade is successful!

"Ughgh." Joe gurgled as the conflicting messages hit his system, resulting in a mini-seizure that left him twitching on the ground.

Havoc kicked him in the chest, sending him sliding across the floor. "I asked you a question, Apprentice; I didn't tell you to make a puddle of drool!"

Joe hit the wall, his Exquisite Shell shattered, and everything went dark.

"...there are many schools of thought on that subject, but the overall agreement is that *no*, there is no single factor that works for physical skills in the same way that Mana Manipulation and Coalescence do for magical skills." Havoc's hushed voice, which Joe only now realized had been droning on into his ears for an unknown length of time, abruptly cut off as he realized that Joe was officially awake. "Hey there, sport! Looks like you took a nasty rockin' to the noggin!"

You have been taught the hard truths of the world by a Grandmaster for the last hour.

Skill increase: Retaliation of Shadows (Journeyman VI -> Journeyman IX).

Skill increase: Mana Manipulation (Student VI -> Student VII).

Skill increase: Mental Manipulation Resistance (Beginner II -> Beginner VIII).

"Were you teaching me in my sleep?" Joe groggily inquired as his Neutrality Aura reactivated and started clearing up his post-unconscious brain fog. "Why was I out for an entire hour?"

"You should stop asking questions." Havoc looked to the side, a small smile on his face, and refused to answer any more questions along that line. "By the way, you should take a gander at the sheer number of permanent residents rushing into this little town of yours. I put out some feelers, and it turns out a whole bunch of people are willing to relocate if a Grandmaster is offering classes once a month for residents."

Joe did not need to check his town statistics in order to understand exactly how many people that would draw. "Havoc, I understand that I managed to complete your assumed-impossible quest and so forth... but why are you going to all of this trouble to help me extensively, while simultaneously throwing me into situations I'm unprepared for?"

"I have my reasons." Havoc offered a hand and pulled Joe to his feet. "The main thing is, the fewer people that know what I'm actually doing, the better. You have a lot of eyes on you, and now you've earned a babysitter from both the Legion and the Oligarchy. You also apparently don't understand what it *means* when I call you 'Apprentice', so let me clearly explain it to you. As my Apprentice, if something were to permanently happen to me, you would be in charge of all of my holdings, including intellectual properties, blueprints, templates, all that fun stuff."

The Reductionist did not know how to respond to the strange openness he was receiving, but before he could think of something to say, Havoc finished his explanation. "So, I need to make sure that you are trained and prepared to protect those things until I am back on my feet. As to what I am doing around the town; let's just say I'm preparing some contingencies for when your plans to achieve peace blow up in your face."

Whumpf!

"The town is under attack!" a voice called out just as a fire started in the 'Orange' sector, the housing sector. Joe started running toward the sounds of battle, but before he took even a dozen steps, everything went quiet.

Your Hamlet has defeated an assault by the Elven-aligned troops!

Quest updated: Ranker II Peerage. Major Elven incursions fended off: 2/5!

"What just happened?" Joe bellowed as he slid to a stop.

Havoc started laughing at the confusion pouring off the human, "Private security from over a hundred high-rank crafters that flooded the area is what just happened! Congratulations, your town has a personal army you don't even have to pay! Let's get over to your Workshop; for the next two weeks, you are studying under my personal tutelage. I'm definitely not trying to keep you away from my secret projects that are going on under your nose and need another two weeks to complete."

"Ah... Havoc, I can understand sarcasm, and you're not even being subtle-"

"Come with me *now*, or miss out!" Havoc started marching into the purple light district, where only Joe's lonely workshop currently stood.

Jaxon suddenly came sprinting into the area, searching around wildly. "Joe! You didn't blow up! But I heard an explosion? How is that possible? *Gasp!* The town must be under attack!"

Joe groaned while simultaneously trying not to laugh. His reputation was starting to get the better of him, and he decided in that instant that he should just give up and roll with it. "Everything's fine, Jaxon. It's already over. Also… thanks for being a good friend."

CHAPTER THIRTY-SIX

Two weeks went by in a flash, if a flash consisted of sleepless nights, intense training, and a relentless instructor. After those two weeks, Havoc finally said that enough was enough. Apparently, there was only so much that could be trained before Joe needed to go out and get real world experience. According to the Dwarf, until he had a long break, the tutelage he received from that point forward would be less than half as effective.

On the fifteenth day after they had begun, Joe slept for a solid eleven hours. When he finally managed to pry his crusty eyelids apart, he pulled up his characteristic sheet and skills, condensing all the changes as much as possible before reading through them. A single glance was enough to let him know that the crash course had all been worth it.

During the training, Joe had reached the threshold in Constitution, Wisdom, and Perception, allowing him to last longer in training each day, notice more details, and better understand the knowledge that saturated nearly every word Havoc spoke.

Name: Joe 'Major-General Pyrrhic, Noble Candidate for Baron' Class: Reductionist
Profession I: Arcanologist (Max)
Profession II: Ritualistic Alchemist (1/20)
Profession III: Grandmaster's Apprentice I (14/25)
Profession IV: None.

Characteristic: Raw score: (Changes since previous marker)

Strength: 158 (+7)
Dexterity: 161 (+9)
Constitution: 152 (+6)
Intelligence (bound): 169 (+10)
Wisdom: 153 (+9)
Dark Charisma: 102 (-1)
Perception: 155 (+13)
Luck: 85
Karmic Luck: 3

Skill increase: Acid Spray, Words of Power (Written), Magical Matrices, Hidden Sense, Polearm Mastery, Natural Magical Material Creation, Ritualistic Forging, Spellbinding, Somatic Ritual Casting , Alchemical Lore, Enchanting Lore, Knowledge and Ritual Lore have reached (Student 0)!
Enchanted Ritual Circles, Enchanting (General) have reached Beginner V!
Battle Meditation has reached Apprentice 0!
Battle Meditation has reached Student 0!
As these skills have been increased using the Grandmaster's Apprentice profession, no additional bonuses can be applied or granted.

Joe had never seen such a massive increase in such a short amount of time. There were only a few reasons it was even possible. First, a Grandmaster had taken him as his direct Apprentice. Apparently, a Grandmaster could only have one designated Apprentice every decade.

The Reductionist shook his head as he remembered how he hadn't even thought that being called an Apprentice was a 'big deal'. It had felt like a nickname; abyss, the crotchety old Dwarf alternated between a half-dozen ways of referring to him, and most were less than complimentary!

Second, the Grandmaster needed to spend nearly the entire day directly training a single *Apprentice* rank skill with him. It didn't matter if the skill itself was at level zero or level nine; after one full day of training the skill or spell, it would increase directly to 'Student' rank. Joe had insisted on spending one of the days on his Enchanting and Enchanted Ritual Circles skills, and found himself deeply regretting what he now considered to be a waste of his potential Profession benefits.

They had originally planned to stop after thirteen days, but it just so happened that the constant stress Havoc kept Joe under had put the human in a semi-permanent state of flight or fight mode. His Battle Meditation skill had increased just enough to cross into Apprentice rank, and the Dwarf had decided it was worth boosting to Student rank.

Stretching out on his bed, luxuriating in the fact that he had nothing that he needed to do today, Joe suddenly went perfectly still as he felt ten tiny blades dig into his chest. His eyes slowly trailed from the ceiling down to his own body, where his blue eyes met with a pair of yellow ones. He started sweating profusely as True Damage began reducing his health bar at a rapid rate. "Cleocatra…! I wasn't trying to get rid of you, or hide from you, I swear! I even have—look over there—I have food and drinks ready for you! I just had no idea how to-"

"Meow." The queen of the Nyandrathals slowly retracted her claws, not bothering to acknowledge the blood that was beading up on his chest. She leaped away from him, transforming into a diminutive, if strikingly beautiful, human. "I saw all of that, and of *course* you would not know where to find me. The pain was because you only bothered to think of me *once* in the last several weeks; nearly a month! I know this because we have already bonded somewhat. Whenever you think of me, I get a notification. No, I simply didn't bother to come here before because it wasn't worth traveling to this backwater you own. Now that there are some amenities, however..."

Her voice trailed off with a purr, and Joe realized that she was once more a cat. Just then, there was a knock on the door and Major Cleave barged in. "I heard voices! Is there someone here? Are you under attack? I swear, the *second* I step out to get some fresh avocado-"

"Just talking to my... cat." Joe explained lamely as he gestured at Cleocatra.

Cleave looked between the human and the cat on the floor, slowly shaking her head. "No. I refuse to allow this. You are nowhere *near* responsible enough to be trusted with a pet. That elemental you've got would've died of neglect if it were a living being that didn't subsist off of the dregs of mana pouring off of you."

"*Thank* you, Major Cleave." Joe directed three of his Ritual Orbs in front of the Dwarf, catching her by surprise and shoving her out the door. He reached over and locked it just before she could push her way back in. "Is there anything I can do for you, um, kitty?"

There was a note on his bed that simply stated: *Don't worry about me; I'll just be following you around and helping whenever I feel you need my assistance.*

PS: Some of your guild members are waiting for you but are detained at your Guildhall.

PPS: Find a way to bring me some fresh fish.

PSPS...

"Psps? What else did you want to-" Joe was knocked over as the cat went sprinting around the room because of the sound he made. "This is why I'm a dog person, you weird *cat*! You creatures make no sense at all! Cleave, I'm leaving!"

"*Help* me, the cat says it'll do. More like blow my face off at every turn and wreck my stuff." Joe opened the door and strode boldly through the halls of the Uncommon apartment building. He reached the exit and stepped into the open, then lurched to a halt. "Cleave, why is there a wall standing in the middle of my town?"

"I believe that is where anyone unaffiliated with the Dwarves is allowed to go," the Major stated calmly. "There are signs posted inside informing all... *visitors*... that if they go outside of that section, they will be subject to the laws of the Oligarchy. The current laws state that anyone found to be Elven-affiliated will be slain on the spot."

"How charming." Joe shivered as he started to realize why there may have never been a chance for diplomacy before. "I'm assuming Stan set that up?"

There was no need for an answer, so the human simply hurried along to the newly erected building. As soon as he stepped inside and saw familiar faces, a large grin couldn't be held back. "Aten! You're here! How have you—wait, why are you under guard? I know you joined the Dwarves...?"

"I did." The Guild Commander reached out for a hand-shake. "I'm just here to make sure none of the others get attacked. I know the Dwarves can be a little over-enthusiastic when there's a chance to get, ah, 'preemptive revenge'. You remember Sub-Commander Mike, of course? We made a plan when we were getting on the Bifrost to make sure to join in on opposite sides of this conflict."

"Good to see you, Joe!" Mike waved at him, and for some reason, Joe felt a little sick to his stomach, slightly disgusted with the man in front of him. It must have shown on his face, because Mike appeared slightly crestfallen. "I had hoped... well, now we know. It's like that for everyone, as far as I can tell. If everyone is sickened just being in the room with each other, I have no idea how peace talks are going to break out all over the place."

"I *told* you, Mike, I have a plan." Aten waved Joe over and they all sat down at the table together. "I'm not sure about you guys, but after our Guild played an instrumental role in taking down the Wolfman King, the way their people were treated after the fact disgusted me to no end."

"You mean how they lost all protection for their young, and people were given massive bounties to hunt them all down like feral dogs?" Joe snorted at the memory. "Yeah, I was just talking to someone about that the other day. I have no interest in seeing that happen here. Elves, Dwarves; they are both fantasy creatures to me, even now. I want to be able to learn from both of them. It sucks that we needed to choose sides."

"I don't know what you have been up to that allows you to own a town like this, Joe," Mike chimed in, waving around at the clearly magical town that was somehow surviving within an active volcano. "Even more, I have no idea how they allowed you to get away with trying to make a neutral town. But I have really good news: I already have the king and queen of the Elves ready to come to negotiations. All we need to do is find a way to ensure that they are protected while we parley, and that they will be respected properly."

"That's going to be pretty hard to pull off." Aten tapped at the marble table as he softly muttered, "We can easily make both sides sign a magically-binding Armistice order, but treating each other with respect? It is literally a racial trait for both of them to see the other side as the most disgusting beings they can imagine. I'm told it actually gets worse as you get to a higher level."

Tap. Tap. Tap. The Guild Commander's finger bouncing off the polished stone surface was starting to get annoying, but it also drew Joe's eye down onto the furnishing itself. He already had planned to place an enchantment on the table, specifically the enchantment he had received from Occultatum for reaching 'Cleric' level twelve on Midgard: Zone of Circumlocution. He just had not realized how important it would be to actually succeed at inscribing it.

"I may have a solution, but I'm going to need some time." Joe shared the information on one of the only enchantments he was guaranteed to know, sending the summary directly to their notifications. "All the way back then, I thought it was a bad reward, that I squandered that improvement. At the time, it was going to be nearly impossible to create this enchantment. Some of the requirements for it, materials such as culturally important items, would have needed to be stolen from museums or private collections."

Mike read a portion of the information aloud. "You create a thirty-foot-radius zone. Beings within the zone that attempt to say something rude, vulgar, or hostile are compelled to say something positive instead. This effect extends to any text which includes rude, vulgar, or hostile language."

"This is perfect!" Aten was already chuckling with gleeful anticipation as he took over. "Looks like creatures who attempt to make rude gestures end up making a similar but friendly gesture. Paintings and drawings which would be considered vulgar change to become wholesome. Oh, this part is going to be important. Since this enchantment doesn't prevent hostile actions, we'll need to figure out private security and such so that people don't attempt to take matters into their own hands outside of official attempts at reconciliation."

"This is… I guess I'm not an enchanter, but to me this looks really advanced." Mike tapped on the strange diagram that was hovering in front of his face. "Do you think you can figure this out in a reasonable amount of time?"

"It's not about figuring it out." Joe cracked his knuckles and rolled his head back and forth. "It's all about sitting down and *doing* the work. I can make it happen, but since you are correct that it is a pretty advanced enchantment, I'm going to need a solid few weeks to knock it out."

"Take a month," Aten ordered him easily, a glint of reflected light coming from his mouth. "It's not going to be easy to get the heads of the Oligarchy and the King and Queen of the Theocracy in the same spot. You've got time."

"We know you can do it. You literally have a silver tongue." Mike slapped the Guild Commander on the shoulder, making all the Dwarves in the room tense up. "Even if you have to buy, beg, or steal, I know you can *invent* a reason for them to be here if you gotta."

The tension in the room started increasing rapidly. Joe leaned forward and whispered, "Mike... move your hand away. *Slowly.*"

CHAPTER THIRTY-SEVEN

Joe was still a Beginner at Enchanting, which made it *highly* unlikely that he would be able to figure out all of the intricacies of a Journeyman-level enchantment designed to force people to act a certain way in time for a meeting of heads of state. At best, the power of the enchantment would push them to be *cordial*, though not as overtly friendly as it would force people that were at a lower power level.

On the plus side, there were still a few options available to him: Joe could hire someone to do it, he could get Havoc to do it, or he could figure out how to translate the diagram over to a ritual that could make the enchantment for him. All of these options had certain drawbacks. The first option was out for sure; hiring someone to create a Journeyman-level enchantment as a rush order, let alone on a large object, was astoundingly and *impossibly* expensive.

"Apparently I should be charging *way* more for my services than I currently am." Joe scoffed as he perused the various options available to him from the Crafters that had come to live in the area. "Probably not a good idea to ask Havoc to do the work either; I don't think a single person would feel safe sitting down at that table. Certainly not the Elves, so that option is no longer... on the table."

Joe wiped away a tear of mirth as he chuckled at his own joke. "Ahh... so anyway, that leaves me with only one real option. I've got to figure out a way to do this work myself. I'm twenty-five skill levels away from being able to perform the enchantment directly, but I figure that a mid-level Expert in ritual circles with experience converting enchantments into ritual diagrams should have no trouble with this at all, right?"

"Yoo-hoo!" Jaxon started pounding on the door to Joe's workshop, not letting up until Joe met his eyes through the tiny window. "All work and no play makes you boring to interact with! Come kill things with me; I have new stuff to show you!"

"But I *am* having fun, I'm playing with magic! This is what fun looks like to me." Joe gestured to his finally-completed ritual that was working on converting cores to Mana Batteries. "Besides, I'm not going anywhere until my weapons are working again."

"Joe, buddy, *friend*... open the door so I can convince you *in person*!" Jaxon demanded, his fingernails scratching at the wooden obstacle hard enough to deal damage. "I found a super fun nest of two-headed turkeys that I'm *itching* to get at. I figure we tear them up until only a few are left, capture some breeding pairs after they are properly tamed, and then I can practice and teach my beast-taming skills when I don't have to work on Chiropractic things!"

"What kind of Chiropractic things do you work on?" Joe called in reply, wincing as the ritual behind him completed and a brand-new fully-operational Mana Battery *thunked* to the table. He tried to stealthily move in front of it, but Jaxon was not having any of *that*.

"Mostly my days are filled with *twisting people* that tried to get out of having fun with me!" Jaxon roared as he scrabbled at the door even harder. Even knowing that it was just his Charisma acting up, Joe still flinched away as though he were facing the zombies in the landfill again. "Looks like you *are* ready, so come on! *Turkeys!*"

"Ugh… fine!" Joe grabbed the glowing stone and checked it for any flaws. Finding no issues, he popped open his icicle Ritual Orb and switched the mostly-empty core for the full battery. "Give me just a minute!"

Ritual Orb of Intelligence. Spell trapped within: Cone of Cold. Bound Core Power remaining: 20,000/20,000 Cost per spell use: 195.

"*Now* let's see if I run out of power in the middle of a fight." Joe tossed the Orb into the air, where it gracefully floated next to two others. He rubbed at his wrists, which felt fairly naked without the control cuffs that he had worn since he had first gotten his Ritual Orbs. With his Battle Meditation at the Student ranks, he had earned a sixty percent bonus to controlling his exotic weapons.

By taking off the control cuffs, Assisted Ritual Orb Usage had automatically upgraded to Combat Ritual Orbs; but the skill level had fallen to Beginner zero. Even so, it was worth it to start empowering the skills that he needed for long-term combat.

Combat Ritual Orbs (Exotic)(Beginner 0): This skill dictates the ease of use for the weapon 'Ritual Orbs'. Each skill <u>rank</u> allows for the skillful use of one Ritual Orb. Each skill level increases damage dealt by 2n%. Damage dealt by non-skillfully used Ritual Orbs is set at 75%.

Even with the reduction in total combat power, Joe was still happy to know that his skills were increasing in a way that seemed consistent and gave him concrete goals. It was also nice to be able to have his wrists free again and still be able to use his weapons. Frankly, he had been somewhat worried that as soon as he took off the control cuffs, it was going to be nigh impossible for him to induce the exotic weapons to work properly.

"Fine, buddy. Let's go out and hunt some turkeys." Joe longingly eyed his workshop and equipment, remembering at the last moment to drop another core into the ritual so that it could begin the next conversion process. "These are birds, right? You are not using some kind of slang for Elves or gullible people, are you?"

"It's kind of hard to use beast taming on something that isn't a beast, Joe!" Jaxon was clapping his hands and dancing in place as he watched his friend gear up to join him. "I don't think I've ever had the chance to fight side-by-side with Major Cleave before! Sure, we *have* been in the same combat, even the same battle, but I don't think we've ever tried out our personal teamwork! It should be fun to see which one of us can take down or capture more of the small creatures! Personally, I like to *rip them apart!*"

"Want to try that last sentence again?" Joe offered without missing a beat, smirking as Major Cleave's eyes widened fractionally; her version of absolute shock and horror.

"What do you mean?" Jaxon's brow furrowed as he looked between the pair. "I said 'my preference would be to capture as many as possible', so how much clearer do you need me to be? I can't even think of how I would say that differently? Really, Joe, if I'm going to learn their anatomy and how best to adjust them for rapid growth and usage in various ways for the betterment of this town, outright killing them is… counterproductive."

"Totally understood!" Joe glanced at his Dwarven babysitter and smiled politely. "Are you also interested in attending? I know you'll feel like you need to go, but I kinda feel like you might like to be asked?"

"It's fine," Cleave stated shortly, her eyes slowly traveling over the mad Chiropractor. "You trust this… human?"

"I most definitely do; he's been on my team and in my life for longer than anyone else in Eternium besides my mother; and she's not much of a fighter." Joe smiled at the wildly grinning man. "I can admit after much shamefaced self-reflection that one of my worst characteristics is that I tend to leave people behind when they want to slow down and live an easier life."

"Don't be down, Joe! It's *only* hard to join in on someone else's marriage." Jaxon offered it as a consolation, but it came out disturbingly inveigling. "Maybe you could talk to Alexis and Bard and see if they—oh, you don't seem interested in listening to me, but I was *going* to say—have a spare room at their house. A room which you could live in to be close to them? Other than that, they aren't even really fighting creatures anymore. Alexis started a small shop, and Bard got a job as a class trainer and performs freelance storytelling."

As Jaxon finished speaking, the small group was joined by the hulking muscleman that was Private Kettlebell. Cleave tensed up once more and reached for her axe, but Jaxon simply continued speaking as though nothing had changed. "Poppy is working on building up an estate and looking into schooling options for his daughter. He wants to get her into an advanced class as soon as possible, and he has a few years until that really matters, but apparently every child needs to start in Midgard. So, unless you want to sit on your thumbs while I keep doing amazing things, you kinda *need* to move on when people slow down around you."

"Jaxon." Joe jerked a thumb at Kettlebell. "Is he coming with us?"

"Oh. Yes!" The limber man practically slithered over to Kettlebell's side. "My trainee is going to be learning how to do adjustments on creatures without snapping their necks! It'll be a big and very *important* step for him. A new experience, even!"

"Yo." Kettlebell nodded at Joe, then much more warmly at Cleave, who was trying to stare the huge man down unsuccessfully as he flexed his muscles at her.

Eventually, she relented and decided to try to make conversation with the huge man that she had been forced to spend time with while locked out of Joe's workshop. "I like your beard, even with as short as it is. I appreciate your attempt to fit into our culture."

"Is *that* why he keeps having to fend off the ladies!" Jaxon slapped his knee as he made the realization. "I should have learned my lesson with the Wolfmen! They're all about body language; here, it's all about hair! I'm betting I can stimulate my hair follicles to match your society better."

Seeing Jaxon start to vigorously poke and rub at his face made Joe laugh. "Come on, let's go. Jaxon. *Jaxon*! You can't just grow a beard on command. It takes-"

"Adjust!" Jaxon snapped his fingers, and a quarter inch of hair burst from his face in the same pattern that most of the male Dwarves wore. "How's that? Ooh! I gained a 'Cultural Understanding' Skill! It lets me learn about other cultures and how to blend in better!"

Joe's jaw dropped, and he shook his head in disbelief. "You have got to be *kidding* me."

"I see no goats around here, Joe." Jaxon reached over and gently pushed Joe's chin up until his mouth was fully closed. "If that's true, then how can I be kid-ding you? Enough jibber-jabber. Let's go fight Pointed Turkeys."

Kettlebell nodded enthusiastically, and Cleave *smiled* at Jaxon. Joe had to rub his eyes just to check that he wasn't seeing things. "Maybe she's uncomfortable around me for reasons I hadn't ever considered...? Maybe it's not because I have trouble remembering that she's around?"

He had spoken his thoughts aloud, even if he had been fairly quiet. Cleave leaned toward him and whispered into his ear, "Be honest with yourself. You know it's *all* of those reasons."

CHAPTER THIRTY-EIGHT

Joe was pleased and relieved to find out that the Pointed Turkeys' nesting grounds were not a terribly far distance from where one of his tunnels opened out of the Shoe. Especially at the speeds all of them could achieve on a straightaway, the others running while Joe vaulted along. There was something deeply satisfying about doing backflips over your friends as they ran along beneath you. He wasn't sure what it was; most likely some form of ingrained competitiveness that he would probably never get over.

Not when it was this fun.

"Pointed Turkeys are one of the mainstay meat animals in this area. Usually, people go ahead and let them run wild, as not only can they fly, but they tend to thrive in the wilderness. The other piece of that puzzle is that they are difficult to tame and *extremely* aggressive." Jaxon was giving a breakdown of his reasoning for going after these birds. Even though it might not affect him very much, Joe found that it was still nice to have conversation going. He had forgotten exactly how pleasant it could be to be surrounded by people, get new ideas, and learn interesting information, even if it wasn't directly applicable to himself.

Humans needed other people, no matter how much they tried to ignore that fact sometimes. Just like that, Joe felt his dream shift. A giant tower where he could study in peace and solitude until the end of time just wouldn't cut it. As the replacement dream settled in, he knew that most of the same elements remained. But there *were* new additions: people. Friends, support staff, even students. His mind still shied violently away from the idea of family there. He figured his mother was happy enough on Midgard, and he had tried the romance route once; it hadn't worked out.

"Bird!" Kettlebell called just before punting a two-headed turkey so hard that it exploded into loose feathers and flying meat. "First!"

Jaxon patted the man on his back, shaking his head slightly. "Good find! Now remember, your goal today is to hold a creature in your hands without accidentally *or* intentionally killing it. Let's work on that, yes?"

"You got it, boss." Kettlebell seemed doubtful about his ability to carry out those instructions, but his clenched fists relaxed into open palms. Joe looked at those hands, uncomfortably reminded of his first version of a table: just hard-edged slabs of stone.

"Takes a monster Chiropractor to make one, I guess?" Joe softly chuckled under his breath as he brushed away the few feathers that drifted down to rest on his shoulders as the group came to a full stop. "Jaxon, 'Pointed' Turkey just means that any sharp object kills it just fine, right?"

"You know it!" Jaxon gave the Reductionist a double thumbs-up before dropping to the ground and scuttling into the long grass like an oversized crab. "I'm going searching for eggs; let me know if you need anything from me!"

Two-headed turkeys sounded like they should be an easy type of prey, since the birds that Joe knew of were animals not known for their intelligence. Here, though? He wasn't sure what to expect. So, when the first of the feathery fiends burst out of the grass with a shock-inducing *gobble, gobble*, he sent his Ritual Orb in, and then *through* it as hard as he could manage.

Damage dealt: 168 penetrating cold!

His next Orb hit for the same amount in blunt damage, then the third hit for only one hundred and twenty-six, though that was enough to send the turkey flying. It hit the grass, its wings spread open, then forced itself upright and eyed Joe with one head, spitting out blood with the other. It wiped a wing across its beak, noticed the bloodstain, then charged at the human who dared to make it bleed its own blood.

Joe settled into position, an Orb in each hand, which he was planning on using to smack the bird. His launched Orbs were coming back, and this bird was going to learn what it meant to fight a full-power Ritualist-

Pow. The turkey let out a mournful gobble as it shot into the sky, Kettlebell's leg following through on the kick so well that he almost booted himself in the head like a ballet dancer. "Inter*cepted*!"

"That was my... wouldn't a kick like that be a field goal?" Joe's attempted correction was ignored as the bird came zooming down at the muscular man like a mortar round, only to be plucked out of the sky and slammed to the ground.

"Spike!"

"*Touchdown!*" Joe yelled at the same time, stumbling over his thoughts as Kettlebell sprinted off to continue the fight against the bird. "Right... why am I even trying to argue right now? I'm just gonna go have my own fight with my own bird."

Finding another bird that was approximately the same size as his first target, he sent his icicle after it. During the half-second charge up, Joe hit the fowl with a Dark Lightning Strike, immobilizing the beast for an instant. His Ritual Orb took the bird in the chest, his follow up Orbs striking the flat end and driving the spike deeper akin to using a maul to split logs. Only a moment later, the bird had been fully bisected, a head on each wildly flopping portion.

"That's a bad idea, Joe. Either burn or freeze it if you want it to die," Cleave calmly warned Joe, who gestured dismissively at the fallen bird halves.

"It was cut in half. That's not enough?" Even as he spoke, fresh meat grew along the wounds, and the birds got up—the halves falling over as they attempted to run at him on rapidly growing legs. "Okay, they have some kind of freaky regeneration. Got it."

When his icicle Orb hit, he directed it to discharge Cone of Cold into the beast. A moment later, only a feathery meat popsicle remained. Joe got an experience notification but ignored it in favor of leaping out of the way of the other turkey, who was already growing an additional head. Cleave was watching from the edge of the path, leaning casually on her huge axe and smirking in amusement. "They aren't all that dangerous. Like one of your cows back on earth."

"Cows killed more people than sharks every year, so that doesn't help." Joe set a new path for his icicle Orb, and it whipped through the air and slammed into the bird, pinning it to the ground. His other Orbs converged and started beating on the wildly flapping monster, but the blows didn't seem to do any lasting damage.

"They don't have regeneration; they have passive flesh magic combined with a lovely Constitution," Cleave informed the consternated human with great amusement. "They're known for attacking *anything* that enters their territory, no matter how much stronger it may be. Only reason they've survived this long is that they're prolific breeders, and they're known to hold a grudge forever. Get too high a percentage of the flock mad at you, and their chicks and grandchicks will hunt you, and perhaps even later generations if you kill those ones."

"These things are *trolls*," Joe whispered as he made the realization. "In all senses of the word. Super regeneration, chasing after you forever just to make your life a *tiny* bit harder, all while knowing that they can't do anything but annoy you. These aren't Pointed Turkeys, they're Troll Turkeys! Are they even good for farming?"

"Oh, yes, they are excellent for meat generation," Cleave confirmed in a matter-of-fact tone. "But there are *reasons* that they are left in the wild. First of all, you only need a single breeding pair to produce a nearly unlimited number of eggs and additional turkeys. Second, as you just saw, you can split the birds apart if you need more of them. However, every time you do that, you lose some trust and gain some aggression from them. Too little trust, and too much aggression, and you'll gain a title that makes their entire species hostile toward you."

"Is Jaxon making a bad move trying to use these?" Joe bluntly questioned her. "Should I put a stop to this?"

"If anyone can get these birds to love them to the point that they don't mind getting chopped up several times a day for someone's meal," Cleave shook her head in wonder at her own admission, "I'm thinking your odd friend can. Even if he can't, something tells me he does not mind drawing the ire of an entire race of creatures."

Joe nodded along, fully agreeing with her. "Totally fair. In any case, this is still active combat. I'm going to work on my fighting skills to see if they progress faster out here."

"As per usual, I'm going to be here to save your skinny rear if you mess with something you shouldn't." Cleave stoically took a position scanning the horizon for *actual* threats.

As the sun traveled across the sky, Joe fought bird after furious bird. Usually, he had to face just one at a time, but every once in a while, he would come across a larger cluster and had to adjust how he fought them. It was excellent training in dealing with creatures that would attack him straight on, although it would not be all that useful against creatures that might use strategic tactics against him, such as humans and Elves. Even so, he learned a few new tricks and found that his control with his weapons was slowly becoming smoother and more practiced.

Eventually, Joe got so used to dealing with the turkeys that he started to try new things, even going so far as to use Omni-vault to get into the air while holding a Ritual Orb in each hand. When he reached the apex of his jump, he mentally commanded both of the Orbs to generate a tiny bit more upward thrust.

There were *extreme* limits to what he could do with the Orbs. For instance, trying to use them to hover in place in the air just did not work, but they *could* function as a touchpoint for his feet to enable him to achieve a classic double jump. While holding a pair of them, Joe found that he could greatly reduce his momentum, though he could never come to a complete stop.

He tried for a follow-up jump after the first, but for some reason, he was unable to keep the Orb in such a position to make it happen. The next time he left combat, he tried one more time, and failed again. Planning ahead this time, he realized that he *might* be able to make a triple jump work if he sent the Orbs into the air, then focused on holding them in position *before* he started his first Omnivault. He sprang into his first jump, followed quickly by his second. "Woo! Ha!"

As his feet touched the second Orb in the sky, a full twenty feet in the air, he pushed off with all his strength and screamed like an Italian plumber. "Yaa-*haa!*"

At the thirty-foot mark, four things happened in quick succession. One, Joe realized that he was thirty feet up and didn't have a landing plan. Two, he noticed a huge column of black smoke on the horizon that had been hidden by a hill. Three, he got a notification that he had surpassed his self-imposed limits and brought Omnivault to Expert nine.

Four, a rafter of turkeys responded to his scream of joyful success by bursting from the long grass and flapping toward him —a feathery promise of painful death by a thousand pecks.

CHAPTER THIRTY-NINE

As the turkeys were coming up to slash him, Joe found a new and interesting application for his jumping. Twisting in the air, he dropped an axe kick in between the heads of the foremost turkey, finding that the motion *almost* gave him enough upward lift to vault away from the resistance that met his foot.

"If these things were heavier, or moving faster, I bet I could use them like a platform to push off of!" Joe heaved with effort as he spoke. An interesting side effect of wildly increasing his characteristics was that he really didn't need to hyperventilate during combat, while running, or engaging in other strenuous activities. Essentially, he was a superhuman in that regard. Even so, his mind told him that he *should* be utterly exhausted and near collapse. This was one of the 'walls' when it came to increased characteristics: until he was able to get his brain to accept the fact that *this* was actually normal, it was going to be difficult to break out of old habits and reach new heights.

He forcefully activated his Battle Meditation, concentrating to make his body fall into a regular breathing pattern as the ground rushed up toward him. Nearly in a trance, he tucked and rolled, his Exquisite Shell taking the entirety of the damage as the flock of malicious turkeys converged on his location. "Dark Lightning Strike!"

Bringing the power down on himself—as he was mostly immune between his defense and mitigation of dark magic—the Reductionist managed to send the entire swarm of birds tumbling to the ground, twitching from the electric damage. He smirked and voiced a thought, "Looks like electric damage is still super effective against flying types."

"You better get out of there before they're up; you should know by now that they're twice as fast on the ground!" Cleave called out in warning, only a hint of concern in her voice.

"Hey! I saw smoke in the distance. What's over there?" Joe pointed toward the horizon behind the hill, and Major Cleave followed his finger. Her eyes locked on the grassy mound, a hint of surprise flickered in her eyes, and her face set into a grim expression.

"Are you *sure* about this?" Her extremely confrontational tone gave Joe pause, but he still signaled yes with a confused nod. In a flash, she was next to him. Her axe lifted into the air, then slammed down repeatedly onto the turkeys until the final chunks of meat stopped trying to regenerate. "If that is the case, playtime is over. The only thing in that direction—or should I say, the only *place* in that direction—that could be smoking is the main Legion training facility."

Cleave started shouting for Jaxon and Kettlebell, zipping over and killing anything attacking them as soon as she had their location. "The three of you need to get back to the Shoe. I will be going to assess the situation at the training facility. If I am *not* back in six hours, alert the capital. Use all the authority and means at your disposal."

"You just want us to go home and-" Before Joe could finish his sentence, the Dwarf was already gone, a trail of torn-up grass flying into the air giving the only indication of where she had gone. "I guess so. *Abyss*, how much do I need to put into Perception to be able to see these people moving at top speed?"

"No idea!" Jaxon cheerfully spoke up as he swung a brace of turkeys back and forth. They were all conscious, but for some reason, every single one of them was completely silent. Jaxon looked at them, and the one he focused on began shivering in fear, continuing for a few moments after the man's attention moved away. "But it looks like the next few weeks will be fun for me, at least! Do you think the Elves' land grab was a distraction? That's what I think. Get the Dwarves all riled up and thinking they're in a resource war, then sneak in a whole bunch of sappers to take down the training facility. Smart. Probably what I would have done."

"I don't think you're that coldhearted." Joe waved his hands to stave off the confusion in his friend's eyes. "All I mean is, for all your lackadaisical attitude toward fighting and dealing damage, I've never seen you launch an attack on intelligent people unless they have done something to you. In fact, now that I think about it, I can distinctly remember several times where you were going out of your way to help people attacking you, even in the middle of combat."

Jaxon shrugged and took the lead, answering Joe over his shoulder, "Hard to get new clients when you're mean to them. Look at these turkeys as an example. Look how well-behaved they are, and all I needed to do was *adjust their attitude* over and over until they stopped being aggressive. It's a beast tamer skill that my trainer back on Midgard had never seen before. Eventually, they will be so afraid of *disappointing me* that they will fall in love with everything about me!"

"Stockholm Syndrome, turkey style. I like it." Joe snorted with laughter, then the three of them went silent as they raced back to the Shoe.

Jimathy Kettlebell almost won, but Joe vaulted past him with a backflip and winked at the huge man as he shot by and entered the tunnel ahead of him by a nose. For the first time since he met him, Joe saw a grin begin to spread across the muscular man's face. There was a sharpness to that smile that made Joe realize that this particular person only really had fun when they were competing with someone else. "Any chance you like board games?"

"No."

The smile was gone, and it appeared that they were now racing toward the hamlet. However, they were in a tunnel, and Joe had the absolute advantage. Ever since the attack on his town had ended with him almost being slain in the tunnels, Joe had practiced bouncing around the enclosed spaces nearly every day. Now he was able to keep his momentum in all circumstances, and corners were simply launch pads for him. When he reached the open airspace surrounding the town, he blasted out of the tunnel like a cork popping out of a champagne bottle.

"*Yeah!*" he bellowed as he hurtled toward the ash-coated igneous stone. Joe had long since been able to ignore the looks that he got from other people that didn't know how to have fun, but now he felt something that had been missing since he had come to this Zone. *Competition.* The fact of the matter was that he could not compete physically with the Dwarves, and achieving a high rank in the military had only required of him what he would have been doing anyway.

With his thoughts on competition, his mind focused on the person that he was most contentious with at present. "You know, maybe I should hunt down Herr Trigger and set up a *real* rivalry between us. I bet setting a hand-sized meteor to follow him and send him to respawn a few times would do it. I *do* need to make a few Student rituals that I've never used before... could I make a homing meteor?"

That reminded Joe to look at his current class quests, and he had some time because he had arrived *way~y* ahead of the others. "Heh."

Beginner Reductionist. Create a Special rank permanent array. Reward: 125 Unique aspects. Array created: 0/1.

Student Ritualist. Congratulations! You are a Student of the path of rituals! Students must learn: for you, this means plenty of fun things to do!

Draw out and activate twenty Student rituals you have never used before. 0/20 rituals activated.

Apprentice Rituarchitect II. Scan five Uncommon structures that you do not have the blueprints for currently. Reward: 5 peak Uncommon Cores. Access to the next class quest.

Joe was struck by an idea and began rubbing his hands together like a fly planning to land on someone's food at a nice restaurant. "You know what? I didn't make my buildings here Uncommon… that means I don't have their blueprints."

There was something nice about using old rewards to earn new and better rewards. On his way to scan the two warehouses, barracks, apartment building, and smithy, he informed one of the Legion members about the pillar of smoke and Major Cleave's departure, giving him an order to send a message up the chain of command about the attack on the Legion training facility. Unbeknownst to Joe, his order was executed with grim efficiency; the Legionnaire ran off looking like someone had stabbed him directly in the heart.

Knowing that he had some time before he needed to verify whether Major Cleave had returned, he decided to spend some time on his new favorite skill to practice: Somatic Ritual Casting. At the moment, he was flush with Rare aspects, meaning he could craft the Student-ranked Architects Fury ritual without any concerns. Well… a few concerns. Namely that his ability to use the skill was only at Beginner nine.

"Well, nothing like shooting for the moon to let you land among the stars. Ahh, that's the stuff. Nothing like a pithy saying to help you ignore the dangers of a task you're working on with your bare hands." As per usual, Joe started the process of making the ritual by using an inscriber in both hands to draw out the diagram. Once he reached the Apprentice circle, he dropped to using only one hand and full concentration.

The circle pulled in closer and closer… then completed with an outpouring of light that allowed him to relax, and the small crowd that had gathered to begin clapping. Joe wiped his forehead and took a few deep breaths, then reached out to start the final piece.

Skill increase: Somatic Ritual Casting (Beginner IX -> Apprentice 0)! Congratulations! Skill information updated! Reward: 100 reputation with the Dwarven Oligarchy, 1,000 Uncommon aspects.

Somatic Ritual Casting (Apprentice 0). This skill allows you to create a ritual in midair! No longer will you need flat land or perfectly smooth paper. When creating Apprentice ritual circles, the stability of the circle is set at 100% for the Novice and Beginner portion, and $80+4n$% where n = skill level in the Apprentice rank. Each rank of ritual circle above Apprentice will be calculated at $80+4n-30T$ where T is each tier above Apprentice.

The tip of Joe's inscribing tool was shaking from nerves. If he had started writing out the next circle, the excitement that notification generated in him would have *absolutely* broken his concentration and resulted in a catastrophic failure. As his Neutrality Aura wiped away the sweat that was trying to drip into his eyes, he took in the new information and let it flow through him. After a few moments, his mind was once more centered and focused on the task at hand, and he began drawing out the Student-ranked portion of the diagram.

"Going by the updated skill information, creating this circle should have something like sixty percent stability." Joe knew that meant he needed to remain absolutely focused, in the moment, while keeping his movements sure and concise. He had a better chance of success than failure, but distraction and cockiness would absolutely wreck him if he let it. As the circle came to completion, he stepped back and admired the Student-ranked ritual with a blueprint floating in the center of it.

"I can swear right now, I will *never* get tired of magic."

CHAPTER FORTY

"Good, now *ease* that line over." Havoc's voice was soft, working to not distract Joe as he set up the model for his enchantment. "You are not putting in an angle, you are listing lazily to the left. Languishing, long lines that you lazily lay down. Keep that imagery in your head; intent matters. These lines will help keep your enchantments steady, stable, and mentally sound as they grow in power. There is nothing like calm, quiet, and laziness to keep a ritual from going insane over the passage of time. That's why dragons sit on their treasure for centuries, straight up laziness so that they don't lose their minds and go on a killing spree."

"Is *that* why it's such a bad idea to steal from their hoard?" This was the first time Joe had heard someone speak of dragons in a serious way, not just some kind of throw away comment.

"Focus! Do you have a *wet-wipe* for that empty bucket you call a brain?" Gone were the dulcet tones and cheerfully relaxed demeanor. "You want to have to kill this table when it goes on a rampage? *Do you?* It's got four legs, so it'll move pretty fast when it wants! If you give it your distractibility, maybe it'll stay so confused that it'll think it's a chair and won't let people put food on it! List that line *lazily* to the *left!*"

They had been at it for hours, and Joe found that he *couldn't* complete the process without making a serious blunder at some point. As soon as something *started* to go wrong, Havoc would grab the paper he was working on and chuck it into a pool of lava. The impact of the crumpled sheet would generate a miniature detonation, a series of cheering from the well-distanced audience, and the flying lava would illuminate the area behind the Dwarf—casting his face in shadow as he inhaled deeply on his cigar.

To Joe, his visage at those moments was absolutely terrifying, as if his figure was about to blossom out into his final golem form and rip Joe in half for his transgressions. The Dwarf *exuded* bloodlust. The fact that Joe *knew* his mentor would not let him rest until he got it right had been nearly as concerning to him… all the way until he listed the line lazily to the left. The diagram glowed golden to his vision for a bare instant, and he was *delighted* by the perfectionism.

"Thoughts, Havoc?" Joe gently handed over the enchantment paper, the most detailed and intricate enchantment he had ever created without direct assistance, which the Dwarf snatched uncaringly and glanced over.

"It looks like a child drew it with crayons during an earthquake… but it will serve its purpose." Havoc tossed it back with a flick of his wrist and stood up. "Let me know when you are going to start working on the table enchantment itself, I will make sure you don't destroy that poor piece of furniture even if I need to destroy it first. Magma doesn't only destroy paper."

Skill increase: Enchanting (Beginner V -> Beginner IX). Direct instruction from a Grandmaster always has benefits!

Joe accepted the paper and nodded. He wasn't going to attempt this behind the Dwarf's back, but he was also not going to go into the Guildhall and try to put this enchantment on the table by hand. As soon as he was alone, or as alone as he could get with Major Cleave always around, the human got to work designing a modified Ritual of Enchantment. "Okay, my ritual that builds Mana Batteries is at the Expert rank, but the Zone of Circumlocution is only at the Journeyman rank. What I'll do is keep the ritual itself at the Expert rank; that should let me power through any issues that crop up with the lower-ranked enchantment."

Now that he had an effective—Grandmaster approved—diagram written out, all he needed to do was replace the enchantment that his ritual would be using. "These five-circle rituals are going to... hey, this will work for my class quest! Technically it'll be a different ritual, since something I've never made before! Technicalities for the win!"

That got him over all of his hesitation, and he sat down to begin designing. The Novice, Beginner, Apprentice, and Student circles were all completed using Somatic Ritual Enchanting, etching directly over the surface of a large chunk of flat stone. When he approached the point where the ritual was too difficult for that newish skill to handle, Joe needed to give up on trying to use his skill and switched to his standard practices to draw the rest out. He was looking forward to the time when the details and symbology that were currently too complex for him to hold in his mind—much less in the air, without losing control and blowing his face off—became second nature and practically effortless to complete.

His Natural Aspect jar had been accruing Expert aspects at the rate of seven per hour, meaning that by now he had several hundred available for use. Yet another reason to find a way to create high-tier Aspect Jars. As always, the hardest part was going to be gathering enough materials at one time to make the initial container, but the return on investment *should* always be worth it.

Since he had all the resources that he needed to complete his work, Joe pushed through the rest of the night and managed to complete both the Journeyman and Expert-ranked circles perfectly. Even though he knew he *could* have created them faster, he also knew he only had one shot at getting them right.

If he destroyed the table, the building, or messed up the enchantment due to carelessness… in order: Havoc would tear him a new one, Stan and Lord Checkoff would come after him, and Joe would miss the opportunity to host the negotiations which his people were using every favor in their possession to make happen.

That meant he triple-checked every portion of his design at every step of the process. When he was absolutely *certain* that the ritual would work, he got to his feet, carefully lifted the tile he had been working on, and started walking toward the Guild-hall at the slowest rate he could manage.

"I *understand* that I could move faster," Joe quietly commented in response to Cleave's annoyed sigh, "But this ritual is only *mostly* bonded. One part is hovering in the air, while the other part is physically attached to the tile. I need to move this with both my hands and my mind at the same time. You just go ahead and let me take all the time I need, and please keep the path clear of obstructions and people."

"You're taking the destruction of our main training center very calmly." Cleave growled as she shifted in place. "Working on projects, trying new things, being all excited."

"You reported the attack, and people in a better position to do something about it than me are on top of things. They're already working on a new training center, and launching a counterattack. What else can I do, but work?" Cleave had nothing to say about that, but he could tell that her restless energy was nearly at the boiling-over stage. When he eventually arrived at his destination, the human slowly sank to his knees and slid the ritual diagram underneath the table, then turned to address the message runners in the room. "Someone go find Havoc."

One of the newly-hired humans stood up, saluted, and sprinted away. It took less than five minutes for Havoc to abruptly appear in the room next to them with a blast of air pressure, as if he had suddenly teleported in. "You are not *seriously* considering creating an enchantment on this table right now, are you? I said that your example was passable! I sure as a horse's mouth didn't announce that it was ready to go on a table that *I* made! You need *way* more practice before you can replicate those enchantments onto an actual item at the scale that it needs."

"Havoc, there's a reason I called you in to see this. I converted the completed enchantment diagram to a ritual. You are welcome to check it, and if you still say no, then I won't do it. But, before we do that, a point of contention: you took *my* pet project and completed only part of what was needed. By your own logic, you can't be too upset if I come back in and actually finish the work on it." Joe grinned as the Dwarf puffed on his cigar consideringly. "Look, I figured you would enjoy seeing this process. Not only do I think this will work perfectly, but I also finally no longer need a huge group of Dwarves to stand around for hours at a time to fuel a ritual like this!"

Joe had been working on converting cores into Mana Batteries ever since he had completed that ritual. He had prepared everything while he was waiting for his persnickety mentor, and only paused long enough for the Dwarf to grumpily nod after he looked at the ritual that was waiting to run. Without giving his mentor another chance to interrupt, the Ritualist activated the ritual. Six circles sprang into being, and the stone table was slowly lifted into the air. A gyroscope of lights began swirling around it, slowly at first, but increasing in speed until the room appeared to contain a twelve-foot-wide globe of light.

"Hope you didn't just mess it up in such a terrible way that everything will go horribly wrong," Havoc ominously warned his Apprentice while staring death at the lights above his head.

Joe waved him off and shook his head with confidence. "I'm not going to stop the ritual just because you're trying to psych me out. Now that you've seen it begin and didn't overtly disapprove, do you *want* to stay for the entire show? This should take about… oh, only thirty hours or so."

That was the *real* reason Joe had taken the time to make a

handful of overpowered batteries. Not only did he care about the other people that would have been forcibly drained the entire time, but *he* wasn't going to stand in the ritual for over a full day while he waited for the table to become fully Enchanted. Automation was key in attempting to create long-term success, and being able to complete multiple other projects while this one was running sounded *fabulous*.

The Dwarf stomped out of the room without another word, and Joe quietly gave the order to triple the guard around and in the building. "No reason to discount the idea that someone will try to sabotage this place before the peace talks."

"You keep bringing up these peace talks as if they're actually going to happen." Major Cleave finally broke down and voiced what had been on her mind. "I think you're truly underestimating how prideful the Elves are, *and* how long Dwarves can hold a grudge. Why are you so sure about it?"

Joe could only shrug and do his best to explain. "Humans just don't give up, I guess. When we set our minds to something, we *will* figure it out. Certainly, we might not get the Oligarchy and Theocracy to voluntarily sit down and sip tea together as soon as we want them to. Even so, I'll tell you this. To me, it doesn't *matter* if humanity has to use every bit of influence or reputation we earn, or if we need to grind through quests until we are absolutely sick of this Zone. So long as we don't all kill each other first, there *will* be negotiations…"

"…and The Wanderers *will* be ready to be a major factor in their success."

CHAPTER FORTY-ONE

"They agreed! The Oligarchy and Theocracy will be traveling to the Shoe to begin initial peace discussions! A treaty for mutual aid and open commerce is on the table!" The runner that was speaking had burst into a meeting occurring in the Guildhall, where Joe was speaking with his guild members and support staff about which buildings were the most important to construct, and *if* he should be the one to raise them.

A deal had just been struck, where Joe would own a subset of the buildings that he raised, receive direct payment for raising a few different ones, and finally set a flat tax for several buildings that were being customized by patrons who didn't want anyone else to see the blueprints or design of the interior. No one was overly happy with the deal so far—which helped everyone agree that it was the best they were getting—but this sudden good news trumped everything else.

Congratulations were given all around, and a new meeting was started right away, in which the defense of the delegations was the only thing that mattered. Joe was tasked with creating several variations of a ritual to restrain hostile people, specifically to teach them the ways of peace as forcefully as possible.

Some of the methods offered up were so novel that Joe wrote them down and promised himself he would find a way to make a ritual out of them.

Within the day, orders had come down from the Legion. An elite unit from both the Elves and the Dwarves was on the way to secure the meeting area. Havoc was ordered under no uncertain terms to leave the area before the first strand of golden Elven hair fluttered into the area. Most low-leveled people were confined to the outer confines of the Shoe's Hamlet, as Joe would have been, were he not the owner of the town.

Joe perused his class quest progress, which had seen a jump in the last weeks' worth of effort.

Class Quests: Student Ritualist. Personally draw out and activate twenty Student rituals you have never used before. 8/20 drawn out, 1/20 rituals activated.

Apprentice Rituarchitect II. Scan five Uncommon structures that you do not have the blueprints for currently. 4/5 scanned!

"I should make time to get that last building scanned before people start showing up. Don't want to be giving out too many secrets if I don't need to, and what's more secret than my ability to raise buildings?" Joe stretched and rolled his shoulders, which felt lighter than they had in weeks. "Heh. Probably almost *every-thing* is more secret than that, but at least maybe the Elves don't know it. Let's see... Havoc had to go, and I can't tell if I'm happy or sad about that. I'm more *relaxed*, that's for certain."

He mulled over the rituals that he had created before running low on Rare aspects, feeling pleased though slightly off-put by the fact that they were merely upgrades of his current rituals. One was a variation that had come to mind after he'd accidentally killed a zombie in the landfill. He had combined Acid Spray and barriers to deadly effect, named it 'Ritual of Acid Bubble', and placed one at each entrance to the Shoe.

He had made a *second* version that he was in love with, which produced the same bubble... but *launched* it. Anything that got caught in its radius would be stuck inside until they either broke free or their form dissolved. The bubble itself only stopped moving upon striking something too large to suck into its confines.

That had spawned a new method of transportation that he wanted to try out: the bubble launcher, sans acid. It was *supposed* to travel in a parabolic arc and burst after stopping completely, leaving the inhabitants safe and protected the entire time. He was *sure* it would work, but he hadn't found any volunteers to test it, and he didn't have the time to try it out on his own.

Another variant was an Oversized Ritual of Stasis, which was designed to take a whole building into stasis if needed; this one, he had set it up around the Guildhall. That way, if an attack occurred, Joe could use the ritual to keep everything preserved for a few minutes. Hopefully, that would render any 'surprises' against the delegations useless.

There had been one surprise for him as well, as he had mostly forgotten that creating *anything* with aspects gave him experience for his class. He proudly and obsessively read over the notification he had gained, as though it were a trophy announcing his hard work to the world.

Class 'Reductionist' has reached level 3! The benefits of mental strength and mana compression will be 30% more effective when crafting.

He wasn't exactly sure how to quantify that reward, but he had a feeling that the next time he went to make a layer in his aspect array, he'd be able to reach a loftier height. Reluctantly pulling his mind back from plans for the future, he continued to pore over what else he had accomplished.

Joe's other rituals had mainly ended up being quality of life things, such as a more efficient heat sink that took the volcano's warmth and redistributed it to the smithy forge stations, as well as back into the magma proper. He was waiting to set that up, as he was sure some fine-tuning would be required, so as to not blow the smithy to cinders.

Finally, the one that he was *really* proud of was already contained in his Ritual Orbs.

It wasn't a 'Student' ritual, but an Apprentice ritual that he was *almost* certain he could reuse with his Orbs... though he only had a single target in mind. His largest problem with Herr Trigger was that the man was *wily*. He was more than willing to wait in ambush until the perfect moment to strike, as well as being swift and agile enough to escape if things started to go badly. Finally… Joe was prepared. There would be no escape for the gunslinger the next time they met. "No escape… hmm. I guess if I use them correctly, these Orbs are basically the Ritualist version of an ultimate attack."

"The advance units are arriving!" someone called out, pulling Joe from his thoughts and forcing him into the moment. Frankly, he was highly surprised that he had been able to relax at all. The room held a good mix of humans that were aligned with Dwarves, as well as those on the side of the Elves. The close proximity created a strangely uncomfortable feeling in all of them, which only compounded over time. Tempers had been flaring, especially as trade goods had begun flowing through their Hamlet.

On the plus side, they had run *extensive* testing on his table enchanted with the Zone of Circumlocution. Whenever someone had gone slightly over the edge and opened their mouth to start a fight or attempt passive-aggressive bickering, what came out instead was a polite redirection of whatever was going on. Sometimes it was even a clear explanation of how they were feeling, and why. That allowed for a level of honesty and openness rarely seen anywhere near such a polarized group of people.

"Places, everyone!" Joe called out as well as clapping his hands. "We've been practicing for this. If you are aligned with the Elves, please make sure to demonstrate all the necessary formalities! Everyone else, buckle up; hopefully this will be anything *but* a wild ride!"

The Elves arrived first, strolling in with haughty attitudes and sneers gracing their fine features as they took in the building around them. One, the apparent leader of the unit, spoke to the room as a whole. "What a… *fine* example of architecture. It nearly appears grown, as though it is a unique combination of Elvish and Dwarven engineering."

Joe surreptitiously studied the walls, a pit appearing in his stomach. He had no idea why he hadn't realized that particular detail beforehand, but it was clearly the truth. He swept his gaze around the structure, suddenly noticing how the stone and wood building had melded together layer by layer, as though it had indeed been grown or perfectly printed. It displayed neither the meticulous specifications commonly seen in Dwarven architecture, nor the organic traits of a building grown using natural Elven methods. "Huh."

The Elf blinked a single time in surprise. It seemed that he had not been attempting to say something nearly half as polite as what had ended up coming out of his mouth. "Is this a Zone of *Truth*? I guarantee to you at this moment, my people will refuse all attempts to make us negotiate within a Zone of Truth!"

Several attendees attempted to make snide comments after hearing that, but each time, their remarks came out as something to the effect of, 'yes, that is understandable'. Joe kept his mouth closed and his thoughts to himself. He wouldn't have any active role in the negotiations, beyond checking in intermittently to ensure everything was moving along smoothly.

His part in this play was over.

The town was built as well as he could manage, every protection he could think of was in place, and dozens of plans and counter-attack strategies had been enacted by actual experts in that field. Everything from small strike groups to a massive assault by an army was accounted for: they were as ready as possible.

After being reassured that the hall was *not* a Zone of Truth and testing it out for himself, the Elf demanded to inspect the area and set out to create his own defensive perimeter after scanning the building for threats and issues. Joe decided he had seen enough and strolled away to go scan the final building he needed to complete his quest.

He passed by the Dwarven Elite unit, nodding as they saluted him. It was strange to be an officer in the military. One oddity that struck him after his time as an enlisted man on Earth was that he had expected to be *way* more annoyed with being saluted than he actually was. "No reason *not* to get respect, I guess."

Since he had been planning to finish scanning the structure earlier but had been pulled into a meeting, the ritual was already set up and waiting for him. All Joe needed to do was activate it and collect the new blueprint. He set it to run, and as the ritual did the heavy lifting, he finished reading over a template for a metal coffee cup. Satisfied that it was what he wanted, he presented it to his sleeve. "Mate, what do you think about this one? It's a Rare coffee mug, and I should be able to make it, but do you think I should hold off longer in order to start with a better one?"

Burble! came the excited reply. That sealed it for Joe; he wanted the source of his caffeine to be joyful at all times.

"Happy coffee means life is frothy and good. We'll start right after we're done here," Joe promised, getting excited non-words in response. The ritual finished, and he stored the lightly glowing blueprint for safekeeping as he waited a moment for the impending notification.

Class quest complete: Apprentice Rituarchitect II. Uncommon structures scanned: 5/5 scanned! Reward: 5 peak Uncommon cores! Record-breaker reward: access to Apprentice Rituarchitect III.

Item gained: Uncommon core x5. Usable exp available: 4,000/4,000.

"Got it. 'Peak' means 'as much in there as possible without getting to the next rank'," Joe muttered to himself as he hurried to the smithy. "Now let's get this all taken care of... oh, the next quest?"

Class quest gained: Apprentice Rituarchitect III. Create three meaningful monuments in your Hamlet. Reward: access to Apprentice Rituarchitect VI.

"I'll get access to the *sixth* quest in this chain?" Joe sputtered as he looked over the message. "What about the other steps-"

Class quest updated: Apprentice Rituarchitect III. Reward: access to Apprentice Rituarchitect IV. How about you just remember that nobody is perfect, Mr. I-forgot-to-make-a-cup-for-over-three-months.

"Right… the system here is alive." Joe chuckled nervously as his stomach knotted into a bundle. He *really* didn't want another random curse. "Look! A task I need to focus on!"

He fled into the smithy as though the omnipresent system couldn't follow him there, diving into his work with a furious and focused vengeance.

CHAPTER FORTY-TWO

Ting. There was a long pause as Joe inspected the cup before hitting it one last time with his Aspect Ingot Hammer. *Ting.*

Congratulations! Under the watchful eye of an Expert Blacksmith, you have created your first ever Rare-ranked forged item.

Skill increase: Ritualistic Forging (Student 0 -> Student I).

Item created: Ebonsteel Eternal Coffee Mug. Durability: 5,000/5,000. This mighty Coffee Mug, made from ebonsteel, offers a nigh-unbreakable defense, especially against coordinated attacks and smaller ballistics. The design was perfected throughout the ages, though this mug was first forged for a General on the front lines of the 58th of 100 waves on Jotunheim, as he struggled to defend that Plane's first and—to this day—final city.

The Coffee Mug's edges are embellished with small metal studs and have been set with decorative gems. Its circumference is ornamented with intertwining metalwork, and the item is ready to receive up to two minor— or one major—enchantments. It's clear this Coffee mug has yet to be used by its master. This mug was created by Joe 'Anti-mage' for his favored coffee elemental.

"That's... different." Joe squinted at his template, noting

that it was indeed an aged document. "Is it just me, or does personal gear have a lot more lore attached to it?"

"Unless you're making new stuff all the time, you're going to be able to see some of the history attached to whatever it is you're making." The Expert smith had a shrewd smile on his face as he looked over the reputation he had just earned for offering a few pointers here and there as Joe worked. "Think of it as a way to always be remembered, yeah? Like when someone makes one of these particle-buildings you're putting up, they'll always be reminded that they weren't the *first* to make it. You were."

"Not bad." Joe's head bobbed as he took all that information in. "I can totally get behind that. Now, at long last… Mate, your new home!"

The coffee elemental swirled into existence from Joe's sleeve stain and inspected the coffee mug. It dripped a few ounces of hot liquid into the opening, then *sloshed* in excitedly. A moment later, the coffee mug and elemental began releasing light, and were soon too blinding to look at directly. Joe threw his hand in front of his face. "What's happening?"

What? Mate is evolving!

"Elementals can evolve? That's a thing here?" Joe looked to the smith, who shrugged and continued to watch the show.

Congratulations! Mate has evolved into AutoMate, and can now use its abilities from a storage device. No more stains on your clothing!

AutoMate has gained new abilities! Here's a handy list!

1. *Auto Over-caffeinate: Similar to a traditional Haste spell, Auto Over-caffeinate increases all effects of physical and mental characteristics by 10% for 10 minutes. Can be used once per day! The negatives of this ability have been removed.*
2. *Proper Presentation: No matter what liquid is poured into AutoMate's Mug, AutoMate will exchange it for coffee and store the other liquid for use at another time of your choosing. Great for dinner parties, tasting amateur brews, and blocking*

attempted assassinations! Try storing your own blood for a handy anti-bleed IV drip at a time of your choosing!

3. *Eternal Ebonsteel Encasement: Once per month, AutoMate can encase your physical form in Ebonsteel and block one attack—a blow that must involve a physical component—that would otherwise reduce your health to zero. Damage absorbed cannot exceed durability, and AutoMate's mug must be repaired in order for the durability to be regained.*

In order to evolve again, AutoMate must be provided an Artifact at minimum. Remaining possible evolutions: 1.

"Abyss, Mate. Er… AutoMate." Joe looked at the jewel-encrusted coffee mug, noting that the liquid within was so dark that peering inside was like looking into the depths of a starless sky. "That was some pretty impressive upgrading. Thank you for being so patient with me on this; I'm sure you've been wanting to get stronger as well."

Bubble!

"Is that actual *ebonsteel?*" The Expert smith stepped forward, hungry eyes locked on the mug. "You used it to make a coffee mug? Are you out of your *mind?* I'll give you five… no, *ten* thousand reputation for it right now! Twenty, if you give me a week to gather it!"

"I… this is a creature now? So, no, but thank you?" Joe regarded the template in his hand, then the panting Dwarf. "I can make another if you want to buy it, though."

"Yes! This will allow for the repair of… ahhh. Right. Listen, don't make it into a mug; just give me the ingots!" the Expert pleaded as he attempted to transfer reputation to the human.

Joe shook his head. "I can't. That isn't how my abilities work."

"Okay, whatever you need!" The Dwarf backed down instantly, waving his hands non-threateningly.

Nonplussed over the situation—the simultaneously demanding and reticent Dwarf—Joe decided that now was a good time to take in some volcanic air. He likely had a few more days before the actual negotiations began, so he decided to take a stroll around the small bazaar that had sprung up in the 'Elf fans' sector which the Dwarves had cordoned off. He was looking at a houseplant—which he was almost *sure* housed a camouflaged listening device—when a voice next to him *almost* startled him into blasting out of pure reflex.

"Oh, so *this* is where you've been hiding, hmm? Somewhere my long-range hunters cannot find you, yes? Inside a volcano?" Herr Trigger stood still and smug, with Major Cleave's axeblade pressed to his throat. He looked at her disdainfully, reaching up to flick the blade uncaringly. "Oh, yes, how *scary*. *Please* show my patrons that this is all a waste of time. I beg you… *press deeper.*"

"Major!" Joe barked as his personal guard moved to follow through on the taunt. "Let him go. If he's here, that means the Elves brought him as part of their Elite unit."

"Hmm, he *can* think, it seems." Herr Trigger's lips were twitching as he watched Joe work to comport himself and his people professionally. "You know, I never thought that my skills and desires would find such a welcome home with the Elves. Everyone told me that guns were useless. That I would never manage to make them viable in a wide market. Yet… here I am!"

"Yeah, here you are," Joe scoffed as he observed the pressed trench coat the man was wearing in the near-sweltering heat and humidity, "using something that only you and your close allies can access. Not exactly a 'wide market', is it?"

"Ahh, but that is why it is oh *so* sweet." The man stepped closer in an effort to loom over Joe, gazing through perfectly round lenses that Joe recognized as tiny auto-focusing scopes which could be set into position in an instant. No wonder the guy's long-range shots were so accurate. "Only I, and those close to me, have the most *powerful* individual weapons in the history of the world in our palms. This gets us access to… ahh… *exclusive* content."

"A whole new world, and you're still stuck on what we

already had." Joe turned and started walking away, only for Trigger to roughly grab his arm and half-turn him.

"*Stuck* on…? You have no *idea* what I gave up to be here. I had the *ideal* life!" The man's accent was gone, but Joe couldn't place the new diction at all. Most likely somewhere in America or England, but he couldn't be certain. The man took a deep breath, and when he spoke again, the now-clearly-fake accent was back. "Do you know *why* I have been able to establish my career here, micro-enchanting bullets? I had an entire *workshop* of my own where I painted competition-winning minis!"

"You…" Joe flexed his Exquisite Shell, and Herr Trigger's hand lost its grip, allowing the Reductionist to fluidly step away. "You mean to tell me that you went from painting dolls for fantasy conventions to being an actual assassin? You're right, that *is* quite the shift. You even modeled yourself after a cartoon character for children? I can't even *begin* to imagine what your life was like. I'd compare backstories with you, but you aren't worth my time. I think I'll just let you read the biography when it's written. Make sure to leave a review; I'm sure it'll be well-received."

Once more, Joe walked away. Three guards descended on the gunsmith, forcing him to return to his delegation, since he had been causing trouble in the town. Joe surreptitiously glanced down at a thin needle, his taglock, which he had managed to poke into Herr Trigger while he had been focused on grabbing at Joe's arm.

Taglock: current storage, 1 drop of blood from [Herr Trigger].

"Now I don't even need to have him in view," Joe muttered softly as he stored the item away. "The minute he starts causing trouble, or this negotiation ends, I get to try out my new Ritual Orb setup."

Now that the Elves had arrived, there was very little that Joe could do to improve the area without setting off alarm bells that would smash the fragile armistice to smithereens. What he *could* do was all the preparatory work for the moment when every-thing was completed. Over the next few hours, he set up a ritual to create the first monument in his town, the Ritual Ziggurat. He was *so* excited to make this small structure, even if he wasn't entirely certain what it would do when it was up. He enthusiastically shrugged. "Can't be *nothing!*"

Cheered up by being inane, Joe decided that he would get his bubble travel ritual ready as well. If he wanted it to work perfectly, he needed to do quite a lot of math. Gravity was different than Earth-normal here, stronger, even if he didn't really think about it too much anymore. After accounting for the strange forces on this plane, he needed to figure out what angle would deposit him *outside* the city that he wanted to approach. There was a good chance that the Dwarves would blast him out of the sky if he accidentally landed too close.

Getting caught up in that plan was a fun distraction, and after a few hours of calculations, he had the ritual ready for activation. Leaving it out in the open risked someone else activating or damaging it, but that was fine by him. In fact, it made him chuckle like a villain from a children show at the thought. "If they activate it, they get sent to the Capital. Damage it... welp, it's a Rare-ranked ritual. They can only mess it up *once*. We should be able to hear the explosion all the way in the Shoe if they do."

CHAPTER FORTY-THREE

"Before we begin…" Aten addressed the room at large as the two groups of leaders for the Elves and Dwarves remained standing on their respective sides of the table. "I would like to address the deal that was made by each party represented here today. Representing the Dwarven Oligarchy, the Council of Five is in attendance."

Even Joe, with his Perception score being… perhaps not the highest in the room, could see that the hand of the Guild Commander was shaking slightly from the pressure of being in an enclosed space with such high-ranked, high-leveled people. Joe was standing in a viewing room, and even there he was being buffeted by the power coming off of the people in waves. It wasn't the same as being in the presence of King Henry and Queen Marie, which had felt like the power of an over-whelming force on the way to slaughter you.

No, coming from the Dwarves was a titanic wash of relax-ation, a heady buzz that made him feel like he was three drinks in, accompanied by a burning desire to let his guard down and *make a deal* with them. All Joe wanted was to give them anything *they* wanted. He wanted to work for them, no... he wanted to *serve* them.

Conversely, the leaders of the Elves in the room emitted a sensation of piercing light, as if he had been adrift on the ocean in a row boat with no protection from the sun for days. It was a feeling of deep scrutiny, as if the surface layer of his body was scorched away in order to allow the Elves to see deeper into what made him tick; as if to delve into his most hidden self and ascertain his true thoughts about... everything.

"I can't tell what's worse, feeling like I would give in to anything demanded of me with no questions asked, or rapidly boiling away just because someone glared at me." Joe's low comment gathered agreement from everyone else in the small room, no matter whose side they were on.

"Representing the Elven Theocracy: the King, Queen, Crown Prince, and Princess Royal are in attendance." Aten continued speaking formally, ending the introductions by placing a sheet of parchment carefully on the table. Lightning was playing across its surface, and the relief on his face when he released it was evident to all. "The Armistice order, which you have all signed, guarantees us all a small period of peace during which all of us can let down our guards enough to have a conversation. From myself and my guild, may I say... we are incredibly honored that you would work with us to engage in a dialogue such as this. Truly, it is a monumental event for the entirety of our people."

"Yes, yes." One of the Oligarchs waved his hand lazily, "We *all* know what the Armistice says. None of us may attack the other through direct or indirect means. Any attacks carried out by our forces that we have any knowledge of whatsoever, or that we approve of either directly or implicitly, will result in a painful, permanent death. Can we move on?"

"I see that the Dwarves are still picking and choosing which traditions they should honor," the Crown Prince commented 'quietly' to his family. "Thank you for this opportunity to observe our enemies, Mother; Father."

"Just like old times," one of the Oligarchs wheezed to his compatriots. "This conversational zone on the table, though lovely and well-made, simply allows the most rigorously tried and tested art form of Elven culture to thrive. Nothing they say can be called a direct insult, and yet…"

"If I may *finish*." The fact that Aten was able to interrupt over the mounting pressure of the two hostile forces, forcefully and with meaning directed at both, stunned the groups into silence. "The Armistice will end either when one side shows not only hostile intent, but takes action to put it into effect; or whenever both parties have removed themselves a minimum of fifty miles from this location *and* each other."

There was a short pause, which the Guild Commander refused to allow someone else to fill. "While we may not be able to reach an agreement immediately, as you are both able to speak for your entire respective races, we might be able to start finding some neutral ground. Speaking of neutral ground, that is our first issue of the day. My guild desires the ability to offer succor to both the Dwarves and the Elves, in addition to those aligned with either faction. As a gesture of goodwill, the Theocracy has moved to request that this town be resettled in a different location and set as a neutral territory for the benefit of both countries."

"Nope, don't like *that*," Joe growled to himself, inadvertently and preemptively mirroring the stink that was raised by the Oligarchy in the next room over. The next several hours slowly devolved into 'you did this' and 'well, you did *that*', while not even a single point had yet to be agreed upon.

Joe was starting to doze off in his chair when he felt a light hand on his shoulder. He turned bleary eyes up to find Daniella's worried face looking down at him. "Can I speak to you for a moment? Privately?"

"I'm really not supposed to leave the building, I'm pretty sure." Joe's brow furrowed as he processed what he had just said out loud. "Actually, I don't know why I said that; that was never discussed with anyone. Can I come back if I leave? Yes? Great. Yeah, let's step outside. Everything okay?"

"Oh, absolutely, everything is perfectly wonderful. I just think we need to *talk*." Daniella's tone made even the people suspiciously listening in shudder and turn their attention and eyes away from the duo. Joe's eyes narrowed; as certain as the sun produced light, he was *not* about to let someone chew him out for some unknown reason. He stiffly stood and marched after the lovely architect, a few people glancing over at him just to smirk.

Once they were fully outside of the building, Joe crossed his arms and glared at her. "I don't know why you're mad at me, but I will tell you this right now… you don't get to talk to me like that. Yes, you are *highly* skilled and strangely alluring, really good at your job, every report about you that comes back is glowing, and all of your co-workers really like you, but I'm *still-*"

"Let's pause while you're still giving me oddly nice compliments." Daniella met his gaze with a tight smile. "My apologies for acting like that in public, but I *needed* to have a good reason to get you out of there without raising any suspicions or making people nervous. Something is going on; I noticed a lot of people I've never seen before coming out of the Guildhall. None of them went in, which means they're coming across the teleporter."

Joe blinked at the sudden shift, then his eyes narrowed and his jaw firmed up. "Who were they? Did you see anyone you recognized at all? Did you follow them? Where were they going?"

"Easy on the interrogation, detective!" Daniella started jogging, waving for him to follow her. "There was only one person that I somewhat recognized from rumors. Apparently, you got in an argument with someone in the market area? Tall guy, blond, black trench coat?"

"Herr Trigger," Joe growled as he pulled up the town administration tab in his character sheet and turned off spawning and teleportation into the area. He also ordered the system to take a screenshot of all the people with access to the teleporter, and anyone who had been activating it in the last few hours. "Let's grab a couple of guards on our way."

"No!" Daniella's quick reply instantly raised Joe's guard. "If we make a mess out of this and everything gets blown out of proportion, there won't be a second attempt at negotiations. Probably not *ever*. We *can't* miss this opportunity. Think of the technological advances the Theocracy could achieve, and the magical advances the Oligarchy would be able to put to good use. Both sides have so much to gain, and *so* much to lose!"

Double-checking his defenses, Joe grabbed three of his Ritual Orbs and set them to orbit around his head. He slowed down slightly, allowing Daniella to pull ahead so that he could keep a close eye on not only the surroundings, but her. Something about the way she had listed the Theocracy first in her point about gaining benefits ruffled his feathers.

She didn't ever look back, fully expecting that he was with her. Taking a hard left, the architect skidded to a halt as they came to the side of a building. Specifically, a warehouse for dry goods that had been smashed into. Joe glared at the hole, wondering why he hadn't gotten any notifications of damage to his buildings. Then he realized that he hadn't even seen the breach until he was standing just a few feet away from it. Something was fishy. He muttered under his breath, *"Essence Cycle."*

The area lit up to his senses, and sprinkles of mana that were already dissipating could be clearly seen. A light ringing also sounded in his ears, one that was different than anything his magical synesthesia highlighted. Joe spoke so quietly that even he couldn't hear himself speak as he pushed a rock aside and settled into a combat stance. "It's my Hidden Sense... what is *this*? A used spell scroll?"

There was more to his Hidden Sense than just the remnants of a destroyed parchment. Now that he was focusing on things that were hidden, the area around him began to chime with the sound of magic. *Muffled* magic. "It's a spell... to hide spells?"

"Looks like the game is up, gentlemen! They found us, so

let's go quietly." Herr Trigger's words were met with sardonic chuckling as people began materializing out of the darkness of the warehouse. A darkness that Joe *should* have been able to see through with his Darkvision, but the spell clearly had messed with his senses as well.

"Why are you people trying to ruin everything?" Daniella took the initiative to bellow at the group of mixed humans and Elves. "Our peoples have a chance at peace! A real chance! It might take a while, and both of them will have to concede small points for negotiation, but the end of this war is in sight!"

"You think your little boyfriend here can just invent a magical table that forces people to be 'nice' around it, and expect that social politeness is enough to get past *millennia* of war? This is *not* what is *best* for the Theocracy!" Herr Trigger's hand blurred, and a revolver appeared in it. Without hesitation, he put three rounds in her chest in under a second. Not missing a beat, Joe caught her as she started to fall and sent a pulse of Lay on Hands into the wounds. "We are going to make sure this travesty of a negotiation dies as the horrible idea that it is… along with everyone else who was involved."

Daniella gasped with pain, then relief almost in the same instant. "You're a monster! Why are you just showing up and, and… not even condoning, but planning to continue *perpetrating* war crimes?"

"Woo, war *cri~imes*!" a Dwarf walking past the area called as he heard Daniella's outburst. He waved at Joe and Daniella, then continued walking. "See ya later, teamkiller bro!"

Clearly, the Dwarf could only see the architect and Major General Pyrrhic through whatever spell was affecting the local area, and he didn't want to interrupt whatever had allowed Joe to catch a swooning lady in his arms.

"I will even *happily* monologue to tell you what we are planning." A wide grin on the assassin's face informed Joe and Daniella that Trigger believed that they could do nothing to stop him. "You do not even have an inkling of *why* the Theocracy chose this place as their secret base, yet you moved right on in as soon as you found it and forced our people away. As if the Theocracy has ever *not* had a backup plan behind their contingency plan, or had to put in place a *final* option behind their plan B and C."

Herr Trigger's people had slowly started to fan out, prepared to attack as soon as they were given the signal. The bounty hunter simply raised his hands as though everything he was explaining was a foregone conclusion. "Right now, we are only waiting for the bait to take effect. Your pathetic little Guild-hall has already been coated in the most delicious smell of *meat*... and *it* is coming for all of them."

"You're going to wipe out your own royal family?" Joe demanded with incredulity, "That will set both of our people back for *months* at the minimum!"

"Oh, it would..." Trigger started laughing as he raised his hand, "If a *Royal family* could truly ever be in charge of a *Theocracy*."

"Abyss, the real ruler of the Elves is some kind of priest." Joe had heard enough. One of his Ritual Orbs opened and unraveled with a metallic *twang*, instantly forming into the Ritual of Remote Activation. His mana touched it, and the wire-made ritual diagram activated. Moments later, klaxon calls began clattering all around the city. He stared hard into Trigger's eyes. "Now the entire Oligarchy knows you're here."

"*Excellent.* Nothing draws out my pleasure like observing someone who knows death is coming... and making them *wait* for it!" Herr Trigger and his team opened up on Joe, who pulled Daniella close and used Omnivault to jump onto the wall of the building, then flipped and vaulted to the top of the next structure over.

"This... is pure..." Just before they were out of range, Joe heard Trigger's voice and looked back, only to lock eyes with the gunslinger. The man had lifted both of his pistols to his nostrils and inhaled deeply, then shuddered with pleasure as he shouted, "... *ecstasy!*"

CHAPTER FORTY-FOUR

"Stop!" Daniella shouted into Joe's ear as he carried her along the rooftops. "We need to get back there and stop him from doing… whatever it is that he's doing!"

"No, we need to get the delegations out of here, right now," Joe told her firmly as he—very easily—continued to carry her. It appeared that having nearly a hundred and sixty points in strength wasn't just for show. "I don't think you have the same kind of ability to jump around as I do, so unless you want me to leave you here…?"

"Just… keep going," Daniella told him after a long, uncomfortable pause. "This was all a trap? Gather the Oligarchs in one place, just to kill off them *and* the Royal family, which are actually only figureheads put in place by the real leader?"

"That's what I was thinking. Even if Trigger fails with whatever is coming, they can use the attacks to justify never going to the table again." Joe shook his head in disbelief. "It just floors me that they would go out of their way to *invent* a reason to continue this war. *Why?*"

"I'm guessing…" Daniella collected her thoughts and gasped as Joe vaulted from the roof, still managing to land gracefully on the ground. "Pressure from the humans? The humans don't want to exterminate people, and I'd say that what you did back on Midgard took the people that *did* enjoy that sort of thing and put some fear into them. As to the Elves, I guess we just can't assume that they'll have the same desires we do. Open trade, advancement of magitech, all of that. They take their cues from the 'gods', so why do they need to want what *we* want?"

"I suppose you never really know what someone wants. What they're *actually* after, even if they seem to be a good person in all other respects." Joe had the Guildhall in view, so he didn't notice that Daniella had sunk into stricken silence. "Since we were able to get them a warning, I hope everyone is in a standoff, rather than actively attacking each other. That'd play right into whatever twisted plan this is."

As they came within ten feet of the doors, the klaxon calls were suddenly just *gone*. Joe jolted to a stop and turned around, stepping away from the building. The alarm was still going. A step toward the Guildhall? Silence. "There's a noise nullification in play? They were never warned!"

Jaxon appeared a moment later, sprinting at Joe and the building behind him. There was a strange look on his face that Joe couldn't interpret, but the larger concern was that his hands had transformed into T-rex heads and were furiously snapping at everything around them. "Joe! *Help*! My hands won't listen to me anymore! They shifted on their own and won't go away!"

"Delicious meat smell…?" Understanding dawned on Joe, and he shook his head to cut off anything more. "Jaxon! A group of people are trying to sabotage the negotiations, and I think they put down some kind of meat as bait, or something similar that is going to draw monsters to this spot. Let your hands be our guide to the meat!"

"But Joe, if my hands get to the meat, with the way I feel right now, they're going to do terrible things in public. If I can't control them *now*, what do you think is going to happen if I let them sink their teeth into juicy meat and go to town?" Jaxon cried out desperately. "Who knows if that will satisfy them? What if it just makes it worse because they got what they want? I'll have to practically start retraining my hands on the spot to keep them from reaching for meat whenever they want it!"

"That's a risk you're just going to have to take, Jaxon!" Joe told his friend in as comforting a tone as he could manage. "The fate of thousands of lives is tied to your hands guiding you to the meat. We'll be with you the whole time, so just let us know what we can do to help you keep your hands under control. But Jaxon, we *need* you to let your hands guide you to that meat. Please?"

"You'll watch the whole time? You'll be right beside me?" Jaxon pleaded as his hands started foaming at the mouth and nipping at his arms to make him move.

Joe healed the damage nearly unconsciously and bobbed his head. "I'll be wherever you need me to be. Beside you, behind you, or in front of you. Anything to make you find relief with your hands and save these peace talks."

"Then let's go!" Lefty and Terror's heads both whipped to stare in a singular direction, their strange eyes dilating as liquid dripped from their orifices. Foam, saliva, blood. The twin heads *screamed* from their pent-up frustration as Jaxon started running toward their fleshy desire. Joe had put Daniella down, and they were soon all running through the Guildhall, rushing madly through the back rooms.

"What's going on? Why are you back here?" Major Cleave appeared and was forced to dodge a bite from Jaxon. "Did you just-"

"Either I bite you, or they do!" Jaxon called as his hands continued yanking him toward what appeared to be a small closet. "Or you get out of the way, I suppose. Joe! Help! A door knob! My greatest weakness when I'm like this!"

"Got it!" Joe grabbed the handle and flung the door open, revealing a pole coated in meat that had been jammed into the floor. "Jaxon! We need to get rid of the bait, so feel free to wrap your mouths around this meat pole!"

"Lefty, Terror, since you've been such *good* hands, Daddy's gonna let you have a treat." Jaxon nervously tried to justify this as *his* choice, and the attempt was so poor that the ravenous hands actually paused to look at him and roll their eyes before tearing into the bait.

An interesting trait of Jaxon's skill was that any food that was eaten was converted to mana, which meant there was no upper limit to what the hands could ingest. In mere seconds, the meat pole had been stripped down to practically nothing. The dinosaurs panted hot, moist air as they snuffled for anything else they could go after. Moments later, they vanished as Jaxon's hands reverted to *just* hands. The man clapped his newly-pink skin and looked at his group, "We did it! We saved the negotiations!"

A group of Legion Elites appeared in the hallway with them, took in their gore-spattered appearance and the bloody closet, then promptly started to hustle them out of the building. Joe could have made a fuss, but he was too relieved to have found the bait in time. Of course, thanks to his Neutrality Aura, he and his team were clean by the time they were tossed out, but the Elites had already decided they were troublemakers.

Joe took a deep, shuddering breath as he scanned the street for any other disturbances. The Elites hadn't seemed perturbed about anything other than *them*, which meant everything else was going as well as possible in the meetings. "Now we need to go find Herr Trigger and his group, then get them tossed out of here. Oh... better yet, I can mess with him at a distance!"

Right then and there, he directed three of his Ritual Orbs to hover in front of him and mentally commanded them to spin open into the ritual circles that he had arranged within their internal wiring. When they were in place, connecting wires sprang up between each individual circle to form the physical component of their sympathetic connections. The circles began turning, and Joe pulled out his taglock. With a flick, the drop of blood flew up to hover in the center of the Novice circle. "I'm so glad I just *tested* to see if I could still use blood as a target...

technically, it isn't used to create the ritual, so no need to investigate the aspect version of his blood."

"What *is* this?" Jaxon flicked the wires, making Joe flinch from a durability damage warning. "Never seen this ritual before, and whenever you use blood in something, well, it always seems to be particularly *nasty*."

"First, please don't touch the wires. These take double damage when they're open like this." Joe swallowed his concern and tried to hone in on the task at hand. "Second, this is the first time I'm using this, and it *is* nasty. This is called the Ritual of Insanity, and it was once considered a taboo ritual. Not anymore, though! I didn't need to involve the things that the original ritual demanded in order to function. Like... you know, it required a finger-sized chunk of flesh from someone the target loves, but *that* requirement just converted into ten Common aspects when I did up the math. Nice and clean, and no one needed to suffer except the target."

"Joe... what does a Ritual of *Insanity* do to someone?" Daniella questioned with a slight quaver in her voice. "Is this what your class is *really* for? Things like this? Not making or breaking buildings?"

"It does it all!" Joe cheerfully ignored her concerned tone and tossed two Mana Batteries into the diagram to power the ritual in its entirety. The circles began to glow, and soon, aspected mana was flowing through the ritual. As more energy was collected, it slowly gathered inside of the drop of blood. The sanguine droplet began to turn gold, and once it was full of energy, the Novice ritual diagram collapsed.

Joe pulled the restored Ritual Orb back to his bandolier, watching as a glowing energy version of the circle shrank down to a fraction of an inch and started swirling around the blood. The second circle did the same thing a moment later, followed by the third. Joe wiped at the non-existent sweat on his head and turned to smile at the others. "The ritual completed without issue!"

The blood dropped into his hand, transformed into a tiny,

perfect sphere with three circles moving around it. An energy barrier kept everything together, allowing Joe to touch the object without interrupting the process within. Daniella stepped forward, her hands clenched into fists. "I asked you a *question*. What does that *do* to a person?"

"Hey now… all it does is make them see and hear things that aren't there. It's a constant distraction, which is especially useful against someone that attacks at a distance like Herr Trigger." Joe stared into her hard eyes and narrowed his own. "Abyss, Daniella, take it easy. It's easy to cancel. Either I just tell it to end, the medallion gets destroyed, or he casts a Student-ranked dispel on himself. Don't forget that right now, he's the *enemy*, Daniella. He tried to kill us all just a few minutes ago, and he'll do it again."

"It isn't right to mess with people's *minds*. Not even if they're the enemy." She crossed her arms resolutely. "If you aren't going to act like you have a moral compass, I'm going to push mine on you."

Bang.

Daniella dropped with a scream as a shotgun slug impacted her leg and shattered her femur. Herr Trigger and his cohorts stepped out of the shadows with cheerful smiles and waves. "Why, hello, Team Joe! Look at all these lovely bounties all in one place."

"Thanks for coming to die and proving my point all in one." Joe snarled as he healed the damage Daniella had just taken. "What is *wrong* with you?"

"Die? No, *no*, I'm here for the show." Herr Trigger pointed at the Guildhall. "I felt the rumblings. My instruments are *very* sensitive to movement."

"We got rid of your bait, Trigger!" Jaxon held his hands up in karate-chop positions. "There's nothing coming!"

"You got rid of all *thirteen* bait packs since last we spoke, Joe? I'm impressed." Trigger's smirk coincided with Joe's team's faces falling. "*No~o~o?* You *didn't?* How shocking."

Rumble.

The ground under the Hamlet shook, and Joe's mind immediately went to the thought that Herr Trigger had managed to set off a volcanic eruption.

"You want to know why I laughed at the fact that you built your little town here?" The falsely-accented man was forced to shout over the vibration.

A massive hand, with curved black talons made of pure obsidian at the tips of the fingers, burst through the ground around the Guildhall. Magma bubbled through the new fissures as the hand continued emerging. Soon, the entire hall was lifted into the air in the palm of a titanic creature's hand. The fingers closed around the structure, and the entire thing was yanked under the magma in an explosion of molten rock.

Herr Trigger finished his thought with a satisfied sigh. "You built your little town right in the center of a World Boss's domain. *Trigger warning*, my exquisite bounty."

CHAPTER FORTY-FIVE

Joe directed an Orb in front of himself and initiated the Ritual of Remote Activation as rapidly as possible. The time from start to activation was approximately one second. Novice rituals didn't need much in order to get going. As the rain of liquid stone started to splatter down, a golden light shone up through the magma. "The building is intact enough that the stasis effect went through. That'll give us ten minutes to figure out how to save them!"

"Yes! *Good*! I highly approve." Herr Trigger clapped as his team leveled their weapons at Joe's face. "Give them *time* to come to the realization that they are in the hands of a World Boss! An area where space is locked, so not even their last-resort teleportation artifacts can function. A creature so much more *powerful* than them that they cannot hope to win in a direct confrontation, even if the Royal family and the Oligarchy were to work together... but they won't. The Royal family will do everything to ensure that the Oligarchy falls in this moment. The *Ascetic* has given them their mission, and they *will* fulfill it."

Something within Joe trembled as the bounty hunter said 'Ascetic'. It took a moment to realize that it was a *hunger*, and it was coming from his title 'Tatum's Chosen Legend'. Somehow, he knew that if he ever managed to find a way to destroy that person, Tatum would make it worth the effort with rewards he couldn't even fathom.

Shouting and screaming was starting to overcome the now-fading sirens that Joe had set off as people began to realize what had happened. The echoes of metal-clad boots filled the air as the remainder of the Legion Elites swarmed the area. Herr Trigger's team looked at him with concern as the troops closed in, but their leader merely shrugged. "We knew it was a one-way trip. Our reward will be waiting for us in our next life. Take them out as well, and the bounty will more than cover our losses!"

"What a very *zealot* thing to say," Joe commented as his group worked to avoid or mitigate the incoming volley. "Have you gone native, Trigger?"

Bang! A clearly enchanted bullet tore into Joe's Exquisite Shell, held in place by the barrier for a moment as it reduced his defense by a third with that single shot. Trigger's grin matched Jaxon's for width and creepiness. "There's nothing religious about this, Joe. We *respawn*; our afterlife is merely waking up and stepping out of a portal in a few hours."

Seeing that all the other enemies were engaged, Joe took on Trigger directly. He sprinted at the man as a barrage of bullets zipped his way, vaulting into the air to avoid the volley, then pushing off an Orb to change directions and dodge the second strike. He threw his icicle Orb out and behind Trigger, though it stopped midair and started spinning in place once it was positioned behind the gunslinger. As Joe landed, he dropped flat and slid under another attack, much to Trigger's frustration.

"Each of these bullets cost me hours of my time! Stand still so I can kill you!"

"No!" Joe succinctly made known his thoughts on the matter. Trigger had apparently anticipated his unwillingness to accept his fate, and left his current position to flow across the ground toward Joe. Bullets created puffs of ash and powdered stone as they missed their marks and ricocheted off the ground. Joe skidded to a full stop as his momentum faltered, and Trigger stood above him, ready to execute the Reductionist at point-blank range.

Thwap! Trigger cried out in agony as Joe's icicle Orb slammed into his right scapula, causing him to lose control of that arm. Fury filled his eyes as he pulled out a revolver with his left hand and unloaded each round, laughing cruelly when his target couldn't manage to move again. "Herr Trigger *always* hits the mark."

Just as he lifted his barrel to sniff the gunpowder residue, his body was flooded with an internal Cone of Cold and hit by a Dark Lightning Strike. Seizing in place and then remaining frozen there, a look of surprise and anger was locked on his face. Joe stepped into his line of sight, a slight grin playing around his lips. "You missed, Trigger. What *were* you aiming at?"

"What… did you… do to me?" Trigger chattered through a mouth he could barely force to do his bidding. Joe was going to answer, but Major Cleave's axe swept through Trigger's neck and sent the man to respawn.

"We don't have time to mess around. You also *never* tell an enemy how you beat them!" She shoved her axes in the direction of the collapsed Guildhall. "We need to save the Oligarchs!"

Joe checked his system clock and winced. "Less than six minutes to come up with an answer. What's a World Boss, and how do we get it to let go of the building?"

"Bad. *Very* bad." Cleave whispered nervously, unable to formulate any other explanation on the severity of the subject. "A World Boss is literally the strongest opponent on each plane; it's also the *only* source of Mythical cores and Sage skills. Just by *existing*, they produce a myriad of effects. Damage dealt to them is a fraction of what it should be, and protections are only half as effective against them. If it has the building, it's guaranteed to be lost. Our only chance is to get in there and get the people out. But there's already a layer of lava in the way, and-"

"Magma," Jaxon chimed in as they gathered around the edge of the new magma pool.

"*Whatever* it *is*, it's between us and the people we need to save!" Cleave barked at the frustrating man.

"Oh! *Oh*! I have a thing for this!" Joe pulled out one of his Ritual of Bubble Travel tiles and started powering it up. "I'll get down there in a bubble, and gather them into one as the building is crushed. I'll be right back!"

"How do you plan to navigate?" Daniella quizzed him with exasperation while pulling at her hair. "You won't be able to see anything!"

"We're all just kinda hoping for the best here, Daniella!" Joe grinned at her, attempting to present a confidence he didn't feel. "Anyone wanna tag along? Kidding, kidding. Jaxon? No? Okay, it's just about ready-"

Quest failed: Shatter the Elven Theocracy. The Elven Theocracy has prevailed against the Dwarven Oligarchy! As your quest has failed, you do not earn anything, nor do you get to see the top contributors!

Anyone with the trait 'Dwarven Superiority' has been given a maximum 'Excommunicated' Title, which can only be cleared away by the King, Queen, Ascetic, or ten deaths followed by supplication at an Elven temple. These people will now glow red to anyone with the 'Elven Superiority' trait. Root out the Dwarf lovers among you!

Title gained: Excommunicated (Mandatory). Magic is the domain of higher beings. All spells or skills that use mana are 20% more unstable. There is a chance for all of these skills or spells to suffer negative effects or a direct backlash when you use them!

The Ascetic of the Theocracy commands all humans to destroy the Dwarves around them! Instead of spending their own lives, any human that kills ten Dwarves will lose their 'Dwarven Superiority' trait as well as their 'Excommunicated' title, and can apply to an Elven chapel or temple for reeducation into Elven ways!

Server alert! Congratulations to all Humans! Your actions have destroyed the racial enemy of the Elves, and the Bifrost will open to Jotun-

heim in the Capital city of the Elves when either 2 of the 3 Dwarven cities have fallen, or 75% of the Dwarven population has been eliminated!

Dwarves, fear not! If you somehow survive against all odds, you will have a very slim chance to reclaim your land!

Quest failed: Ranker II Peerage. No Oligarchy, no way to be one of their nobles. Hold your land through absolute force, or not at all!

"What... what just happened?" Major Cleave whispered as she gaped around at all the equally shocked faces. "We... *thousands* of years of fighting, and humans made us lose within a year of arriving? Why did we ever listen to your calls for peace? We got *annoyed* into becoming a Shattered race? You've gotta be kidding me!"

"But..." Joe was staring at the ritual, which was right on the *cusp* of activation. "But how? I had at *least* five more minutes until stasis wore off. I had time! This isn't fair!"

"Defenses are only half as effective against World Bosses." Daniella repeated Major Cleave's earlier words in a hushed tone. "The system must have considered the ritual as a defense and cut the effective time in half."

"What... what are we going to do?" Jaxon let out an uncomfortable whimper. "I don't like being on the losing side. I'm not used to it. Makes me all itchy."

"You're going to defect? I'm surprised, but not shocked." Cleave whirled her axes around. "Just *try* and come after my people so you can get rid of a pesky *title* you don't like!"

"Stop it, Cleave," Joe ordered with a soft sigh. "None of us are going to go after the Dwarves. *Listen*, all of you."

The steel in his voice made the entire group go silent and turn to look at him with hope in their eyes. He took a few deep breaths, doing his best to keep his simmering rage below the surface. "We're going to *survive*. When we get the chance, we're going to strike back and destroy the Elves. I refuse to let the Dwarves be the Shattered race, especially since the Elves forced this in such a dishonorable way. We're going to turn the Shoe into an unbreachable fortress, the last bastion of the Dwarves. The first thing we're going to do is get out there and bring back the best and brightest of this race, and prepare ourselves for the long haul."

He met each of their troubled eyes and pointed to his workshop. "Somebody find anyone that is in charge of *anyone*, and get them to my workshop. We're going to go make a plan."

CHAPTER FORTY-SIX

"Joe, the fact of the matter is… even though you've done all of this, we simply don't have the option to trust you. For our own safety… you need to leave." From the way the other Dwarves nodded, Bauen spoke for the entirety of the assembled Dwarves. "We all got the message. There's no more chance of coming back for us. Every time one of us goes down from now on, we're going to come back for the other side… as an Elf."

A collective shudder ran through the group, and the Dwarves stood to continue doing what they had been doing: packing up and preparing to flee to the city. The Elves would be reckless in the coming days, willing to sacrifice themselves in droves since the only losses that were permanent were now on the shorter, hairier side. Even with all their concerns and the information arrayed against him, Joe persisted. "What can I do to win your trust? How can I modify this place so that it'll be somewhere you'll all want to stay in comparison to somewhere more well-established?"

Bauen and some other familiar faces grimaced at each other uneasily as Joe mentioned 'modifying' the place. The various crafters, professionals, and highly-skilled people conferred for a short while, then seemed to come to a decision. Once more, Bauen was selected as the speaker for the group, "Look, Joe. There's a whole slew of Towns, Hamlets, and Villages… but like the notice stated, there are only three Cities. A City is a Tier-five place and has countless protections and such… but they're also well-known locations and are going to be under constant attack."

"Just tell me what you need from me," Joe insisted once more, trying his best to project a confidence he didn't have.

The Dwarf nodded and started outlining some requirements. "Each of these Cities has at *least* one Grandmaster. If you can get them to relocate here, at least three Grandmasters, then the core of Dwarven Society—our heritage—can be saved. In the Capital, there are two known Grandmasters… Havoc and his brother McPoundy."

"I already have an in with McPoundy." Joe nodded and got to his feet. "I'll get going right now."

"You get McPoundy, and the rest of us will stay here until we know for sure that you *can't* get the others." Bauen offered as graciously as he possibly could. "We can give you a couple days, but…"

Quest gained: Gathering confidence. Your entire population is planning to abandon the 'unnamed Hamlet' in the Shoe. Get one Grandmaster other than Major General Havoc to promise to relocate within 2 days. Reward: Population will stay and work to fortify the Hamlet to the best of their abilities. Failure: Hamlet will be abandoned.

"I've got this, Bauen. Everyone, get ready to start working as soon as possible. I'll be back with plenty of time to spare." Joe ushered everyone away from his workshop and locked the door. The Dwarves were muttering in discontent and disbelief as they dispersed, but Jaxon was clapping loudly.

"I loved it! How are we gonna make this happen? I'm betting the Grandmaster isn't going to be super open to leaving everything behind and coming here, so I can't wait to hear how you plan to coerce him!" The excitable Chiropractor cheerfully enthused. "Are we going right now, or-"

"Dude, *chill*," Joe hissed at his friend, noticing that many Dwarves had also stopped and were waiting on the answer. "Let's get going; I want to talk to McPoundy in the next few minutes."

"But… Joe, the teleporter. It was eaten by the World Boss," Jaxon reminded him carefully. "I'm not sure how you think we're gonna travel a four hour's sprint without a teleporter."

"I have a plan for that." Joe grinned as they started racing toward the exit, only to come to a screeching halt as they found their path blocked by Daniella and Major Cleave. "Pardon us, we're in a hurry-"

"Yeah, well. We're going with you," Major Cleave informed him, falling in step with the once-again-running duo. "I was ordered to watch out for you, and I'm gonna do it."

"The government has fallen, Cleave," Joe quietly reminded her. "I have no idea what the city is going to look like, I have an untested transportation system, and you don't get any spare lives. If this all goes down in flames, I don't want you to vanish forever."

The Dwarf studied him, looking for mockery, and found only concern. Her posture relaxed slightly, but she shook her head. "I don't know what you humans do when your authority figures fail, but my people fall back on tradition. The worse things are, the more important our way of life becomes. My people are on the chopping block for extermination… you'll never see us more orderly and ready to sacrifice ourselves for each other."

"There are a *lot* of humans in the city, Cleave," Joe warned her worriedly. "There's no way they're taking this well."

"All the more reason to make sure you have a Dwarven escort that can attest to the fact that you aren't killing our people," she informed him with a growl, avoiding meeting his eyes as she asked a question she was dreading. "This conversation is over… unless you're trying to sneak off and get rid of your new title?"

Joe didn't have anything to say about that, so they continued to the exterior of the Shoe in silence; all but for Daniella's huffing and puffing. An architect's lifestyle didn't leave much room for boosting physical characteristics.

They took a hard left at the exit to the tunnel, continuing on for about fifty feet before coming to the flat rock that Joe had designated for a launchpad. The ritual was ready to go, so he had everyone stand as close together as possible and hold on for dear life. "This is totally untested. We could lose our protection halfway there, or hit like a meteor and get crushed like bugs. It could kill us all just by getting *activated*. That means that this is the last chance for anyone that wants to opt out."

No one said anything, but Joe could see that Daniella at least considered it before firming her resolve. Without any protests to stop him, he cracked his knuckles and got to activating the ritual. Mana flowed out of him and the barriers began crackling to life. As it charged, the entire ritual shifted to orient in the directions Joe had plotted out for the travel trajectory. "Three... two... *one!*"

A huge figure appeared next to the stone just as the bubble fully materialized. The 'bubble' made of mana barriers shot forward like one of Herr Trigger's large caliber rounds, smashing the group and sudden addition against the interior plane of force until their bodies acclimated to the speed. Just by the crushing feeling, Joe could tell that their Constitution was the only thing keeping them from sustaining serious injuries. In fact, his Neutrality Aura was needed to fix up some minor injuries among the less hearty.

His attention turned to the newest addition, Jimathy Kettlebell. The first thing Joe noticed was the lack of rank; it appeared that lower-enlisted humans had been expelled from the Legion. The huge man spoke before Joe could berate him, staring at Jaxon with shark-like puppy eyes. "You were just gonna leave me here? I thought you thought I was a good learner. You said that we would work together until I was fully trained."

"Of *course*, my young friend!" Jaxon patted the swollen bicep pressed against his face reassuringly. "I had just remembered that you weren't a fan of heights, and I thought that you might want to sit this one out!"

"Heights?" Kettlebell looked around, only now noticing that they were already a quarter mile off the ground and still ascending at a speed which commercial airlines would have envied. A high-pitched howl tore from his throat, cutting off when Cleave delivered a sucker-punch to the trachea.

She met the disapproving stares with a scowl of her own. "Too loud. That was reverberating in here."

"It's *fine*! Let's not get into any kind of fights in the bubble that's traveling at several hundred miles per hour above monster-infested countryside, *hmm*?" Joe's distracted tone earned him a few concerned glances, but he was watching the readout of the ritual to ensure that they weren't about to be trapped in an imploding bubble barrier, though he did make a note to turn that into a combat ritual in the future. "We have maybe three minutes until we land, and I'm not sure what sort of speed we'll be moving at. I need *all* of my concentration so that I can cancel the ritual in time if we're about to hit something."

"Yes, let's not use our own blood to paint the inside of this small space, please!" Jaxon cheekily tossed out an 'okay' hand gesture. "Going quiet now!"

They could already see the city getting closer, and by the time they laid eyes on it, the view had expanded dramatically. Joe's eyes kept flicking between the ritual and the ground that they were now dropping toward. "Steady... *steady*...!"

When they were about ten feet off the ground, Kettlebell lost control of himself. "We're all gonna die! I don't wanna die alone!"

He launched himself at Jaxon and swept his mentor up in a hug, inadvertently slamming into Joe and sending him bouncing around the small space.

Two seconds later, the bubble walloped into the ground and dug a deep furrow as it expended all remaining energy, tossing the group around like pinballs before popping and scattering them across the ground.

Moments later, Kettlebell sat up and grabbed the leg in front of him, "I can't feel my legs!"

"Let. Go. Of. Me." Cleave slapped the human off of her and sent him spiraling into a tree.

"Hey! Alright, I'm okay!" Heaving himself upright, Kettlebell felt at himself. His oversized muscles were unblemished, and his legs were working just fine. Joe could only glare at the man with pure malice in his eyes as he waited for his broken spine to fix itself.

Neutrality Aura for the win.

CHAPTER FORTY-SEVEN

They moved through the city as easily as Major Cleave had promised they would. She had been correct about many things, such as how the Dwarves weren't going wild or attempting to loot stores, and the fact that they were incredibly standoffish toward any humans walking around without a Dwarf in their party. A cluster of humans that were stalking the streets with blood dripping off of them and sizing up solo Dwarf travelers certainly wasn't helping matters, but Joe's party had more pressing concerns.

"You've *gotta* let us in." Joe kept eye contact with the Expert smith Dwarf that was blocking his path with a spear tip nearly brushing Joe's throat. "We need to talk to McPoundy; he knows me, and I've come to collect a favor."

"Nope." The Dwarf sucked gently on his teeth and spat to the side, neither deigning to say more nor explain himself.

Joe sighed and motioned for Cleave to take over. She stepped forward and glared into the Dwarf's face, then slapped the spear out of the way with practiced ease. "Look here, you little *crafter*. If you don't get out of our way right now, I'm going to pry you open like an overloading golem and shove a wrench in you to try and fix what's broken!"

"Woah." The Dwarf had a gleam in his eye as the tasseled ends of Cleave's mustache waved in front of his face. "You seeing anyone? I figure we gotta get started *now* if we're gonna save our species-"

Jaxon was suddenly next to the Dwarf, poking him thirty-six times in rapid succession. The Dwarf blinked and tried to turn to face him, but he ended up being unable to control his body, followed by slowly slumping and falling flat on his face. Each member of the team took a turn walking over the face-down, prone Dwarf.

It would have been more satisfying if he hadn't giggled whenever someone's foot landed on him.

"What are you doing in here!" The demand was followed by dozens of intensely glowing weapons being unsheathed and pointed at the vital points of everyone in Joe's party. A Master smith that Joe had met in one of his previous visits stepped forward and inspected each of them, his eyes narrowing fractionally when he saw Joe. "You... I know you. You're the human that kept coming in here and throwing himself down the trash chute while wailing about how we mistreated you."

"Always good to be remembered," Joe replied cheekily. His liveliness was met with dark looks and a tightening of hands on hilts, so he dropped the humor. "I'll cut to the chase. I'm Major General Pyrrhic, here to see Grandmaster McPoundy on matters of survival of the Dwarven race. Lower your weapons, *now*."

Not a single Dwarf complied.

"Well, that's just great." Joe sighed as a few Dwarves even started edging in closer to be the first to attack. "Here I thought that the Dwarven people had honor and were going to fall back on *tradition*, Major Cleave?"

"Not my fault that some people are a little more overprotective than they should be." Cleave waved gently at the room.

"Clearly, there's been some threat to the Grandmaster. Read the room, would you?"

"I liked you better when I didn't know you were around," Joe muttered under his breath as he took her advice. Recognizing that everyone in the room was prepared to die before giving up the Grandmaster, he could only grunt and pull out a trump card. "How about this? I'm Joe, Apprentice of Major General Havoc—Grandmaster Golemancer—who is also the brother of Grandmaster McPoundy. I'm here in an attempt to save the Dwarves, and I need to speak to McPoundy."

No reply was forthcoming, so Joe narrowed his eyes and started speaking to the actual room. "You know what? No Oligarchy means that any oaths sworn have lost the ability to punish people; deals once made no longer apply! I have great information on swords designed for attacking feet, and a whole *bunch* of stories which the Experts in the room and I can discuss!"

A door appeared in the air, and a hand came out and pointed to Joe, then made a 'come' motion before vanishing into the open doorway. Joe pushed forward past a row of hesitating Dwarves, some of which didn't move their weapons fast enough and earned a shadowy slap across the face as the edges brushed against his Exquisite Shell. As soon as the human stepped into the smithy's subspace, the door vanished behind him.

McPoundy was standing in the odd room, tapping his toe on the ground and glaring at Joe. "I am *busy*, and threats against my reputation are neither appreciated nor welcome. This is the last time I'll respond, as It won't matter what people think of me if we are unable to survive the coming onslaught, so use this opportunity to speak with me *wisely*."

"Didn't want to have to do that, but what I do have to say is important." Joe sent along his quest information to the Grandmaster, who read it and shook his head. Before the Dwarf could speak up, Joe began laying out his reasoning for the Grandmaster to join him. "Listen. We need to keep as many Dwarves alive as possible, but the quantity won't matter if we aren't able to train them up to be powerful enough to have a fighting chance of taking back the Zone. You *know* that it is only a matter of time before the Dwarves get taken down. It doesn't matter if it's three days or ten years. Having a secure fallback point is *essential*."

"One Grandmaster isn't enough," McPoundy informed him instantly. "Just *me* being there is nothing. I may as well stay here and continue beefing up the defenses of the city."

"I don't need you there all the time. I just need your promise that you won't go down with the city, and that you'll fall back to the Shoe when it becomes necessary," Joe wheedled as he tried to think of how he could make this work. "I'll make it easy for you. You're a Grandmaster in Enchanting; do you know how to make a linked portal?"

"I do," McPoundy snorted impatiently. "I *don't* have the time to make it. Linked portals need to be made *exactly* the same, and they require Unique resources that I just don't have."

"Do you have the template?" Joe wondered hopefully. "If you have that, I can get them made, and I have a way for you to come back and forth to get everything set up. Also, you'll be able to evacuate as many people as you can when the time comes."

McPoundy considered the offer, but ultimately shook his head 'no'. "I'm sorry, Joe. I *can't* just give those templates away. They're too hard to make, and your Hamlet is, frankly, a bad escape plan. My workshop is here. You have minimal defenses. The Elves know *exactly* where it is, and the land is already *proven* to be dangerous. Most importantly: you never passed your peerage test, so your Hamlet doesn't have a Guardian that can prevent Elven teleportation, infiltration, and easy access. If you had let it remain a fort, a normal Guardian would have appeared or been assigned. So, *no*. That is my answer."

As McPoundy pointed at the door, Joe was struck with sudden inspiration. "Wait! I can *get* a Guardian!"

"It doesn't *matter*, Joe! The other reasons are still valid."

McPoundy was starting to get angry, and he grabbed at Joe to start moving him out the door.

"Then pretend to be a human and help me cheat!" the human demanded just as the Dwarf was reaching for the handle.

The bearded Grandmaster paused and sighed. "I'll let you speak. Explain."

"Help me convince my villagers to stay. I can recreate this worksop that we're standing in *exactly* the way it is, and no one will be able to tell if you're staying in it or not." Joe started counting off his solutions to the issues. "Then you at least have an *option* as a fallback point. Since we've failed so badly with the Oligarchs, the Elves would never expect it to become the bunker that will house the greatest of our people. Our failure becomes our greatest protection! Defenses are easy, I just need time-"

"Stop." McPoundy took a deep breath and looked Joe in the eyes. "You haven't failed *me* yet... so I'll give you just one chance. Get a Guardian for your Hamlet, and I'll make an appearance. I'll give you the linked portal templates, and it'll be on you to create and install them. If you manage that much, I'll pop in once a week or so. Everything else? It'll be up to you to make a convincing argument. There's your time, which has ended here."

The door was pulled open, and they stepped into the workshop. McPoundy waved the others forward before turning to Joe. "What do you need to get started?"

"Got any food?" Joe shrugged and waved his team over to the garbage chute. "I have a lot to do, and not much time."

The Grandmaster tapped Joe's ring with his own, and a screen appeared asking Joe if he wanted to accept the transfer of two weeks' worth of dry goods. He accepted and hopped onto the edge of the trash chute after the transfer completed. The Master that had recognized him saw his position and shook his head, muttering darkly.

"Okay, team! Everyone in!" Joe didn't wait for a reply, instead crossing his arms and leaning back like he was going into a waterslide. "We've got a civilization to save!"

CHAPTER FORTY-EIGHT

Joe landed in the muck below the garbage chute, concerned at how much *longer* of a fall there had been. He scanned the area, spotting literal tons of garbage in the air being directed to the distant A.S.P.E.C.T. and being refined into something. "Good, that means everything should still be moving along nicely... I wonder how far everything settled after taking a lake's worth of liquid out of here?"

Bulky objects were far more numerous on the top layer of the landfill than thay had been even a few weeks ago, and the small things that Joe could see each looked to weigh more than fifty pounds. All of this together meant that his ritual had been doing excellent work. Now it was time to see what he had gained in the time he had been absent. Joe heard a shout and vaulted out of the way as Jaxon impacted the sludgy ground and sank all the way down to his chest.

"Pardon me, Joe, but what in the ever-lovin' abyss did I just get myself into?" Jaxon shimmied and shot out of the muck without using his hands to touch the 'ground'. "I'd like to stand very close to you for a few minutes, as I think I just got very sick."

"Ohh… right." Neutrality Aura was practically the only thing that kept Joe from dying down here, and his team obviously had a different skill set than his. "Range of my aura is ten feet, but that was doubled at the Journeyman rank. Stay within twenty feet of me, and you'll be okay."

"You failed to mention that we would be spending time in a dump, Joe. I'm not a huge fan of throwing myself away." Jaxon's head turned to the side like a dog hearing a call for a treat. "I think Daniella was coming right behind me; you may want to try and catch her."

He gestured at the space where the two of them had landed, which had compressed into a pit of agitated ooze. Joe looked up, then jumped straight up and caught not Daniella, but Cleave. As they were moving into position to land safely, Daniella shot past—almost instantly followed by Kettlebell. She hit first, then was covered in a wave of… um, *mud*, as the much larger man impacted the surface and sank in. The group helped to extract them, and Daniella slumped to the side, staring in horror at her soiled clothes and letting out intermittent whimpers.

After a few seconds, the ick was cleaned away, and the accumulated debuffs began vanishing as well. Joe was glad that they most likely couldn't see the litany of diseases and parasites that had attached to them in the brief amount of time that they'd been in this area. "So, everyone, being down here is utterly terrible for your health. I have an aura that will keep us going, but you all need to keep an eye on your total hit points all the time. Whenever you see them start to dip, come and stand with me for a while."

"How… how often are you in this place?" Daniella pointed to what looked like an animal path that led into the distance. "Was this you, or is there something down here that we need to watch out for? Also… *why* are we here?"

"Ahhh, *little* of both." Joe's eyebrow ticked a bit as he realized that he hadn't told anyone what was going on. "I made that path, but yes, there are dangers down here. Lots of animals, as well as a whole *lot* of Dwarven Zombies. So long as we're careful, they shouldn't be too much of an issue. Oh, and every one hundred feet is a barrier that will appear if you are moving too fast, so when you need to run away, don't go at top speed other than a dire emergency, at least until you understand the grid squares. Last thing, we're here to kill a hidden Guardian that was malfunctioning or something. Once we manage that, we'll get to install a top-of-the-line Guardian in our Hamlet."

Cleave had gone pale *long* before Joe finished explaining, so when he was done, she choked on her words a few times before managing to shout at him. "You... *abyssal* corn-filled chunk of fecal matter! Do you have any idea what you're saying? The zombies alone...! If I get bit, the city won't need to worry about the Elves!"

"Then perhaps we shouldn't be yelling?" Joe interrupted before she could build up a full head of steam. "Like I said, it shouldn't be too much of an issue'; I've had some practice with them now."

"When there was a *Dwarf* with you?" she hissed at him while her eyes were darting around the area. "Zombies of the same race are a *hundred times* more aggressive against their original kind! If they get a whiff of me, they'll hunt me until either I escape, or none of them are left!"

"Okay, but in all fairness, I didn't know that was a thing." Joe could only throw his hands in the air and start walking. "We need to get to shelter right away, in that case."

"So... do we just follow the floating debris?" Kettlebell pointed up at the moving garbage.

"Yes. In case we get separated, go to the vanishing garbage, and we'll meet you there." Joe agreed with the mountainous man. "Very good observation, Kettlebell. I'd give you a cookie, but I recommend not putting anything in your mouth here if you can avoid doing so."

"One last thing, Joe. A *Guardian*? There's five of us!" Cleave was pulling at both ends of her mustache as she whisper-screamed at him. "It can take an entire battalion of Dwarves *dying* before we make headway against the Guardian, and that's in a minor fort. How big is this one? Where had it been located before being sent down here?"

"Well..." Joe thought about the best way to answer the question. "If my guess is correct, it used to be up above us."

"It's... you found a City Guardian. A malfunctioning one that attacks Dwarves." Cleave nearly fainted as she took in Joe's suggestion. "You want us to kill a City Guardian, surrounded by zombies, while fighting off constantly-refreshing debuffs in a dump-sewer combo."

"Yes, and we have less than two days to get this back up there and get McPoundy on board, then return to the Shoe." Joe summed up the information she was missing.

"You gave me a chance *not* to come with you, and I just... came anyway!" Cleave giggled wildly as her eyes dilated. Her words dissolved into odd ramblings and chuckles, but she managed to keep up, so the rest of the team couldn't spare the effort to worry too much.

The dump was eerily quiet, which Joe decided must be due to the animal population losing easy cover and subsequently being decimated by the roaming zombies. The loudest noises were the squelching of their shoes, and objects floating around bumping into each other intermittently. The several-hour journey passed quickly since there had been no interference, and soon Joe was staring up at his barriers and wondering how his team was supposed to get into the A.S.P.E.C.T., since the ritual had concentrated on the garbage nearest to it first. There was now a thirty-foot deep pit beneath the tower, which, while great for defense, posed an issue in terms of ease of access.

"Got it." Joe snapped his fingers and turned to his team. "Anyone have some rope? I think I can manage to get up there, and then I can lower the rope and you can either climb or get pulled up."

It turned out that Kettlebell—of all people—was the only one that had any rope at all, as he used it for cross-training exercises. Joe stored everything in his Codpiece of Holding and took a few deep breaths to prepare. Once centered, he started running around the excavated area, then used the momentum to jump up as high as he could.

An Orb was waiting for him, and he pushed off it for more lift. He barely needed the second one as he grabbed onto the ladder built into the underside of the building and easily held himself there as steadily as if he were standing. Joe felt a moment of nostalgia, wishing that he'd had this kind of upper-body strength in the old days. After scrabbling up the side to a more secure spot, he lowered the ropes and waited for the group to climb.

As they clambered into safety, Joe was already pausing the Ritual 'Little Sister's Cleaning Service' and inspecting it for wear and tear. "Yikes… this is already practically dead. Good work, little ritual. Time for you to rest."

With that, he dispersed the ritual and watched fondly as it faded away. He ignored the howls of discontent that sprang up from nearly every corner of the dump as all of the levitating filth rained down on the locals, too immersed in the bittersweet moment that always arrived at the end of a successful ritual. "Well… with that all done, I can turn off the aspect array and set up the Special layer, then get the Student ritual in place."

"What just happened?" Jaxon called as the sounds of the dump slowly returned to silence.

"I canceled the ritual that gathered trash! I'm gonna set up a more robust version soon, but I need to clean out the container here and do some work first." Joe didn't want to let on how concerned he was with the impending time limit, but if he wanted to create the rituals he knew he would need against the Guardian, he required more potent resources than he currently had on his person. "Let me know if you have any issues!"

With that, he dove headfirst into the A.S.P.E.C.T. and got to work setting up the Special layer.

He could only hope that it wouldn't go terribly wrong and force him to find a different strategy that would work just as well, or even better, than his current plan.

CHAPTER FORTY-NINE

"I literally cannot believe that went so well. It *had* to have been thanks to achieving Reductionist level three." Joe pondered the shifting curtain of light that composed the Special layer of the aspect array. It had been difficult to create, but was only marginally more problematic than the Rare layer had been. It was also much smaller, formed of multiple geometric planes of aspects that weren't highly detailed, but were very difficult to hold in position.

The most dangerous moment of creating the layer had been when Joe had lost focus on one of the hexagonal portions, and it had snapped back from a sheet of energy into a single strand —the Reductionist had *barely* managed to keep it under control long enough to reshape it and lock it in position.

The long-awaited message came right as he was wondering how he could do this better if he ever had to do it again.

Class quest complete: Beginner Reductionist. Reward: 125 Unique aspects.
Record breaker bonus: access to Beginner Reductionist II.
Class quest gained: Beginner Reductionist II. You're about to get rewarded for doing something that you were going to do anyway! Spend 10,000

aspects from each category of Rare and below. Reward: One Rare template for any craft you practice. Aspects spent: 0.
Class quest gained: Apprentice Reductionist. Collect and use 10,000 Rare aspects! Reward: +5 levels to any crafting skill under Master rank.

Joe couldn't speak for a long moment, too enthralled by the fact that he could gain multiple class quests at the same time for the same class. That had been a shock, but a very happy one. "Special layer is up, sso let's at least get a *look* at the Unique layer…"

After placing his palms on the dais and taking a peek, he gently removed his hands and tried not to feel terribly sick to his stomach. "That's a *whole* lot of array to make. I don't have days or weeks right now… or a quest for it."

Swapping out the full Aspect Jars for empty ones, he climbed out of the container to join the others atop it, sitting down and watching the zombies that were swarming the space below them with great concern. "So, *that's* not great."

"Nope," Jaxon agreed as he pointed out an extra-large Legionnaire wandering among the others. "That one showed up first; it looked like it was sniffing the ground like a dog. We're pretty sure it followed Cleave's trail *exactly*, and when it lost her, it screamed. Then all the others showed up to help it search. Some horror-show stuff going on down there!"

"Let's hope not," Cleave sighed as she stared at the ceiling far above them. "I had no idea this place was so infested. It's a danger to the entirety of the Zone."

Joe decided not to acknowledge the pouting, and instead began using his new collection of aspects to create all the rituals he could think of that would be useful against the Guardian. By the time he was finished, more than half of the time they had in which to complete the task was gone. He stood and stretched, feeling as rested and prepared as he could be without taking an actual nap. "Two more things to do, and we can be on our way."

The others nodded with varying degrees of hesitation.

Cleave looked like she was going to be sick, Daniella looked like she was about to refuse to come with them, Jaxon looked excited to have a goal, and Kettlebell sat staring at the sky, trying to find some kind of pattern that might indicate when and where garbage would drop into the dump. Joe wanted to do his best to let them all have whatever time they needed to prepare, so he went to the top of the container and began pushing mana into the new Student-ranked ritual he had created specifically for use in the underground waste cavern.

"Little Sister wasn't designed to clean a place like this." Joe gleefully made up a backstory as he activated each circle, watching as they expanded and began warping space around themselves very lightly. "That's okay… now we have the Ritual of Big Brother's Moving Company to take the pressure off of her!"

A very minor shockwave rippled through the entirety of the landfill as the ritual activated. Moments later, heavy garbage that had remained still for countless years began to shift off the ground and hover into the air. Joe moved like a whirlwind, pouring mana into the activation of the permanent aspect array. Moments after he succeeded, the first item was shoved into the container, and two massive columns of gray smoke erupted from the top as the object was reduced to pure energy.

The tradeoff for the new ritual being able to move all of the bulky gear was that the items were being collected *significantly* slower, but that wasn't an issue for Joe: he had no idea when he would be here next. So long as the work was getting done, he didn't care about the speed. Now that things were happening, the team looked lively once more. He waved at the floating items, his grand gesture pulling their attention to him. "Just like that, we now have a way to get to the Guardian and away from the zombies. You guys most likely don't have the Jump skill like I do , but I think you'll all be able to manage this with your phys-ical stats alone."

"I have so many things I need to explain to you about why this is a bad idea that I'm not even going to try. I'm just gonna do what you say and hope I survive long enough to kill off a few hundred Elves before I go." Cleave stood, brushed off her pants, and set her resolve to participate.

"Glad you're back with us!" Joe looked around, put his hand in the air, and tried to gauge the distance to the last place he had seen the Guardian. "That's the way we need to go; is everyone ready?"

"Yes!" Jaxon shouted in excitement, causing all the zombies below them to go still. The majority of the group shushed him, but Joe just nodded in acceptance and jumped onto a large broken safe that was flying toward him, then started running. Muffled curses rose behind him as the others realized that with him gone, the air around them was not only disgusting again, but deadly even in the short term.

Even if he had wanted to stop—and he didn't—losing his momentum now would mean that the ritual would see the item he was on as 'in use' and drop it. Joe moved at a constant pace, just above jogging, and made sure to pick out his path well in advance. "Whoop, can't use that one; they don't have Omni-vault. Someone tries to follow me, they're dropping. There's a couch, it's turning… perfect!"

Joe jumped from the edge of a bathtub onto the back of an overstuffed couch, then scuttled along a few tables, then pushed off doors with fist holes punched through them. He looked ahead once more, slowing down slightly. The reach of the ritual was still expanding, and if he went at top speed, he'd get to the edge of the floating gear too quickly. A glance back revealed that the rest of his people were following him, but also that the zombies were slowly trailing behind.

It appeared the scout among them didn't have a good read on where they were, and none of the creatures seemed to think to look up. They were zigzagging all around in an attempt to follow the scent, and sometimes even backtracked. "Gonna need a way to lose all of them…"

He moved this way and that for the next half hour before approaching a ridgeline of garbage that his ritual just hadn't been able to make any headway against. He jumped and landed safely, then waited to pull his companions in as they jumped at him. Once everyone was together, he pointed into the distance, and they began moving as fast and silently as possible.

The land began to slope down, and Joe noticed a few steam vents pumping scalding water away from the area. He stopped and began setting up the first of many rituals, this one being an acid bubble launcher. The five of them circled the area placing ritual after ritual, slowly drawing closer to the center, where he knew the Guardian was lying under the surface.

When his final circles were in place, he pointed out three different glowing diagrams that were hovering in the air. "If we are getting wiped out, run over to any of those and activate it. The bubble that forms will send you straight up and out of this area in a single second, then slowly drift to the edge of the dump and drop you by the wall so it doesn't set off any barriers."

"What's the actual plan here, Joe?" Cleave questioned the human as he started drawing out a ritual in midair, leaving the glowing lines hanging from it like acid-filled lasers.

"Rituals aren't spells, technically, and we're going to have to hope that that technicality will let us get away with using them, even though we're all Excommunicated. Technicalities matter," Joe explained in a fretting, distracted manner as he drew the final line of the fairly simple ritual. "Cleave, can I get access to a drop of your blood?"

"Not a chance," she refused instantly. Joe pleaded with her in hushed whispers for almost a minute before she allowed him to poke her with his taglock and insert the blood into the ritual. "I think we're going to need to stop hanging out after this."

"Don't be like that. It'll be important later," Joe promised her as he turned his attention to a gleaming bronze pipe that was poking just above the surface of the trash. "Here we go; everyone get ready to hunker down and stay hidden. I'll be right back."

Barely making a noise, Joe crept to the pipe and started

stuffing what he now knew to be Warped Rituals of Exquisite Shell into the piping. After blowing himself up with them way back when, he was excited to see what they could do to someone else. After all, it was hard to examine the results when he kept ending up unconscious at the start of the experiment. "I need to do this... for science!"

The tightly rolled scrolls fell through the pipe without issue. Just to be *extra*, Joe stuck a Ritual of Streaming Acid to the opening as well. He positioned the ritual flow to pour directly into the pipe—setting it up so that it couldn't move away from its position relative to the pipe itself. Then he turned and overly-stealthily tiptoed his way back to his team.

"Everyone ready?" Joe questioned his group, then began creating a few Novice Ritual of Remote Activation in the air. He set them up in the order that they should be used, then dumped mana into the first.

Warped Ritual of Exquisite Shell (Linked x5) activated!

There came a series of five explosions, and concussive blasts tore from various exit points under the garbage, revealing dozens of pipes identical to the first one that he had targeted. "Next one activates... now!"

Ritual of Streaming Acid activated!

Quest updated: Student Ritualist. Student Rituals activated: 4/20!

"Looking good, looking good..." Joe realized just then that his group was currently standing unprotected in the wide open. "Whoops, should have restarted this one first."

The Reductionist slapped his hand onto the ritual they were huddled around. He had activated this one a few minutes previously, then paused it until their opening salvo was ready.

Ritual of Concealed Defense. When activated, it creates a set of barriers that wrap over a small area and protect anything within from damage. Conceals its presence and the presence of the contents.

In the same moment that the shields winked to life around them and they 'vanished' from the spot, the bronze pipes began to frantically shift around. A howl of acidic steam shot from the pipe, coating the area directly adjacent with acid that was hot enough to melt skin, even if it *weren't* already acidic.

A tinny bellow of madness-filled rage shook the heaps of filth away from a house-sized Dwarf-made creature, which unfolded and stood to its full height as it began searching the area for whatever foolish creature had such a strong desire for respawn that they would assault it. An axe appeared in one hand, a glowing sphere in the other. It slashed at a nearby upward slope, sending metric tons of destruction flying away, only to crash against the one-hundred-foot barrier; most of the items turned to small chunks, or were reduced to sludge that slid down the rapidly dissipating plane of force.

The entire time this was going on, acid was being poured down the pipe that had been exposed. As far as Joe knew, that was a steam exhaust—therefore, his acid was draining down right into the center of the creature. There would be no outlet for the caustic material. Not until it created its own escape route.

Daniella nudged Joe. "Good thinking with the acid, Joe, but it isn't enough. We'd need an army to fight that thing!"

"You know, I thought of that." Joe beamed at her as he activated a Ritual of Remote Activation. "You have *excellent* timing."

Predator's Territory activated!

A chill went down their spines as the ritual they were exempt from came online. Jaxon, who had experienced this feeling before, looked at Joe quizzically. "You know that won't make the Guardian leave, right?"

"I know. But I found out something super-duper extra neato about that ritual." Joe cocked his head to the side as a cacophony of howls and shrieks filled the air. "It carries the 'scent' of whoever's blood is used to activate it… and just like Cleave told us, the smell of Dwarves makes Dwarf Zombies go nuts."

CHAPTER FIFTY

"Donuts make *me* go nuts." Jaxon broke the silence in the little bubble as everyone stared at Joe in horror. The Chiropractor took in all the strange expressions, and his face shifted into realization. "Ohh, this is the first time you're doing something paradigm-breaking with Joe. Yeah. *Yeah*... eventually, you'll just go with it. Solid fifty percent chance of success. Half the time, it works every time."

"I'm going to die here. Gonna go ahead and make peace with that right now." Cleave's eyes were flat as she stared out at the swarm that was approaching. "*Uuggghhh*. I'm gonna have pointy ears."

The Guardian wasn't waiting for the enticed zombies to close in; the metal Dwarf lifted the hand that ended in a glowing sphere... and mana began rushing into it. After a three-second charge, it fired a beam of liquid flame in a laminar stream, passing it over the front wave of the encroaching zombies.

Dozens of undead became dead-dead as the intense heat purified their mortal forms. Joe had a notebook in hand and nodded as he watched the flames wash out. "Three second charge, range of about seventy-five feet. Noted."

"Did you do all of *this*... just to see what sort of attack patterns this thing uses?" Daniella glanced at Joe with a hint of admiration in her gaze. "I thought the zombies, the rituals, the diving into the garbage... was all just a spur of the moment thing."

"It isn't going to be anywhere as useful as you think it is," Cleave warned them as she waved at the Guardian. "That thing wouldn't be the defender of a *city* if it were easy to plan against."

The automaton's hand was in the air, shining with a bright new light. As the rotting Dwarves started throwing themselves against the metal body, a tornado came into being around the Guardian and effortlessly tossed them away. Joe's quill twitched as he counted each second that the tornado lasted, but it simply didn't vanish until even the most stubborn zombie had been thrown. Once its legs were clear, the giant stomped, creating a shockwave that caught anything still in the air and threw it further.

A wave of waste material was flung into the open space when the tornado began, and after the shockwave, it zipped out and tore apart even more of the zombies. Joe had seen enough for the moment, so he carefully stored his notebook and began drawing power into the third and final hovering Novice circle he had set up in advance. "They can't even get close. Time to give them a fighting chance."

He activated the Ritual of Remote Activation, and one of the pre-charged rituals created a bubble of force and started filling up with acid. The barriers were unaffected by the caustic material, and as the sphere became *full*, it was launched at the Guardian from the side, arcing through the intervening space as though a trebuchet had taken the field.

The bubble struck the left shoulder and stuck there, keeping the acid mostly concentrated on one spot, though it leaked constantly where the semi-permeable side had allowed the metal to infiltrate the barrier. The Guardian stumbled as the huge weight attached to it, then reached over with its right hand and *slapped* the pustule on its side. The acid-filled sphere popped from the force, sending hundreds of gallons of liquid pouring down over its body.

Joe was hoping for more, and watched in calm satisfaction as the ground under the Guardian began to smoke and foam. Fractions of a second later, a second bubble from the same ritual landed on the Guardian, only slightly off from where the first had hit. Speaking before the others could ask, the Ritualist pointed at the ritual that was already filling another bubble with acid. "It just keeps going until destroyed or it runs out of energy. It'll get, at most, ten shots."

As the Guardian hit the second bubble, releasing caustic death that rained from above, the zombies attacked. The distraction that Joe had instigated proved perfect, and soon scores of undead Dwarves were attached to the behemoth, punching, clawing, and battering it with weapons if they had one. Acid from the second ruptured bubble flooded over a solid quarter of the zombies, as well as the bronze Guardian. The oversized protector let out a mechanical bellow, swinging at the attacker on the ground with his massive axe and cleaving charging creatures with a vengeance that left even the jaded Major Cleave impressed.

Then the group heard a *thump* and turned to look behind them. A slew of zombies were charging down the slope that they were hidden on, and several of them had just tripped over the practically invisible barrier. When Cleave turned, she was less than an inch away from a zombie's face. Joe expected to see fear or startlement, but all that crossed her face was a slight sadness as she sighed, "I don't know who would do this to so many of my people. If this many are already here, there must be *thousands* in the landfill. How many each year were murdered and shoved into the garbage to hide the evidence?"

"Some kind of serial killer?" Joe tried to offer an explanation.

She shook her head. "I doubt it. Not from my people. Though it might be more likely that there is an Elven presence in the city that attacks unwary Dwarves. The fact that so many of them are in armor tells me that they must attack near the Legion barracks, or along a route that the Legionnaires follow often. It's just too bad that… well, this place is deadly dangerous, even with our high Constitutions. No one *ever* comes down here."

"That thing is looking in our direction!" Daniella squeaked out just before an icy mist blasted out of the magical-attack hand. The temperature along the entire slope hit sub-zero in under a second, turning the mounds of domestic refuse around them into a sheet of ice. Any zombies that weren't flash-frozen to the ground started sliding straight into the waiting axe of the Guardian, who was slamming its weapon into the ground like a Swedish chef preparing vegetables.

"We're going to need to move soon," Cleave informed the others. "That ice won't melt; it'll just continue to get colder. At some point, the Guardian will send an attack that shatters this area and turns all the ice into razor-sharp projectiles."

"I thought you said we couldn't tell what was coming?" Kettlebell quizzed her with narrowed eyes. "If you know a punch is on the way, you should either prepare to take the hit or block it. If you know someone else is about to be hit, you should let them know."

"There *aren't* any patterns," Cleave explained as she watched zombies comically slipping and sliding around them. "Not when it's getting attacks *ready*. But when it puts out a hazard, you know that at some point, that hazard is going to be actuated. Even you should know how this one works."

"Great!" Joe chimed in as their tones started to get heated. "Whenever you see something you recognize, call it out! I'm going to drop the barrier as soon as there aren't any nearby zombies, so-"

"Wait, there's something else you should know." Cleave took a deep breath. "I didn't think it would matter, since I assumed we'd already be dead by now. But you've gotta understand that a Guardian has as many stages to defeat as its tier. This, as a City Guardian, will have five layers of protections that we need to destroy."

Joe paused as he listened to her speak. "Why tell us this now?"

She pointed to the Guardian, which had three bubbles and at least two hundred zombies attached to it. "If I'm correct, you've done so much damage to it that it's going to shift out of the first form any second. Each form is more powerful than the last; right now, it's about to go from tier five to tier four. That's the form with the most variation, but it almost always shifts to a mobile, long-range attacker."

"You mean to tell me that this metal man is a *transformer?*" Jaxon clapped his hands a single time. "I *loved* those in my fifties! You could bend their frames in so many new and interesting ways."

"I think it's starting!" Daniella called as all three acid bubbles burst at the same time. The Guardian's body became malleable, and it began rotating at high speed. Joe had a sudden realization and panic-dropped the barrier. Without a word, he jumped forward onto the ice despite the fact that he started accumulating freeze debuffs. He picked up speed as he slid, and even though his legs were frozen nearly solid, he ended right where he needed to be.

Joe reached out with his will and mana, *shoving* the Ritual of Predator's Territory at the shrinking-down Guardian. The ritual floated at it, getting caught on its bronze chest plate and pulled into the inner portion just before it finished morphing. Sparks flew, and he felt a pull at his mana...

Then the newly-made bronze phoenix pushed its powerful legs down and leapt into the air with a mechanical screech. Joe checked his active ritual tab, full of pure relief when he discovered that the ritual remained active. A glance around reassured him even more: even though he was far closer to the zombies than the mechanized bird was, the vast majority of the zombies kept their rotting eyes on the flying prize. Practically the only ones that *didn't* follow their target appeared to be the strongest and smartest of the bunch.

That part was less exciting for the frost-coated Reductionist.

Jaxon slid in next to Joe, grabbed him, and spun both of them like he was an alligator trying to drown its prey. They hit the ground and started rolling, not very fast, but distance was being generated. After a few seconds, Joe's Neutrality Aura managed to fully remove the frost, and they hopped to their feet and ran.

"We can lure the zombies onto the ice and let them get frozen and shattered!" Jaxon offered as they ran so quickly that paper bags exploded into shreds in their wake.

"No! We need them!" Tossing his arm in the air and waving it while pointing, Joe directed the group to fallback point number three. He knew the trio would get there before them, and he could only hope that they'd set up a proper defensive position. Joe and Jaxon ran in a wide circle—needing to buy time, avoid the frozen areas, and keep the ever-growing following of zombies off of them. "Wasn't planning on that thing being able to fly, but I can reconfigure the ritual of…"

"Down!" Jaxon grabbed Joe and they dove headfirst into a huge mound of moldy fruit. Ignoring the maggots in their way, they pushed forward as a series of concussive blasts came from above, turning the ice into icicles and forming a hurricane that tore apart anything that had been in range.

The flyover ended, and most of the gunk had been blown off of Joe's body. They got to their feet and kept running, though Jaxon whirled around and redirected a vicious zombie's bite into another of its kind. The attacker tore off an entire rotting arm, barely managing to rescue Jaxon from an incoming hammer blow to the skull. The humans resumed running as the zombies reset their position, and soon, Joe could see Daniella's well-conditioned brown hair.

Charging into the rear of the formation, Joe opted to tinker with the aiming settings of his ritual as the others engaged the zombies. Cleave took point, using her namesake to split several attackers in twain over and again. Jaxon redirected everything coming at him, only rarely sending a full-force blow of his own into the ravenous flesh eaters. Conversely, Kettlebell sent an endless barrage of straight punches into the zombies. It didn't do too much damage, but the attacks did send the much smaller beings flying, and it bought the team some breathing room.

Daniella… was an architect. Joe noticed that she was standing in a ready position, but he didn't even know if she had a proper weapon or method of attacking. He genuinely hoped that he didn't need to find out. He risked a glance around, noting the alcove that this ritual had been set into. They had all known that it was likely that things would go poorly, so he had tried to ensure that he placed his rituals in at least semi-protected places.

"Sure, the terrain has been shifting rapidly during the fight, but that just added an element of *excitement!*" Joe joked as he finished altering the trajectory of the bubble's arc. He activated the ritual, and a bubble barrier began forming in the same instant. "Everyone get back to me!"

"Finally!" Cleave noted the glowing blue light and started retreating. "Let's get out of here; there's no way we can-"

"Nope, sorry! *Don't* get in the bubble!" Joe called a warning almost too late. "Go around! *Around!*"

There was barely enough time to get past the bubble as it continued growing to full size. No longer blocked by anyone, zombies piled into the space and charged at Joe and the others. Then the bubble fully formed, and the zombies began slamming into the barrier on the inside, gnashing their teeth as all of them pressed in as close as they could get, some even crawling over the others in an effort to get access.

"*Joe!*" Daniella screamed as the barrier flickered lightly, a result of too much damage in too short of a time.

Understanding precisely what needed to happen, Joe manually activated the movement portion of the ritual and sent it flying out and up. The bubble knocked over dozens of zombies that had been right behind the first group, then rocketed into the air and began zooming around the one-hundred-by-one-hundred-foot space.

The Guardian was flying slow enough that it didn't have the same limitation, and it had been bombarding thousands of feet-worth of landfill. Still, Joe knew that it would come back to its space, that it wasn't going to abandon its territory or stop assaulting its attackers. The Reductionist turned his attention back to the ritual in front of him and hoped that his modifications would do the trick. Another bubble started forming a moment later, and he let out a massive sigh of relief.

Holding off the zombies for even a few moments was difficult, but the expanding bubble added a layer of protection that meant they needed to defend themselves in a smaller and smaller space; all the way until the barrier stabilized, and a massive sphere of zombies went rocketing up toward the ceiling to give them a moment of relief. Four bubbles had launched into the air before Joe's plan finally bore fruit.

Screaming in mechanical rage, the Guardian blasted a bubble. It detonated and sent every zombie within to the after-life. Its focus on a single target was its downfall, and one of the other randomly moving bubbles slammed into it from the side. As the phoenix faltered from the strikes, another hit and clung to it. The third bubble continued moving aimlessly, missing over and over.

The Predator's Territory that had been absorbed by the Guardian in such close proximity caused the zombies to lose whatever self-preservation instincts they had remaining, and the creatures were doing everything in their power to get at the succulent siren song of *blood* just beneath the surface. The phoenix continued blasting, but it appeared that it had no way to hit itself or remove the attackers from its own body. Flipping in barrel rolls, rapidly turning, even slamming itself into the ground did nothing: the zombies were encased in a barrier that kept them from exiting, as well as protected them from outside forces.

In an act of pure self-destruction, the bird turned and dove directly at the collection of acid spheres that had collected a few dozen feet away from where it had stood in its previous form. The acid destroyed the bird, lighting the liquid on fire at the same time. The resulting storm of destruction melted and burned everything within a few dozen feet, but the Guardian also stopped moving.

Everything was silent for a few moments, and the team took a moment after the most recent bubble fired into the air to investigate what was happening. Cleave took a deep breath and nodded with cautious enthusiasm. "I think that was the second form being destroyed. The next one should take into account what has happened so far, and thus work to counteract the forces that have been at play."

"What does that mean?" Joe instantly inquired of his resident subject matter expert.

"Since we've been using mostly swarm tactics and physical damage to take it down, it'll likely be something that can fight a huge number of opponents and be resistant to acid," Cleave replied hastily as she shoved a zombie away. "We'll only know for certain when-"

The ground rumbled, and a pillar of light shot straight up to the ceiling of the landfill from the space where the Guardian had originally lay. The pillar expanded, and the terrain was cleanly swept away. For the first time, Joe was able to see the *floor* of the landfill as it was scraped spotless. Hundreds of feet were voided as the light expanded, including the space where the team was standing. They fell into the light, doing their best to keep their footing as the ground shifted away under them.

As far as Joe could tell, anything without a will was shoved away. All inanimate objects, starting at the top of the pile and then lowering, were compacted and moved. He was thankful for this, as otherwise they would have fallen hundreds of feet instead of tumbling dozens of feet at a time. A much less deadly descent, it was easily handled by their powerful bodies. Joe's eyes caught the telltale gleam of enchanted objects, and resolved to move his A.S.P.E.C.T. here after the fight had concluded.

When the ground in a two hundred and fifty foot radius had been entirely cleared, dozens of portals opened across the floor. Golems began pouring out of various subspaces that the death of the previous Guardian form had created. Five large crystals grew out of the floor, which Joe recognized as the telltale sign of a pentagram-style ritual at play. The crystals lit up, hundreds of zombies began toppling into the open area from far above, and a blue sheen coated each of the golems as they began moving to attack.

"Ah. I see. Something that can fight against swarm tactics. How do you do that?" Joe gulped as zombies and golems alike started to charge. "You make your own swarm."

CHAPTER FIFTY-ONE

"We need to destroy the crystals!" Daniella called as she saw one of the golems tank a hammer blow from a zombie without gaining a scratch. "That way! Go! Stay together!"

Perhaps it had something to do with the fact that there was no way out of the landfill, no escape, and that all of Joe's rituals were out of reach that pushed her over the edge of fear and into action. He wasn't sure, but he did find it a nice change of pace not to be the one calling the shots.

The first crystal wasn't far, so they charged through the swarm and Cleave swung her axe at it with her maximum strength. A hairline crack appeared on the surface of the object, but the crystal also turned bright red. Every golem in the area also had their shield turn red, and they pivoted to protect the enchanted object that was generating their shielding.

They wielded their edged weapons with brutal efficiency, cutting through the ever-increasing number of zombies that filled the new arena. As Cleave hammered away at the crystal, breaking off flakes of its faceted surface but not making a lot of real progress, the rest of the team was forced to hold off the zombies that were coming for them from all sides. Kettlebell bellowed a question at his group as he grabbed a zombie in each hand and threw them at the incoming golems.

"Why aren't we being overrun?"

"Why in the *abyss* are you asking questions like that?" Daniella wondered as she shifted her stance and let a zombie fling itself over her. Joe caught the move out of the corner of his eye and wondered where she had learned judo to this skill level. "Just take the benefit and don't think about it too hard!"

But Joe *was* thinking about it. As his Orb activated a Cone of Cold that slowed the tide of hungry flesh, he peeked at his active rituals and got a shock.

Predator's Territory (Blood of Major Cleave) has been absorbed into a greater enchantment during a moment of change.

Predator's Territory (Blood of Major Cleave) has become a trait of an evolving creature. Ritual dissipated as the effect has become permanent.

"Ha! *Ha!*" Joe's barked laugh made the others question his sanity, but he explained what had happened between attacking and dodging. "The Guardian absorbed the ritual! It's *exuding* the scent of strong, healthy Dwarf from every single one of the golems! It has to be overpowering, and it's confusing the zombies enough that they're only attacking us if they are right up on our group!"

A squad of golems broke through the horde and charged at the mostly-human defenders. Their terrible weight shook the ground, and their shields rebuffed all attempts to stop them. Cleave reared back and put everything she had into a final attack, "*Break*, abyss you!"

The zombie barrier had lasted long enough, and her final attack was enough to shatter the heavily damaged crystal. The red shielding around the golems in the immediate area vanished, leaving the golems out of the range of the other crystals finally vulnerable to attack. Joe's team didn't wait around, try to hold the line, or break down the golems.

As soon as the first crystal broke, Kettlebell started running at the next one, forcing his team to follow him. The massive man acted as a wedge, barreling through distracted zombies and sending them sprawling. Spaced at one hundred feet apart, the crystals weren't too difficult to get close to, but the sheer number of combatants flooding into the arena made everything hectic.

Dozens of glancing blows landed on Joe's Exquisite Shell, but he powered through, knowing that they would all be given a hearty slap and rocked back. The next crystal came into range, but Jaxon blocked Cleave from attacking.

"One moment, if you don't mind! I'd love to test something!" He gently touched the crystal and received no reaction from it. "Good, good. Now, please, do make sure nothing bites me on my juicy toosh!"

With a wink, the man began tapping on the crystal as quickly as he could manage. Joe dropped a Dark Lightning Strike on some zombies that were rushing at them, getting a nasty surprise as the spell rebounded and hit *only* him. His Exquisite Shell was on its last legs, and they had only been able to take down a single crystal so far. "Ah! Abyssal *Excommunication* title! Jaxon, whatever you're doing, please hurry!"

"Slow is smooth, smooth is fast!" Jaxon countered as he increased the pace of his already frenetic tapping. "Wouldn't want this effort to all go to waste now, would we?"

"Don't know what you're doing beyond touching a rock, so I wouldn't even know what you were wasting!" Cleave roared as her axe lashed out at some exceedingly *rabid*-looking creatures. They fell into chunks, but the top halves continued crawling at her.

"Not rocks, *crystals*!" Jaxon informed her jovially. "If metal is the bones of the earth, then crystals are the *joints* of the earth. Joints can be *adjusted*!"

With his proclamation, the crystalline structure within the huge object shifted slightly out of place, and the entire stone shattered. Throughout the entire arena, the shields that were covering any of the golems vanished, and they began accruing damage.

"No one has *ever* called crystals the joints of the earth!"

Daniella tried to point out, but Cleave clapped a hand over her mouth to keep the words out of Jaxon's ears.

"If it works, you just *sprint* with it, human!" Cleave removed her hand and they ran toward the next crystal. "You just don't inspire doubt in something that needs to be done!"

Joe's team shattered the third crystal and then repeated the procedure, until only the fifth and final one remained. The Reductionist had slipped back into his role as a healer and was doing everything he could to keep the group topped off as they were torn up by the zombies. His Neutrality Aura helped as well, keeping them free of debuffs and healing minor damage in no time flat.

Jaxon started tapping at the crystal, and Joe took a moment to look over the battlefield as a whole. Firstly, the waterfall of zombies had reduced to a slow trickle as they lumbered into the area. As for the golems, destroying the third crystal had slowed their attack speed significantly, and the fourth had decreased how rapidly new golems managed to come through the portals.

"When this one goes down, the portals should close!" Jaxon confidently proclaimed as he tapped away. "Major, what will we need to look for in the next form?"

"Next will be something with overpowered physicality and defense! It's meant to hold off all attackers while any remaining defenders escape. Then the final form is always *random!*" she informed the group as she sliced the head off an undead Legionnaire. "Get ready; as soon as the last golem goes down, the next battle will start!"

"Here we go! *Adjust!*" Jaxon stood perfectly still with his finger on the crystal for a long moment, then exploded into chunks of meat and shards of bone as his mana-using skill rebounded on him.

Party member 'Jaxon' has been slain!

"Oh, for Celestial's sake," Cleave growled as she whipped around and started beating on the crystal, which instantly turned bright red. A half-dozen portals appeared within ten paces of the crystal, and golems excessively larger than the originals in the area stepped out. They turned as a unit to face the group as Cleave swung again.

Joe decided that it was time to get involved. He pulled out his icicle Ritual Orb and set it to attack the spire. After a half-second spin-up time, it shot forward and slammed into the final power source of the golems. The tip was clashing with the surface, its armor penetration working overtime as the Orb spun like a diamond drill. Sparks flew, and Cleave changed targets. Using the flat of her axe, she slammed it into the Orb and grunted as it broke through the surface and didn't stop spinning.

"Keep it up, baldy!" She swung again and again as the larger golems were swarmed by zombies searching for the source of the dense 'Dwarf smell' that erupted from the steam-powered fighters. A final hit on the back of the icicle sent it deep into the center of the structure, and the crystal shattered.

Instantly, all portals closed, and Joe's team retreated to the utmost of their ability. The white light that had compacted the garbage began to fade, and the heaps began to shift forward and tumble back into the arena space. Daniella saw that the walls were collapsing, and her eyes snapped to Joe. "We need a barrier! Now!"

Joe nodded and dropped a ritual tile on the ground, pulling out two Mana Batteries and pouring mana into them. The light of the arena faded faster with each golem that fell, and soon, the final one was starting to drop. It hit the ground and shattered. For a moment, all went still as the lingering effects of the Predator's Territory trait vanished.

Voom.

The nearly inaudible sound of Joe's stationary barrier activating couldn't be heard in almost any other context. But in the eerie silence of the landfill, it was a dinner bell calling out to the far-too-close masses of undead. Their heads all turned toward the party of four, hungrily staring at the Dwarf in the center of a translucent bubble. An unholy screech came from one of them, and the hoard charged...

…only to stumble to a halt as a wave of bloodlust and *fear* washed through them. An apparently Dwarf-flavored bloodlust, judging by the way the zombies stopped in their tracks and whipped around in full salivation mode.

A mote of crimson light was hovering in the air where the center of the arena had once been, and it rapidly expanded out into a huge, spiked, armored form. Joe's eyes narrowed as he realized that he recognized this creature. "Is that a *Hammer Beast?*"

His audible query was too slow; already, the creature had begun to spin in place. Hundreds of zombies charged at the armored Guardian, only for it to charge *them*. It rolled over the closest ones, then released a red mist that started to rapidly fill the area.

"No!" Cleave gasped as she recognized the tactic. "That's the unblockable ability 'Taunting Fumes'! Any creatures in range that are hostile to the Guardian will be taunted!"

The red mist hit them, passing through the barrier without issue, and Joe's mind went blank… all but one thought.

"I will do *anything* to fight that creature!"

CHAPTER FIFTY-TWO

Debuff 'Taunting Fumes' has ended.

Joe closed his mouth, which for some reason was hanging open and ached terribly. "What in the…?

He scanned the open space that had been cleared, spotting the massive Hammer Beast, which was still zooming around squishing zombies. His team was holding their own, their health keeping them together while their strength was put to good use against the heavily armored sides of the creature. They even managed to pin it for a moment, and a few zombies took that time to wedge their entire bodies into the small openings in the shell of bronze that the Guardian was protected by.

Then the Guardian broke free and started *bouncing* as it rolled, creating tremors that not only knocked over the zombies, but destabilized the walls of detritus. The last Joe recalled of the fight was a dozen zombies reaching up and catching the Guardian in midair, holding it there while others started scaling the spikes that coated its body. Then their small space was buried under the tsunami of slop, and he looked around at his equally confused teammates. "Why does my jaw hurt?"

"I think…" Daniella was rubbing her own face as well, "I'm pretty sure I remember trying to *bite* the barrier?"

"Taunting Fumes makes you forget your weapons and skills, then use brute force in an attempt to take down your target," Major Cleave informed them as she peered around the dark space, which was lit only by the soft blue glow of the screens of energy holding a mountain of muck off of them. "This bubble saved us twice there. Once from the collapsing rubble, the other by keeping us from charging in and attacking that Guardian with melee attacks. *Excellent* usage of your abilities, Joe."

"Thanks!" Joe turned and fist bumped the Dwarf with a wide smile, hoping that it could be a turning point in their relationship. He turned to Kettlebell next. "How are you holding —*wha~a~at?*"

Letting out a whine like a kicked dog, Kettlebell wiped his face clean of blood and bone chunks. "Why isn't it getting cleaned? Everything *else* vanished!"

"Wait… I recognize that finger… this isn't filth, it's a usable material." Joe's eyes went wide as he saw the largest chunk, which was a long middle finger. He took the flesh and held it in the air, hoping that he had enough to work with.

"Are you… are you gonna *eat* that?" Kettlebell looked positively green at the thought.

"No! *Ew!* Why would you think… why would you *say* something like that?" Joe shuddered and set the finger down, moving his hands through the somatic portion of casting Resurrection. Power began to gather in the air and mana started to flow through his body, forming a connection to both his deity and to Jaxon's respawn waiting room. Over the next few seconds that it took to complete the spell, Daniella voiced a concerning issue.

"Joe, I don't know what you're doing, but what happens if that spell backlashes on you because of our new title?" Her question was enough to make Joe tense up, but he did his best to simply complete the divine spell.

He did manage to speak quietly, though haltingly so that he didn't mess up. "Can't live in fear. Gotta go ahead and keep living. Things can always go wrong, so we just gotta do our best and hope it's enough. *Resurrection!*"

A swirling, golden portal appeared over the finger, which vanished as soon as Jaxon's foot touched the ground. Kettlebell sighed in relief as the tacky blood covering his front turned to vapor and left his body and gear clean once more. "Well, that was unexpected, wasn't it! How did you beat the next two forms already... never mind, I'm all caught up. We're in a bubble, and the thing is rampaging, yes?"

"Got it in one, Jaxon." Joe waved in the direction of the pounding noises. "I'm always glad to be around a quick study. The boss is over there somewhere, going to town on zombies. We have a couple minutes to prepare, but I think we should get in there sometime soon. This place has *got* to be running out of zombies by now."

"Thank the Celestials," Cleave muttered with great discomfort. "Anyone need gear patched up? Weapons sharpened? Spells touched up?"

"Oh, yeah. Good idea." Joe dropped his Exquisite Shell and allowed his mana to return to maximum before he started rebuilding it, wary of whatever spell failure would look like. When it was back to max capacity with no complications, he let out a small sigh of relief and shuddered. "This title is unpleasantly insidious. Makes me think about it all the time, and do everything extra cautiously. Here's a thought, though... do you think the fact that it makes skills and spells unstable perhaps means we'll progress in them faster when we are successful? Since we need to hold the mana structure with more control to counteract the new inherent instability?"

Wisdom +2!

"That would make sense," Jaxon agreed as he rubbed his hands together excitedly. "Can we go and take our revenge against whatever is out there now? I'm hoping to catch a few zombies and test their reflexes to see what sort of differences need to be accounted for."

"I think we should just wait until all the sounds have been

gone for a while." Joe offered his two cents, his hands twitching. He needed to continuously stop them from pressing together and rubbing against each other greedily.

"No, the creepy Chiropractor's right. How about we keep our eye on the prize," Cleave grumbled as Jaxon began limbering up. She watched him for a few moments, the discomfort on her face growing more apparent. "I don't know how you're moving like that… but when you get to the Master rank, I'd love to learn."

"*Really?*" Jaxon paused and regarded her with bright eyes. "A second student even before I'm officially practicing? Absolutely!"

"Fine. Then I'm going to shut off that side of the barrier and start melting our way out of here," Joe informed the group as the discussion turned to fees, expectations, and accountability when training someone. He was glad they could talk, but… they were in a boss battle! "Who talks about *cash flow* when there's a major moment happening?"

The duo didn't acknowledge him, so he looked at the other two and shrugged, then got to work. Joe only removed enough of a section for everyone to squeeze out of, then began casting Acid Spray over and over. Soon he was creating a tunnel, even though acid washed over his Exquisite Shell three times as the spell rebounded against him.

He wasn't concerned, but instead felt pleased that his shell was what was drenched. There had been a concern in the back of his mind that the spell rebounding would hit like true damage, bypassing his preparations. As he wormed his way through the midden heap, he tried to think on the bright side of being hit by his spell. "You know, all this is doing is helping my Neutrality Aura to keep me clean. It's nice, like a shower for my shell."

With that thought helping stave off claustrophobia, he kept worming forward. A final cast allowed light to filter through the hole, but it wasn't like he could shout that back to his team without alerting his enemies to his location. Joe pushed his head out of the cavity and looked around, his eyes landing on the Guardian as it ever-so-slowly rolled over the last zombie still standing.

The Guardian was leaking fluids from all sorts of cracks in its bronze carapace, and terrible grinding was coming from its internal components. Turning his attention to the arena floor, Joe found that *thousands* of zombies had been ground to paste by this last defender, and he was truly impressed. As the Guardian steamrolled the final zombie, it came to a halt with a shuddering **hiss**. If he were ascribing human emotions to the machine, he would have absolutely called that a sigh of relief.

"No time to waste... who knows if that thing has a self-repair function?" Joe tossed his Ritual Orbs into the air, directing them to attack as he pulled himself fully from the heap. Hands held out, he prepared to begin casting.

The icicle Orb shot forward the fastest, guided by his intent into the largest crack in the armor, specifically where Joe had been hearing the cacophony of damaged gears. Upon shooting into the space, the scream of tearing metal was all that could be heard.

Damage dealt: 168 penetrating cold!

"Cone of Cold!" The spell, which originated from an object and not himself, didn't seem to be under the same restrictions as he was with his Excommunicated title. A frigid blast of arctic ice coated the internals of the steam-and-magic-powered Guardian, preventing it from speeding into action once more.

Damage dealt: 1,394 (268*520% Magical Critical hit!) cold damage!

While he wasn't sure what the battle had looked like until this point, and he was somewhat glad to have missed out on it, he was pleased to see that his enemies had devastated each other to the point of total impairment. The Hammer Beast crumbled open, displaying its internals as it powered down.

Trait gained: Karmic King! You have avenged over a thousand creatures killed by a single opponent in less than an hour from their death! +5 to all stats! The secrets of Karmic Luck will be far more receptive to being understood by your fragile mind.

Last hit! You have killed an enemy at a much higher level than yours, which was taken to the brink of death by unaligned parties. Solid kill steal! Luck +5.

One-hit kill! You killed an enemy at a much higher level than yours with a single blow! Once combat is concluded, all experience gains for the entire battle will be increased by 5%!

"That counted as a single attack?" Joe lost focus and took a deep breath as his body became heavier, denser, more perceptive, more reactive; his mind cleared of fatigue and showed him the next steps forward more clearly. He hadn't passed any thresholds, but he was happy to see that he was finally getting close to the Luck threshold. He was almost certain that things had gone wrong due to the differences in tier among some of his characteristics, but he hadn't been watching his notifications as well as he should have been lately.

He looked over his character sheet as he waited for his team to join him and for the final Guardian phase to begin.

Name: Joe 'Excommunicated' Class: Reductionist
Profession I: Arcanologist (Max)
Profession II: Ritualistic Alchemist (1/20)
Profession III: Grandmaster's Apprentice (14/25)
Profession IV: None.

Character Level: 21 Exp: 237,109 Exp to next level: 13,296
Rituarchitect Level: 10 Exp: 53,700 Exp to next level: 1,300
Reductionist Level: 3 Exp: 8,836 Exp to next level: 1,164
Hit Points: 2,122/2,122
Mana: 3,662/7,585
Mana regen: 63.2/sec
Stamina:1,698/1,705
Stamina regen: 6.56/sec

Characteristic: Raw score

Strength: 158 -> 164
Dexterity: 161 -> 166
Constitution: 152 -> 157
Intelligence (bound): 169 -> 174
Wisdom: 153 -> 158
Dark Charisma: 102 -> 109
Perception: 155 -> 161
Luck: 85 -> 95
Karmic Luck: 3 -> 18

"That's... that's a lot." Joe let out a low whistle as he looked over all the changes. "That Karmic King thing... I got that for avenging *zombies*? Maybe for working to put them to their final rest as well?"

Someone popped through the tunnel he had made. Joe looked back, expecting it to be Jaxon, but found Cleave instead. "Everyone okay back there?"

Major Cleave's face was as pale as a sheet, and she raised a shaking finger to point behind Joe. He whipped around, finding himself inches away from a pair of flaming eyes that seemed to be staring into his soul.

CHAPTER FIFTY-THREE

"Interesting." The Guardian took a step away from Joe, the glowing ruby eyes being hidden for a bare moment as he blinked. His beard was intricate and tasseled, his hair thick and well-arranged. Every bit of his body was made of some kind of metal, though it was so well done that his bronze hue was the only thing keeping him from appearing as a regular Dwarf. "*Singularly* interesting."

Joe looked over to Cleave, who was still pale and staying *far* away from the Guardian. She met his eyes and drew a finger across her neck, shaking her head at the Reductionist as if to show her apologies for not coming to help him. The human turned back to the automaton, gathering his courage. "You are the fifth form of the Guardian?"

"I am." The metal Dwarf rubbed his beard consideringly. "Your friend there is staying back and holding back your other companion, because she recognizes me. Somehow, miraculously, this is the form that managed to manifest in the random rolls that decide the fifth manifestation. I am *Corey Digger*, the concentrated will of the first Dwarf to sacrifice themselves for my people. You aren't dead right now only because you have three things going for you."

"I'm-" Joe swallowed so that he could moisten his terribly dry throat, "-so happy to hear that."

The Guardian didn't make him guess what he meant. "I've reviewed the information that I've missed out on while I was trapped by the tacked-on enchantments in my previous forms. First, you released me from the shackles which others imposed on me, simply by adding another trait to my earlier forms. This broke the enchantments that had been in place by creating a variable they couldn't account for. For the return of my sanity, I thank you."

Joe bobbed his head without saying a word. How was someone supposed to respond to something like that?

"Second, you were instrumental in releasing *thousands* of my brethren from a state of undeath. Even if they are to come back as Elves, it's so much better than the cursed life they had been living. For breaking through the horde and saving my cursed brothers and sisters, I thank you." The Guardian's ruby eyes leaked a small tear of purest fire that vanished in a flash of light.

"It had to be done." Joe knew what to say for this one. "Even if it were not with your help, I had planned to come here and completely cleanse this area."

"Good." The Guardian's bright gaze bored into Joe's eyes, then washed over his team where Kettlebell had crawled out of the tunnel. "Finally, you clearly have the power you'd need to remove the title that is restricting you. Yet, you've stayed true to your oaths and the people around you. The people I've observed, whom you surround yourself with, are true of purpose and have nothing to hide from you. For keeping your honor when it would be so much easier not to, I thank you a third and final time."

"I… can't tell you how much that means to me-"

"But now I must issue my challenge." The Guardian's eyes narrowed. "You are the only person still standing in the arena that has dealt damage to my previous form. You may leave now and accept the lesser rewards as they stand, or you can receive my blow. I warn you; I will strike with the intent to kill. If you fail in this challenge, I will revert to my first form, and you will be dead."

Joe considered for a few moments, but finally cracked his neck and stepped forward. "I'm not about to stop at the last moment, after all of this. Bring it on."

"Brave, indeed." The Guardian tapped the air, and rapidly climbing numbers appeared overhead. "The challenge is thus: all others that have damaged me have been slain in their attempt. Only you, who has dealt damage and accepted my trial, remain standing. My previous body had five hundred thousand health, as well as eighty percent reduction from all edged weapons. You will need to be able to survive ten times the pre-mitigation damage that you personally dealt to me, or you will fail my challenge. You may prepare yourself. When you tell me to strike, I will. Until then, I will not attack unless you attempt to flee your accepted trial."

At that moment, the spinning numbers stopped and displayed their result.

Damage to be taken by the challenged: 15,620.

Joe looked at his health, sitting at two thousand one hundred and twenty-two. Sighing, he dropped his Exquisite Shell and returned it to maximum after the slight acid damage it had taken. After the refresh, the shell sat at ten thousand three hundred and ninety-one. "Well, abyss, those numbers don't add up. I'm about to die. No escape… hit me, I guess."

He waited for the strike, eyes closed, then slowly opened them to see the Guardian still staring at the number in surprise. The ruby eyes flashed to Joe, then the number, ultimately coming to rest once more on the human. "…How in the *abyss* is that number this low?"

"That? Oh. I only hit you once." Joe's explanation made the mechanical Dwarf's jaw drop. Then he snorted, and his shoulders began to heave.

"You... you only hit me *once?*" The Guardian began laughing uproariously. "Can you... *ha!* Can you imagine if you hadn't hit me even a single time? I would have appeared, free and clear to revert back to my first form because there were no surviving damage dealers! You truly have some uncanny luck!"

Luck +1!

Even the *thought* of that made a pit appear in Joe's stomach. All that work, gone, if he hadn't actively participated. He fervently praised himself for getting a move on and not lounging around while waiting to scoop up rewards like he had originally wanted to do. The Guardian smiled at Joe and raised his fist. It began to glow as the numbers hovering in the air started counting down, growing brighter and vibrating intently as the numbers were sucked away into his fist. "Because I like you, this will all be blunt damage. No pain; you'll just pop like an overstuffed waterskin. Here I come."

The smiling Guardian was in front of Joe in the next instant, slamming his fist into the human's chest as though his hand were a maul, and the Ritualist's rib structure was a particularly stubborn walnut that he didn't even want to eat anymore: he just wanted to prove he could destroy this too-tough nut.

For Joe, the damage came almost in slow motion. His Exquisite Shell flared, brightened, tried its best, but still shattered into motes of glittering light that faded away.

Exquisite Shell: 0/10,391

Then his chest started to crumple, and his health faded like the last sip of soda being drained through a straw.

Health: 1,900/2,122

1,100.

800.

100.

Clang!

Joe was unable to breathe as he was sent flying into the soft garbage cliff, leaving behind a startled-Reductionist-shaped hole as the blow drove him deep into the recesses of the pile. The shockwave that erupted in the next instant left him and the

Guardian standing in a five-foot cleared space, with the human desperately holding himself back from using Mend or Lay on Hands. He had no idea if the spell might backlash and kill him in this state, and Neutrality Aura was already healing him at eighty-four health per second.

A huge globule of blood shot from his mouth and landed with a splash, and his eyes leaked bloody tears as he opened his eyes to find the now-dented body of AutoMate surrounding him as a bathtub-sized coffee mug and letting out a *burble?* of concern as it took the blood pouring into the coffee and recirculated it into his body.

AutoMate uses Eternal Ebonsteel Encasement! This ability is now locked for the next month!

AutoMate durability: 3007/5000.

"I've had dreams of waking up like this. Just swimming in coffee." Joe wheezed through a bloody smile, only then looking up to find the Guardian watching him.

"Look at this! A proper cup of Joe! Ha! You *do* choose your companions well." The metal Dwarf sighed in contentment and patted the elemental on its mostly-liquid head as the suddenly massive cup containing a whole person somehow shrank to be normal mug-size once more, without squeezing Joe. "I look forward to guarding whatever wondrous place you station me. I consider your challenge fulfilled."

The Guardian collapsed in on itself, converting into a huge bronze button, then automatically entering Joe's Codpiece of holding.

Quest complete: Hidden Guardian. You have defeated the five forms of the Guardian hidden in the landfill. Reward: Guardian Activation Button. While this Guardian is designed for a City (Tier 5), you are able to place it in any settlement that is not considered a fortress.

Benefits:

- *The Guardian will fight on behalf of the residents of the settlement.*
- *Each person entering the range of the Guardian will be*

scanned for hostile intent toward the residents of the settlement. The landowner and delegated individuals will also be notified.

- *Space is locked down in the area around the Guardian. Only the owner of the Guardian may permit artifacts, spells, or other abilities that allow teleportation or flight into or out of the area.*
- *This Guardian has five forms, and each of them must be defeated for the settlement to transfer ownership.*

"Alright. Neat." Joe tried to take another step forward, but fell to the ground gasping for air. A goodly amount of his blood was soaked into the trash around him, so it made sense that he didn't have a lot of oxygen moving through him at present. A glance at his health made him decide to risk a heal, so he began pumping mana into himself in the form of Lay on Hands and Mend.

He was taking extra care with the spell structure, and got himself back to half health before he decided to just let Neutrality Aura take care of the rest. As he let out a long sigh of relief, notifications crowded his vision, all of them vying for his attention.

You have defeated form 1, 2, 3, 4, and 5 of a City Guardian! Experience value is based on contribution to the kill: 2,400 (6,000*40%) + 8,000 (10,000*80%) + 1,200 (15,000*8%) + 65 (21,000*.31%) + 28,000 (28,000*100%) for a total of 39,665 experience.

You gain 2,883 experience as kill contribution credit for Zombified Dwarf x7,213. Click here to see each individual value.

Joe avoided even *looking* at that button too hard, as he was sure the combat log would blow away everything else that he actually wanted to see.

Karmic King reward applied! Total experience gained increased by 5% for a total of: 44,675 experience. (39,665+2,883).

You have reached Ritualist level 23! Current experience: 281,784 Experience needed for next level: 18,216.

Joe was lifted off his feet as the double level increase sent golden light and utter euphoria through him. It took another minute before he could move. The waves of emotions he usually surfed had swollen into tidal waves and spelunking, so he read over the final notification while he collected himself.

You have completed a hidden quest: Remains to Be Seen. Requirements: release at least 99% of the Zombified Dwarves in the landfill from their otherwise unending torment. Reward:

- *10,000 Zombified aspects that can be claimed at any time. 10,000 Reputation with the Dwarven Oligarchy.*
- *Automatic reputation rank of 'Friend' with every Dwarf from the Dwarven Oligarchy.*
- *You may now enter and exit the landfill from any point in the Dwarven Capital and choose where you appear, so long as you are not in combat.*
- *You may now exit the landfill from any point inside the landfill, to any exit point in the Dwarven Capital.*

Reputation with Occultatum +2,222. New reputation rank: Extended Family! Seek out a space dedicated to your deity for a reputation-based reward!

"Thanks, Tatum." Joe got to his feet and properly stretched, then walked through the smoking hole in the cliffside that the Guardian had created by punching him a single time. When he stepped into the open area, he found his team waiting for him and offered a tired smile as they cheered for him. They rushed in for a group hug, all of them jumping in excitement over having completed their quest and collecting such a windfall of experience.

Finally, Daniella broke away and motioned at a small stone pad in the exact center of the area that was undamaged and *not* covered by gore. "Is that an elevator teleport pad?"

Major Cleave went over to take a look, nodding in agreement. "Sure is… but this isn't Dwarven-made. This is Elven for certain. I want you all to stay down here for the next hour. I'm going to check this out, and if I don't come back, I want you all to exit elsewhere."

"Cleave! No!" Joe called at her, but she had already gotten on the teleport pad and jumped, vanishing into an unknown point in the city. They argued back and forth about doing what she asked versus joining her, but eventually decided to honor her wishes.

At the forty-minute mark, she reappeared—absolutely *engulfed* in blood. Joe sent a heal her way, but quickly found out that the blood wasn't hers. She gave them a quick explanation. "There was a secret Elven compound near a house of ill repute. It appeared that they would lure unsuspecting Dwarves into an illusion and kill them. There were also a few NecroSpecialists in the building. My guess is that they were creating a zombie outbreak and were planning to unleash it on the Capital to soften it up when the main army was at our gates."

"You sure you got all of them?" Joe quizzed her with great concern.

She nodded wearily. "I am *most* certain."

"In that case," Joe stepped on the teleport pad and smiled at his group, "let's go turn in this quest. Step one of saving the Dwarves: complete."

He jumped slightly, vanishing from the landfill.

EPILOGUE

Joe was still laughing from the others' reactions to once again traveling by bubble, this time to get *to* the Shoe. He felt that he had a better handle on the Ritual now, and had been able to make the takeoff and landing far more comfortable for everyone involved. To make it palatable for Kettlebell, he even figured out how to make the bubble opaque when it was within a certain distance from the ground.

But he hadn't told the others any of that before taking off, and they had all screamed and thrashed around when they lost the ability to see. Apparently, there was nothing like thinking you were about to ram into a volcano at full speed to pull the high-pitched screams out. The time limit was coming up quickly, so as soon as they landed, Joe took off at his top running and Omnivault speeds to get to the Hamlet.

"Guess we'll catch up, then!" Jaxon called as Joe dove head-first into the tunnels.

By the time the Ritualist got to the open area, there were already dozens of wagons starting to rumble toward the exit. He sucked in a deep breath and bellowed, "Everybody, *stop!*"

That caused several eyes to point in his direction, but effected no real change in trajectory. With a flick of his wrist, he drew out a Ritual of Alarm and activated it, sending a shriek through the entire town that pulled every Dwarf out of their shelter and paused each wagon as they waited to see what was happening. "Hello, residents of... this Hamlet! I come with important information, and news I guarantee you will want to hear."

"Get out of the way, Joe!" a waggoneer yelled back at him. "This place is a deathtrap, and I'm getting out now!"

"You're free to leave." Joe stepped aside and sketched a mocking half-bow. "For the rest of you, I just wanted to let you know that Grandmaster McPoundy is on his way as we speak!"

With a flourish, he pulled out a metal disk and held it in the air. An enchantment revealing the maker's mark of McPoundy shimmered in the air for a long moment before vanishing. Anyone in the know would understand that a token like that meant that the bearer was speaking on behalf of the Grand-master, and that such an enchantment was not given out lightly.

"It's not enough!" another person called, this time from a crowd so that Joe couldn't pinpoint them. "This place is gonna get wiped off the map!"

"I have a few solutions to that as well," Joe explained in a forthright manner. "I came back with an *enormous* number of resources. Let me explain what I'm going to do *today*. I'm going to rebuild the Guildhall. I'm going to build *Grandmaster McPoundy's* workshop. Lastly, to help with defense of the area... I brought a City Guardian back with me."

The muttering dropped into shocked silence, and then returned as shouts and jeers of disbelief. He didn't waste another word, simply walking to the plot where he was planning to rebuild the Guildhall, atop the resolidified magma where the original one had stood. "This time, we're going to be protected against treachery! We won't fall for the tricks of the Elves ever again. Our eyes are open to what needs to be done!"

At the end of his speech, he pulled out the bronze button

and pressed it down. The token flew out of his hands and into the air, where the bronze rapidly morphed into a fifty-foot-tall City Guardian, nearly twice as tall as the one Joe and his team had taken down. As the process completed, steam roiled off the mountainous metal creature.

A moment later, its eyes opened. Like massive spotlights, they swept around the area and across the gathered crowd. It raised its left arm, and the implanted sphere of power began to glow. Stone spikes shot up out of the ground, impaling a half dozen people in an instant. Joe gaped in horror for a moment, thinking that he had made a terrible mistake. "Did it break again? Is it attacking Dwarves?"

Then the impaled people slumped, and their illusory disguises faded away to reveal Elven Elites that must have never left the area after their Royal Family had been slain. The cavern fell dead silent for a long moment, and then the Dwarves broke into excited cheering and chattering. They scampered back to shops and apartments, offices and slaughterhouses, pulling their wagons with them.

Quest complete: Gathering Confidence. After securing promises from 2 Grandmasters, the people that have already gathered in your Hamlet will now stay and fortify the location. Additional reward: +2 Charisma!

Quest gained: Not Lost, but Hidden. Convince at least one more Grandmaster of the Dwarven Society to join your burgeoning settlement. Reward: the location of 'The Shoe' will be lost to the Elves and anyone with positive ties to them. This will greatly aid your efforts to return the Dwarven Oligarchy to its position as a Unified race. Failure: The destruction of this settlement.

A cloud of smoke wrapped around Joe, and he turned around to find Havoc standing near him. The Dwarf was beaming at him while distractedly chewing on the end of his cigar. "Nice work, kid. C'mon, I got a surprise for you."

They traveled to the edge of the town, finding Bauen, Stan, and Lord Checkoff shouting orders at dozens of Dwarves whom Joe had never seen before.

"You! Get over there, and make sure, the temperature readouts, aren't approaching red! You! Get over there, and make sure, that piping isn't going anywhere." Lord Checkoff was in fine form, marking completed tasks and adding new ones to his clipboard at breakneck speed.

"I did something abundantly illegal," Havoc admitted to Joe with a light chuckle that set the human's hair on end. "I've been setting up violently deadly, intricate defenses and protections for this area. I tell you what: as soon as we activate these, we're going to become an absolute deathtrap to anyone that tries to get inside. Couldn't do it without you completing your peerage quest first, but... ya know. The Oligarchs getting beaten down tends to shift the definition of 'moral', 'decent'... and what even *is* 'lightly evil', amiright?"

"Ah... we still want people to join us, Havoc," Joe stated with no small concern. "We can let people in that we *want* to let in, right?"

"Yeah, these bad boys will make sure that we're undisturbed. Not even a *fly* will be able to get in from outside and remain in anything *resembling* a single piece, let alone ready to attack us."

"*Havoc.*" Joe forced his mentor to look at him. "What about all the Dwarves that are going to come here? Will they be trapped outside? If we don't take them in as planned, they'll call us monsters."

"Don't you worry your pretty little head about that." Havoc chuckled lightly, wiping imaginary dust off Joe's shirt and straightening the collar. "Once we're all sealed up, the volcano will be soundproofed. That'll take care of your worries about hearing 'mean words'."

"*Not* what I meant!" Joe called helplessly as Havoc waved and walked over to join the group of workers. "Abyss. This is basically his town now, isn't it?"

"We're beginning, sealing procedure test, number eight!" Lord Checkoff frowned as a cloud of ash sprayed out of a section where only clean air should be flowing from. "Everyone stop! What was *that*? Who was supposed, to clean and install those? We're starting over, from list item, number one! You! Check the out vent! You! Check the in vent!"

ABOUT DAKOTA KROUT

Associated Press best-selling author, Dakota has been a top 5 bestseller on Amazon, a top 6 bestseller on Audible, and his first book, Dungeon Born, was chosen as one of Audible's top 5 fantasy picks in 2017.

He draws on his experience in the military to create vast terrains and intricate systems, and his history in programming and information technology helps him bring a logical aspect to both his writing and his company while giving him a unique perspective for future challenges.

"Publishing my stories has been an incredible blessing thus far, and I hope to keep you entertained for years to come!" -Dakota

Connect with Dakota:
MountaindalePress.com
Patreon.com/DakotaKrout
Facebook.com/DakotaKrout
Twitter.com/DakotaKrout
Discord.gg/mdp

ABOUT MOUNTAINDALE PRESS

Dakota and Danielle Krout, a husband and wife team, strive to create as well as publish excellent fantasy and science fiction novels. Self-publishing *The Divine Dungeon: Dungeon Born* in 2016 transformed their careers from Dakota's military and programming background and Danielle's Ph.D. in pharmacology to President and CEO, respectively, of a small press. Their goal is to share their success with other authors and provide captivating fiction to readers with the purpose of solidifying Mountaindale Press as the place 'Where Fantasy Transforms Reality.'

Connect with Mountaindale Press:
MountaindalePress.com
Facebook.com/MountaindalePress
Twitter.com/_Mountaindale
Instagram.com/MountaindalePress

MOUNTAINDALE PRESS TITLES

GameLit and LitRPG

The Completionist Chronicles,
The Divine Dungeon,
Full Murderhobo, and
Year of the Sword by Dakota Krout

Arcana Unlocked by Gregory Blackburn

A Touch of Power by Jay Boyce

Red Mage and
Farming Livia by Xander Boyce

Space Seasons by Dawn Chapman

Ether Collapse and
Ether Flows by Ryan DeBruyn

Dr. Druid by Maxwell Farmer

Bloodgames by Christian J. Gilliland

Unbound by Nicoli Gonnella

Threads of Fate by Michael Head

Lion's Lineage by Rohan Hublikar and Dakota Krout

Wolfman Warlock by James Hunter and Dakota Krout

Axe Druid,
Mephisto's Magic Online, and
High Table Hijinks by Christopher Johns

Skeleton in Space by Andries Louws

Dragon Core Chronicles by Lars Machmüller

Chronicles of Ethan by John L. Monk

Pixel Dust and
Necrotic Apocalypse by David Petrie

Viceroy's Pride by Cale Plamann

Henchman by Carl Stubblefield

Artorian's Archives by Dennis Vanderkerken and Dakota Krout

Vaudevillain by Alex Wolf

Made in United States
North Haven, CT
17 April 2024

51451533R00226